TARGET STEALTH

TARGET STEALTH

Jack Merek

SIDGWICK & JACKSON
LONDON

First published in Great Britain in 1989 by Sidgwick & Jackson Limited
Originally published by Warner Books Inc, New York

Copyright © 1989 Jack Merek

ISBN 0-283-99859-8

Printed by Richard Clay Ltd, Bungay, Suffolk
for Sidgwick & Jackson Limited
1 Tavistock Chambers, Bloomsbury Way
London WC1A 2SG

This book is dedicated to the spirit of those who risked all or sacrificed all so that the rest of us might fly safely and sleep soundly.

To the memory of...
Glen Edwards, Iven C. Kincheloe,
Doug Benefield, Chuck Sewell.

To the everyday courage of...
Chuck Yeager, John Glenn, and all those
who probe the limits of the envelope.

A debt of gratitude is acknowledged to A. Arthur and the parachutists and patriots of 3rd Bde., 8th Inf. (Abn): Stu Watkins, Ron Sinclair, Terry Sorsby, Rich Ryan, Mike Perry, and Phil Villa.

Finally, for Susan.

TARGET STEALTH

PROLOGUE

WASHINGTON, THE EXECUTIVE OFFICE BUILDING

Madeline Murdoch, the president's assistant for national security affairs, lit her fifth thin brown cigarette of the morning and cursed silently at her most recent failure to kick the habit. She was comforted only somewhat by the cup of Morning Thunder herbal tea and the early arrival of the morning's action memo. It would give her a few moments head start before she walked across the street to brief the President at 1600 Pennsylvania.

Madeline Murdoch respected the opinion of E-23 (name excised), the National Security Council analyst who prepared the morning action memo. She realized, however, it would have to be her own ideas she carried into the Oval Office. She puffed quietly and her hands trembled slightly as she skimmed the page.

CLASSIFICATION: MOST SECRET-BLACK
DISTRIBUTION: MURDOCH ONLY, EYES ONLY
SOURCE: MAGIC 13, DESK E-23
SUBJECT: Renewed Instability in Persian Gulf Ops Area

The breakdown of the latest cease-fire between Iran and Iraq poses risks, opportunities and a grave threat to United States interests. Council staff strongly believes a diminished U.S. naval presence would only increase the risk. There may be opportunity for diplomatic progress if fighting further weakens the current regime in Tehran.

A threat of U.S. security is imminent. Communications intercepts foretell preparations for fresh attacks on U.S. Forces. However, intercept is unable to determine whether the anticipated attack is state-sponsored or the work of the regime's most radical factions, which may be operating without sanction from government in Tehran.

In an event, the danger is clear and present. A pre-emptive surgical strike against terrorist resources, or back-channel notification to the hostile regime is indicated. The fleet, and our embassies in the region, are in peril.

Sincerely,
E-23 (name excised)

Madeline Murdoch dropped E-23's memo into the burn box. It incinerated with a dry popping sound, not unlike microwave popcorn. She wished her decision on whether to recommend bombing the terrorist stronghold in the Bekaa Valley could be disposed of as easily.

THE PLAN

1

BEIRUT

The lone patron of the sidewalk *maqha* signaled the tea shop owner to bring him another glass, his gesture displaying the impatience and arrogance of the young. The old tea vendor disliked having to cater to every youth with a 9-mm automatic in his waistband, but what young man did not have one these days? Or a Kalashnikov or some equally deadly thing. Beirut was, after all, a city of guns. The old man wiped sweat from his graying stubble and brought tea for the sullen young man.

Despite the cease-fire, all other shops near the Green Line that divided Christian East Beirut from Muslim West Beirut remained closed as the noon hour approached. No one believed in cease-fires anymore—it was safer to close up and watch the soccer on television. The tea vendor had been closing his own shutters when the young man approached, opening his light Italian-cut sport coat to expose his pearl-handled Browning and staring coldly at him from behind his Vuarnet sunglasses. With the fatalism characteristic of all capitalists in the fallen Paris of the Middle East, the tea vendor had yanked the chain on his shutters and propped up his ragged awning, a green-striped testament to better days, and, without a word, had gone to make tea and nurse hopes that the young man would leave.

They spent the rest of the morning that way, sharing the dead air and watching the rubble in front of the listing high-rise apartments. A truck full of Amal troops rumbled by, the militiamen waving their Russian rifles and occasionally letting fly with a pop-pop into the sky. The young man sneered as the truck vanished, leaving a trail of dust. From behind the counter the tea vendor watched him, wondering at his political affiliation. As the old man wiped his tea glasses, he dreamed of an American visa and a reunion with his cousin in Detroit. All who could go from Beirut were gone, and the tea vendor asked Allah, if it be His will, that he might go, too.

The young man sipped his tea and waited. His feet, clad in silver Nike running shoes, tapped nervously against the tiled floor. He folded his arms and unfolded them and inspected his Rolex watch. The tea vendor wished the young man would tire of this and leave. Iraq was in finals with Mexico for the World Cup, and he wanted to see the match.

A dull thud erupted in the distance, rattling the glass in the cabinet behind the counter. A car bomb, not artillery, the old man decided. When the echoes of the blast faded, the city was silent, except for the sound of a cricket chirping in the rubble.

A sudden screech of tires from a gray Mercedes-Benz interrupted the young man's nervous meditation. The powerful car swayed round the street corner at full bolt. Another Mercedes pursued, its driver making a confident turn practically atop the skid marks of the first. The cars appeared to be bearing directly on the old man's shop. As he dived behind the counter, he saw the young man stand and pull a grenade from the pocket of his sport coat. For an instant he regarded it as he had his Rolex a few moments before. The label on the small green canister read, "Grenade,

Smoke, Yellow. Made in U.S.A." He smiled at it, pulled the pin, and tossed it into the boulevard at the careening vehicles. Drawing his pistol, he ran into the street. Billows of smoke blossomed from the grenade, and the two-car convoy braked sharply to weave through the clouds. From a side street, a Peugeot sedan racketed forward in front of the cars, its worn diesel engine sounding like a machine gun. A Toyota pickup truck emerged from an alley behind the cars, and a gang of young unshaven men armed with submachine guns leaped from the truck bed and blasted away until the tires of the two Mercedes were useless masses of exploded rubber.

A breeze from the Mediterranean cleared the smoke. From behind his counter, the old man peered at the activity in the street. He knew that if Allah chose this moment, he had no further part to play in this world. But he had to see.

Methodically the gunmen smashed the windows of the cars and opened the doors from the inside. Then they stepped back, raised their weapons, and sprayed the first Mercedes, full automatic, sending a spatter of blood and flying glass into the street. The cordite smell mixed with the sulfurous odor of the grenade. The old man's ears rang. He was terrified, but he could not turn away. He murmured a hasty prayer.

Before the firing stopped, the three occupants of the second Mercedes emerged and the gunmen shoved them roughly into the waiting Peugeot. They were pale foreigners, heavy men, the tea vendor noted.

The Toyota pickup and the Peugeot vanished as quickly as they had appeared, the gunmen in the truck firing wildly in the air. The tea vendor saw that the young man he had served remained in the street, and he watched him put the pistol back in his waistband, straighten his sport coat, and look at his watch once again as he strolled back into the *maqha*. The young man peered over the counter, lowered his dark glasses, and whispered, "Look upon the beloved of Allah."

The tea vendor sighed resignedly as the young man

drew the Browning from his waistband, laughed, and fired careless shots into his neck and chest. Dying, the tea vendor realized his killer's affiliation. He was of the Islamic Dawn faction.

THE BEKAA VALLEY

Pink streamers of thin cirrus clouds floated above the low hills of the Bekaa Valley near the ancient ruins of Baalbek. A gentle breeze cut across the camp as the sun began its daily pilgrimage from the east, but it was not brisk enough to whip the red, white, and green flag of the Islamic Republic of Iran, which hung limply from an iron pole secured by sandbags.

Colonel Asrar Ajami Avadek of the Islamic Republican Intelligence Directorate leaned against a wooden bunker post and smoked. He enjoyed the quiet moments that attended sunrise. He watched the men in their faded field jackets prostrating themselves before the cleric who led the morning prayers. The mullah sang out the ageless song of pain and promise, stopping occasionally to glower at Avadek. The meaning of the mullah's hostile stare was clear. Avadek did not pray. He was the mullah's enemy and so the enemy of Allah.

Avadek returned the mullah's stare. His weathered, bearded face bore no expression of contempt or amusement, even though he felt both emotions. As an intelligence officer, he had made a career of rendering his face a mask. Avadek field-stripped the remains of his cigarette, crumbling it into flakes between his fingers as he had learned at the infantry school in Fort Benning, Georgia, so many years before. Then he reached for his crumpled pack and lit another Gauloise as the cleric attempted to return his attention to the faithful.

Avadek slapped some dust from his green army field jacket and stepped down into the bunker. He walked along the little passageway to a dugout where a younger man sat watching the glowing green scope of an American-made ground-surveillance radar left over from the days of the shah's regime. The man was not a Pasdaran, a Revolutionary Guard. He was regular Iranian army, a technician. His mission was to maintain equipment and to help those brothers who were busy exporting the Islamic revolution into the Lebanon.

"Said your morning prayers, my colonel?" the army captain asked in their native tongue of Farsi.

"Of course."

"Me too. Got a smoke?"

Avadek handed the captain the pack. The officer took one and put another behind his ear to save for later.

"They hate you, you know. Those beloved Pasdaran out in the exercise yard hate all of us from the service," the captain said, monitoring the scope for any indication of penetration of the camp perimeter.

"See anything out there?" Avadek asked.

"There have been Syrian trucks on the road lately," the captain said. "There was a movement of T-55s rolling toward the city earlier."

"There will be more."

"You think so?" the captain asked as he lit the cigarette and turned to Avadek. "The beloved of Allah who lead the men out there won't like that."

"They don't like the truth."

"My colonel, you should be careful of what you say," the captain admonished. "They will have the Imam cut off your hand. They hate you."

"What I offer the mullahs is more valuable than ten thousand boys who clear mine fields with their feet. Like you, I possess something the holy men need, the ability to find the enemy before he arrives."

"That may not save you, if you are not of the faithful. I know this," the young man said.

"What I lack in faith, I make up in hatred of the foreigner."

"What will you tell the Majilis when you return home?"

"That we should quit this place," Avadek exclaimed with what for him was an unusual level of emotion. "We have no business here in the Lebanon until the jackal of Bagdad is vanquished! Defeat the Iraqi first. The Americans are helping him. He must be beaten like a dog."

"They will never abandon this place. The mullahs want to carry the sword of Islam across the region. They have planted the flag here in Baalbek and will never go home. They want to fight America. They want to fight the Israeli. They want to fight everybody."

"Why fight America here? They are all gone home anyway."

"No. The mullahs want to destroy the embassy."

"Again? What will be accomplished by another martyr in a truck? It's been done," Avadek snorted.

"Sure. The guards don't know how to fight in an order of battle, but they know how to die with a smile," the captain said bitterly.

Avadek dropped his cigarette butt carefully into the dirt and crushed the glowing ash with his dusty combat boot. He shook his head and turned to leave the bunker.

"Peace, my colonel."

"Peace be unto you," Avadek said softly.

Walking out the tunnelway under the bare electric bulbs, Avadek wondered if one day his head and its impeccably groomed gray-black beard might indeed grace the plate of a mullah. He grinned strangely at the thought. What he lacked in devotion he made up in a value he shared with the clerics, an acute hatred of the foreigner. Russian, American, French. It did not matter. His variety of contacts and mentors in the craft of intelligence only convinced him of the contempt they held for ancient Persia, his homeland, adopted kingdom of Alexander and heir to history. In Avadek's eyes, the foreigners brought only misery and danger with them. Either they wanted to invade like the Russians or to buy Persia and corrupt it like the Americans. They left his nation ripe for the mullahs to carry it back to a new dark age.

Avadek's sentiments were secular but nationalistic. He wished for his nation only a competent regime independent of foreign rule. But it was foreigners who schooled him.

Once, a training officer at the CIA installation known as "the Farm" called him a "camel jockey." The insult came as the instructor, a man named Angus McCain, tossed him hard on the mat while teaching a judo throw. Avadek, then a young man, laughed. But he never forgot the slight. It was just one among hundreds he would endure from arrogant Americans or brutish Russians.

Avadek's value as an intelligence officer, however, lay in his ability to cultivate friends, especially among the despised foreigners. And being a Persian, of an ancient, noble race, he was able to demonstrate amity of the warmest sort. Because no one was really his friend, everyone became his brother, even the mullahs he disdained. When the hated shah departed, Avadek had already long been helping his most recent sponsors, even before the holiest of the Imams returned from exile in France.

He pondered how to explain the folly of wasting troops, money, and matériel in Baalbek to a leadership that often found virtue in apparent folly. It was not time to spread revolution, he believed. It was time to beat the invader from Bagdad. He stood in the passageway, watching the men on the parade field begin their calisthenics.

Avadek was lighting yet another cigarette when he heard the rush of the hollow wind, like a devil sucking all the breath in the sky from the west. It was a faraway roar, sounding closer by the second. His ears, tuned by years of war, heard the whine of powerful turbofan jet engines a long way off. He dived into a slit trench and pressed his face to the earth.

Avadek's ears rang and his hearing went fuzzy as the camp shook around him. The bombs exploded in great balls of yellow flame and plumes of blue-black smoke. Buildings collapsed. Trucks blazed. Wood, fabric, rubber, and flesh burned. The young men on the parade ground shrieked and died or tried to run away, burning. The mullah, stunned, wandered aimlessly on the athletic field while an infant held in the death grasp of its dark-robed mother cried.

The bodies and limbs of the guards unfolded in flowerlike patterns, drifting through the air on the vibrations of the shock waves, then falling to earth to be crushed by a rain of American-manufactured aluminum bomblets. Heat waves fluttered toward the sky, followed by a sudden quiet, punctuated only by the transonic whine of the fighter bombers disappearing in the distance.

Avadek lay choking on dust that clouded the slit trench. His ears hummed and hurt him. He felt a hand grasping his leg and looked over his shoulder to see the captain from the radar station pulling at his boot. The captain bled at the nose and ears from the concussion.

"The Zionists," the captain gasped.

"No," Avadek said, coughing, "they flew Intruders. It was the Americans. Sixth Fleet, I'd say."

"Why?"

"Only Americans fly Intruders. Somebody must have talked. This time they got us before we got them."

They lay in the trench for a while, listening to the cries of the wounded. They knew they had to wait against the possibility of a second strike. The radar captain reached to his web belt for a canteen. He handed it first to the colonel, who took a sip and returned it to him.

"Thank you, my brother."

Avadek said, "Let's climb out of this hole and see if there is help for any of these martyrs."

They emerged from the trench and walked among the wounded and the dead. The captain stooped down to pass a drink to a boy dying from burns. The boy looked up at him, moving his lips in a wordless prayer. He died.

The two officers surveyed the ruin of the camp and knew it for what it was, a new shrine of the revolution.

"Once again, the cowboy Americans," Avadek said. "I've known them all my life. They think nothing of our lives. They bomb us from positions of comfort."

In the distance a vehicle drove wildly on the road into camp, whipping up dust like a dervish. It was a Land Rover.

"Like the American movies," the colonel said dryly. "The cavalry arrives. Only too late."

A Palestinian driver wearing his kaffiyeh scarf to filter the dust wheeled the vehicle into the camp at high speed, braking on the hard, dry ground with a screech of worn tires and brakes. From the passenger side, a fashionably dressed young man in Vuarnet sunglasses emerged and walked briskly toward Avadek and the radar captain.

The man in the sunglasses embraced the colonel, kissing him twice on the cheeks.

"Do you bring the ambulance, Issam?" the colonel asked, returning the gesture of affection.

"The damage is already done here," the young man called Issam said excitedly. Pointing to the dying, he added, "These are already in Paradise. You must come with me to Beirut. We have found something of value."

Avadek surveyed the camp for an instant. Without another word, he climbed into the vehicle. Issam clambered over the side, and the trio sped away, leaving the captain staring dumbly into the cloud of dust that receded in the distance.

WASHINGTON, D.C.

David Willers of *Flight World* magazine strode briskly down the hallway toward the White House press room, his running shoes squeaking and propelling him nearly to a run. Saturday news conferences were rare, so he was anticipating a breaking story. He presented his press credentials to the blue-jacketed officer of the uniform branch of the Secret

Service. The security officer noted the picture on the press card, matched it against Willers's face and waved him in.

A few old hands like Leon Chapman and Joe Daniels hovered over the buzzing wire service printers. Veterans of every administration since Truman, they always seemed awake and alert before their younger competitors. Even on a Saturday the veterans wore their rumpled suits. They loved reading the wires, though their pleasure had diminished when the old clattering Teletypes were replaced with electronic printers.

Willers poured coffee into a Styrofoam cup from a pot at the service bar and walked over to the printers. Other reporters were elbowing into the briefing room, but Willers, with the luxury of writing for a magazine, walked over to the printers to see what the old hands were reading.

"What's up?" he asked Daniels, whose hair had gone white watching the world go crazy too many times to count.

"We're back in Lebanon in a big way. The chief seems bent on repeating the previous tenant's mistakes."

Daniels unrolled the growing pile of printer paper and found the addition to the bulletin Reuters had moved from Beirut about ten minutes earlier.

"The Lebanese radio is reporting a bomb and missile attack at that Shiite camp in the Bekaa," Daniels said.

"Can those guys be trusted? Isn't their stuff usually pretty flaky?"

"This sounds right."

"How can you tell?"

"It just sounds like the way it would happen," Daniels said. "Don't worry, you'll have plenty of time to write up whether the smart bombs worked."

"You guys think you're the only deadline writers," Willers said jovially. *"Flight World* goes to bed day after tomorrow. They're going to want the wrap on this tonight, latest."

"Tough working for those high-priced magazines, huh?" Daniels grunted. "Sounds like sheer hell."

The noise level in the press room rose with the arrival of the camera crews, who dressed and acted like a pickup softball team as they bumped into each other while stringing their cables.

Press secretary Harold Roberson entered the briefing room looking slightly annoyed, as usual. He often said he likened the job of administration spokesman to being pecked to death by ducks.

"Hal, what have ya got for us?" demanded one reporter.

"Calm down, Ira. You'll all get it at the same time," Roberson said, taking a sheaf of memoranda from an eager-to-please, nicely coiffed blond assistant.

Dozens of reporters filled the seats opposite the podium. The white lights for the television flashed, and Roberson was bathed in a brilliance not his own.

"I suppose you're wondering why I gathered you here," he said, repeating his fondest joke to a cacophony of groans from his captive audience. "I'll make a brief statement for the cameras, then we'll go off the record. Is that all right?"

"Do we have any choice?" the reporter called Ira asked.

"Can it, Ira," a television reporter called out. "You can mix it up after we roll tape."

"I don't have to roll over for you guys just because you're in television," the print reporter snarled.

David Willers grinned and shook his head as he watched the running spat. He scribbled a few questions on his notepad, concerning the weapons systems aboard the American jets.

"Can we get on with this? I'm just going to start reading," Roberson declared testily. "You can roll tape or not." He gave his stack of briefing papers a final shuffle.

Everyone, including the disgruntled print reporter, piped down.

"Elements of the U.S. military have attacked and destroyed a terrorist training base in the Bekaa Valley of Lebanon. The action was taken after reliable intelligence determined the foreign units stationed there intended new terrorist actions against our embassy in Beirut.

"The mission was carried out by attack elements attached to U.S. Navy units carrying out normal security duties in the Mediterranean. It is action that we regret the necessity for, but will not hesitate to take in the face of continued terrorist affronts.

"Aircraft, personnel, and weapons performed satisfactorily, with all planes returning safely to their base of operations. That's the end of my statement. Questions?"

The reporters waved their arms wildly and began shouting their questions, which were as often as not statements. Roberson folded his arms and shook his head petulantly. "It's one at a time, or not at all, folks."

"What is the suspected country of origin for the terrorists we bombed today?" one reporter asked.

Roberson shuffled his briefing papers as though he needed to check again in order to remember, then answered, "We believe the terrorists to have originated in the Islamic Republic of Iran."

"First we send them missiles, then we bomb them. What's going on?" shouted the *New York Times* reporter.

"We have no diplomatic relations with the Iranians. As you know, we have no embassy there," Roberson said sarcastically.

"What are we likely to do with or about the Iranians? Are we ever going to have a clear policy on that nation?" another reporter asked.

"We have done what we believed proper, which is to measure appropriate response to appropriate provocation. As we have announced time and time again, that will be our reply to terrorism."

"But this was a preemptive strike. Nothing had happened. Is that our policy from now on? We hit first?"

"There may be other such strikes. We will do what we feel to be appropriate. We will take the actions necessary for our national self-interest."

Willers, waving his arm furiously, was finally recognized. "You say all planes returned safely. Is it true that the Intruders got a new coat of radar-absorbent paint? Wouldn't that be why Syrian radar missed them coming in? Was this a new test of some Stealth technology?"

"That was three questions, Dave," the press secretary said, grinning crookedly. "And you're a damn fool if you think I'd answer any of them."

One reporter waved his notebook and asserted, "Harold, we are getting reports of massive chemical shelling on the Iran-Iraq front near Abadan. We also hear that missiles from Iraq are hitting cities deep in Iran and making the place look like Dresden. In light of this morning's raid, would we intervene on behalf of one side or the other?"

Roberson shook his head vigorously. "Our position is one of neutrality in the Gulf War and the desire for a speedy conclusion of hostilities."

Another reporter stated: "A Lebanese radio report quoted on the wires says two American planes were shot down."

"We have nothing on that. I have no knowledge of any American casualties. I think that's wrong."

One reporter, a woman with a floppy hat, waved her arms wildly and shrieked, "Wait a minute, Harold! The Soviets have walked out of arms talks in Geneva. What are you going to do about it?"

Roberson held up his hands helplessly. "What do you want me to do, Molly?" he said.

THE WHITE HOUSE, WEST WING

The president of the United States clicked the remote-control box in his hand, switching off live coverage of the briefing carried on Cable News Network. He liked CNN, considering it the most patriotic of the networks.

Clad in his comfortable khaki slacks and polo shirt, the president settled back into the deep leather of his favorite chair and kicked his deck shoes up onto a hassock in his private office, which he preferred to the more spacious Oval Office because it reminded him of his former office in the Rayburn Building. Unlike his Rayburn office, this was a secure room.

The president packed tobacco carefully into a favorite pipe, signaling to CIA chief Brady Daniels that it was all right for him to light up his own briar. Madeline Murdoch, the national security adviser, lit her thin, brown custom cigarette of a kind enjoyed by people who, like herself, preferred Harris tweed jackets and were frequent lecturers at Georgetown University.

"Your opinions of our vaunted White House press corps?" the president asked, filling the room with the aroma of a burley mixed at a smoke shop in nearby Alexandria, Virginia.

"They're at their usual best, Mr. President," Professor Murdoch ventured acidly. "It's a few hours until the evening news. By then they should have the satellite film of the widows and orphans."

"It always makes me angry when they do that," the president said. "What else could we do? They were going to kill our people again. They are an impossible people."

"You're right, Mr. President," said Daniels. "The intelligence was solid. They were going to do it. Another truck bomb, another dozen American foreign service workers. The only Americans left in that godforsaken place. They are determined we should leave."

"And we are not going to leave," the president said grimly. "Many terrible things have happened there, and we have paid a great price with the young men and women who have given their lives there. Marines, State Department workers, CIA, our finest. We blundered when we tried to strike a bargain with Iran. We must not do that again."

The president paused to puff his pipe. "I wish that

we could reason with those people," he continued. "But force appears to be the only language they understand."

"My guess is that the Eastern papers and the networks will have us missing the targets, with stray bombs hitting surrounding villages," Murdoch said, reviewing a checklist on blue paper attached to her briefing folder. "We will want to respond to that."

"Did we hit villages?" the president asked.

"Most likely we did not, Mr. President," the owlish Georgetown professor said. "At least, not in the sense of its being a real village. There may have been some residual damage, but the bombs were precision, laser-guided explosives. They hit what they aimed at, and the pilots overflew to confirm damage with cameras. The problem, of course, is that a village is often used to shield a camp from an attack, so there may have been some civilian casualties. We must be ready to explain the distinction."

"And those poor people in the villages," the president said, running his fingers across his thinning hair. "Did they have any choice?"

"The terrorists don't give choices, Mr. President," Brady Daniels interposed hoarsely. "They go where they want, and civilians are convenient for their purposes so they can make the top of the evening news with the casualties and the stories of American atrocities when we hit them."

"If there is one thing that makes me grieve, it is the absence of a solution in that part of the world. We've worked so hard, with so little to show for it after these many years...." The president sighed and shook his head, then looked up wearily. "What else do you have for me, Brady? I didn't expect you to come out all this way, even with the events of this day. You could have stayed in Langley."

"I had a matter I did not want to discuss over the telephone, Mr. President. Not even on a secure line."

"What is it, then?"

"It's an espionage matter. And it looks graver by far

than the Walker business during the Reagan watch. It concerns Plant thirty-six in California."

"Oh, spying. Not that again. Well, I suppose I'd rather get it from you than the *New York Times*."

"They don't know about it yet, sir. We haven't solved this one. We don't have an arrest. But the exodus of materials from one of our Southern California defense plants is perilous."

"I certainly want to hear about one more danger to our nation's security," the president said. "Can we hear it over lunch, though? I don't think the nation will cease to exist over lunch, do you, Brady? How about you, Dr. Murdoch?"

"I hope not, sir," Murdoch replied, but she had her doubts.

Because the classified briefing would take several hours, luncheon was brought in. Madeline Murdoch and Brady Daniels smiled weakly as though they were both suffering gas pains while two White House waiters in their spotless whites carried in food and an urn of fresh coffee.

To each waiter the president uttered a gracious "Thank you." The pair, who had served two previous chief executives, murmured, "You're welcome, Mr. President," as they crisply turned the linen and laid out the service on a foldout table.

As the waiters departed they opened the French doors and walked past the stolid Secret Service men and the solemn uniformed colonel who waited in the hallway, wearing his ribbons and the weight of the world. The colonel carried the "Football," the black bag with the series of "go codes" that the president could use to initiate nuclear warfare. The waiters closed the French doors, and the briefing continued.

"So tell me a spy story," the president said with mock cheer. "You know how I love Le Carré."

Brady Daniels coughed. "I'm afraid it's almost that bad, sir. We fear there may be a soft spot in security on the low-observable technology."

"Damn, Brady," the president snapped. "Speak plain English. Have we lost something related to Stealth?"

"We don't think so, Mr. President, but we are not sure," Madeline Murdoch interposed, taking a birdlike bite of Maryland crab cake. "We have reason for suspicion, but not undue alarm."

"Well, I'm alarmed," the president growled, sounding like the defense committee chairman he once was. "The Stealth Technology Bomber is nearly operational. Are you going to tell me that after a dozen years we've been wasting our time? This isn't another one of those goddamn technology transfers like the Toshiba case, is it?"

"Rather more direct, sir," Daniels said. "FBI spotted someone they believed to be a Polish trading officer in Southern California. His identity was later clarified by some people in counterintel who did a first-rate file job. He was a Russian, from the San Francisco consulate, traveling well outside his permitted area."

"Get to the heart of it, Brady."

"The man was spotted leaving a restaurant in Downey, California, where we believe he consorted with someone from Mercury Aviation."

"Well, hell, man. Who did he 'consort with,' as you put it?" the president demanded.

"We don't know. All we know is that the Pole—that is to say, the Russian, disappeared," Daniels said.

"We do not know if there has been a leak, Mr. President, but we feel we must be certain," said Madeline Murdoch. "Particularly in light of the sensitive stage of talks with the Russians on long-range nuclear forces."

"This is disheartening," the president said, pushing away his untouched lunch and taking a sip of ice water. "If the missiles are traded down, Stealth is our hole card should we ever have to counterstrike or, God help us, preempt."

"I know it, Mr. President," Daniels said. "That is the reason for the weekend briefing. We know you already had a full plate with the Bekaa strike, but we thought you should know."

The president sighed. He folded his arms and closed his eyes for a moment. Although he was a robust and cheerful man by nature, the loneliness of the job sometimes discouraged him. Finally he opened his eyes and grinned, maintaining the poise needed to keep the world stitched together.

"Well, now that you've brought me a new brainteaser, what do you suggest, Madeline? Can the FBI handle this?"

"The needs of this operation are somewhat unique," Daniels said. "We think we should go outside the loop, sir."

"Absolutely not," the president said, shaking his head vigorously. "The last time we did that, we got involved in a can of worms. Running guns to terrorists and so forth. I won't have it."

"We didn't mean like that, sir," Madeline Murdoch said. "The operation should be FBI-supervised. But we need someone from the air force. Someone who knows the technology and has credibility with a contractor."

"Give me some names," the president said, packing his pipe and motioning Daniels to let him know he could do the same.

"Well, there is General Secord," Daniels said, grinning wryly, looking something like a mummy in bow tie and tweed.

"You're joking," the president exclaimed.

"Sorry, sir. Actually, I just meant he has the sort of background we need. A top-grade hardware man who has done covert operations. We could get the same sort of aid from General Yeager. He did some outstanding courier work in Switzerland during the war and some camera work for us over in the Soviet Union when he went to Moscow with Jackie Cochran."

"Oh, boy," the president said. "That's a pair. But isn't Yeager too involved with his business commitments? I'm also afraid his profile is a bit too high."

"You're probably right, Mr. President," Madeline Murdoch said. "We have another man, also retired. But he's still on flight status with the reserve and has enormous respect in the industry."

"We're referring to General Cartwright," Brady Daniels said, puffing carefully on his malodorous blend of Latakia tobacco.

"The astronaut? What does he know about spying?" the president asked, looking somewhat puzzled.

Daniels laughed. "It appears he has preserved his background quite carefully, sir."

"What do you mean?"

"When I met him, he had had his butt shot out from under him by a Messerschmitt over France. I jumped in with an OSS team, and he jumped out of the trees with a gang of Maquis, the Resistance. He landed on his feet all right. We blew a bridge or two together."

"That's fine, Brady. But it was behind-the-lines stuff and a long time ago. Is that the sort of thing that will help now?"

"I think so, sir. We need someone with the common touch, someone friendly. But we need someone who can be cold-blooded if it comes to it."

"And that's Cartwright?"

Daniels smiled, thinking back across the decades. "While we were behind the lines, sir, it became apparent that there was a Gestapo informant in the Maquis band. The Resistance fighters flushed him out all right, but there was fear there would be bad feeling over who would have to kill him. The man had family in the area who could betray the entire band."

"What are you getting at?" the president asked, now clearly fascinated by the older man's tale.

"Cartwright took the heat off the band. He killed the informant. With one shot, straight and true. Then he hiked to Spain, carrying me half the way. I had a bum ankle. It got all torn up with a blasting cap on the bridge job. I wouldn't have made it alone."

"Sounds like a remarkable man."

Reading from a thin file, Madeline Murdoch said, "General Cartwright also performed certain tasks during

Operation Overflight—the original U-2 missions—that put him in contact with the intelligence community."

The president pursed his lips and ran his fingers through hair that was running ever higher on his already high forehead. "He sounds ideal."

"I'll get Defense to cut new orders for the general, then," said Madeline Murdoch.

"Fine," the president said, pressing a button to call for removal of the largely untouched luncheon. "Now let's see what the news has on the Bekaa strike."

The satellite film was in. The emphasis was on the civilian casualties.

BEIRUT

The Land Rover sped through the ruined streets of Muslim West Beirut, past the shuttered shops, and past the black-veiled women hurrying from door to door on their mournful searches for relatives. The aged vehicle rolled past the walled-in, garbage-strewn shantytowns of the refugee camps, where Amal was trying to pin down the Palestinians.

The truck maneuvered through the twisting side streets, then crossed an open space near the museum crossing, where an antiaircraft battery nested atop a Russian truck, the boys behind the guns twirling the gun platform as though it were a toy carousel. Occasionally the Land Rover sped past a corpse.

Finally the driver wheeled the Land Rover into an alley in one of the deserted buildings that made the city appear a collection of tombstones. The driver dropped off Issam and Avadek, who stumbled over the rubble blocking the doorway to a basement entrance.

"What have you got here that would take me away from evaluation of the Bekaa operation?" Avadek demanded in guttural Arabic, following the young man as they descended into the musty darkness below ground.

"I do not know, exactly, except that it is your specialty, not mine."

"You mean information, not slaughter," Avadek said, almost shouting over the throbbing pulse of a generator that pumped air below the earth.

"No," Issam said, laughing. "I mean it is technical. You've got to talk to a Russian. This man we got was carrying documents."

"Why would you take Russians captive? That is madness."

"The Saiqa militia took our chief, and we want him back. The Saiqa gang likes the Syrians and does not care if we take a chief of theirs. So, we take Russians instead," Issam reasoned simply. "The Russians, they also like the Saiqa fighters. But mostly they want their own man back. So they will give us back our chief."

"Madness," Avadek muttered, following Issam through the labyrinth of hallways and tunnels. Finally they turned in a small passageway, and Issam called out through a slit in a steel door.

The door scraped as it opened, scratching along gravel and crumbled concrete particles that carpeted the damp floor. The room smelled of must and garlic, sweat and urine. These odors Avadek's keen nostrils dismissed. There was another he detected immediately. It was the tangible smell of fear emanating from the pale, balding, fleshy man seated on a chair that leaned against the wall, propped on its back legs. The man squinted and blinked, attempting without success to see his captors, several bearded militiamen who shined a powerful flashlight beam in his eyes.

"How long has this man been here?" Avadek asked.

"Since a day," Issam said.

"Where are his things?"

Issam pointed to an attaché case and an airline bag resting in the corner of the bare, bunkerlike room. Avadek picked up the man's passport and examined it with interest. "You told me there were documents," he said.

"There must be. One man, with this one, tried to run with that case. We shot him."

"You did not open the case?"

"We feared it might explode."

"That is good," Avadek said, patting the younger man on the cheek. "If you had tried to open that case, it would have done worse than explode. It would have dissolved. It is triggered to release sulfuric acid that will destroy its contents."

"You know this?"

"I am sure of it. It is of KGB manufacture."

Issam's jaw dropped, and he exclaimed, "You are sure?"

Avadek nodded and asked, "Whom did you think you were taking?"

"Embassy trash. Diplomats."

"You got yourself a bigger fish, and more dangerous to you," he said. "Have you got his glasses?"

"Sure, no problem," Issam said. He muttered to one of the militiamen, who produced a pair of bifocals and handed them to the colonel.

"I will also need a pitcher of water," Avadek ordered. Another militiaman stepped out and returned with a pitcher and glasses on a Cinzano tray, which he set on a table.

"Have these men leave, my young friend," Avadek instructed Issam. The fighters shifted uneasily, several fingering the safety catches on their Kalashnikov rifles, eyeing the colonel suspiciously.

"I must be alone with this man," the colonel said softly.

"The others will go, but I must stay," Issam said, an edge of defiance in his voice.

"That is well. But he and I, we must be able to talk quietly."

Issam uttered his orders, and the bearded ones shuffled out. Avadek turned to Issam and embraced him, whispering, "Now, my young friend, you must wait at the door so I can do my work."

The younger man regarded Avadek sullenly. "You know, except for my chief, I usually kill someone who tries to give Issam orders."

"I know this, my brother. That is why I ask you to do this, with the utmost affection and respect."

"Let it be so, then. Allah aid you in your efforts."

Issam walked out of the room but left the door halfway open. The man tied to the chair watched Avadek, blinking and shrugging as though to shake a kink from his neck. Even in the bright light his pallor was noticeable beneath the patches of reddish stubble. The captive was dressed in American-style sport clothes, wearing the shirt with the little alligator on it. He looked like a man unused to discomfort.

Avadek stared expressionlessly at the man for a long time. One of his articles of faith as an interrogator was that if you looked at a man long enough, it was likely he would talk, just to fill the silence.

He gently placed the Russian's glasses on his face so that the man could see his captor. The Russian watched Avadek with the peepish intensity of one who needs bifocals. Avadek returned the stare and after several minutes brought the man a glass of cloudy water, which he poured, almost lovingly, over the man's lips. The captive slurped at the water and pursed his lower lip over his upper so as to get all the drops. Avadek stepped back and regarded him again. *"Est-ce que vous savez qui je suis?"* he asked in impeccably accented French.

"I know that you are responsible for my safety," the balding man rasped in a jumble of mangled French.

"I know that you are Russian," Avadek replied.

"You are mistaken. I am a Polish commercial officer. Any harm that comes to me will be of gravest international incidence."

"What is your name, Polish commercial officer?"

"I am Jerzy Kazanowicz, principal trade officer for Polamco. We are an exporting firm of equipment that would be useful to the cause of socialist advancement worldwide. You have no right to hold me. I demand my freedom immediately."

"You Russians are always arrogant."

"I insist to you, I am not Russian. I am Polish!"

Avadek reached for his blue package of cigarettes. He favored the brand of the French paratroopers, Gauloise. He inhaled the stale-smelling, strong tobacco deeply, then exhaled through his nose.

"You want one of these?" he asked.

The captive refused the cigarette.

"Come on, trade officer," Avadek said, smiling gently. "There's no treachery in accepting a cigarette. You will feel better."

The man shook his head again, but Avadek approached him and placed the cigarette between his captive's lips. He lit the end with a Zippo lighter, and the man puffed.

"I ask you again, do you know who I am?" Avadek demanded quietly.

"I do not know who you are. I do not care. Your best course of action is to free my comrades and myself. Prove yourself a friend of socialism, and no harm comes to you."

"Your comrades are dead. You make threats like a cursed Russian. Now, you must know who I am," Avadek said, pressing the glowing stub of his cigarette out on the bound man's left hand. The man yelped once, in surprised agony, then gritted his teeth, sensing what was ahead. "Fuck your mother," he gasped.

"In case there is any doubt, I am the man who will singe your eyelids and notch your nose," Avadek whispered in the man's ear. "And that is before I become imaginative."

"You do not know who I am," the man said, still groaning from the burn on his hand. "Your last mistake will be to harm me."

"Now it becomes clearer," Avadek said, striding a few steps away and regarding the man in the glare of the flashlight's beam. "No trade officer of a satellite country talks in such a way."

"Look to save your own life now," the bound man said. "You are in graver peril than I."

Avadek smiled. "You do not understand my people," he said. "We are not as afraid of death as you. Many of us rush to it, as to a bride. It is our gate to Paradise."

Issam burst into the room, his face pale and angry beneath the glasses that he wore even in the dimness of the basement labyrinth. "The Saiqa, they give us their answer," he exclaimed.

"What have you got?" Avadek demanded gruffly. "I told you I need privacy with this man."

"They give us this," Issam said, anguish filling his voice as he unwrapped a handkerchief with a human finger in it. There was a gold ring on the finger, which Issam recognized as belonging to his chief.

"Listen to me," Avadek said in the curt, clipped tones of a field commander. "The matter of your chief means little. This man we possess and whatever it is that he carries are of great importance to the nation and Islam."

"Kill him now," Issam blurted out in anguish.

"You talk like a donkey. Do as I say. Prepare transport for myself and this foreigner. And what he carried. The satchel must be protected. I need security and guaranteed arrival in Tehran this night."

"I cannot make these arrangements just so that you may go home with one spy. It is not worth it," Issam said.

Avadek placed his hands on Issam's shoulders. He looked through and seemed to penetrate the glasses. "This man is more than a spy. He has been to America, and I believe he carries secrets."

"How do you know this?"

Avadek showed Issam the passport. "His last visa was for the United States. His identity is the common cover for a Soviet spy. I have been to America, and I know the Russians. Believe me, I know what I say I know. We must hurry him away, or the KGB will lose no time to engage in active measures to recover this man and his things. Do as I say. Arrange transport."

MOSCOW

Under normal circumstances, Major Volodya Romanovich would enjoy the morning drive past the village of Teplyystan, a dozen miles southwest of Moscow. He relished any escape from the crowded offices of the KGB headquarters at Lubyanka, the six-story Gothic building where Lavrenti Beria once shot his enemies and tortured his friends.

This morning's drive down the narrow road that led into the dense forest that hid the offices of the KGB's First Directorate for Foreign Operations was hurried. The call that woke Romanovich from his vodka slumber was urgent. By the time he pulled his clothes on and looked out the window of his apartment down to the street, a driver was waiting in a big black Zil, the elephantine car usually reserved for highest officials. The sight of the car filled him with dread. As soon as Romanovich seated himself on the deep, comfortable rear seat, the driver departed and jetted onto the connector highway leading out of the city at a speed no Moscow traffic cop would dare question.

The Zil shot past the highway sign that forbade trespassing on the grounds of the "Water Conservation District." The driver braked and stopped just a kopeck's length short of the militia post so that Romanovich could show his buff-colored plastic pass. The driver dropped Romanovich off at the parking lot next to the guardhouse, where KGB personnel were checking in at the turnstile to begin their daily chore of subverting imperialism.

An officer in the trim khaki uniform of the KGB Guards division matched Romanovich's pass photograph with his face and waved him through the turnstile. The major walked briskly past the flower beds and lawns, ignoring the green shoots of earth that signaled the coming of spring in Moscow. He looked ahead with mounting anxiety at the seven-story structure of aluminum and glass.

On a normal day the major might have stopped at the cafeteria for a beer and admired the pretty village girls who worked there. As it was, on this day he hurried across the length of the marble foyer, barely acknowledging the flower-laden bust of Felix Dzherzhinsky, the Cheka man who was the Bolshevik state's first chief of secret political police. Flashing his pass to yet another officer of guards, he rushed to the main bank of elevators in the center of the building and pushed the button for the floor that housed the offices of the American desk.

A middle-aged secretary looked down her nose at the major and nodded her head of gray steel wool toward her supervisor's door.

An older, equally severe-looking man waited within, reviewing a stack of papers in the company of a young woman who had apparently traded on her good looks until she was able to secure employment in Moscow and finally in the world's largest secret agency. The man looked up from his papers, eyeing Romanovich through his steel glasses in a way that recalled a general on the parade ground who has spotted lint on a junior officer's collar tab.

"Another difficult night, Volodya?" he queried. "The party no longer approves of such indulgence. Even from officers of the organs of state security."

"I am well, Comrade Director. Thank you."

"That is good. There will be many hours, many days, of work ahead, Comrade Major. There has been an accident."

"What sort of accident?"

"Project Aurora has been blown."

Vassily Rudenko, the director of the American desk, never changed expression as he relayed the information, but Romanovich felt beads of cold sweat trickle down the nape of his own neck that he knew could not be attributed to vodka. Because of the director's terse announcement, he felt as though he were watching his career swim away from him, and ahead lay nothing but the horizon of a drowning sea.

The pretty assistant stacked file folders, yellow, blue, and white. She left the director's office with the folders in her arms, walking crisply in a way that indicated the energy of youth and her apparent utter ignorance about what had been discussed. Romanovich wondered why she was in the director's office at all.

"The Aurora material is no longer in our hands," Rudenko said, wiping his glasses with a handkerchief.

"The Americans have retrieved it, then? The FBI?"

"My dear Volodya," the director said, replacing his glasses, "that would be a relief. If the FBI regained control of Aurora, our task would be clear. But the material, in effect, has been hijacked."

"But how, Director? Was it the French or the Israelis, or some free-lance outfit?"

The blond assistant returned, carrying a videotape. She pushed a button by the door, and a wall console opened, revealing television, stereo, and videocassette recorder, all of latest Japanese manufacture. She drew the curtain on the window that allowed the excellent natural light to flow into the director's spacious office.

"Sit and watch, Volodya. You always liked the Western newscasts. It's not like that cheery crap we see on Vremya. There are no crop forecasts or folk dance festivals. It's exciting. We are going to watch the evening news."

Romanovich sat on the chair that faced the director's desk. It was constructed, of course, so that the director could look down at whomever he wished to address. But both men had a good view of the television in the wall console. The assistant popped the videotape into the VCR, pushed the forward button, and again left the office.

The VCR clicked and whirred. Then the newscast began.

"And in tonight's top story, we go to Rome, where yet another airliner has been hijacked after terrorists were able to carry weapons aboard," the American anchorman said in his calm, controlled tone.

The satellite film followed the airliner's departure, its refueling in Algeria, and its final landing in Beirut, where the American network's local correspondent, a young, sandy-haired Englishman with a mustache, picked up the report. He stood in the foreground of the drama as a gunman standing on the passenger ladder of the plane waved a pistol in the background.

"The Austrian Airways plane was bound for Vienna," the journalist reported in his clipped BBC accent. "It is believed that several Americans were aboard, but their fate, like the others', is not known. When the Boeing 727 jetliner landed at Beirut International Airport, several passengers, apparently Europeans from East-bloc countries, were escorted from the aircraft."

The director tapped a remote control mounted in his desk, and the tape froze the British correspondent's slightly pained features.

"Are you getting the idea, Volodya?"

"Who of our people held the Palestinian account in Rome? They did not know this piracy would occur?"

"The Rome KGB resident has already purchased a

one-way ticket to Yakutsk. After they freeze him a bit, he will be liquidated."

"But I do not understand. Our team was escorted from the aircraft. Why are they not at the embassy?"

"The bandit-terrorists of Beirut have taken our people, Volodya. Who can know their crazy minds? They are more interested in fighting each other than they are in making war on the Jews. Our people were on safe passage, in high-speed convoy to the embassy, when they were intercepted."

"Who intercepted them?" Romanovich asked, wishing he could smoke but not daring to without first asking permission.

"We do not know yet. The Beirut resident is working on it. That is the worst problem we know of. Because there has been no ransom demand."

"We need an action team in Beirut. And we need to take measures to protect our asset in California."

"You are ready to travel?"

"Of course."

"What are your intentions?"

"Recover what we have lost without fail."

"And failing that?"

"Steal it again, if I must."

"I thought so. The Aurora material is of utmost necessity to the Soviet state. You must not fail."

The major pulled at his collar and wiped a few beads of sweat from his forehead. The need for alcohol and tobacco could extract effects from him at home that no adversary abroad could accomplish, even in interrogation.

"If you must smoke, go ahead and do so, for the good of the state," the director said wearily.

Romanovich nodded his thanks and reached for his cigarettes, beloved Marlboros that he had snagged *na levo*, on the black market, when his supply from his last trip abroad ran out. Even a privileged KGB major needed a little help from his friends occasionally. He lit and puffed greedily.

"You should have better control of your personal habits, Volodya. You are allowed your excesses because you are imaginative and resourceful, but you really should quit, you know."

"It's one life I've got," the major replied. "I'm going to live it."

"I was like that, in the NKVD, with the partisans behind the fascist lines in the Ukraine," the director said, his lips pursing into what passed for a smile. "That was 1942. A quiet smoke was more valued than a roll in the hay. Well, enjoy your vice, then prepare to work. You will need all of your resources now."

"I know it."

"And one more thing, Volodya. I've gotten you some help."

"What do you mean, Comrade Director? You know I work alone."

The director pushed a button, and the blond assistant reentered the room. She didn't look like a girl from the republics anymore. She was dressed for travel, and Romanovich suppressed an impulse to whistle.

"I am Tatiana," she said. "My English is excellent. So is my French."

The director smiled again. It was a ghastly expression. "If you need to steal the material again, she will get it."

"This swallow?" Romanovich asked, almost dropping his cigarette from his lip as he laughed. "This one is for an evening's pleasure. She is not for active measures. And this assignment could go wet. I don't think you want me to bring her along for bloody work, Director."

"I can get anything," she said calmly. "And I can kill anyone to get it, if the organs of state security require."

Romanovich looked at her again, taking in the opaque beauty of her green eyes and the slenderness that hid a taut muscularity. This time, he whistled.

THE CALIFORNIA DESERT

The plane sailed nearly silent in the clear, azure air ten miles above the floor of the Mojave Desert. Inside the cockpit of the B-20X prototype bomber, the crewmen murmured quietly to one another through their oxygen masks. Their calm voices reflected the contentment experienced only by men who fly high-performance military aircraft.

The pilot, co-pilot, and the defensive and offensive avionics systems officers each had separate functions, but they worked together as a team. It was the team, not an individual, that flew the machine. Each face, beneath each mask, differed little. The men were as sure of themselves, or that which drove their inner impulses, as members of a Trappist order. Theirs was the religion of flight and of competence.

"We've been near the ceiling," said Richard Moody, the chief test pilot, nudging his control handle slightly. "Let's bring her down to the deck."

Moody's co-pilot, an air force major, nodded. The bomber descended with the apparent ease that is the result of thousands of mechanical and electronic components working in perfect harmony at zero defects efficiency. The camouflage-coated bomber dropped down to the deck and sped along, almost noiselessly, flying nap of the Earth, the way it would on penetration of Soviet airspace.

As the defensive avionics system operator worked out his electronic warfare calculations on a glowing green screen, only rabbits, coyotes, and a few stray prospectors standing in the vast aloneness of the desert took note of the bomber's progress. It zoomed down at twice the speed of sound, with its eighty-six-foot wings swept back like a prehistoric bird's, leaving sonic cracks in its wake.

The only creatures that might have sensed its approach before it soared overhead were rattlesnakes, using their pitted nostrils to detect the radiant heat of an infrared signature.

More than twenty years before the advent of the B-20X, it had taken a dozen unwitting herpetology students from UCLA months to gather the snakes needed for dissection and analysis so that witting engineers could copy their complex heat-sensing biology in order to design an efficient heat-seeking missile. The result was named, appropriately, the Sidewinder. On the ground the namesake reptiles flared their pits, detecting the dreadful creature sailing overhead in the clear desert air.

Ignorant of the bomber's progress were the six million people living a hundred miles to the south in Los Angeles. Millions of motorists driving to work on smog-choked freeways were mercifully unaware of the aircraft that carried enough destructive power to end civilization. As they drove to their jobs, tuning in to the radio and tuning out the traffic, they did not know that hundreds of bombers assigned to the Strategic Air Command had made thousands of flights during four decades of operation, each carrying their deadly complement of nuclear weapons within commuting distance of most major American cities.

Only twice had the unobtrusive presence of potential atomic ruin displayed itself during the uneasy nuclear peace that prevailed since Hiroshima and Nagasaki. In March 1958, a B-47 on a training exercise over South Carolina dropped an atomic bomb on Walter Gregg's vegetable patch. It was a mistake. The TNT used to arm the device exploded, blowing off Gregg's roof, but the atomic weapon itself thudded harmlessly to earth. The bomb's arming device, not yet engaged by the pilot, was fail-safe, the Defense Department declared.

In 1966 a B-52 exploded over Palomares, Spain. Four H-bombs fell, three of them scattering to earth and one falling in the sea. Again, because of the complex series of arming mechanisms, catastrophe was averted. Three B-52 crewmen and four fliers from a KC-135 tanker that was refueling the bomber died. The Spaniards were shaken, their tomato and bean fields strewn with radioactive material. But the nuclear peace endured.

The crashes underscored General Curtis LeMay's demand for zero defects. The architect of SAC didn't want excellence. He demanded perfection. In creating the "complex and beautiful instrument" of the Strategic Air Command, LeMay told his fliers he was "unable to distinguish between the unfortunate and the incompetent."

The men in the supersleek B-20X, soaring above the Mojave Desert floor, adhered to LeMay's credo no less than any others who held apocalypse in their hands.

"Change the wing sweep," chief test pilot Moody quietly ordered. "Let's try the stall mode."

His co-pilot nodded and threw a switch to move the wing from its swept-back configuration into its fully extended mode.

Up to that moment the bomber represented the ultimate in manned strategic weapons delivery technology. Its chief strategic advantage was that it existed in reality, not on a drawing board, as a computer model, or in the minds of designers. Its reality hovered in the nightmares of Soviet air defense officers and members of the Politburo.

Already some men in the Kremlin were aware of characteristics of this bomber. When the Kremlin's air defense minister, Dimitri Antonov, gave his report on defense development progress of the "main foe," he spoke only fleetingly of the plane. He knew its radar signature was only one percent of that of the still-feared B-52 bombers that were being replaced by the B-1 fleet. He also knew of its advanced terrain-following radar that allowed it to fly so low, it might well reach a missile base in Kazaksthan or, for that matter, the Soviet capital before anything could be done about it. These were matters he did not want to go into in great detail before the Politburo until or unless his designers had an effective copy of the bomber. This they were working on furiously.

But the bomber flying in California that morning did not make up the worst of Antonov's fears. His continued frustration over three decades had been the geometric pace of U.S. technological development. The Soviet state, he knew, was a mighty war machine. All its possible resources were poured into making Soviet weaponry the world's best. He'd once read a wire service article attributed to the great

American test pilot Chuck Yeager. He remembered the anger he felt upon reading of Yeager's contempt for Soviet air power. The American who broke the sound barrier had said all Soviet aircraft were copies of American aircraft.

Antonov had hated reading those words but knew there was too much truth in them. And now the Americans were working on a new, nightmarish device. A radar-invisible bomber they called Stealth. Antonov realized there was little hope of inventing a Soviet Stealth. Its construction was complex and involved miniaturization and materials available only in the West. It would have to be copied, and the materials needed for its construction would have to be bought or stolen.

The Soviet bomber fleet, fearsome to any other nation, could be checked by the Americans. Antonov knew this, and knew also that the best hopes for progress lay in the technology-theft capability of the KGB's First Directorate. The Soviet Backfire bomber was effective, but barely equivalent to the earliest version of the B-1 and not possessing its range or awesome combat characteristics. At the arms control talks in Geneva, the Soviet state was implacable in its opposition to deployment of new American bombers. Meanwhile the Americans saber-rattled about the Soviet Blackjack bomber, which Yeager contemptuously considered an ersatz B-1. Now the B-20X, and next the Stealth. Antonov hated and envied the American designers.

The B-20X piloted by Moody reared back from Mach 2 to Mach 1 flight and finally slowed to the speed of a World War II bomber, its wings spreading from the swept position. The object of flight test lay not only in determining how fast an aircraft would fly, but in how slow it might go. The envelope of test flight had many edges to it.

Their oxygen masks removed, the pilot and co-pilot grinned at each other like boys. It was often said that pilots were boys who never grew up.

"Put her in full stall," Moody said, winking at his counterpart.

"Roger that," replied the major.

Moody depended on the co-pilot to act as pilot so

that he might observe all of his actions. He let the major fly the plane fully, realizing that one day Moody the teacher would not be in the aircraft. He surveyed the banks of instrument panels, display screens, and gauges, feeling confident his colleague knew his way around nearly as well as he.

Moody had flown since the early days of the jet age. He was old enough, in fact, to be his co-pilot's father. He calculated the major to be capable of all actions demanded in test flight. Even with the computer models and the advanced telemetry accounting for much of the test flight regime, there was human interface with the technology. Such interface demanded zero defects. The pilot expertly brought the variable-sweep wing into stall position. Moody waited an instant for the major to throw a manual fuel transfer lever that would shift jet propellant at the bomber's center of gravity. That the procedure was manual reflected a design glitch already noted on the new bomber's flight card. The younger man looked at Moody, a question mark in his eyes. In that instant Moody felt a shift, a slight wobble. He shouted, "No!"

For an instant there was a terrible shudder of buckling aluminum alloy crunching into titanium supports. Like an elevator out of control, the aircraft plunged. It dropped so quickly none of the men could cry out as Moody threw the eject toggle and the crew were fired their separate ways from dynamite-propelled ejection seats.

Only desert creatures heard the rumble, the fire, and the explosion of America's most advanced experimental bomber. A plume of black smoke rose above the wreckage.

A remote U.S. Forest Service fire station observer spotted the smoke rising in the skies above San Bernardino County. The firefighter adjusted his binoculars and found the wreckage. He scanned the area and spotted the bodies, scattered but lying within a hundred yards of each other. One of them was crawling. It was Chief Test Pilot Moody, the only survivor of the single defect in that morning's flight.

2

CALIFORNIA,
THE ESCONDIDO SUMMIT

Scott Cartwright enjoyed driving with the top down. Ever since his days as a fighter ace in England, he had driven hell-for-leather. He was a teenaged lieutenant in an Austin Healy then, speeding to an airfield to jump in a P-51 Mustang. He loved the feeling of the wind blowing back his hair almost as much as he loved the feel of the stick during a dogfight. He still had his hair, but it had gone snow white, and a general's star had replaced a lieutenant's bar, but he still loved driving with the top down.

As he approached the peak of the Escondido Summit in his sleek black Corvette, he put the pedal to the metal and gunned it a good one. The 1969 L-9 model's 427-inch engine was revving well, and the rack-and-pinion steering held the angry car true to the rim of the road. His concentration fixed on the road, he paid little heed to the sheer sandstone and granite cliffs that tumbled hundreds of feet down, just a few inches away from the edge of his racing tires. He just wanted to catch that bastard in the red Porsche with the "Fly Navy" bumper sticker. And he was confident he would.

The car soared easily over the peak of the three-thousand-foot grade and glided into the gentle sloping curve of the road that linked the Los Angeles basin to the edge of the Mojave Desert on the other side of the San Gabriel Mountains. The 'vette gained momentum as the road straightened. Cartwright grinned as he watched the speedometer edge toward 110 miles per hour. He was going to have navy for a light snack before lunch. The needle topped 108 MPH as he spotted the red lights from the Highway Patrol cruiser in his rearview mirror.

"Damn," he muttered, and throttled back so he could pull gracefully onto the gravel highway shoulder.

The black-and-white cruiser edged onto the shoulder about fifty feet behind Cartwright, who remained seated in the Corvette's deep bucket seat. The patrolman was lean, rangy, and tall and less than half Cartwright's age. Cartwright hated taking orders from a badge worn by a youngster, almost as much as he hated deferring to generals with more stars.

The officer already had his ticket pad out and was beginning to write as he approached the Corvette. Like Cartwright, the officer wore aviator's dark glasses, and they met each other's bug-eyed stares with equanimity. Without a word, Cartwright handed the officer his driver's license in an oft-repeated ritual.

"I had you clocked at a hundred and five miles per hour," the officer said casually.

"You were wrong, son," Cartwright said. "It was closer to a hundred and ten. I'd have topped that too if you hadn't shown up. Did you see the navy guy in the Porsche?"

The officer shook his head from side to side. Then he looked down at the older man, grinning easily as he sat in the cockpit of the car that was too hot for many men half Cartwright's age. On his flight jacket, the general sported a shield-shaped patch, with an orange plane blazing past a barrier line over a field of cacti on the desert. The patch read, "Ad Inexplorata," Latin for the words "Toward the Unknown." It was the mark of the test pilot.

"Say, aren't you Scott Cartwright, the astronaut?"

"The same."

The officer looked regretfully at his ticket pad.

"Gee, I hate to do this. I'd rather get your autograph, but, damn, sir, this is my job."

"I understand perfectly, son. You go right ahead. A man's going to play, he's gotta be willing to pay," Cartwright drawled. "You gotta notebook?"

"Sure."

"Well, give it here."

Cartwright took the notepad from the officer and scrawled his easy autograph signature, "Scotty Cartwright, Oldest Man in Space."

"My boy's gonna go nuts. He won't believe it."

"You just tell him you did your duty as you saw it. You wrote me a ticket, and I told you you was doing your job, like any good American."

The officer took the autograph and handed over the ticket in return.

"Take it a little easy heading into town, General. We got radar posted along here, all the way through the Antelope Valley, out onto the desert. We got planes now, too. They'll probably get that guy in the Porsche."

"I know it, son," Cartwright said, grinning like the small devil that was always in him. "But, you know, beating the radar's been half the fun in my life. Don't matter if it's you Chippies or a MiG. I just gotta push my luck a little further. Sometimes I go too fast. I can't help it. Now, if you're done administering justice, I gotta go."

The officer put his hands on his hips and watched the black speedster glide back onto the highway. As the Corvette accelerated toward the desert horizon, the officer whistled.

"Hot damn. There goes the legend," he muttered. "And I gave him a ticket."

TEHRAN

Yazdi's widow dropped the liter of precious cooking oil she had bartered for in the bazaar and dived for the ground. As she clung to the dying brown grass of Farah Park, the liquid in the polyethylene container gushed from the bottleneck like oil from a bombed refinery. The empty hollow rush of devil wind in the sky above her told her she was close to death.

Even as she hugged the earth, she bounced off the ground from the shock wave as the missile struck a few blocks away. Yazdi's widow blinked through the grit in her eyes and looked beyond the dying trees of Farah Park near Tehran University. Quickly she stuffed the veil of her chador into her mouth, fearing that this time, as promised in the leaflets, the Iraqis would have put gas in the latest missiles to rain on the besieged capital.

She heard the singsong horns of the firefighting brigades mixing with the wail of the air raid sirens. She lay on the ground, waiting, lest another rocket smash her like the small creature she was. Across the street from the park, she could see a few people beginning to venture out of their apartments and gazing toward the threatening sky. They trudged over the broken glass and appeared furtive, stunned, and directionless. Yazdi's widow stared at the half-empty bottle of cooking oil. Carefully she crawled toward it and replaced the stopper. Half a liter would have to do, for a week or more, because of the rationing. She would have wept but was grateful to Allah that any oil had been saved.

Yazdi's widow got up, gathered her chador about her, and began to walk toward the sound of the shrieks and screams. She wanted to run the other way, but curiosity commanded her to look.

As she turned the corner her eyes filled with horror. The children were burning. The missile, unguided and unknowing on its flight path from Basra, had struck the Orphanage of the Martyrs.

A mullah stood in the street, waving his arms and shouting orders at no one in particular, one lens in his steel-frame glasses shattered. Meanwhile the firefighters poured water on the wreckage of the building, and others, grim, bearded young men, carried the wreckage of little lives out of the building. The sound of the boy children's screams was horrible.

Little boys lay broken and burned on the pavement, much as they would have a few years later after being sent to the front. A wave of hate consumed Yazdi's widow. These orphans were plucked for this fate much as her Yazdi was in 1983. Much as her little boy Hamoon was last year. They were piled into buses festooned with holy green streamers and carried to the front. Yazdi. Hamoon. Yazdi's widow cried the name of her husband and her boy until her throat was hoarse. She fell to her knees, keening and wailing.

Chaos reigned about Yazdi's widow as the firemen ran back and forth into the building, carrying more bodies and weeping, screaming children.

As Yazdi's widow kneeled on the pavement, hugging her half-liter of cooking oil, she did not notice the young fireman running toward her. He carried a little boy, perhaps three years old. The boy, filthy, dusty, and bleeding from the wreck of the orphanage, wailed hopelessly.

The fireman, holding the boy with one arm, shook Yazdi's widow, bringing her out of her tormented reverie. With an arm strengthened from wielding fire hoses, the man grabbed the polyethylene bottle from the woman. Roughly he thrust the child into her arms, and she instinctively hugged the boy to her bosom to comfort him. His crying subsided somewhat.

"Take the boy," the fireman whispered fiercely into her ear. "Take the boy and run. No one will know you have him in all this chaos."

Yazdi's widow looked dumbly at the young man, then

nodded that she understood as he handed her the precious plastic bottle of oil.

"All revolutions eat their children," he grunted, and turned away to fight the fire.

Far away and overhead, Yazdi's widow heard the hollow whistle of another rocket. And another. She squeezed the child and began to run toward home.

As the curtain of darkness descended on Tehran, another twenty missiles fell on the city like the devil's rain. Many areas were untouched. Others resembled the city of Dresden after the firestorm that turned night into day. One missile fell near the shack of Yazdi's widow. She and the boy never knew what hit them.

IRNA, the Iranian News Agency, broadcast to the panicked capital that the war for the cities had begun, and that all must prepare for sacrifice.

THE PERSIAN GULF

The Green Flight leader led his patrol within maximum visual range of the carrier USS *Saratoga*, and the four planes he commanded performed a playful wing wave as they sighted the patrol of A-18 Hornet attack fighters at nine on the clock. The Hornets, still gaining altitude from the heaving *Saratoga*'s deck, answered the Green Flight leader's greeting in kind.

"This is Green Flight leader to Tex. Let's break off and climb."

"Roger," Tex, the leader of the Phantom flight element, replied evenly.

The brace of F-14 Tomcats, trailed by the older Phantoms, throttled up and ascended toward the sun in a gradual climb over the deep blue of the gulf. The backseaters in each of the aircraft busily monitored their radar screens, scanning their cathode-ray horizons for friendlies, bogeys, and bandits. The Green Flight leader noted approvingly that the Hornets were holding a tight patrol formation near the *Saratoga.*

With the Phantoms trailing the F-14 flight element, it fell to the radar intercept officers of the Tomcats to track possible targets at maximum range, using their newer, more powerful avionics systems. With their eyes on the powerful AWG-9 track-while-scan system, the Tomcat operators stayed busy watching radar sweeps that ranged out more than one hundred miles from the Green Flight formation.

"It sure is a beautiful day," Tex declared solemnly in his microphone.

"Tex, this is Green Flight leader," the F-14 pilot said gently but firmly. "We're going to enter a radio silence mode unless we get some action. You read me, over?"

"Roger, Green Flight leader."

The four planes flew on in transonic silence, ascending gradually to an altitude of about sixty thousand feet above sea level. Heavy cumulus clouds rolled by beneath them, now and then revealing patches of blue water far below.

"Green Flight leader, this is Hot Dog," the pilot flying the second F-14 announced, breaking radio silence. "We've got a bogey flight at six on the clock and low."

"Green Flight leader. Roger. My backseater confirms, over."

"This is Hot Dog. My guy confirms an Exocet engaging a tanker. Looks like the Exocet separated from a Mirage flight, over."

"Roger, Hot Dog. Green Flight leader to Tex. Let's bounce 'em."

The four jets banked into a half barrel roll, with the Tomcats leading. As they zoomed toward the deck, the Phantoms fell back so the attacking planes trailed into a finger-four formation favored by Luftwaffe pilots a half century before. On the sea, a plume of black smoke rose from a flaming tanker. The Green Flight leader grunted as the G-forces mounted. He gritted his teeth, half in response to the accumulating gravity pull and half from anger that the flight was already too late to prevent the tanker attack.

The Green Flight leader dived through the clouds and closed range on the departing enemy formation. The Mirage F-1 fighters were accelerating away from the tanker at maximum speed, and the Green Flight leader called to his intercept officer for a range estimate.

"Their lead fighter has a hundred knots on us," the backseater said calmly on the intercom.

"Illuminate bandits one and two," the Green Flight leader ordered.

"Bandits one and two illuminated," the radar officer said, firing the beam that would allow the Phoenix missiles to home on a radiation beam launched from the Tomcat and reflected by the target aircraft.

"Launching number-one Phoenix," the Green Flight leader announced. A second later he said, "Launching number-two Phoenix."

"Roger. Launch verified on number-one and number-two Phoenix," said the backseater.

The long-range Phoenix missiles sailed away from the lead Tomcat, their semiactive homing radars following the fleeing attack aircraft.

"We've got a lock-on," the radar officer declared, concealing the jubilance he felt at hearing the acquisition tone.

"Roger."

"We've got kills on bandits one and two. Three and four are still wild."

"Green Flight leader, this is Tex. Let's close and nail bandits three and four."

"Roger, Tex. Let's go for it."

The Green Flight skimmed above the surface of the waves, all four pilots zooming with their throttles wide open on military thrust, leaving four sonic cracks behind them as the flaming tanker faded in the distance. The four fliers of Green Flight knew they could close on the bastards quickly enough to get in range for a Sidewinder salvo. Each pilot grinned while the radar operators stared in intense concentration at their CRT screens.

Suddenly, out of the sun behind them as they began another slow climb, a brace of enemy fighters descended. The Green Flight leader's radar officer heard an alarming buzz and announced on the intercom that a missile had locked on their tail.

"Green Flight leader, you're going to take one in the ass if you don't break off," Tex announced.

"I'm out of here," replied the Tomcat pilot, rolling over and pulling up into a steep climb. The missile overshot, and the Green Flight radar officer whistled shrilly in appreciation.

Climbing toward the sun, the Tomcat pilot spotted the tailpipe of his most recent attacker and let fly with the reliable Sidewinder. The predator became prey and shattered in a burst of flame as the Green Flight leader zoomed by the wreckage, watching the clear plastic window screen of his heads-up display for other foes.

He pitched the Tomcat into a nose-down attitude and spotted another bandit fleeing. Tex, the Phantom element leader, was on its tail. He launched a Sidewinder that arced after the escaping plane but suddenly fizzled and pitched harmlessly into the gulf. The fleeing plane, sensing its escape from the missile, pulled a sharp turn, but the Green Flight leader's wingman opened up with a long burst from his Vulcan cannon, disintegrating his foe.

The four planes of Green Flight were suddenly alone over the gulf off the shore of Iran, along the coastline that stretched from the Strait of Hormuz to the border with Iraq.

"It's a good day's work," the Green Flight leader said. "Let's go home."

"It would have been nice to have saved the tanker," Tex said.

"Can't have everything, Tex," declared the Green Flight leader. "We need better coordination on the ground."

"That'll be the day," Tex said.

The Green Flight passed over ships of the patrolling Sixth Fleet, maintaining the appropriate distance prescribed since the U.S. Navy announced that its Phalanx guns were on automatic and would shoot down any aircraft passing within two miles. The planes tightened formation into a welded wing, passing over the twisted, blackened steel of the half-destroyed refineries at Kharg Island.

The flight turned inland and headed north, toward its home field, just south of Hamadan in the Islamic Republic of Iran. The planes of Green Flight touched down gracefully, taxiing onto the dusty airfield in western Iran.

Each plane turned its own way, toward its tactical hangar, buff-colored bunker edifices covered with camouflage netting. In the distance, the needle points of Hawk antiaircraft missile batteries bartered from the Americans pointed skyward under the brown spidery netting that concealed them.

Mehdi Mahan, the Green Flight leader, descended gingerly down the ladder that the ground crewmen steadied. As he stepped onto the tarmac, he tried to shake out the stiffness.

Hossein, Mehdi's radar operator, followed him off the airfield, offering him a Marlboro cigarette from a carton that he'd cadged from a Lebanese smuggler. Mehdi accepted gratefully and lit it with the Zippo lighter with the U.S. Air Force enamel insignia presented to him a dozen years before, in another life, by the American general.

As the two fliers smoked peacefully beneath a dome of camouflage netting, an Islamic cleric approached them, looking at them reprovingly from behind his glasses, which, like those of all the mullahs, appeared to be the thickness of a Coca-Cola bottle. The mullah was the squadron's officer for Islamic purity, and he was an ever-present, if unwanted, presence in the squadron.

"You have failed," the mullah shouted. "A tanker was destroyed, and it is your fault."

"Go to hell," Mehdi Mahan declared evenly. "What

we did today was shoot down three Iraqi Mirage fighters. You get us an AWACS and we'll save your precious tankers."

The mullah glowered and pointed to the ghostly remnant airframes of F-14 fighter planes draped under the netting that lined the furtive desert airfield.

"Muslims have died and gone to prison to get you your airplanes," the mullah shouted. "Men have died to buy you your weapons. Your job is to protect the oil."

Mehdi Mahan flicked the cigarette and crushed it in the dust with the heel of his flight boot. "My job, little man, is to kill the enemy," he said, smiling. "I think I'm pretty good at it."

"We give you the weapons," the mullah pressed.

"You mean that Korean shit? One of my men almost died today because you bought bad goods. That imitation Sidewinder couldn't hit Tehran University."

"You complain, and your pilots speak the satanic tongue of English. Your attitude is noticed, Mehdi Mahan."

"We speak English in the air because that is the flier's international language," Mehdi said evenly. "You should come up with us one day. You might learn something."

"You should learn how to pray, Mehdi Mahan," the mullah snarled. "I will report this to the Islamic Council. Your attitude is noticed, I promise you."

Mehdi Mahan did something that few in his position would dare. He laughed at the mullah. "We don't need to pray, here, little man," he said. "Don't you remember? We are already dead men."

With that, Mehdi and his flight officer turned and walked toward their tent, which had a green banner over it, festooned with the words, in Farsi, "Patrol of the Doomed."

Inside the tent, Colonel Avadek of the intelligence service waited. He was heating tea on a small field stove. As Captain Mehdi Mahan entered the tent, Avadek smiled warmly.

PLANT 36,
THE CALIFORNIA DESERT

The red light snapped on, and a buzzer groaned on Andy Roberts's console at the Security Control Center, a complex designed to monitor all movement at one of the nation's most jealously guarded defense plants. The lumbering former deputy sheriff paced nervously from one screen to the next.

"This is Site One," Roberts announced nervously into his microphone. "See if the tower can't give us a better fix on the origin of the intruder aircraft."

"Roger, Site One," answered Sergeant Duane Peabody, Roberts's counterpart outside on the airfield. "We are setting a line around the aircraft, and Captain Booth should be en route to your location."

As Roberts paced, he hitched his Sam Browne belt a notch tighter to pull in his expansive waistline. He restlessly scanned the console of twenty television screens and hundreds of alarm buzzers. The remote cameras attached to the outbuildings and inner hallways at the plant whirred quietly as they scanned the building and plant perimeter. Inside the security complex, with its multiplicity of warning lights and buzzers blinking and moaning, Roberts sweated.

Scanning the console's multiple screens, the retired deputy couldn't spot anything amiss. But he worried nevertheless. Interruption of routine was an ill wind.

"Where the hell is Captain Booth," he muttered to himself and the large German shepherd that nestled by the door, patiently awaiting a command from his master.

On the tarmac, a squad of U.S. Air Force Security Police augmented by half a dozen civilian guards armed with shotguns warily circled a Learjet, an unauthorized aircraft that landed on the main taxiway at Plant 36 after its pilot announced engine trouble. The engine trouble referred to had not been immediately apparent as the Lear plane taxied down the runway and the plant's security detail scrambled.

A loud alarm horn droned insistently, the noise carrying for miles through the clear desert air that surrounded the plant. Thousands of workers inside the huge buildings of the plant's assembly lines and test hangars froze at their stations as the horn continued to sound.

As the horn maintained its mournful wail, work stopped at the assembly complex for the new space shuttle *Victory* in Hangar 20. Work stopped at the maintenance hangar for the Ultraflite spy plane in Hangar 8. Work stopped in the engineering complex for the Advanced Tactical Fighter in Building 12. Work on the Stealth bomber prototype stopped in its unnamed, unnumbered, windowless hangar. The horn blared, and at thousands of workstations and desks within the sprawling complex, the day's work on the bulk of the nation's aerospace programs stopped.

The horn wailed, and within the desert plant thousands of engineers, assemblers, accountants, and clerical workers looked at each other anxiously and awaited instructions.

Inside the Site One security complex, Andy Roberts scanned the television screens hooked to cameras monitoring the fence around the plant. He felt reassured as he watched a security police pickup truck making an uninterrupted circuit outside the high chain-link fence, leaving the usual cloud of dust as it wheeled along the frontage road passing sentrylike spiny Joshua trees and signs that forbade flightline photography.

As Roberts reached reflexively for a cup of coffee that had gone cold, the screen went dark. In succession, all the screens went dark.

The electronic door to the Site One security complex swung wide, and three men wearing gas masks walked smoothly into Andy Roberts's office. The first fired a silenced pistol that made a *punk* sound and ruffled the fur of the police dog, which slumped immediately to the floor.

The second man through the door lifted and fired his pistol three times in a smooth, continuous motion.

As he lost consciousness, the last muffled words Andy Roberts heard from his masked attacker were, "Bang, bang. You're dead."

The third man through the door busied himself shutting down dozens of switches on the console. A long horn sounded outdoors and within the plant's walls, signaling that the drill was over.

When Andy Roberts awoke, he found himself looking groggily at a shaken and pale Captain Booth, his immediate supervisor. The captain's arms were folded, and he was nodding somberly as he stood in the presence of a hard-looking man wearing blue coveralls, and Thomas Gunston, the secretary of the United States Air Force.

Two other men stood in the doorway of the Site One complex. Like the hard man who stood by the secretary, they wore blue coveralls, and Roberts guessed they had been the gas-masked assailants. One of them, seeing that Roberts had stirred, carried him a paper cup of water from the cooler and gave it to him wordlessly.

After Roberts took a few sips, the man in coveralls took him gently but firmly by the arm and escorted him from the Site One office. Still groggy from the tranquilizer darts, Roberts sighed. The other man in coveralls followed, escorting Captain Booth. Roberts knew that neither he nor Booth would ever see the inside of the Site One complex again.

"Where's my dog?" Roberts asked.

"Don't worry. It's all taken care of," said the man in coveralls.

Inside the Site One office the secure telephone on the console rang, and the hard-looking man who had accompanied the secretary picked it up.

"Mr. Secretary, it's the president," the man said to Gunston, who nodded and picked up the receiver.

"Mr. President? This is Tom Gunston. Yes, sir. I am on

site." The secretary listened for a moment, then replied, "Yes, sir. I'm afraid the operation was a success, but the patient died. The plant was penetrated by the air commando team and the Delta elements."

Listening again, the secretary waited politely, then responded, "Yes, sir. I agree fully. The security overhaul contemplated will take time to implement, but we must begin immediately. I have Lieutenant Colonel Donegal assisting me. The Delta element will secure the Mercury facility, where they will be assigned cover as civilian operators. They will also provide an unseen screen of additional security during your visit."

The secretary hung up the phone. He sat down at the console and methodically dialed the combination on his attaché case, removing a sealed envelope as he had been instructed to do by the president. Opening the envelope, he showed two photographs to Lieutenant Colonel David Donegal, who commanded the combined detachment of Air Force commandos and Delta troopers.

"During your tenure as interim security manager at this facility," Gunston said, "there are only two men who will be given total unrestricted access to the plant. You are looking at their photographs, Colonel. I want you and your men to memorize them."

"A lot of people will know who this guy is," Donegal said, pointing to the photograph of an older man. "Who's the young guy?"

"He works for the president."

"Good enough for me."

"They will not be briefed on your assignment or your presence. Nor are we briefed on their mission. But you are to provide any assistance they should require if it becomes a matter of direst need. Those are your orders, Colonel."

"I understand, Mr. Secretary."

One of the men in blue coveralls monitored the screens on the console. "Sir," he said quietly, "here comes the bully beef express."

The colonel and the secretary leaned over the console

and watched an eighteen-wheel tractor-trailer pass through the gate and lumber slowly toward the Mercury Aviation complex.

"There are eight nuclear weapons on that truck, Colonel. Hot enough for you?"

"Mr. Secretary, I once humped a nuclear weapon on my back," Colonel Donegal said casually. "That was in Germany. We carried backpack nukes."

"Well, I'm glad you're experienced, Colonel. There's enough firepower there in that one truck to erase the United Kingdom. Guard it well."

"With my life and the lives of my men," the colonel said, nodding.

Outside, the tractor-trailer rumbled, and its gears made a high-pitched grinding noise as it turned a corner into the towering Mercury secure hangar, the only one without a number on it.

THE AIRFIELD AT HAMADAN, IRAN

The briefing room at Hamadan Military Airfield was a large tent of heavy waterproof canvas manufactured in the United States. Like the hangars, it was disguised with camouflage netting. The mosquito net windows that would have allowed some fresh air into the musty structure were covered with blackout curtains. Inside, a kerosene lamp burned, casting eerie shadows across Colonel Avadek's bearded face.

The pilots and backseaters of Green Flight lounged in their metal chairs, each in the various angles of repose assumed by airmen drained by the rigor of a day's combat flying.

"Welcome, friends," Avadek said, smiling. "It is not every day one is able to greet such fearsome patriots."

"We are not friends," said Sidi, the youngest flier. "Soldiers and fliers do not befriend the secret police."

"So, you think you know more about me than I do about you," Avadek said. "You speak quickly, young one. What makes you decide that I am, in fact, a policeman?"

Sidi gazed at the impassive face of the intelligence officer. "You wear the simple boots and field coat of the Revolutionary Guard. But you are older than they." His face twisting in hatred, he continued, "You look like the men who took my father away. I would guess you were once SAVAK."

"You are apt and bright," Avadek said cheerfully. "Now let's see what I know about you." He opened a drawer on a small field table and removed a stack of brown file folders.

All the fliers gathered in the tent shifted uneasily on their chairs. They knew the presence of files could not bode well for them. Avadek leafed through the folders and picked one. He lit a cigarette and exhaled noisily as he read the contents. Then he gazed at the young pilot named Sidi.

"Your nickname is 'Tough Guy,' isn't it? Are you a tough guy?" Avadek asked, switching from Farsi to nearly unaccented English.

"Who wants to know?" Sidi demanded, also suddenly speaking in English.

Avadek looked down at the file again and burst into spontaneous laughter. "You must have seen too many thrillers at the cinema when you attended the Air Force Academy in Colorado," he said, chuckling. "The 'Fat Man' gave you that nickname, didn't he?"

Sidi looked down at the dirt floor of the briefing tent, deciding for the moment to keep his mouth shut.

Captain Mehdi Mahan of the Islamic Revolutionary Air Force stood up and stared at Avadek until the intelligence officer returned his gaze. Mehdi's face was handsome, open, and intelligent, defined by an aristocratic Persian nose and a razor mustache that was the opposite of the shaggy features of the Revolutionary Guards. He frowned with concern.

"Colonel Avadek, why is it that you wish to see my men? Surely you know everything you need to know about them. Half of their families are your prisoners. Still, these good men fight every day for the defense of the homeland. What more do you want from them?"

Avadek rose. Although he was nearly a head shorter than Mehdi, his solid bulk and confident manner made him an intimidating presence. Again, he smiled. He exhaled cigarette smoke through his nostrils, walked toward a map of the battlefront, and turned to face the Green Flight leader.

"They call you 'the Old Man,' don't they? Why, I would wager you have not yet seen thirty-five years on this angry planet," Avadek said, squinting at Mehdi. "You are young. Yet when the American general Secord trained the shah's air force, you were considered the best pupil, were you not?"

"I have paid for that distinction," Mehdi said bitterly. "I pay for it every day."

"That is true," Avadek said, folding his arms and inclining his head as though he were in deep thought. "You certainly are special, Captain Mahan. You, like all of your men, are under sentence of death." He paused and added, "What a group."

Avadek walked over to the map of the battlefront and traced his finger along the line of trenches and battlements that separated the marshes of western Iran from the siegeworks of the Iraqi border. "If we should lose this war, you will no doubt die in battle," he declared. "Time runs out for all fliers, eventually. But if we should win, you will die anyway. It is not easy to escape a sentence of death from a revolutionary regime. The leaders of such movements use a hot iron to burn out the sins of the past. Believe me, I know."

"We are not afraid of death," Sidi blurted out.

Avadek turned to him and chuckled again. "No, of

course not. But you do not believe in Paradise, either. That is why the mullahs arrested you. You were religiously impure. And you were polluted by America."

"America," spat Hossein, the radar operator. "We would not have had all this trouble if not for America. I wish to God I had never gone to that place. My family would be free now."

"Yes," Avadek said wistfully. "Those are the fortunes of war. In the day of the shah, you were the pick of the crop. But the shah fell. Suddenly your former ally and teacher becomes the hated enemy. Your former commanders flee to exile. Your new leaders hate all men of the twentieth century. The new commander is your jailer and someday, perhaps, your executioner."

"Fuck them all," shouted Reza, the flier who had been nicknamed "Hot Dog" by his American flight instructor. "We will do what we can as long as we are able. If we die, so be it."

Avadek barked a short, bitter laugh. "How proud the mullahs would be of you," he snorted. "That's the attitude that has cost this ancient nation a million lives over just a few years."

"It's out of our hands," Captain Mehdi Mahan said stoically. "We will fly and fight until we die. We are professionals. That is all that's left for us. Perhaps when we die, our loved ones will be shown clemency."

Avadek nodded his head. "Perhaps. But maybe there is another way to regain favor."

"What have you got in mind?" the Green Flight leader asked, his voice filled with suspicion.

"I must know first if you are willing to face danger, grave danger. I propose a mission, a mission that could turn the tide of this bloody war in our favor. But many of you might die, even if it succeeds."

"Who do you think you are talking to?" Mehdi demanded. "We are fliers."

Avadek smiled. "Then I think you should fly with me to the Zagros Mountains."

"The Zagros?" Sidi exclaimed quizzically. "But there is nothing there. It's a wasteland."

"There is something there now."

"You speak in riddles, Colonel," Mehdi said. "What is it that we are going to?"

"Security bids me to be silent, for the moment," Avadek said. "You are familiar with the American term 'need to know.' You will understand me sooner than you think. Go get your things and prepare to leave this place."

Mehdi motioned to the other men in the flight. They knew an order when they heard one. Avadek seemed to carry his rank within him, rather than on the collar of his simple Revolutionary Guards' field jacket.

THE IRANIAN CENTRAL PLATEAU

The men of Green Flight piloted their motley collection of fighter aircraft over the Zagros Mountains to final approach at the isolated airfield and touched down on the perforated metal landing strip in a tight formation that would have made the U.S. Air Force Thunderbirds precision flying team proud.

Captain Mahan, "the Old Man," flew a special prize that had been gathering dust in a secret hangar. It was a two-seater training version of the F-16 Fighting Falcon, the last fighter plane purchased by the shah. The rest of the lot of some sixty of the General Dynamics planes never made it to Iran. Instead they were sold to Israel after the Pahlavi dynasty fled to exile. This plane, refitted lovingly by Mehdi's personal maintenance crew, was the jewel of what once promised to be one of the world's greatest air forces. It was a remnant of the former riches and power of the man who aspired to be the "Policeman of the Gulf."

The mysterious Colonel Avadek had demanded the

best of the reserve equipment and, to Mehdi's amazement, had gotten it. Green Flight's formation, touching down at the isolated airstrip, resembled a history of the last thirty years of American fighter development, an F-16 Fighting Falcon leading two F-14 Tomcats, followed in by an aging but worthy F-4 Phantom.

The turbofan engines of the warplanes of Green Flight whined at a high pitch as they rolled across the metal sheeting toward the makeshift hangars, which were little more than spidery collections of netting. A hot desert wind blew in sandy gusts across the eleven-thousand-foot airfield, which was surprisingly long for such a makeshift facility. The hastily improvised base, if it could be called that, made the military field they operated from at Hamadan seem a luxury.

"This looks like hell," said Hossein, Mehdi's backseater, as he descended the metal ladder from the F-16.

"I agree," Mehdi said matter-of-factly as he scanned the barren facility.

Oil field workers had hastily leveled out the airstrip. A U.S. Army surplus "water buffalo" tank was parked at the end of the runway to meet the basic needs of thirst. Two fueling trucks stocked with JP-4 and JP-5 were hidden in the netting, and a maintenance facility had been carved in the ground and covered with corrugated metal and earth. That was it.

From behind the fuel trucks, a jeep pulled out and drove toward the fliers. Avadek sat in the passenger seat and Issam, incongruously outfitted in designer civilian clothes and sunglasses, drove the jeep. Avadek, smiling, stepped down from the vehicle and embraced Mehdi.

"What does this mean?" Hossein shouted as the other fliers gathered around behind him in an anxious circle. "Why do we come to this hellhole? We could have trained for any mission at Hamadan."

Avadek walked to Hossein and, patting his cheek, said, "Little brother, what did the Americans call you?"

"Dead Eye," Hossein replied.

"I know," Avadek said. "It's in the file. They called you this because of your keen vision. You are, in fact, the finest radar intercept officer trained by the American Military Assistance Advisory Group. Look around you. What do you see?"

"I see a place in hell," Hossein cried, gesturing wildly. "There is nothing here but dust and wind."

Avadek smiled gently and nodded agreement. "Precisely," he said. "Listen to the empty howling wind. It is the sound of secrecy."

Their conversation was suddenly interrupted by the whine of approaching jet engines.

"Air raid!" yelled Ali Rezai, the pilot code-named "Tex." The eight fliers, including Mehdi, began running to scramble their aircraft in the instinctive response of highly trained airmen.

Avadek stood by the jeep, laughing. The sullen young man in the jeep grinned.

"It is no air raid," Avadek shouted. "These airplanes belong to us, to our little group."

The airplanes materialized, black dots growing larger in the haze that draped the Zagros mountain range. One was a DC-8, a commercial airplane, painted with the colors of the Iranian national airline. The second, following the first in as though on approach to Mehrabad International Airport in Tehran, was a military version of the airliner. It was a KC-135 tanker.

"What's the meaning of this, Old Man?" Reza asked his commander.

"It is not for you to ask immediately," Mehdi said with uncharacteristic curtness. "All will be made clear to you by and by."

"I don't like this," exclaimed Sidi. "Always we have done everything with our eyes open. We want to know the risks. We should be told what is happening."

"Soon enough you shall know everything," Avadek said, folding his arms. "At this point, secrecy is paramount. If there are objections, you must leave this place, now."

Sidi, Reza, Ali Rezai, and the other fliers looked at each other uneasily. Sidi gazed a moment at Avadek, then turned to Mehdi as the large aircraft taxied onto the field.

"We will do as you say, Mehdi," he declared. "You are our leader."

"Then I say we follow Colonel Avadek. His plan will be made clear to us soon."

As the large aircraft rolled to a halt, a team of a dozen men in mechanic's coveralls sprang from the maintenance bunker and ran toward the airliner. Some of them rolled a universal step toward the airliner. As the pilot, co-pilot, and engineer emerged, they were taken into custody by three of the men in coveralls, who put pistols to their heads. The fliers looked dismayed at their fate.

Issam slipped from the jeep and sauntered toward the group by the airliner. Almost casually he pulled a P-9 automatic pistol from the waistband of his slacks. Wasting no motion, the men in coveralls pushed the flight crew toward the end of the airstrip. Followed by Issam, they disappeared behind the jetliner. The men of Green Flight looked at each other in horror and disbelief as they heard three sharp cracks. Another three shots followed as Issam administered the coups de grace.

"What is the meaning of this?" Ali Rezai demanded of Mehdi and Avadek. "What sin did those men commit?"

Avadek replied coldly, "For this mission, security is everything. The military tanker crew will instruct us on how to fly the large plane. We must learn well."

"We are not hijackers and assassins. We are fighter pilots!" screamed Reza.

"You are wrong," Mehdi said simply. "For this mission, we will become hijackers."

With his arms folded, Avadek regarded the men of Green Flight. "And if assassins are needed, you will do that also," he said. "You have pledged yourselves to follow Captain Mahan. Do what he says and you will be rewarded. Fail, and the penalty will be severe and immediate."

"We have never failed," Sidi boasted, all the while

using his peripheral vision to try to see what had happened at the end of the airfield.

"Good," said Avadek. "But in case any of you should have thoughts of leaving this place, remember this: there are no guards here. They are not needed. This airstrip is on a plateau surrounded by salt flats. Run out onto the flats and you will drop through the ground. First you will be cut to shreds by the salt crust, which is about three meters thick. After you have been sliced by the salt crust, you will fall into salt water and drown in the marshes below." The colonel lit a cigarette and offered the pack to the fliers, who all declined. "This is a secret place," he continued. "The only way out of here is that way." He pointed to the sky.

Issam walked back from the end of the runway, replacing the automatic in the waistband of his trousers. He was grinning broadly, like a boy lighting firecrackers.

Days at Avadek's secret airfield passed quickly, even in the dizzying heat. Avadek made sure that the men of Green Flight drank enough water to keep from passing out, nearly a quart an hour. As the men woke in the darkness each morning, they heard the sound of a bulldozer moving earth at the end of the airfield. Neither Mehdi nor Avadek would tell them the purpose of the giant hole being dug in the ground.

Sporadic shipments of fuel made practice with the tanker aircraft episodic. But when there was fuel, Mehdi drilled the pilots relentlessly on touch-and-go flying from the eleven-thousand-foot airstrip. In the skies well back from the war front, the fliers practiced flying a tight formation pattern. The tanker pilots would align their aircraft with the DC-8 flown by Sidi and Ali Rezai for air-to-air refueling exercises. Reza piloted one of the Tomcats on the starboard side of the airliner.

Mehdi directed the exercise from his F-16, watching Sidi bring the probe on the nose of his aircraft toward the boom snaking from the tanker. It was a perilous airborne ballet sufficient to challenge the aptitude of any flier.

"Tighter," Mehdi commanded over his cockpit radio. "You are flying like old women."

"We are encountering some turbulence, Old Man," Sidi radioed from the airliner, which had just effected the hookup with the tanker.

"Give me results, not excuses."

"You sound like the American general," Hossein joked on the intercom, which he activated by pushing a button with his foot to speak from his backseat position.

"Forget the American," Mehdi ordered curtly. "If we fly well, it is because we know we must fly with excellence in order to survive."

"I speak of the American only because he was our teacher, and a good one," Hossein said, sounding slightly hurt at the reproach.

"If the shah had lived in Iraq, the Americans would have helped them instead of us. We have no friends in the world. It is the fate of a great people."

As Hossein pondered his commander's words, the tanker completed its refueling operation and pulled away from the airliner, its fuel boom retracting into the aft section.

Almost immediately, the radar scopes of the escorting aircraft lit up simultaneously with the image of an approaching aircraft. Their cockpits buzzed with warning tones from their identification friend-foe panels.

"I've got a bogey, approaching at three on the clock and high," Reza announced from his Tomcat, relaying the information his backseater had deciphered on the Grumman plane's powerful radar.

"This is Green Flight leader. No friendly aircraft are cleared for flight in this sector. I identify as a Mirage. Do you roger, Hot Dog?"

"Affirmative, Old Man. Who will watch Mother and Father while we engage?" Reza queried, referring to the large aircraft that had just completed the refueling operation.

"This is Green Flight leader. I have them under my wing. You are free to engage, Hot Dog. Watch your six."

Reza banked to meet the approaching hostile aircraft, a swept-wing Mirage F-1. Mehdi, diving in his stubby-winged F-16, flew a scissors pattern between the tanker and the airliner. Completing his maneuver, Mehdi climbed to thirty thousand feet to command a protection zone around the two large aircraft. As he climbed to position, Hossein coolly announced a missile separation from the Mirage.

Mehdi made his decision instantly, transmitting his warning to Ali Rezai, who was piloting the airliner. "Tex, this is the Old Man. Break right. Break right. Break right."

The airliner dived, shedding altitude as the Mirage fired a Matra Super R550 Magic missile, the French equivalent of a Sidewinder. The missile sailed past Ali Rezai's airliner and struck the tanker's starboard engine. The tanker's wing caught fire, and the large plane plummeted crazily toward the desert floor in a flat spin. It crashed seconds later, shaking the earth and shooting a fiery plume of flame and smoke a mile into the sky. There was a new hole in the desert war zone.

Ali Rezai turned the airliner sharply about and dived toward ground level, flying as low as possible in hopes of evading another missile. The Mirage dived, apparently attempting to fix the location of the second large plane. The Iraqi pilot either ignored or missed the Tomcat piloted by Reza. Reza's radar officer got the acquisition tone on the Mirage, and Reza fired a Sidewinder missile that sailed faultlessly to the tailpipe of the Iraqi plane, blowing it to fiery pieces across the sky.

"This is Hot Dog. Bull's-eye, one Mirage," Reza announced calmly, all the while scanning the skies for other hostiles. The horizon was clear, and he headed for home with the drug of victory pulsing savagely through his veins.

Feeling sick at heart, Mehdi landed the F-16, taxied up to one of the makeshift hangars, and climbed down the ladder. Avadek approached him on the tarmac, his expression grim.

"You lost the tanker," Avadek said.

"I preserved the integrity of Green Flight. Which is more important?"

"Yes, of course," Avadek said, waving his hand dismissively. "Sooner or later, for security reasons we would have had to liquidate the tanker crew. None but yourselves can know of this mission or this place."

"What do you mean, liquidate?"

Avadek snorted and lit a cigarette. "It is an American CIA term. Eliminate. Sanction. Terminate with extreme prejudice. The Russians have the same terminology, with variations. They call it 'wet work.'"

"But it all means the same thing, to kill in cold blood without mercy or regret, right?" Mehdi snatched the cigarette away from Avadek, threw it to the ground, and crushed it with his flight boot. "Do not smoke on the flight line, my colonel. You could liquidate Green Flight with a single cigarette."

Avadek stared coldly at the flier. "You should be more careful. About how you behave, I mean, young captain. I could liquidate Green Flight with a wave of my hand."

"I suppose I should be more careful. Look where being reckless has got me. Meanwhile, you be careful on my airfield. Jet fuel and cigarettes do not mix," Mehdi said, wagging his finger.

Avadek looked at him again and laughed. "Did anyone ever tell you that you look like the American cinema actor Errol Flynn? You do, you know. Now, where are your wayward children?"

They turned toward the jagged horizon line of the Zagros Mountains and watched Reza flying in aboard the Tomcat, trailing the DC-8 piloted by Ali Rezai on final approach.

"You were right, of course," Avadek said, lifting a pair of binoculars to watch the horizon. "The integrity of Green Flight is paramount."

"We needed more refueling practice, and we needed the expertise of the tanker captain."

"I can't get you another tanker, but there is something that will help you even more, I think."

"You were able to obtain the package you described, then?"

"Obtaining the difficult is my specialty, Captain Mahan."

Mehdi whistled thinly between his teeth. As they spoke, the airliner taxied to the far end of the runway and pulled onto the apron, where Avadek's hand-picked maintenance crew moved it into a hangar constructed of camouflaged corrugated steel on the sides and netting on the top.

The men of Green Flight marched toward Avadek and their leader, shedding their parachute harnesses and looking relieved that they had lived to fly another day, even if the tanker crew had not. But the tanker crew mattered not so much, thought Avadek; they were not men of the Green Flight.

Sidi, the one called "Tough Guy," looked agitated, his young face turning several shades paler than its normal olive hue.

"I do not like to be in an airplane that has no missiles to defend itself," he said.

"You mean you are not up to the job of co-pilot on the big plane?" Mehdi demanded.

"I did not say that," Sidi declared angrily. "I can fly anything! But by all that is holy, I want to be able to defend myself."

"The plane you will fly will not need missiles to defend itself," Avadek said, smiling. "Follow me, holy warriors."

Avadek walked from the apron into a tent, where Issam lounged on a camp bed. In one hand he held his ever-present pistol. In the other he held the case seized from the Soviet courier in Beirut.

"Doesn't he ever talk?" Mehdi asked Avadek, gesturing toward Issam. Issam gazed at Mehdi from behind his reflective sunglasses.

As the other fliers approached the tent, a rat raced

from under some wooden planking out toward the desert. In one smooth motion Issam raised his pistol and fired a single shot, making the rodent sail into the air. It was dead before it hit the ground. The men of Green Flight scrambled aside.

"That is the way Issam usually speaks," Avadek said. "Pay him no mind. He is a rogue."

"Are all those who work with you rogues, Colonel Avadek?" Sidi asked.

"No. I also work with spies and assassins. And an occasional idealist. Do not worry about Issam."

Avadek bade the fliers follow him and walked outside the tent, talking as he walked. "By the time we extinguish our lamps this evening, you will know many things," he said, lighting his Gauloise and blowing foul-smelling tobacco smoke through his nostrils. "You will have knowledge of the tree of good and evil."

As he spoke, the ears of all the men of Green Flight pricked up. They could hear the turboprop engine noise of an approaching C-130 Hercules.

The metal container delivered by the Hercules was the size of a small house. It was rolled down the ramp of the cargo aircraft by the Hercules crew and settled on a massive wooden pallet. The maintenance team that Avadek commanded shrouded it immediately with netting, and the bulldozer was used to push a large dune of sand behind it against the possibility that the airfield might be spotted and strafed by a Mirage or MiG returning home to Iraq.

The crate sat exposed in the waves of heat that shimmered off the apron until evening. The pilots relaxed in their tents, drinking tea and making reports on the morning's action for Mehdi, who maintained his reputation as a strict administrator even in the distant camp. Once again they heard the sound of an approaching aircraft. This time it was the whirring drone of a large dragonfly-shaped army helicopter, a Sky Crane used for moving artillery pieces.

The men of Green Flight walked out to the flight line

and watched wordlessly as the crew chief of the Sky Crane attached hoists and straps to the metal container. Taking orders from Avadek, who directed the operation using a walkie-talkie, the crew chief completed his work in about fifteen minutes, and the container was hoisted about twenty feet in the air. As the sun sank behind the western horizon, the giant copter lowered the container into the earthen bunker that had been dug for it.

"I bet we don't have more than one of those Sky Cranes operating," Sidi remarked quietly. "I thought the Iraqis had gotten them all before the big push on Basra."

"You are looking at the last one," Avadek said.

"You must have a lot of pull to requisition such a machine," Reza remarked.

"My precious patriots, there is no more important mission for the homeland than the one you are assigned to perform."

The Sky Crane eased the metal container into the ground. The crew chief separated the hoists and rode the cable back up to the cockpit like a genie returning to a bottle. The helicopter flew away into the gathering darkness.

Avadek gestured, and the men of Green Flight followed him like children. Issam followed also, carrying the ever-present attaché case. They walked toward the bunker in the earth and descended on a metal ladder that had been placed in a slit trench leading into the bunker. The bearded mechanics were busy placing cables from generators and auxiliary power units into the plugs placed at intervals along the outside of the container.

With Mehdi's help, Avadek opened a metal door and swung it wide. There was a metal ladder leading to yet another, smaller door. Avadek climbed up first and opened the small door. Mehdi climbed up behind him and gestured for the others to follow him into an air-locked room about the size of a kitchen. Avadek walked across the room to another inner door and opened it, beckoning the fliers to follow. "Step inside, holy warriors," he said. "Now the serious lessons begin."

As the fliers crowded each other to get a view of the chamber, there was a collective gasp of awe from all of them. In all its features, the chamber duplicated the flight deck of a sophisticated transport aircraft. If it had been on the European continent, it would have been a suitable centerpiece at the Paris Air Show.

"I've seen nothing like this since the academy in America," Hossein exclaimed. "What airplane is this?"

"It is a cockpit simulator for an Aeronautiquebus transport," Avadek said matter-of-factly. "But with your help, it will be used to simulate the aircraft you are being trained to fly."

"How did you get this?" Sidi asked incredulously.

Avadek smiled. He lit a cigarette and puffed thoughtfully. "The Europeans want our oil, all of it that we can sell them, anyway. And they so badly want to sell their commercial airplanes. This flight simulator was presented to our government as an inducement to buy. A gift, really. Once it was in Tehran, I had only to ask for it. I usually get what I ask for."

Captain Mehdi Mahan sat on the pilot's chair of the simulator, which was a perfect working model of an airliner cockpit. He pointed to Ali Rezai and bade him sit next to him on the co-pilot's chair.

Together they surveyed the instrument panels in front of them. In place of conventional dials and needles, there was a row of six video display screens. Above the cockpit window there were more than one hundred caution, advisory, and warning lights. Outside the cockpit window, it was dark.

Mehdi threw a yellow switch next to the throttle control, and outside the cockpit the window glowed an eerie green. Then forms outside the window took on color and shape, like those on a television warming up. Suddenly the men inside the cockpit were looking down the runway of a major airport, which had been digitally programmed for the flight simulator.

Mehdi turned to his men and grinned. "I believe we

are ready for takeoff." Saying this, he moved the throttle forward, and the mock aircraft appeared to speed down the runway. Expertly Mehdi maneuvered the control yoke, and the aircraft was "airborne," with all the men grabbing bulkheads as the plane quite convincingly lifted off from the taxiway. They could sense the climb from the hydraulic systems that pushed the nose of the simulator upward.

"We are in league with the devil," Reza declared, and Hashemi, his radar operator, nodded vigorous agreement.

Mehdi maneuvered the simulator into a final approach pattern and brought the "airliner" in for a gentle landing, the aircraft's hydraulic simulated landing gear thumping along as he approached the end of the video landing field.

"It is good," Mehdi said, tapping the control yoke in satisfaction.

"That is the mission, then," declared Sidi. "We are to hijack a plane full of OPEC diplomats and hold them for ransom."

Avadek, relinquishing his grip on the bulkhead, laughed, his nearly finished cigarette dangling from his lips. "My friend, what you are going to take is more precious than a planeload of old farts with briefcases. And what you are going to take is finally more precious than the oil, which becomes more difficult to send every day the Iraqis increase their attacks."

"What is it, then, this holy mission?" demanded Reza.

"Learn your component of the mission first," Avadek declared. "At this moment, yours is not to reason why. As the Americans would say, knowledge will be given only to those with a need to know. Or it will be earned."

Mehdi threw switches and shut down the video scenery that hovered outside the cockpit simulator, so that the only light in the chamber came from the glowing green cathode-ray tubes on the control panel.

"You have much to learn," he told his huddled subordinates. "The flying is only half of it. Colonel Avadek, will you instruct your subaltern to pass me the materials we discussed?"

Avadek, switching from Farsi to Arabic, murmured quietly to Issam, who opened the Soviet courier's case and passed forward a file jacket and a plastic container for computer diskettes.

"Ali Rezai, tell Colonel Avadek why it is that the American general decided to call you Tex."

"I already know why," said Avadek. "You attended Texas A&M University. Refresh my memory, Lieutenant. What was your course of study?"

"Computer engineering," Ali Rezai replied. "I was an honor student."

"See if you can do honor to these materials," Mehdi said, passing the box of diskettes to the younger pilot. "I want you to program this cockpit chamber to achieve interface with this software package provided you. Can you do it?"

Ali Rezai grinned. "I need a Randomware computer with a data conversion cable. The cable is Japanese."

"That should be no problem," Avadek said. "We have good commercial relations with the Japanese. Now tell me something. Do you think you could fly a plane as complex as the one laid out before you in this simulator?"

Captain Mehdi Mahan rose from his position at the flight controls. "There is no need even to ask, Colonel Avadek," he said resolutely. "The Iraqis have nearly dominated the air war. But we men of Green Flight have denied them dominion and harried their ships and cities. We are as good as the German pilots who flew outnumbered against the Americans and Russians. We are better than the Zionists. If it came to a fight, we could beat the Americans."

Avadek lit a cigarette and puffed thoughtfully. "I hope that you do not boast, young captain. If we fail in this mission, we could lose the war and our existence as a nation. And the fight with the Americans you speak of. It could come to that."

He turned to the group. "I must now ask you—are

you capable of performing an impossible mission? If you are less than capable, I must find others who are up to the task."

The pilots eyed each other sullenly, resentful that their competence was questioned by this outsider. They looked to Mehdi, who returned their stares and then nodded somberly.

As one, the fliers rose, clenched their fists, and pounded their chests. Their arms shot out from their chests with the fists clenched. Together they shouted: "Green Flight, the nation, and victory!"

Avadek surveyed the young men, with their fervent eyes and clenched fists. He bade them sit and offered them smokes from his pack of cigarettes. This time, each man accepted.

OVER THE CALIFORNIA DESERT

About ten thousand feet off the deck, in the skies above Rogers Dry Lake, Cartwright put the needle-nosed X-29 aircraft into a gentle roll. With blue sky above him and an endless expanse of buff, brown earth below, he reined back the control stick and brought the plane close to stall. When the aircraft had done its trick, he tapped the stick forward, and it dived, like an obedient steed handled by a world-class rider, which of course Cartwright was.

As the plane zoomed a few hundred feet above the prehistoric lake bed, Cartwright followed his lifelong habit and gunned it, leaving the sharp crack of sonic thunder in the jet's wake, the same way he had more than forty years before, when he was a young stallion chasing Yeager's tail smoke. Yeager had been the first, breaking the invisible sound barrier that defeated all men and machines before the Bell X-1 he'd dubbed "Glamorous Glennis." But Scotty Cartwright stayed close behind Yeager's tail until he passed him, climbing up to the edge of space in the X-15 and then, one fine day, clear outside the envelope in the space shuttle.

After his X-15 exploit, which put his face on the cover of *Time* magazine, Scotty Cartwright, who was never one to hide his light under a bushel, dubbed himself the first man in space. Now, with a chuckle, he called himself the oldest. It had taken plenty of congressional pull to get his ride on the *Columbia*, but he'd done it. Cartwright had piloted a space shuttle back onto the hard, cracked earth of Edwards Air Force Base at an age when most men were piloting golf carts through retirement. Unlike most men, who allow the physical prowess of their youth to fade and their reflexes to slow, Cartwright seemed to improve with age. Like his rival Yeager, he aged like hickory wood.

Thundering above the dry desert floor, he pulled the

stick back and climbed. A voice crackled in his earphone. It was an engineer, wanting to know about the plane's roll characteristic.

"She's sweet," he told the ground engineer, who monitored each microsecond of the flight, recording the telemetry that would decide if the plane represented the next century's generation of fighter planes.

"How's that wing, Eagle?" the chief engineer queried.

Cartwright nosed the X-29 higher, his body tingling for any signal that the plane with the strange, forward-swept wing would begin to shudder and part at the seams of its wings, made of a combination of alloy and plastic.

"The wing's snug," he radioed back. "Snug as a tick in a puppy's ear. I'm coming in."

"Roger that, Eagle. You are clear for approach."

Cartwright put the plane into level flight, then banked and swooped down onto a heading for home base. He loved solitary morning flight over Rogers Lake. Actually, it wasn't a lake at all; it was millions of acres of prehistoric silt deposits that made it the largest landing field in the world. With that margin of forgiveness, he had landed countless aircraft, including a spaceship. A few times, after an un-lucky flameout, he had landed on his own two feet on the dry lakebed. It pained him to have to use a parachute. After his feet-first landings, his wife, Gloria, would remind him gently that he couldn't walk on thin air any more than he could walk on water, and he would tell her he wasn't so sure.

Leaving behind the dry lake at Edwards Air Force Base, he banked left and thundered a few miles south to Plant 36. There the X-29's wheels bumped onto the tarmac, and the sleek plane eased to a stop. The bubble opened, and Cartwright emerged from the cockpit, looking like the fa-miliar figure on the high-performance tire commercial and at the same time looking startlingly like that young fighter ace who'd climbed out of a prop fighter a generation earlier.

On the airstrip, two men waited for him to descend from his airplane. It was easy for Cartwright to see that they did not belong there. They were not engineers with pens in their pockets. They were the sort of humorless fellows who wore dark suits and little earphones and stayed close to the president. The only outward characteristic that distinguished them in appearance from Secret Service was the absence of sunglasses. The wind whipped their suit pants, and if the heat that shimmered in waves off the desert bothered them, they did not show it. Their poker faces might have belonged to guards at Buckingham Palace.

Several engineers ran from the tower like schoolboys to greet Cartwright and congratulate him, slapping him on the back in hopes that some of what he had might rub off. The men in the suits watched all the pleasantries, unimpressed by the general's mystique. As Cartwright finished shaking hands with his admirers and turned to walk toward the hangar, the men in the suits approached him.

The general saw them coming and waved. "You fellas must be FBI," he said cheerfully. "What's up?"

For just an instant, both agents lost their perfect composure. They never believed they were so easily recognized, despite the fact that by their mere presence they could only be FBI or corporate lawyers who had lost their way.

"That's correct, General," said the senior agent. "You're to come with us, sir."

"Fine, but what for?"

"We don't know, sir. It's not our party. But I would say that judging by the names on the guest list, it's pretty damn important."

"Well, I've got the whole day open for the FBI."

The trio marched into a large, low-slung building that looked like a dozen others on the cactus-patch grounds of the Plant 36 complex. The men stopped at a checkpoint just inside the building, and the uniformed security guard, recognizing Cartwright, waved him through. The guard then painstakingly examined the plant identification the FBI men had been provided with, matching photographs to faces.

Cartwright, still wearing a flight suit, caught the stares of secretaries, computer programmers, and middle-management executives alike as the three men walked down the twisting hallways in the labyrinth.

"General, if this were a ballpark, this bunch would be mobbing you," the senior agent observed sourly.

"Nope. Not these folks. We all know each other. We're in the same business, making airplanes for Uncle Sam and driving 'em where he needs 'em."

After clearing another checkpoint, they walked through an air-lock door that quietly *whoosh*ed shut behind them. They stepped into an elevator that sank down through a twelve-foot layer of hardened concrete several stories beneath the earth.

They waited outside a steel door where an air force security guard in a blue beret peered from behind a bullet-proof window, with his M-16 at the ready. A red light changed to green over the door, and it swung open. Once again the guard checked the passes and this time was just as thorough with the general's ID.

The trio passed through a final air lock and stepped into a small conference room, where the president of the United States sat at a sturdy oak table reviewing a stack of files with the directors of the FBI and the CIA and Madeline Murdoch, the national security adviser.

The president, wearing a formal navy-blue pinstripe suit that highlighted his broad shoulders, adjusted his half-frame reading glasses and smiled at Cartwright.

"General, I'm glad you could come," he said, offering his hand. "We're in a bind, and I told these fellows here that I thought you could help out."

Of all the postwar presidents, Cartwright genuinely liked this one and considered him the best since Eisenhower, who conformed with Cartwright's liking for competent generals. He approved of the president's war record in Korea.

"I'll do whatever you need done, sir."

"Good. Have a seat. These good people have put together a little show for us."

Cartwright shook hands with Daniels, Dr. Murdoch, and the austere-looking FBI director, who was known as "the Judge." He knew Murdoch and Daniels through their joint efforts to press Washington to adopt a "high frontier" defense system that would protect the United States from space. He knew the Judge only by reputation.

From the pocket of her gray suit, Dr. Murdoch produced the hallmark of her profession as the nation's top briefing officer, the telescoping pen pointer. She walked over to a stand and removed a blue flannel cloth covering a flip chart.

"General, you are about to witness a brief review of a sorry history of security breakdowns. Breakdowns which unfortunately we have been unable to prevent."

"I don't know if that's entirely accurate," snapped the Judge. "If Americans were not actively engaged in selling their country's secrets, this briefing wouldn't be necessary."

"Judge, let Dr. Murdoch proceed without interruption," the president said in a tone of such quiet authority that for a few seconds the only noise in the room came from the air-conditioning ducts.

On the first laminated panel on the flip chart was a color photograph of an F-14 Tomcat supersonic fighter, still a formidable aircraft. Next to it was a grainy photograph of a similar-appearing aircraft, but the red star on its tail indicated it was a MiG.

"The Soviets got the Tomcat away from us because we handed it over to them piece by piece," said the former Georgetown professor, flipping to the next panel, which displayed charts depicting cruise missile components of U.S. and Soviet manufacture.

"Look familiar, General?" she asked, using the pointer to match areas of similarity between the two diagrams. "They got that from us, too. And thanks to a Mr. Bell, formerly of Hughes Aircraft, and Jan Zacharsky of the Polish intelligence service, the Russians were able to get the radar that would allow them to shoot down a cruise missile.

"Of course, the MiG Fulcrum fighters will use an air-to-air missile to fire at the cruise weapon that was also thoughtfully provided by Mr. Bell to his friends," she added.

"We should have taken Bell when he was in Switzerland," Brady Daniels said, punching his left fist in his right hand like a catcher who'd blown a key play. "We should have grabbed him the same way the Mossad got Eichmann."

"That's water under the bridge, Brady," the president said. "Bring us up to date, Doctor."

The next display looked like a rogue's gallery in a post office. It consisted of photographs of sour-faced men, stubbled and grim in their middle age. Cartwright recognized a few of the faces from the news. Walker, the wisecracking ex-navy man who'd handed over the secrets of the fleet for thrills and cash. He recognized a picture of Richard W. Miller, a pudgy, failed FBI man who'd handed over his country for nothing but a few afternoons in cheap hotels and rented rooms with an alcoholic Russian émigré woman. And there was Jonathan Jay Pollard, doing life for giving the navy store of secrets to an ally, Israel.

Murdoch pointed at Miller's photograph. "Remarkably, the conviction of an FBI man as a spy aided our cause," she said in her detached briefing voice as the Judge shifted uncomfortably in his chair.

"Judge Kenyon threw the book at Miller, and it was good for the country. Too many traitors were getting a slap on the wrist and a promise of immunity in exchange for cooperation. Miller won't get out for many years."

"Begging your pardon, Professor, what's this got to do with me?" Cartwright asked. "I read the papers, like anyone. But I'm no spook. I'm a flier."

The president turned slightly in his chair and put his hand on the general's arm. "Just a little more patience, Scotty," he said in his warm, deep tone. "You don't suppose I flew out here while all those fool reporters think I'm up at Camp David to waste your time, do you?"

"No, Mr. President. Of course not."

Both the Judge and Brady Daniels fidgeted with their arms folded as the professor flipped to the final chart, a map of the Plant 36 complex. The diagram looked like a maze for Pavlov's rat.

"General, there is a mole working right here in Plant thirty-six. This country's top-secret strategic weapon is under development in this complex, and some son of a bitch is trying to move it to Moscow," Madeline Murdoch said crisply.

"You mean the Mercury project, the Stealth bomber."

Murdoch nodded grimly, crossing her arms in her sensible sturdy jacket.

"We want you to catch the son of a bitch, Scotty," the president said, gripping Cartwright's arm tightly. "And we want it done before he hands our friends in the Kremlin a gun to hold at our heads."

Cartwright looked at the president and nodded his slow, sure nod of understanding. "I'll do what I can, sir. But I don't yet see how I figure in."

"You will, Scotty. Brady and the Judge will tell you what you need to know to get started," the president said, patting the general's arm. "When they finish briefing you, you'll be pretty much on your own. We don't have a lot of time. Things aren't at a good stage in the latest round of arms talks with the Soviets. If we ever went to hostilities, we wouldn't want them to have this weapon."

"I understand, sir. It's a first-strike weapon."

"Not for us, Scotty," said the president, shaking his head sadly. "But it certainly could be for them. You've got to keep them from getting it. You've got to."

The president, who always sounded so warm and sure, sounded a desperate note that was out of character.

"You've got my word that I'll try my best, Mr. President."

"There won't be any medals for effort, Scotty. You've got to do it."

"Sir, I've never served my country for medals or rank

or privilege," Cartwright said, effecting a sharp salute. "It has been an honor to do my part."

The president nodded gravely, signaling the general to drop his salute. "We're both old soldiers, General," he said, offering his hand. "We know about duty."

The men shook hands, and the president got up to leave, rising as though he carried a heavy weight.

IRAN, THE DESERT AIR BASE

The ancient Mercedes-Benz truck rolled up to the tarmac in the gathering dusk, and the men of Green Flight dropped down from the tailgate. Like sailors running down a gangplank for shore leave, they hit the ground running. In pairs they raced toward the flight line. The machine guns at the other end of the airfield lit up, spitting bullets along the apron as the men ran lightly, their flight boots barely touching the perforated metal of the airstrip.

The bullets pinged and ricocheted, threatening at any instant to drop the three teams of fliers who appeared to be running a pattern for a soccer game. From the tower that looked down on the airstrip, Captain Mehdi Mahan kept one eye on a stopwatch as he monitored the men's progress while they ran serpentine over a pattern of rubber tire obstacles. Avadek watched the exercise through binoculars.

The rate of gunfire from the sandbag bunkers on the far side of the airstrip accelerated, and pink tracer fire lit up the evening sky as the men fanned out to run to their separate aircraft, the Tomcat, the Falcon, and the DC-8 airliner. As the machine-gun fire continued chattering, the turbofan engines of the three aircraft began turning over, and soon the aircraft were taxiing down the runway.

Standing at Mehdi's side in the crude tower was Hossein, the Green Flight commander's radar intercept officer. As the planes picked up speed toward the end of the runway, he fired a red flare, signaling the end of the exercise.

"Three minutes forty-seven seconds," Mehdi announced matter-of-factly, watching the sun sink behind the mountains in the distance. "That is thirteen seconds better than last time."

Avadek clicked his tongue in disgust. "They will never have that long. We will need them on the taxiway in three minutes."

"It cannot be done, I fear, my colonel."

Avadek glowered. "It must be done, Captain Mahan! If the nuclear bombers of the American Strategic Air Command can scramble in three minutes, why cannot the men of your little command?"

"The Americans will not face hostile fire running to their bombers."

"So you can't do it, then," Avadek hissed, for the first time looking angry.

"I think they can," Hossein interposed. "I think we can, my colonel. We will need more practice."

"They must be better soon, Lieutenant Hossein. The clock is running."

"Hossein," Mehdi said abruptly, "retire the men and recite the evening prayers. I must talk further with the colonel."

Reluctantly the radar officer climbed down the steel ladder leading up to the tower, which was little more than a collection of steel pipes and wood.

Mehdi turned to face Avadek and gazed at him levelly. "It is time to be frank," he said.

"How so?"

"Stop it! Do not answer my statements with questions. I need the truth, and now. What exactly are my men being trained for?"

Avadek lit a cigarette and puffed. "Surely you must have guessed."

"What I see before me is a training session for a suicide mission. What I don't see is the reward. I see that my men are running naked onto a flight line that is raked by machine-gun fire. Who is to be the attacking force? What are we getting into?"

Avadek ran his fingers through his thinning hair. He placed the Gauloise so it dangled between his lips and lowered himself onto the ladder. "Follow me, young captain."

Descending the ladder, Mehdi Mahan trailed Avadek as he walked briskly toward his quarters, a low tent near the end of the apron. Inside the tent, Issam lounged on a bunk. Avadek motioned to him, and the young man pulled the courier's case from under the bunk and set it on a small field table. Avadek adjusted the oil lamp hanging in the tent so that it burned evenly and brightly, casting shadows on his weathered face.

Avadek seated himself on a chair and bade Mehdi sit on a spare bunk. He opened the case and carefully began removing papers, all stamped "Top Secret: Aurora."

"It is a good thing, Captain, that the SAVAK was trained by the CIA," Avadek said casually. "You see, the CIA expected the shah to be America's policeman here in the gulf."

"Spare me the history lesson, Colonel. What is your point?"

"My point, Captain, is that the CIA planned for us Persians to be their cutting edge against the Soviets. We were trained, you see, to enter into combat with the KGB. We did exactly that."

"And so?"

"And so, these materials you see in front of you would have been destroyed except for the fact that I received such thorough training at a faraway place called 'the Farm.' It's in the American state of Virginia, some distance south of Washington, D.C. It was there that I learned how to deactivate a KGB courier's carrying case so that it would not destroy the secrets inside."

Avadek motioned to Issam, who stepped outside the tent into the darkness and took up his post as sentry.

"What were the contents of this particular case?" Mehdi asked.

"Many things. It staggers the imagination. You trained with the Americans also, did you not, Captain Mahan?"

"You know that."

"Tell me, did you like them?"

"They were friendly enough. I liked some of them. But they always wanted to be boss."

"Precisely," Avadek said, rising from his chair and

pacing with his hands drawn together behind his back. "That is their way. It is the road of empire. They were the boss, and we were...what would you say? We were the little guys. The little brown brothers, I believe."

"It was them or the Russians," Mehdi said, curling his lip in distaste. "I would rather dine with the devil who lives far away than the devil who is close."

"Maybe it doesn't have to be either devil," Avadek said, sitting down again and spreading the documents in front of him. "Could you drop a nuclear bomb, Captain?"

"What are you saying?"

"I am saying that if you can give me the correct answer, you may save the children and widows who are being bombed daily in Tehran. And you may save some of the old men and boys who are marching to Paradise in the marshes."

Avadek gazed at the documents in front of him as a jeweler might look upon an array of fine gems. For a moment he appeared nearly hypnotized. Then, he spoke.

"What I am showing you is not sorcery. It is real. We took these from the Soviet courier in Beirut. They are stolen American documents, belonging to the Mercury Aviation Corporation."

"What documents?"

"In a word, everything," Avadek said, an edge of excitement entering his voice. "They relate to production of the American Stealth bomber, which is code-named 'Aurora.' The courier was carrying the schematic drawings of the aircraft and the draft operations manual."

Mehdi's eyes widened, and he whistled thinly. Then he furrowed his brow. "How did he obtain such materials?"

"The Americans are a corrupt people. Someone stole them and sold them to the highest bidder. Obviously that bidder was the Russian courier, whose flight we interrupted."

"Of what use are these documents to us?"

"In addition to the drawings and the computer software package for the flight simulator, there is the schedule for the prototype aircraft's flight trials at the Flight Test Center in California. In effect, it is an itinerary of when the bomber will be fueled and armed. There are also drill instructions for the arming sequence of the weapons system."

"Why would a prototype aircraft be armed? And with what armament?"

Avadek sorted among the papers on the field table. He pulled a document that was evidently a photocopy. It was pink and topped with the words "Classification Top Secret–Black: Aurora."

Mehdi's English was excellent, and he read quickly. In simple block letters, the memo read:

MR. PRESIDENT:

PURSUANT TO YOUR REQUEST THAT THE NEGOTIATING TEAM AT GENEVA BE PREPARED WITH THE WIDEST RANGE OF OPTIONS, IT IS DEEMED ADVISABLE BY THE MAGIC-13 WORKING GROUP OF THE NATIONAL SECURITY COUNCIL THAT THE AIRCRAFT CODE-NAMED AURORA RECEIVE ITS FULL COMPLEMENT OF B-83 GRAVITY-DELIVERED SINGLE-MEGATON WEAPONS. IT IS THE NSC'S OPINION THAT THE SOVIET COUNTERPARTS IN GENEVA WILL BE APPRISED OF THIS DEVELOPMENT AND MODERATE THEIR NEGOTIATING POSITION ACCORDINGLY, CONSIDERING THE AIRCRAFT'S CAPABILITY TO SUCCESSFULLY PENETRATE SOVIET AIR DEFENSES. UNTIL SUCH TIME AS SECURITY AT PLANT 36 CAN BE GUARANTEED BY AN EFFECTIVE COUNTERINTELLIGENCE OPERATION, IT WOULD SEEM PRUDENT TO HAVE THE OPTION TO USE AURORA IF NEEDED, RATHER THAN LOSE IT DURING AN INITIAL STRIKE.

DR. MADELINE MURDOCH
NATIONAL SECURITY ADVISER

Avadek leafed through another pile of documents until he found a second single-paragraph memo. It read:

Top Secret–Black
Subject: Aurora

Confirm receipt of Magic-13 report and agree. Approval is hereby affirmed for installation of armament package on Aurora project.

The memo was signed by the president of the United States.

"This is the aircraft we are going to hijack?" Mehdi asked incredulously.

"If you can do it, Captain Mahan."

Mehdi whistled again.

"The plane carries eight nuclear bombs. Qaddafi tried to buy a bomb. He couldn't. Saddam Hussein tried to build a bomb. The Israelis stopped him cold and left his reactor in ashes at Osirak. We will take our bombs, and the aircraft that carries them," Avadek declared, his eyes glowing in the lamplight. "Like thieves in the night, we will take the plane and the bombs from under the Americans' noses. Within a month we will win the Gulf War, and then we will assume the same power and stature in the world as France and China. With eight bombs and a sophisticated delivery system, we will not be the little guys anymore. We will not be a regional power. We will deal as equals in this dangerous world."

Mehdi looked at the lamplight playing on Avadek's leathery face. He decided he was sitting at the devil's own table.

3

TEHRAN

Colonel Avadek surveyed the slums of Tehran with distaste as his driver sped south toward the holy city of Qom. There were so many city dwellers now. Most were dirty and hungry, and the capital could not support them. They were the legacy of the shah's great leap forward. The peasants had abandoned the countryside in search of city wages. The hungry people, and the idle cranes that stood like rusting gallows, were like ghosts of the shah's rule. Pahlavi was many years gone, but the mullahs still invoked his hated name to stir the masses against the many enemies of the Islamic Republic. And because the city and surrounding slums were crowded, many young men piled into the buses that would carry them to the front.

The car sped past Beheshteh Zahra, the martyrs' cemetery, where bulldozers prepared the way for the latest harvest of the dead. There, at the Fountain of Blood, where the water gushed red, the boyish Basij shock troops were exhorted by a holy man to fight for their own ticket to

Paradise. To Avadek, the fountain represented an artery, pumping away the lifeblood of his ancient nation.

The Mercedes-Benz rolled south on the bumpy road, and Avadek gathered his thoughts. He would need to be careful in his presentation to the Imam. Who could know the thoughts of the most revered? The wrong suggestion and a man's short life could abruptly end against a wall in a basement. Yet Avadek did not expect that to happen. Even though he had given such orders many times, he survived.

"What will you tell the ulama?" Issam asked.

"I do not speak to the mullahs," Avadek said. "I will confer only with the holy one."

"I am amazed he would grant you audience. There is the matter of his son."

"I was not involved. It was SAVAK, but not me. I can assure you, if I had played a part in the young man's disappearance, I would not be speaking to you today."

Issam lit a Marlboro from his last carton, which he had bartered for with a friend at the American University Hospital in Beirut. He smoked with relish, realizing that when the carton was gone, obtaining another would be difficult. "I still do not understand how it was that you were spared, when so many of your comrades who served the shah perished," he said.

Avadek turned and smiled at the younger man as the car drove on in the gathering dusk. "I will always survive," he said. "If you do not understand that, you do not know Avadek at all, my little brother."

"In any event, you will also have to contend with the Imam's other son. If he is not convinced, your plan will surely fail."

"He will help us. For survival, we need victory. And if the holy one listens to me, we will have it."

The sun was setting over the low brown roofs of the holy city of Qom as Avadek and his protégé arrived, passing the Hawk antiaircraft missile batteries purchased at great price from the minions of Reagan. The driver slowed as he entered the narrow, twisting streets that led to the university. A loudspeaker blared in the distance, calling the faithful to their evening prayers. The colonel was hungry and would have liked a kebab and some rice, but there was no time for food.

After the driver showed his pass, the car rolled past a barricade manned by Revolutionary Guards. The car drove into a gated courtyard. Avadek, always alert, could sense the tension in the air. He looked up to the roof and saw more guards, hoisting Stinger surface-to-air missiles onto their shoulders so they could scan the horizon.

"Has there been an air raid?" he asked the driver. The driver shrugged.

The colonel leaned forward from the backseat, so that he could hiss in the driver's ear. "Listen to me, dog," he whispered, punctuating each word as he twisted the driver's collar with his powerful hands. "When I ask you a question, you turn to face me and give me an answer, or I will have you on a martyr's bus faster than you can say 'Praise Allah.' Understand?"

The driver nodded fearfully while Issam laughed.

"There has been no air raid, Excellency," the driver gasped.

"That was the right answer, little brother. Now, wait for us, and pray that we are happy when we return."

Issam's laughter died down, and he assumed a somber expression as he followed Avadek from the car across the courtyard. Escorted by a pair of Pasdaran, the Revolutionary Guards who enforced the will of the Imam, Issam and Avadek passed through a wooden door and walked down a hallway with walls painted white, the color of purity.

At each turn of the hallway a guard armed with a West German G-3 rifle waited like a statue. At last the Pasdaran who escorted Avadek and Issam opened a tall, heavy door into a large room. As one, the four men sank to their knees and bowed their faces before the scowling portrait of the Ayatollah Ruhollah Khomeini. They then looked up into the stern and meditative face of the old man's designated successor, a bespectacled cleric who sat with his knees crossed beneath the portrait that hung from the whitewashed, undecorated wall.

The eyes of the Imam Haman Safavi were brown pools that appeared to first absorb all detail, then probe the inner thoughts and feelings of his visitors. Issam shivered as the old man's glance shifted toward him.

Next to the holy man sat his son, an equally austere presence, only younger and not possessed of the aura of power that appeared to radiate from the old man.

"What is it you have brought me?" the old man asked hoarsely in Farsi.

"We have a treasure, Imam," Avadek replied graciously.

"Will it aid the faithful and banish the evil ones?"

"With the aid of Allah, it could destroy them."

The old man blinked and gazed impassively at Avadek. The colonel was not a religious man, but he still felt a chill as the holy man stared at him. The old man blinked again.

Finally the Imam spoke. "The military and the intelligence services always promise more than they can in reality provide. But it is the holy warriors who defend the republic."

Knowing his life could depend on his response, Avadek said simply, "We have come into possession of plans for a weapon that could annihilate the foe at a single stroke."

"I would hear more of this," the old man said.

"Better, Imam. Let us show you."

The old man nodded. Avadek took the attaché case that Issam held, opened it, and leafed through a manila file. He left the photocopied documents in the file but began handing the Imam's son a series of sketch drawings and computer-aided designs and artist's conceptions of a wing. The classification printed in bold black letters on the photocopied documents was "Top Secret." The letterhead on the documents was Mercury Aviation.

The ayatollah studied the drawings, then looked to the blue veins on his slightly palsied hands. He was a mystic. Issam's heart pounded as he watched the old man who appeared almost to float on the cushions beneath him. His robes encircled him like dark clouds gathering. He gazed at the kneeling men and addressed Avadek after a silence of many minutes.

"Tell me more of this treasure."

"We have documents indicating it is a weapon of great ability. It is an aircraft, Imam. A plane superior to any used thus far in the holy war."

"A plane cannot be so powerful as the legions of the faithful who sacrifice themselves daily," the ayatollah pronounced simply. "We have airplanes, but they have not prosecuted the war to great effect. They cannot even protect Tehran from the rockets given to the enemy by the evil ones."

"It is our martyrs who carry the war to the foe," the ayatollah's son said sharply, speaking for the first time.

"This plane would vanquish the foe," Avadek said.

"Where is this weapon?"

"It is in America."

"Of what use is it, then?" the holy man's son snapped.

The Imam's features darkened. The lines of his face became sharpened creases, each as deep as canyons. "The Great Satan," he murmured. "We have their planes already. They are of little use. They are always breaking."

"Imam," the colonel said, turning his hands up in supplication. "This aircraft is singular. It would end the war with glory for the faithful."

The old holy man shook his head, appearing for the moment strangely puzzled. "How is it that an airplane that is in America can help us? The land of the devils is many thousands of miles away."

"Imam," said Avadek, turning the palms of his hands upward in supplication, "I have a plan that will deliver the plane into our hands."

For a fleeting instant the ayatollah smiled and regarded Avadek with open curiosity. Before he could ask a question, his son spoke.

"How did we come by knowledge of this?" the ayatollah's son demanded.

"This little one from the Lebanon brought it to us," Avadek said, gesturing to Issam, who swallowed so that his Adam's apple bobbed nervously.

"Who are you?" the Imam's son asked Issam, switching easily to Arabic.

"I am only a follower of the Imam," Issam replied. "And I am a fighter for the memory of Imam Musa Sadr, who was taken from us poor folk in the Lebanon."

The old ayatollah's face brightened suddenly. A trace of a smile crossed his face as though he were sharing a pleasant memory with himself. "Musa Sadr," he said quietly. "Did you know him?"

"I knew only his teachings and that he loved the Shia peoples. I know I would die for him."

"He was my friend," said the old man. "He was the fruit of my life. One day we will avenge his disappearance. Now, little one, tell me how you came to possess these American documents."

"We took them from the Russians, in Beirut," Issam blurted, glancing sideways at Avadek.

The ayatollah's face brightened, this time into a beneficent smile. And he laughed softly. "A gift brought from America by way of Russia. Both Satans," the old man said, chuckling. "Truly, then, this was a gift from Allah."

The ayatollah's son glowered at Avadek, evidently not pleased that a suspected heretic had brought a prize to his father. "Plans are mere pieces of paper," he said. "They mean nothing of themselves. What do you propose to do? Can we trade them for weapons?"

"Is it not true that we have many followers who go to university in America?" Avadek asked.

"You know it is true," the son answered. "Do not speak in riddles."

"If it is true that we have such people, people who already help us to obtain parts for our planes in the war with the Iraqis, then there are people who may help us with what we will do."

"Which is what?" the son growled.

"We will go to California and take the plane."

"That is absurd," the ayatollah's son snapped.

"With a few good men, Imam, I can do the job."

The ayatollah rocked back and forth on his knees. As he did this, a thin stream of breath exhaled from behind his ancient teeth, making a noise like the hissing of a tea kettle. It took Avadek several moments to realize the old man was laughing.

BEIRUT

Major Volodya Romanovich's car never stopped as the driver sped toward the embassy. This driver was fast, but precise. He looked tough.

"We could have used you a couple of days ago," Romanovich told the driver, shaking a Marlboro from his pack, which the man gratefully accepted.

"*Spasibo*, Comrade Secretary," he said, nodding his thanks and slowing just a bit as the powerful Mercedes entered the deteriorating grandeur of the once fashionable Hamra Street shopping district.

Romanovich watched pairs of Syrian paratroopers strolling the boulevard, casually cradling their Soviet assault rifles as they inspected the wares in the shops and the people hurrying. The major also noted the beauty of the women, who stepped lightly in their spiked heels, attracting the stares of the soldiers.

"All is not Islamic law in West Beirut, I see," the major said wryly, noting to himself that one dark beauty had legs as strong and smooth as those of his new colleague, Tatiana.

"Many here do not wear the veil, unless the radical Shiites are in control. Personally, I do not care what they believe," the driver said with a leering smile. "I like a bit of leg."

The car passed quickly through the fortified gate of the embassy. Romanovich stepped out of the Mercedes, entering the main building through a side entrance, as was his habit. After showing his pass, he walked quickly to the office of the KGB resident for Beirut, whose cover job was that of secretary for cultural relations with the Lebanese, a high priority in the Kremlin.

Romanovich stepped into the ornate outer office that was graced with a large portrait of Lenin and Marx advancing beneath the huge red flags of socialist internationalism. The KGB major wondered what the long-departed Cheka chief Dzherzhinsky would have done about the hapless Beirut resident who had allowed a Soviet diplomatic convoy to be hijacked by Arab terrorists. He decided quickly the first Cheka chief would have spent one bullet to solve the problem.

A pretty secretary, obviously a Moscow-imported mistress, rose gracefully as Romanovich strode into the room. "Identify yourself," she said sternly.

"Don't bother to announce me," Romanovich said carelessly. "Your boss knows I'm coming."

She stood dumbfounded as he brushed past her. No one had ever entered her chief's office that way.

The portly, balding resident was shuffling a stack of papers as Romanovich marched in.

"On your feet," the major ordered. "The day of accounting has come."

"You cannot address me in this fashion," the resident snapped. "You are just a major. I am the resident for Beirut."

"You are the resident for about another five minutes, unless I say differently. Don't talk to me about rank, Malenkov. I am not an apparatchik with an uncle in the Party. I am from Moscow Center, and you will answer every question to my satisfaction, or you and that woman out there will be shoveling coal in Siberia. Understand?"

The resident sank in his chair and held his head in

his hands. "What am I to do?" he murmured, more to himself than to Romanovich. "No one understands. This city is mad. Never before have I failed. No one can accomplish anything here."

"Snap out of it and tell me what happened," Romanovich said, seating himself on a gold brocade chair and lighting another Marlboro. He did not offer one to the resident.

"Those men, the ones from the plane. They have vanished. That is all."

"No one vanishes. The KGB can find anyone. Where do you think they went?"

"That is the crime of it, Comrade Major," the resident said, attempting to win Romanovich to his point of view. "We know where they went, but still they are vanished. They were taken to the Shia slums near the airport. It is a warren of sniper nests and snake pits that no one can enter."

"What did the American marines call that place before they all died?" Romanovich asked, waving his cigarette. "It was a pretty bad place as I recall."

"You remember, then," the resident said, sounding relieved. "It is a no-man's-land."

"What are the Syrians doing for us? I assume they must have intelligence assets here, even if the Soviet state does not," Romanovich said caustically.

The resident got up and paced, clasping his chubby hands behind his back. "No one can go there, not even the Syrians. Those Shia keep everyone out."

"They sound pretty tough."

"They are not tough, Comrade Major," the resident said in his pleading tone. "They are just crazy."

"No. They are just tough. Tougher than the KGB in Beirut. Not a trace of fat on them. How does that make you feel, Malenkov?" Romanovich asked, poking the resident in his ample waistline.

The resident wiped his forehead with an embroidered handkerchief. "Who can be prepared for men, and women, who drive trucks filled with dynamite and laugh as they explode themselves in the blast? Not the Americans. And how are we to stop such an attack?"

Without answering, Romanovich lifted a Russian cigarette from a silver tray on the resident's desk. He lit it, spat a few leaves of tobacco from the loose wrapping, and regarded the resident with contempt. "Comrade Resident, you are dealing with people who are truly committed. It was Soviet people with similar commitment who won the revolution and beat Hitler," he said, stubbing out the cigarette. "To defeat such people, we have to be bigger bastards than they are."

"What do you suggest?"

"Grab a couple of their people. Then give me a sharp knife and we will see how powerful their God is."

Romanovich shoved the ornate desk telephone toward the resident, and the portly man began to make hurried telephone calls to friends, allies, and enemies who owed the Soviet state a favor.

PLANT 36
THE CALIFORNIA DESERT

After the president departed the conference room, Cartwright noticed his three advisers exhale a collective sigh, and he wondered whether it was from relief or exhaustion. The FBI director leaned back in his chair with his arms folded, regarding Cartwright. Brady Daniels fumbled with a briar pipe, packing flakes of tobacco from a leather pouch. Madeline Murdoch pulled a pack of brown cigarettes from her coat pocket and offered one to Cartwright.

"No thanks, ma'am. I quit after the surgeon general's report," Cartwright said easily. "Besides, smoke's not good for the eyes. Visual acuity is what kept me on flight status all these years."

"I understand, general," said the whiskey-voiced adviser. "Seems like everybody's quitting these days. I can remember when smoking was quite smart. Now even a university professor can't light up without getting a lecture."

"Well, I won't try to make a convert of you," Cartwright said.

"Let's finish briefing the general," the FBI director snorted. "That way we can all get back to work."

"We are working," said Brady Daniels, blowing great puffs of smoke that were immediately sucked into the underground air-conditioning system. "And if the FBI was working a little faster, we wouldn't need the general's help."

The Judge started up from his chair, moving toward Daniels. "I won't stay here and listen to this," he said.

"Gentlemen," Madeline Murdoch said in her firm professorial tone, "we aren't here to squabble, or to debate the merits of the nation's intelligence apparatus. We are here to serve the president, so let's get on with it."

"Amen," Cartwright said. "Now, if you don't mind, I've got a question."

"Certainly, General. What is it?" Murdoch asked.

"Where's my point of contact with the air force? What level is the air force briefed at? I'm an old blue-suiter, and I can't imagine them not being in on this."

"Let me be blunt, General," Madeline Murdoch said. "The air force has not and will not be briefed. Neither has Mercury Aviation been informed. Because that is where the problem lies. You are the only blue-suiter—well, you are almost the only blue-suiter with a need to know."

"Are you telling me the branch of service most affected is not aware that you've got some kind of half-assed James Bond operation going?"

"It better not be half-assed, and it better not be a James Bond operation, General," the FBI director snapped.

"One air force officer other than yourself has been briefed. He is a major from the Pentagon."

Cartwright rose from his chair and paced, brushing his shock of silver-white crew-cut hair in a habitual gesture.

"A major. I don't get it," he said, shaking his head. "You say the commies got their hand in the air force till. And you say they're trying to get their mitts on the hottest project we've got. And now you say you're running this investigation with a retired general and an officer who is barely field grade?"

"We think we have a plan that will work. Will you listen to it?" asked Madeline Murdoch.

"I already told the president I would."

"Good. Brady, will you buzz for Major Glassman? I think we're ready for him now."

The electronic door popped open, and an officer in a light blue summer uniform entered. Cartwright immediately noted the silver master pilot's wings above the breast pocket on the lean young man's shirt. The major stood at attention until Cartwright told him to stand at ease.

"General, may I introduce you to Major Adam Glassman," Murdoch said, and Cartwright offered his hand.

"Glad to see another pilot in this spy ring," he said, evaluating the major's grip.

"It's good to meet you, sir," Glassman said, returning the handshake tentatively. "I recognized you from the commercials."

"Hell. I guess that's how anybody born after 1950 knows me."

"Nearly everyone is familiar with your exploits, sir."

"Not all of them," Cartwright said evenly.

"Let me give you a little background on Major Glassman," Dr. Murdoch said. "He has been an air attaché with the Israeli government, and flown test evaluations on their Lavi fighter plane."

"I'm impressed," said Cartwright. "Anybody who's flown with those guys must know his way around an airplane."

"More recently, he's been assigned to the Defense Intelligence Agency."

"I'm a paper pusher now, General," Glassman said, his lip curling a bit. "I evaluate the threat. My specialty is Soviet aircraft, their capabilities and research and development progress."

"Sounds like interesting work, son," Cartwright said.

"Well, it's delayed until we're finished working together."

Cartwright's ears tingled. He detected hostility from the younger man. It was a kind of resentment he often ran into during his career when he encountered rival officers less accomplished than himself or people who had been turned down for assignments he had drawn because of his skills and abilities. But it was rare for Cartwright to run into a younger officer with a chip on his shoulder. They were almost always in his corner, eager to learn from the old master. This guy, he felt, seemed to think he knew it all.

"You can finish the briefing, Major."

"I won't show you any charts, maps, or photographic overlays, General," Glassman said, sticking one hand in his pocket and brushing back a shock of wiry black hair with the other. "This is an oral briefing on an intelligence matter. For your ears and eyes only. Essentially, we want to bait a trap. We believe we will be approached by someone at Mercury Aviation Corporation, here in the Plant thirty-six complex, after we have presented their top engineers with some tantalizing data on a new project being developed by a rival firm. That is the bait."

"And you are hoping that will snare your game," Cartwright said.

"Yes, sir. You catch on quickly."

"That's why I'm a general, Major," Cartwright said, smiling.

"That is why you were deemed most fit for the assignment," said Madeline Murdoch. "It is the Pentagon's desire that the person who is a Soviet deep-cover agent in Plant thirty-six take note of your personal involvement in a high-security project. We hope your presence will make the project an irresistible target for espionage."

"Sounds just like hunting ducks with a decoy."

"Just so, General," Madeline Murdoch said. "With aid from the FBI, Major Glassman has designed a series of briefings that should tantalize several people with a high-level access to the project. And your presence will create

enough stir to let middle-level employees know that something is in the wind."

"That way," said the Judge, "we can surveil upper
management and the middle rank for any extraordinary
activity. We would use your act, if you please, in the same
way that our agents posed as Arab sheiks a few years ago
during the Abscam sting."

"Do you folks think I can act?" the general asked,
grinning.

Brady Daniels coughed and said, "Let's hope so,
General."

"I think that about wraps it up," Madeline Murdoch
said. "You two will be on your own, for the time being. The
Judge has a top field agent, however, to act as our liaison.
Until you hear from him, good hunting."

"What happens now?" asked Cartwright.

"Major Glassman is running the operational end,"
Brady Daniels said. "Can you make arrangements with
your family to let them know you're needed in Los Angeles
for a few weeks?"

"Gloria knows my duffel bag is always packed. I'll tell
her I'm flying test on some new executive jet."

The presidential advisers rose and shook hands with
Cartwright. The Judge pushed a button, and the door buzzed
open. Cartwright noted that all their shoulders appeared to
sag as they trooped out. He never regretted his career
decision to remain on flight status. He knew it denied him a
second star, but it kept him young.

"Say, Major, I gotta hike out to the pad and get into
that X-29 jet NASA loaned me this morning, so I can drive
it over to Edwards," Cartwright said, walking briskly down
the hallway. "You want to fly chase?"

"With all due respect, sir, I don't think so. Our mission is priority. I think the Pentagon would frown if I busted
my ass on a joyride when we were supposed to be plugging
the leak here. Maybe another time."

The major saluted respectfully and held the salute
until Cartwright returned it. "If it's all right with you, sir,

I'll reserve a room for you at the Desert Inn and call you there about ten hundred hours tomorrow."

"That will be fine, Major," Cartwright said.

Major Adam Glassman executed a smart about-face and strode off, tapping his heels on the high-gloss floor, marching away as though in search of an opponent.

Cartwright headed toward the building entrance and the tarmac. As he walked to his waiting airplane, he wondered what kind of a bug Adam Glassman had up his ass.

As he neared the final security checkpoint, a secretary, roughly the age of his daughter, rushed at him. "All my supervisors told me not to, but I had to, General Cartwright. Could you sign this for my little boy and my husband? They'd be so thrilled," she said, thrusting a notepad at him.

"Sure thing, darlin'. Here, let me write this one for you specially."

As he ambled out toward the flight line, the secretary gazed lovingly at the three signatures, which all read: "Scott Cartwright. Oldest Man in Space."

WEST LOS ANGELES

Khalil Ali Musawi was watching *Good Morning America* with his feet kicked up on the coffee table in his apartment when the FBI arrived. The loud rap on the door roused him from his near doze, and he spilled his cup of tea.

"Mr. Moosawee? Mr. Moosawee, are you there? This is the FBI," the agent announced in his best megaphone voice.

Khalil rolled off the couch and crawled on his belly to his bedroom. The banging on the door continued as he hurriedly pulled papers from one filing tray and stuffed them in another. There was really nothing he could do.

"Mr. Khalil Ali Musawi," the agent bellowed. "We have a warrant, and we are coming in."

The apartment manager's key turned in the door as

Khalil ran to the bathroom with a pile of papers in his arms. He tried to light the papers with a Bic lighter as the agents' feet thudded through the living room into the hallway. It was too late. They were on him.

One big agent pulled the sheaf of flaming papers from the slight Khalil and shoved it in the toilet to put out the fire. Two other FBI men grabbed Khalil and shoved him onto the floor in the hallway. One man held him by the hair, and the other yanked his arms back to put the handcuffs on him.

"Mr. Khalil Ali Musawi, we have a warrant for your arrest," one of the agents said as he snapped the cuffs so they pinched the young man's wrists. "You have the right to remain silent. You have the right to an attorney. Anything you choose to say may be used against you in a court of law."

"Mr. Musawi, do you understand English?" the supervising agent asked as another held Khalil's face to the floor by resting his heavy wingtip shoe on the back of the young man's neck.

"I am a student," Khalil yelled, half in anger, half in pain. "I am an innocent student. I go to UCLA. With what crime am I charged?"

"Mr. Musawi, you are named in a complaint that charges you with violating sections of the Export Administration Act that pertain to the movement and sale of restricted items. In short, Mr. Musawi, Uncle Sam thinks you are an arms smuggler, trying to ship the goods back to your bloodthirsty camel-jockey friends. There is no offense more vile than unauthorized arms dealing."

"I am an engineering student. I love America," Khalil protested as the trio of big men hoisted him to his feet and pushed him to the door.

Neighbors clad in housedresses, robes, and bikinis gathered in little groups by the swimming pool as the agents hustled Khalil toward an unmarked government Plymouth parked outside the apartment building's security gate. Several black-and-white patrol units from the LAPD blocked off the street, their red-and-blue lights flashing. The cops stood by the cruisers with their arms folded. Several of them sneered and smiled as the FBI agents pushed Khalil into the car and read from a Miranda card.

"Where to, Chief?" the agent behind the wheel asked his supervisor.

"Downtown. Hall of Justice jail. We've got a few more weenies like him that Terminal Island wants brought over in one bunch. The sheriff can watch him for a couple of hours."

"I want my lawyer," Khalil demanded, squirming in his handcuffs. "You torture me. These handcuffs are too tight."

"Settle down, Ahab," said the agent sitting next to Khalil in the back of the car. "You'll get to talk to your attorney soon enough. But first you're going to get a look at a real American jail."

The car pulled up to the Hall of Justice on Temple Street in downtown Los Angeles. The agents hustled Khalil into the building, where a U.S. marshal signed him over to the Sheriff's Department for temporary custody while transport was arranged to Terminal Island Federal Prison. Khalil's wrist shackles were replaced with a pair of disposable plastic handcuffs. Two deputies, larger even than the FBI men, marched Khalil into an elevator, which carried them to a holding room behind the second-floor court chambers.

Khalil found himself seated on a bench next to several prisoners wearing orange jail fatigues and the disposable plastic cuffs adopted as an economy measure. The prisoners were mostly black and Latin, and there were a couple of heavily tattooed white men. They all watched him with empty, hostile eyes.

"What you in for?" inquired a bald, powerfully built black man.

"It is nothing," Khalil replied. "I will not be here long."

"He's got a federal beef," said a white prisoner with stringy blond hair. "I saw the marshal hand him over."

"He's probably dealin' dope from Pakistan or some-place," a Latino said, flashing a gold-toothed smile. "Hey, buddy, can you get me some Lebanese red? I could dig some hash."

"He look like a faggot to me," said a black with a voice like sandpaper. "Somebody going to have to break him in. Likely it be me."

"I am none of those things," Khalil half shrieked. "I am a student. I am in America for studies only."

"Hey, brother," the bald black said, "are you Muslim?"

"Of course, I am Islamic," Khalil said sullenly.

"Leave the brother alone," the black said, tugging at his plastic cuffs in what appeared to be an isometric exer-cise. "He's with me."

"Says who?" demanded the black with the sandpaper voice.

"Says Akim Ali Hakim, and all my brothers," the bald prisoner said, smiling sweetly. "You do read me, don't you, man? The little Muslim brother here is mine."

"I do not know of what you speak," Khalil said uneasily. "I will not be among you long."

"Never mind, child," Hakim said. "You under my protection."

The heavy door swung open, and a stocky deputy leaned in. "Everybody up," he barked. "Stand on the white line."

All the prisoners stood.

"You're moving outside in five minutes, for bus trans-port to the main jail. When the trustee walks in here to chain your legs, you will hold your hands forward. Your legs will be spread apart, two feet exactly. You will keep your heads down. Understand, assholes?"

The prisoners murmured.

"Give it to me again," the deputy demanded. "With feeling."

"Yes, sir!" they shouted.

"Now line up, assholes. Shortest to tallest, and don't wear me out," the deputy ordered.

The group sorted itself out, and Khalil found himself second in line, behind the white prisoner with the stringy blond hair.

"What's your name, little brother?" asked Hakim.

Khalil turned to see the Muslim standing behind him. Powerfully built though he was, Hakim was barely an inch taller. "It is Khalil," he murmured.

"That's a good Muslim name," Hakim said, his breath hot in Khalil's ear. "You stick with the brother here and you be all right."

"It is a mistake. I am not supposed to be here."

"I know it. It always be a mistake. You just stay close to Hakim."

Somebody in the back of the line pushed, and the heavy line of prisoners pitched forward like dominoes, the heaviest onto the smallest. The white prisoner at the front of the line yelped in pain and tried to push himself up, grabbing the door handle. The door opened. He looked out into the hallway, and he looked back in amazement at the pileup of prisoners.

"The fucking door opened," the shortest prisoner gasped. "The asshole didn't lock it."

The prisoners whispered to each other, and Hakim hissed, "Shut the fuck up. Look on down the hallway, white boy. Who be out there?"

"There's nobody out there, man. There's no one."

"Then let's get our asses moving," Hakim said, pushing past the white prisoner and pulling Khalil along with him.

Some followed Hakim into the empty corridor, and others stayed behind.

"What are you doing?" Khalil whispered as the muscular Hakim pulled him along.

"What's it look like? I'm busting out. You with me?" he demanded, hauling Khalil around.

"How can we get out of this place?" Khalil asked breathlessly.

"We don't know till we try, little brother. Let's go this way."

They heard an alarm bell sound and glass shatter in the hallway behind them. Suddenly the corridor filled with the noise of deputies shouting and prisoners swearing. A canister the size of a grenade sailed past Khalil's ear as he ran after Hakim. The canister popped, and the corridor filled with the acrid odor of tear gas.

"Let's haul ass," Hakim yelled as he rounded a corner with Khalil close behind him. They turned into an alcove full of cleaning equipment next to a window covered with white paint. Hakim smashed his powerful shoulder against the glass and found that it was the kind with wire mesh in it.

"Take the broom," Khalil shouted. "Smash the window with the broom."

Hakim took a large push broom between his bound hands and thrust it through the window as though he were harpooning a whale. The pane blasted out, showering the men with glass. Hakim leaned over the window ledge and looked down. The sounds of battle in the hallway were getting nearer.

Hakim climbed onto the window ledge and jumped. Khalil leaned over to see the prisoner land, rolling over expertly like a paratrooper. The window ledge was only one floor above the ground, in an alley. Hakim looked up at Khalil for an instant and smiled. "Allah will find us a way," he said.

Khalil took a deep breath and jumped through the window.

THE CALIFORNIA DESERT

Major Glassman rapped on the door of the hotel room for the fourth or fifth time, then smashed it with a flat-handed slap of frustration. He paced past the pool to the front desk and approached the desk clerk.

"General Cartwright is registered here, is he not?" Glassman asked.

"Yes, sir, he certainly is," the clerk said. "And if you are Major Glassman, the general left a message for you."

The clerk handed Glassman the desk memo. It read: "See you at Edwards. Got a loose end to tie up at test pilot school. Cartwright."

The major stalked out of the hotel and climbed into his rental car. Driving the twenty miles of empty desert past the ramshackle hotels and neon-lit truck stops that had been in decline since they were built in the 1950s, he simmered, wondering why the general refused to cooperate with him. Brooding, Glassman sped along Rosamond Boulevard, the finger of deserted highway that led to the base and ran parallel to Rogers Dry Lake, where Cartwright had brought in the space shuttle.

Glassman parked his car in the lot by the low, buff-colored, cinder-block building that housed the air force school for test pilots. He marched into the building and showed his access badge to the charge-of-quarters sergeant, a beefy, middle-aged man who stood and saluted.

"I'm looking for a general," Glassman said, returning the salute. "Can you help me with that, Sergeant?"

"There's been a couple of generals through here this morning, sir. Which one do you want?"

"Cartwright."

"Hangar eight, sir. He's with the commandant."

"Thank you, Sergeant. Stand at ease," Glassman said, heading down the corridor that led out to the tarmac.

He strode across the flight line past several sleek-looking aircraft of various dimensions, shapes, and sizes. The hangars at Edwards formed the crucible through which America's combat aircraft passed. The aircraft would be tested, evaluated, and flown, and sometimes they would crash there. The ones that performed best passed into the air force arsenal for service in South Korea, West Germany,

Spain, England, the Philippines, and all the places where warplanes were needed to defend American interests.

Glassman spotted Cartwright. He was in a flight suit, conversing warmly with a two-star general. The major walked up and saluted. The two generals returned the salute smartly.

"General Donovan, meet my aide, Major Adam Glassman," Cartwright said. "General Donovan runs the flight school here. You know, when I had the slot, it was for a bird colonel. Now they need a two-star to get the job done."

"Morning, sir. Pleased to meet you."

"Good morning, Major. You're flying with General Cartwright, I see."

"No, sir. I don't think we're flying together this morning. We were to be at a meeting at Plant thirty-six."

"That meeting's in the afternoon, Major," Cartwright said.

"But you were to be briefed, sir. By me."

"That's fine, Major Glassman. We can do that after we take a ride in that airplane General Donovan has parked over there," Cartwright said, pointing to a needle-nosed two-seater F-104 built by Lockheed. "The NASA boys rolled it over here as a favor for an old astronaut."

Donovan clapped Cartwright on the shoulder and shook hands with Glassman a final time. "You men have a good time, and don't bust up any expensive government property," he said.

"I don't understand this, sir," Glassman said, placing his hands on his hips.

"What's that, son?"

"General, I am not your son. And this is not a glory ride for a magazine cover. We are on a national security mission. We have been briefed by the president and are at his disposal. And I cannot get this job done if you are not where you are supposed to be when you are supposed to be there."

Cartwright met the major's stare head on. Each man appeared to stare right through the other's aviator glasses.

The heat waves radiating off the Mojave Desert bounced in the lenses of the mirrored frames both men wore.

"Major, can you hear me?"

"Of course I can, sir."

"Then you snap to attention, and I mean now," Cartwright said quietly.

"What?"

"I said attention, damn it," Cartwright snapped. Major Adam Glassman locked his heels and stood stiffly on the sizzling tarmac.

"I don't know who you are, Major," the general said as he walked a slow circle around the younger man. "I don't know why you've got a king-sized chip on your shoulder, and I don't care. Understand this, you little bastard. I am a general officer returned to active duty. Next to me, you've got about as much rank as a heat sensor."

Cartwright thrust his chin close to the taller man's face as though he were a drill sergeant. "When you were in knee pants, I had already killed more men and shot down more enemy airplanes than you likely will ever see. And if you want to know about the James Bond bullshit, I aided OSS behind the lines. That was the real war, when Uncle Adolf was busy putting your people in ovens. I helped put a stop to that, see?"

Glassman maintained his rigid position, but his lip curled defiantly. "I fail to see what your presumption of my heritage has to do with the success of this operation, General."

The general continued his slow circle around the major. "When you were a tiny baby, Major, I ran spy flight missions out of Iran, just inside missile range of the Russkies, and came back to tell about it. I brought back film of MiG bases and missile pads in the Urals and gave it to Ike. Can you match that?"

"No, sir."

"The people I handed my film over to were in the White House, too, and they were not, I might add, junior officers, majors, lieutenant colonels, and the like. Are you reading me, Major?"

"Loud and clear, sir."

"Good. Stand at ease."

Glassman let his shoulders rest just the slightest bit. Cartwright turned his back to Glassman and adjusted a strap on his harness. "Now, from the way I read it, Major, for our mission to succeed, my task is essentially to be myself," he said. "I am supposed to be way out in front, to tempt the enemy in until we got the rascal in our sights. Is that correct?"

"Yes, sir."

"Okay, then. That's the way we'll do it. I have got to assume you were tasked for this mission because the president and his advisers thought you could do the job. But you will understand one thing."

"What might that be, sir?"

"You will live and breathe every moment in the knowledge that I am the general, and you are my subordinate. Are you with me?"

"Yes, sir."

"Fine. Then go draw a G-suit. The maintenance sergeant will fit you out."

"That will be impossible, sir."

"What did you say?"

"I am saying, with all due respect, General, that we are expected to be at Plant thirty-six in a couple of hours. I need the briefing time, General."

"Well, that's fine, Glassman. Because we'll be at the plant in about forty minutes after we take off. When I travel on air force time, I fly an airplane. Go suit up."

Twenty minutes later Glassman marched out from the hangar, looking awkward in his bulky suit. Silently he followed Cartwright to the fighter plane parked on the flight line, where maintenance crew members gave it a few last, loving looks and marked off the forms on their clipboards.

Cartwright walked over and shook hands with a chief master sergeant. "I see you took good care of her for me," he said, grinning and shaking the sergeant's hand heartily.

"Haven't I always, sir?"

"Damn right."

Cartwright climbed the ladder and hoisted himself into the cockpit. Glassman stood on the tarmac, looking up at the general.

"Come on, Major. We haven't got all day. You've got to brief me, right?"

Reluctantly Glassman ascended the ladder and seated himself in front of Cartwright. After lowering the cockpit bubble, Cartwright radioed the tower for clearance and steered the needle-nosed craft onto the runway.

The General Electric J-79 turbofans rolled over and began to whine as their RPMs increased. The engine noise rose from a rumble to a roar as Cartwright gently pushed the throttle and rolled forward. He accelerated, and the jet glided from the runway into the thin, high air of the desert.

"Look at her go," the chief master sergeant said as the plane disappeared, a thin blip of silver light in the morning sun.

The chief and his mechanic shielded their eyes from the glare as the plane vanished. They walked to the hangar to get Cokes while Cartwright goosed his airplane quickly to fifty thousand feet. The men on the ground sipped their drinks while the Starfighter went supersonic, rumbling a crack of sonic thunder as it rocketed toward the heavens.

Cartwright was in his element, nosing the plane down so he could see all the way from the Tehachapi Mountains to the Mexican border. "You ever check out on a 104, Major?" he asked through the microphone in his oxygen mask as he put the plane into a gentle bank high above the blasted volcanic mountains that pointed the way to Nevada.

"No, sir. It's an old airplane. I flew F-16s."

"Well, when they rolled out the first Starfighter, we called it the missile with a man in it," Cartwright said, pulling out of the bank and nursing the stick so the aircraft began to climb.

He guided the aircraft up and up until gravity forced him back hard in his seat; then he pushed the nose over into a dive, and the plane plunged from its fifty-thousand-foot perch, plummeting toward the desert floor.

"What the hell are you doing?" Glassman shouted into the microphone as the brown earth rushed toward him.

"Checking a pitch-up problem," Cartwright replied calmly. "I want to see if they ever got it fixed."

As the plane plunged and the blue sky turned to aquamarine in the fliers' peripheral vision, the Starfighter's nose began to pull back from the dive. As it reached its angle of attack, it began weaving and yawing.

"Yup. She's still doin' it," Cartwright said.

The indicated altitude on Glassman's altimeter dropped as the sinking plane shuddered and turned, being pulled into the centrifugal force of a flat spin. The jet fell crazily as the dragon's teeth of the jagged San Bernardino Mountains below opened hungrily.

"We gotta get out of this," Cartwright said. "You want to take the controls, Major?"

"Goddamn you, Cartwright!" Glassman screamed. "It's your plane!"

"You're goddamn right it is," Cartwright growled, pushing the throttle forward until the jet built up a surge of new RPMs in its powerful engine and sailed out of the uncontrolled spin.

"There's plenty of sky between us and the old six-by-two farm," Cartwright said happily as the Starfighter leveled off. "We musta got us three thousand feet between this old plane and the deck."

The F-104 wagged its tiny wings as it passed once again over Rogers Dry Lake at the air base and sailed off toward the landing field at Plant 36. Cartwright radioed for permission to land, and the tower cleared him.

"You want to set her down, Major?" Cartwright asked, loosening his oxygen mask.

"I already told you, sir. It's your airplane."

"Suit yourself."

The Starfighter's wheels tapped the tarmac, and Cartwright set her down as lightly as pastry. The jet eased to a stop, and Cartwright climbed down the ladder the ground crew provided. He took off his helmet and walked toward the tower. Glassman ran to catch up with him.

"That was some fancy flying, sir," Glassman said. "What if you'd drilled a hole in the desert just to impress me? That would deep-six the real mission."

"Major, you're about the last guy I need to impress. I wondered why you traded in flying for flying a desk. You must have gone sour. You're afraid."

"Got it all figured out, have you, General?"

"I think so. Now let's mosey over to your little conference room so you can pull out your charts and pointers," Cartwright said, turning and walking toward the building.

BEIRUT

The Soviet embassy driver pulled the prisoner's head from the bucket of water. The young Lebanese hung limply, suspended from the driver's heavy arms.

"Revive him," Romanovich ordered.

The driver dropped the prisoner on the floor in the dimly lit basement room. He dropped to his knees and crisscrossed the young man's arms to pump the water from his lungs. After a couple of minutes a few gulps of water spurted from the prisoner's lips, and he coughed and gagged.

"Hit him."

The driver smacked the young man sharply with an open hand, and his eyes opened. Romanovich shined a pocket flashlight in his eyes and, satisfied that the man was sufficiently coherent, kneed him in the groin, causing him to double over.

The KGB major uttered a few demands in Arabic. He waited and listened, then repeated his questions in French. The young man, huddled on his knees on the cold concrete floor, made no response.

"Give him the mineral water," Romanovich instructed the driver, who smiled as though someone had just presented him with a woman.

The driver ambled over to a wooden table where his tools were assorted like surgical instruments and retrieved a bottle of Vichy water. He popped the cap, then picked up the young man like a rag doll and sat him down on a chair. He tied his hands behind him. Holding his thumb over the opening of the bottle, he gave it a good shake so the water sparkled, then tilted the young man's head back and poured it down his nostrils.

The young man shrieked and begged for mercy from Allah. But there was no mercy for him. The driver poured another draft of water down his nasal passage.

Romanovich asked his questions again, wearily. He did not like torture. He preferred drugs and hospital surroundings for such work, but he had to make use of the tools at hand, which consisted of the things on the table and the driver from Kiev.

A loud banging on the steel door interrupted his train of thought. He pulled aside the steel shutter to see the Beirut resident waiting anxiously outside. Romanovich nodded to the driver, who opened the door. The resident pushed his way in, blinking like a mole in the dim light.

"Has this one spoken?" he asked Romanovich.

"He doesn't know anything. If he did, he would have spoken. Your man is efficient."

The driver smiled appreciatively.

"I was upstairs, and the liaison for military affairs demanded to know why we were holding this man without informing him."

"Fuck your mother," Romanovich snapped. "The last thing we need is military intelligence getting their long snouts in this."

"They are GRU," the resident said helplessly. "If they suspect the mission is of a military nature, they will become involved."

"Since when does KGB take any shit from GRU? Listen to me, Malenkov. I don't know what relative got you your job, but you better remember you are a Chekist. You are KGB. And KGB takes shit from no one, especially those dogs in the military."

"But what do I tell the military attaché?"

"Well," Romanovich said, sneering sarcastically, "you could tell him that you are the luckless dog responsible for losing the most precious technology transfer secrets ever obtained by the Soviet state. You could even tell him that this suffering boy here was plucky enough to take them from you. You could tell your colleague that. You could also tell him it was you who failed to find this little bandit, and that it was I, a visiting Chekist, who made the payment and arranged for his presence here."

"Comrade Major," the resident said, looking horrified, "I would be arrested and shot."

"After they finished laughing at your incompetence, yes. Lie to the GRU man. Tell him the matter is out of his jurisdiction. Try not to be an idiot."

The driver hoisted the young man by his hair and shrugged with his free hand, as though to inquire if further treatment were needed. The prisoner's eyes rolled in his head.

"Another day, Comrade Major, and I will have all the answers you need," the driver said.

"I haven't got a day."

"What will we do with this one?" Malenkov asked, pointing his finger accusingly at the helpless prisoner. "He will create an incident. We will have the bandit militias to deal with. They will want revenge."

"I don't give a shit what you do with him, Comrade Resident. He's your problem. I'm leaving for California. Maybe the resident in San Francisco knows his job better than you know yours."

IRAN, THE INNER CHAMBER

The old man's fit of laughter subsided, and, clearing his throat noisily, he regarded his hands with great concentration. All in the room waited upon his words, as did all in the Islamic Republic of Iran.

"Describe to me the attack on the camp of the faithful ones in the Lebanon," he said finally.

"The aircraft were those of the American navy. They are called Intruders," Avadek said.

"The name is deserved," the old man said. "Certainly, they are intruders in the lands of the Shia. What did these American airplanes do?"

"They dropped from the sky so quickly that they were upon the camp before the Pasdaran could know of their arrival. And then they dropped many small bombs and burned the camp and all who were in it."

"Then there were many martyrs?" the old man inquired.

"Many," Avadek replied, noting what seemed like a strange gleam in the eye of the Imam.

"Were there women? Were there children?"

"Some."

The Imam clicked his tongue. He shook his head slowly and folded his hands. "How many women and children have the American devils martyred?" he said, turning his hands upward in a beseeching gesture to his just God. "How many were killed by the shah, the Americans' puppet?"

The holy man dabbed at his eyes, then regarded Avadek anew. "Tell us now of the plans for this American plane you describe," he continued. "What is it that makes this plane different from the others?"

"It is invisible, Imam. It flies, it fights, and it drops bombs without being seen."

The ayatollah's face darkened, and his liquid eyes

fixed on Avadek, who shuddered the slightest bit, hard man that he was.

"Do not speak such a falsehood to one who reveres Allah and the Prophet," the ayatollah said, glaring at the colonel. Behind him, the portrait of old Khomeini also glowered.

"Oh, Imam, I speak the truth. The plane, for the purposes of the radar and antiaircraft weapons, cannot be seen. At least that is the declaration of the American engineers whose documents we seized from the Russian jackals."

"This would be truly satanic," the Imam murmured. "And if we were to acquire this engine of destruction, the Americans would surely attack us with great force."

"The plane, Imam, is its own defense. Whoever holds it would possess great power. We would finish the war with the infidel and decide the fate of nations."

"No single weapon could do such a thing," the Imam's son snapped. "This is folly. My father, this man is a charlatan."

Avadek, recognizing the son as his enemy, spread his hands upward in a gesture of entreaty and said, "I am no charlatan, Imam. I am a vessel of the will of Allah, and of yourself as the keeper of the laws. Are we not trod upon by the intruders and the infidels? Have not we, the Shia, suffered at the hands of all the great powers? Let me propose to serve you, as I have served you before."

The Imam waved his hand, and all became silent. Once again, enwrapped in his robes, he seemed almost to float within the room. He closed his eyes and appeared to sleep. Avadek, Issam, the son of the Imam, and the guards waited on their knees. Finally, one of the old man's eyes opened and then the other.

"I have pondered this," he said. "Now hear my words. The weapon of the Great Satan shall be delivered unto us. Because our cause is just, because we are of Islam, we will use it well."

"My father," the son said, beginning to utter an objection, but he ceased speaking at a wave from the hand of the Imam.

"You will help these vessels of Allah, my son," the old

man said, pointing to Avadek and Issam. "Whatever they shall ask, you shall provide. So shall it be done."

The son, seated next to his father, bowed deeply. He raised himself up and addressed Avadek. "What is it you will require?"

"My own men. And with them, I shall need the best pilots from the Iraqi front. I will need the best that are still alive."

"And what else?" asked the son of the Imam, barely concealing his distaste for Avadek, whom he considered an opportunist.

"I need an American. His name is McCain. He once served the CIA."

"Those devils," the son gasped. "You would seek their help?"

"This one, Angus McCain, serves only himself. And he will help us, for gold. I need him."

"We will use the devil to vanquish the devil," the Imam said. "So shall it be. May Allah aid you in your just endeavor."

The elder raised his hand beneficently, signaling that Avadek and Issam could stand. Doing so, they bowed and turned to leave. But the old man raised his quivering, melodious voice.

"Wait," he commanded. Both men stopped and turned, again lowering their heads.

"You may go, my faithful officer," the old man said, pointing his bony finger at Avadek. "You have served our cause well. But I would wish to speak further with this young one. I wish to hear more of the Lebanon."

Even as his head was lowered, Avadek's gaze shifted quickly to Issam, and from the corner of his eye he caught the unguarded smile of the holy man's son. The intelligence officer immediately assumed that the old man and his son were intending to co-opt Issam, to intrigue with him. Surely the young man would be awed at such attention. He had never been in the presence of such powerful men. Or had he? For a second, Issam caught Avadek's inquiring gaze. In the mullahs' chamber, minus his dark glasses, the features of the young Lebanese softened from the cruel mask of the assassin. His long lashes drooped guiltily, and he turned his face suddenly from Avadek. The colonel understood. The soul of a traitor was always detected in the eyes. Issam might be loyal to the mullahs, but he could not be trusted by Avadek. The colonel smiled gently at his fellow traveler. Issam grinned uneasily.

Closing his eyes and nodding humbly, Avadek turned to the mullahs and raised his hands. "This young one has been my comfort," he said, smiling. "Take your pleasure in his company. I must prepare the way for our departure." He turned and strode out of the room.

4

LOS ANGELES

Khalil raced after Hakim down the alley. Stopping abruptly, Hakim stepped into an empty alcove meant for a dumpster, and Khalil followed him. In his bloody hand Hakim held a glass shard from the shattered courthouse window. Crouching, he picked up a wad of soggy newspaper and, using it to grip the glass shard, sliced the plastic strap connecting Khalil's disposable handcuffs with a few furious slashes. Wordlessly he bade Khalil to reciprocate. Then they ran on.

Khalil was momentarily blinded by the bright sunshine on Hill Street and bumped into a cluster of workers leaving the county buildings for lunch. Somehow he kept his eye on Hakim, who ran ahead through the crowd. As he pushed and shoved he seemed to be nearly invisible in the crowd. Khalil shuddered as he heard sirens screeching and the low drone of a helicopter.

He scrambled after Hakim, who climbed a wall and brushed his way through a urine-soaked hedge that filled a large planter behind the Criminal Courts Building. Hakim ran the hundred-foot length of the planter and dropped down from the wall onto a metal ventilation grate, where he found what he was looking for, a pair of sleeping bums.

"Here they be, just like I thought," he said happily.

"What are you doing?" Khalil asked as Hakim started stripping the jacket from one of the passed-out drifters.

"Just help me get the motherfucker's threads, will you? We ain't got all day."

Hakim pulled off his overalls and tied the sleeves at the waist. He put the derelict's coat on and sniffed. Then he grabbed the old man's hat and pulled it down on his shiny head.

"You do the same, brother, 'less you want to go back."

Khalil, catching on, started taking a tattered sport coat off the second bum, a grizzled creature who emitted a toothless, alcoholic groan.

"Hurry up, man. I'll help you," Hakim said, pulling the coat from the second victim and handing it to Khalil. Then Hakim methodically pulled the pants from both men. He put on the pair that looked closest to his own size and motioned for Khalil to don the others.

A few feet away, hundreds of people walked by, hurrying to the takeout restaurants and not seeing, or ignoring, the larceny in progress. Even the victims appeared not to notice.

"Let's go," Hakim said, trotting off the grate and weaving back into the sidewalk traffic. Khalil followed, suddenly realizing that the black man was wise.

They crossed the street and walked over to a dried patch of grass outside City Hall East, across from Parker Center police headquarters.

"You go over there," Hakim said, pointing to a tree. "Flop yourself down like you was one of those bums. Like you was passed out. I'll be doing the same thing. But when I give you the signal, man, you get your ass up and run after me like a rabbit."

"What is your plan?" Khalil asked as he dropped on his stomach.

"Just do what I say and I'll snag us a ride."

They lay on the lawn in the smoggy heat, inhaling vehicle exhaust as buses and cars rolled by. Khalil watched the sidewalk traffic through a little mask he made with his fingers as he feigned alcoholic unconsciousness. Once, he spotted a pair of deputies walking by. But they didn't appear to be searching. They just walked and talked while Khalil attempted not to shake uncontrollably. Helicopters passed overhead, their rotors making a menacing dragonfly racket, and it was all Khalil could do not to bolt.

It seemed an eternity of heat and noise. Khalil saw that Hakim watched the street, as though he were searching for some signal. As the noon hour ended, the sidewalks filled again with people returning to their offices. Then the traffic thinned. The light at the intersection of First and Main changed to red, and a big laundry van pulled up at the light. It was an open truck, with the driver sitting on a high seat. Like a sprinter, Hakim was up and across the lawn, with Khalil running after him. In seconds Hakim was in the truck. He shoved the startled driver off his seat, dumping him into the street. Khalil hung on to a metal grip on the dash, and Hakim pulled away as the light changed. Khalil looked back to see the driver running after them.

"Crazy bastards!" he shouted.

"We free, ain't we?" the black man said gleefully as the truck careened south onto Main Street.

"Yes. Yes, we are free," Khalil replied. "But for how long?"

"That all depends. You see how we gave 'em the slip. Now we gotta hide ourselves good. Got any ideas, little brother?"

"It could be I have an idea," Khalil said, noticing that Hakim was maintaining an even speed and stopping for all the lights. "I've got a girlfriend."

"That's a start."

"This girl does what I say," Khalil boasted.

"That's the only way. Point me to her crib and we'll make a plan, my man."

Khalil grinned at his new companion. "It is good," he said.

"I knew this was going to be a good day," Hakim said. "I said my morning prayer, and I knew that, Allah willing, I would be delivered from the hands of the infidel. So where do we go, little brother?"

"Westwood. By the university."

TEHRAN

Avadek and Issam climbed out of the battered Peugeot the Revolutionary Council had given them and walked toward the entrance of the former Tehran Hilton, now the Independence Hotel. Scowling clergymen had replaced the well-dressed multitudes of foreign businessmen and beautiful women who once frequented the establishment. Avadek, now dressed like Issam in an Armani suit, walked quickly through the hotel's revolving doors. Issam, however, was careful to stop and stamp twice on the American flag that was painted on the sidewalk outside the entryway. A Soviet flag was painted next to the Stars and Stripes as a convenience to those who felt equal enmity toward the other satanic superpower. In a gesture of fairness, Issam spat on it.

The pair rode an elevator to the twentieth floor and stepped into the hallway, which was dim due to lights that failed and were never replaced. They found the room, and Avadek knocked carefully and stepped aside, the habit of someone who wishes to avoid being shot from behind a door. The door swung open, and the tall blond man in the room made a mocking half bow and gesture of welcome.

"You got here fast," Avadek said in barely accented English. "You must have smelled money." Issam followed Avadek into the room and closed the door, regarding the ex–CIA field officer warily.

"McCain can always travel in a hurry for old friends," the American said, grinning with large white teeth that looked like headstones. "It's been a while, Major," he said, offering a massive, callused hand.

"I am a colonel now," Avadek said, embracing the American. "When I was a major, we both had more hair, and it was not so gray." Issam watched the foreigner as though he were tracking the movement of a poisonous snake.

"No need to search your old buddy," McCain said, still grinning. "I'm clean. The only thing I got past the customs boys at Mehrabad Airport was this bottle of Jim Beam. Care for a taste?"

Avadek shook his head while McCain poured a generous serving into a water glass. Issam frowned.

"Got a cigarette?" Avadek asked.

"Sure, take the pack," McCain said, handing him a pack of Winstons. "Don't imagine you see these as often anymore, with the new team in charge."

"The regime is not so new as you say," Issam said in his halting English. "It is many years now that we have guarded the revolution against you imperialists."

"Who's the kid?" McCain asked.

"He will kill you if I ask him to," Avadek said, smiling.

"Aw, shoot, Avadek. Lighten up. You didn't bring me all this way to kill me. You could've done that in Paris. Let's us drink to your promotion, and you can tell me what the revolution needs from old Angus McCain."

McCain raised his whiskey glass, and Issam knocked it from his hand. Before the glass shattered on the floor, McCain's powerful hand gripped Issam by the throat. The youth pushed his nine-millimeter automatic into McCain's ribs, but the American smacked it aside and knocked Issam off his feet with a sweep kick. He then pinned the youth to the floor, with his knee in the young man's throat. Avadek stood back, watching, his arms folded. He sighed as though bored by the spectacle.

"Any killing to be done here, old Angus is likely the one to get it started," McCain said.

"Let him go. Your point is proved," Avadek said.

McCain released Issam, who picked up his pistol and glared at the American. Ignoring him, McCain retrieved another water glass from the bathroom and filled it with whiskey. "You people don't know what you're missing," he said, smacking his lips in satisfaction.

"Do you still work for Qaddafi?" Avadek asked.

"You know I never discuss clients."

"Qaddafi took our Imam!" Issam shrieked. "Did you help him?"

"I don't discuss religion, kid. I stay on the technical end of it. I've got no idea where the old boy is."

"Issam, be quiet," Avadek ordered. "If you cannot work with me, you will return to the Lebanon." He turned to McCain and said, "So, tell me, are you done with the Libyans?"

"It's like I told you, Avadek. I don't discuss clients. Look, you know me, buddy. Time is money."

"The Islamic Republic needs your skills."

"I'm available," the big American said simply.

"We do not need this mercenary," Issam blurted out. "How much will it cost? The mission is dangerous."

"My usual fee."

"One million dollars, is that it still?"

"Or the equivalent amount in Krugerands, deposited to my account in Switzerland. Not bad for you, considering inflation."

"Consider it done."

"Fine. That's how I like to deal, with a stand-up guy. Now, what do you need?"

"First, kill this one," Avadek said, pointing at Issam.

Issam stared at Avadek in an instant of disbelief. Before he could turn to face McCain, his look of horror was transfixed in the shock of death. He fell to the floor, his hands moving to his neck in a reflex from the single lethal blow to his throat.

Avadek offered McCain a cigarette and lit it for him. "Now, we get down to business," he said, puffing smoke through his nostrils.

"Suits me," McCain replied. "You sure you don't want that whiskey?"

"A short one. Make it two fingers."

LANCASTER, CALIFORNIA

General Cartwright stepped from the shower in his hotel room and toweled himself down briskly. He pulled on a clean, soft pair of faded jeans and buttoned up a checked rancher's shirt with a crease in the sleeve so sharp it could cut paper. The fresh socks and tooled-leather boots completed his wardrobe. He felt good.

He settled himself on one of the room's two wing chairs and kicked his boots up on the floral-patterned spread on one of the room's two double beds.

Picking up a copy of *Time* magazine, he leafed through it until he came to the article about Mercury Aviation, which described how the aerospace firm had lost thousands of classified documents from the offices of the "Beaver Works," its top-secret engineering complex in the gray stucco Los Angeles suburb of Downey. He clicked his tongue in disgust and turned to other newspapers and magazines arrayed on the table beside him. So many aerospace contractors stayed at the hotel that the newsstand sold everything he needed: *The New York Times, The Washington Post, Aviation Week, Popular Science, Flight World, The Air Force Times.*

Hurriedly he scanned headlines and topic headings, leafing through dozens of pages. Finally he found what he wanted. He began reading a *Future Science* article on the use of infrared radiation tracking devices as a possible substitute for radar detection. The chief benefit, the article stated, was that a passive detection system would not emit beams to alert attacking aircraft. Infrared radiation could not be masked in the way that the radar signature of an aircraft could be disguised, the article declared boldly.

"Years ahead, but technically feasible," Cartwright murmured. "Well, if you don't break eggs, you won't get an omelet."

Sunlight from the fading day filtered through the

windows of his room. In the time just before twilight, the pale blue of the desert sky turned a deeper shade, almost aquamarine, preceding the riot of violet and pink that would play across the heavens as the sun set. Cartwright watched a Lockheed Orion sub patrol plane make a lazy turn in the fading light. He considered the prop plane a pretty thing, and there was some glow deep inside him that warmed from the memory of days when all aircraft rumbled from the noise of pistons and propellers. He stood, hitching his jeans so they were comfortable, and stepped out of his room.

The general descended the steps and walked gingerly past the pool and lounge and out of the hotel onto the sandy hardpan of the desert. A lizard skittered from his path, and a cricket chirped. The symphony of evening was beginning.

He looked up toward the sky and watched the Orion disappear, lazily, beautifully, into the glowing western horizon. The heavens had turned deep violet, then purple. The sun, sinking behind the Tehachapi Mountains, threw back a brilliance of pink-and-orange light. Then, as gracefully as the plane, it disappeared behind the jagged peaks, and all was the shadow and whispers of dusk in the desert.

The towering Joshua trees cast ghostly shadows, like spiny sentries guarding the empty land. Cartwright breathed deeply the scent of sagebrush and wildflowers. He spotted the first bright star of evening, and the rush of hidden feeling that welled within him was filled with remembered dreams of piloting a rocket ship home from space. He realized suddenly that he had lived the best years of his life on this desert, and that the desert was the beach that rolled out to the ocean of space.

"I was the astronaut," he whispered to the desert and himself. "It was meant to be me, through all this time and trouble. I was the star voyager."

For an instant, the star vanished. Cartwright shook his head and blinked rapidly, and it reappeared.

"You must be getting old," he whispered to himself, chuckling. "Talking to yourself like some farmer."

Night cloaked the desert like a velvet blanket studded with the billion blinking diamonds of the Milky Way. The general took a last loving look at the heavens, then turned to hike back to the hotel, where the lights were electric and worries were earthly.

THE PLANE

5

LANCASTER, CALIFORNIA

Cartwright walked over to the desk and asked for his morning messages. There was nothing from Glassman, but there was a message from his wife, Gloria, who was at their home near Marysville. With a spring in his step, the general returned to his room and dialed his home number. When Gloria answered he noted with pleasure that her voice still betrayed a faint English accent.

"Is this that pretty little gal I shared doughnuts and coffee with in the Hyde Park tube station during the blitz?"

"Is this the fresh bloke? I remember him," she said liltingly. "He was rather nice. But fresh all the same."

"I was wonderin' if you'd like to see America someday?"

"Me mum told me never to date Yanks, unless of course they were terribly handsome and knew better than to try to buy a girl with sweets," Gloria Cartwright replied demurely.

"Seems to me your mum was a pretty smart gal."

"She was that. She even liked the Yank flier from the tube station, as I recall. Where the dickens are you, General?"

"Aw, I'm doing contract work with some weenie out here that can't tell a slide rule from a pocket calculator. The Mercury boys want to fly an airplane ass backwards and I won't let 'em."

"How long are you going to be? If it's more than a couple of days, I'm going to San Francisco with Beverly Jennings."

"What's in San Francisco? You got a Jody you're keepin' quiet about?"

"Better than that, flyboy. Bridge tournament."

"Well, hell. I know better than to stand in the way of bridge. You go right on ahead and have a good time. Don't spend too much."

"I've got my own money."

"Then buy me somethin'. And do me one more thing. Get me Stu Felton's phone number in Virginia. I've gotta talk to that old boy."

Gloria Cartwright gave him the number that was filed lovingly in a recipe box, amid the numbers of a hundred other hot pilot buddies on Scott Cartwright's old-boy line. She recited it to him twice.

"Anything more you need, buster? I might not be here when you get back. They say Omar Sharif's playing my tournament."

"I knew it. There had to be a Jody out there someplace."

"No, I don't think so. He's a sweet-looking man, but he can't fly a hot plane. Don't bust your behind, General."

"Keep the wind at your back, darlin'. I love you."

"Love you, too. Sleep tight."

Cartwright rang off, then dialed Stu Felton's Alexandria, Virginia, number.

"Felton here," a sleepy voice answered.

"Colonel Felton, this is your old fishing buddy. 'Member me? Don't say my name."

"Hello, old man. How the hell are you?"

"Fine, fine. I need a favor. Bear in mind that this is not a secure line."

"I'm listening."

"I'm gonna give you a Social Security number. I want you to run it through the computer and give me everything you've got in the file. You can ring me up in the morning at that old coffee shop we used to stop at on the way out to the fishing hole. You know the one?"

"Hell, yes."

"Make it zero seven-thirty hours. Now here's the number," Cartwright said, and read off the nine-digit number.

"Consider it done."

"Thanks."

Rather than going straight to bed, Cartwright went down to the lounge. He considered calling one of his many pals from the Society of Experimental Test Pilots but decided against it. They'd just want to know what he was flying and who for.

He sat down at the bar and ordered Wild Turkey with a water chaser. He was savoring its golden, smoky glow when a man carrying too much weight under his polo shirt approached.

"Excuse me, sir, you are General Cartwright, aren't you?"

Cartwright absently signed an autograph on a cocktail napkin and handed it to the heavyset man.

"No, sir. I don't want your autograph. What I mean to say is, I want an interview. I'm David Willers, for *Flight World.*"

Reluctantly Cartwright accepted Willers's handshake. "I'm not doing interviews tonight, son. I'm just having a drink."

"Well, let me buy you one, then, General."

"Look here, young fella. If you and I get to drinkin', suddenly we're friends. Then before you know it, I'm spilling my guts and the nation's secrets to you. And I can't do that. Why don't you just run along?"

"I just want to know what one of the country's most

famous astronauts and test pilots is up to. I'm just a reporter, see? If I didn't ask you for an interview, what kind of reporter would I be?"

"Son, I'm just out here in the Antelope Valley to hook up with a couple of old fishing buddies. That's all. So, no media interest. Okay?"

"What have you got against *Flight World*?" the reporter demanded. "Haven't we done enough to promote your career?"

"Sonny, right now I'm gentle-natured. One more crack like that and I might not be so tender. Let's just say you work for a good magazine, but I'm not doing an interview tonight, and leave it at that."

"What have you got against the press, General?" the reporter persisted.

Cartwright set down his drink and twisted in his bar stool so he faced the reporter. He stared a long moment at Willers with his cold blue eyes. The reporter's shoulders shrank, and he walked away.

At the other end of the counter, the bartender clapped solemnly. "Right on, General," he said, and Cartwright nodded to him and signaled for one more drink.

"Well, Scotty Cartwright, you haven't changed much," announced a woman sitting near the bartender's station.

Cartwright looked at her and cracked his flyboy grin. "Well, I'll be. You haven't much changed, either, Glenda Moody. You are a sight for sore eyes," he said, getting up and walking over to her stool to embrace her. "What are you doing here?"

"I'm still in town, flyboy. And you're still the straight shooter, aren't you, Scotty," she said, slurring her words only slightly.

"Old dogs don't change. I just didn't want to have to slug that guy."

"You wouldn't have done that, Scotty. You could see he was pretty harmless."

"Where the hell is Dick? You drinking alone?"

"Dick," she said, twisting a curl of her abundant

blond hair, "is not here. Dick, my dear, sweet Scotty, is not with Glenda. Having a quiet drink alone is something I seem to do a lot lately."

"I heard about that business with the B-20X. Tough break."

"Yes, my darlin' Scotty," she said, patting him lightly on his leathery cheek. "That's just what it was. A terrible break."

"I always figured Dick would dust himself off and get a new airplane. He's not the sort to let an accident bust his ass."

"That mighta been the air force way, but it didn't work like that with the contractor. Dick's not gonna fly any more hot planes, Scotty. Connaught Aircraft had to stick somebody. It was negligence, they said."

"Aw, shit. Where the hell is he?"

"I don' know. We aren't together," she said, her eyes misting.

With a finger Glenda stirred her drink, a pink thing with a lot of melted ice in it. She licked her finger, then signaled for another. The bartender looked doubtfully at Cartwright, who shook his head.

"Come on, Glenda, honey," he said. "I'll take you home."

She looked at him and attempted to focus her beautiful green eyes. "I always loved you both, you know. All those bases. All those moves. Both of you so strong and tall and true. Scotty, will you make love to me?"

He hoisted her onto his shoulder and started walking her quickly from the bar. He did it so hardly anyone huddled over their drinks would notice he was carrying her. She passed out on his arm.

Cartwright's radio alarm buzzed at 5:30 A.M., and he swatted it to the off position. With more than forty years of military life behind him, he awoke alert, swinging his legs off the bed into his rubber sandals. Hitching up his skivvies, he walked to the bathroom and turned on the light. He regarded the beautiful woman who slept peacefully in the other bed. With her long blond hair spread across a pillow, she looked like a girl of twenty. He clucked his tongue regretfully and stepped into the shower.

Glenda Moody awoke as Cartwright finished shaving. He stepped across the room to the closet and pulled on a pale blue Arrow shirt, some comfortable tan slacks, and a pair of brushed leather Dingo boots.

"Could you please tell me where the hell I am?" Glenda asked, holding the sheet up over her breasts.

"You're with your old pal Scotty. 'Member me?"

"Scott? Scott Cartwright? Is that you?"

"The same as ever, Glenda. I didn't know where to bring you last night, so I brought you here."

"Scott, did I do anything I should be ashamed of?"

"You had a snootful, but I don't guess it's the first time that ever happened. You weren't too bad."

"Scott, did I come on to you? Tell the truth."

"Maybe it was the other way around, and you gave me a slap and told me to mind my own business."

"Don't bullshit me, Scott. You wouldn't hit on me while Gloria's alive. For one, she'd kill you, and for the other, you just wouldn't do it."

She shook out her hair, pulled the sheet around her, and stepped into the bathroom to inspect herself in the mirror. She made a face at her reflection.

"It's not fun anymore," she murmured. "Scott, I'm humiliated."

"Let's just say I didn't have my way with you, and leave it at that. You seemed to have another fella on your mind, anyway. What about Dick?"

"What about him? We're just through, that's all."

"It ain't that simple, Glenda. Nothing is."

"Look, after he got burned for the B-20X fiasco, he took to drinking. He'd been drinking anyway, but it got worse. Now he says he's flying for the money. He never talked like that before. I think he was going to meet that magazine writer. I don't think he would have told the guy anything, but he'd have listened. That's not like him."

"Shit. You know where he is?"

"He's at one of those hole-in-the-wall Mojave air-freight services."

"I don't like the sound of that. Why'n't you freshen up and we'll go get some eggs."

"I think I'd die," she said, holding her head in her hands.

"Look, Glenda, I gotta run. When I get back, we'll talk." Cartwright grabbed his jacket, left the room, and headed for the parking lot.

He gunned the Corvette the thirty miles to Mojave, feeling confident that the Highway Patrol was lurking in the southbound lanes, lying in wait for the Los Angeles commuters. He made the thirty-minute drive in a little over fifteen.

It was just after 7:00 A.M. when he arrived at Droopy's, the desert greasy spoon where he always stopped for eggs and toast on the way to fishing forays in the Sierra Nevada. He sat at the deserted counter, ordered coffee, and read the paper. A front-page article had the Pentagon halting payments to Consolidated Technologies Corporation because of a kickback scandal. The article went down about as well as the coffee. A pay phone at the end of the counter rang, and the cashier, a grizzled desert dweller, answered it and asked if there was a Scotty in the joint. Cartwright walked over and took the phone.

"Stu, what have you got?" he said.

"Shoot, Scott, if you'd have given me the guy's name instead of his dog tag number, I could've briefed you last night. I know all about that guy."

"Lookit, Stu. I'm working something a little weird. I don't want to get you in trouble at the Pentagon, so the best I could do was trick up a little subterfuge. What have you got on this guy?"

"Well, Major Adam Glassman was probably one of

the hottest fliers we had outside of flight test at Edwards, or since Vietnam."

"You're puttin' me on."

"Negatory. He was hot. And he is also an ex–POW."

"I thought you said he didn't fly Vietnam. He's too young."

"He flew in Lebanon. He was flying with the Israelis while they were doing a photo recon. He went in low to get a picture of a Soviet missile battery in the Bekaa Valley, and he went down in the weeds. Syrian SAM got him."

"How long did they keep him?"

"Couple of months. I understand he stayed frosty. Kept his mouth shut as long as he could. It was the usual drill. Dark, musty room. Bad chow. Isolation. I don't care how frosty you are—when the thumbscrew boys go to work on you, you'll spill. But State got some help from the Reverend Andrew Clayton Washington. He was moving through the area on his latest campaign swing, and it turned up lucky for our boy. He was sprung, and the Eastern papers took back all that stuff about the reverend being an anti–Semite, or some such."

"Tell me somethin', Stu. If Glassman stayed so cold, how come he didn't fly again after that?"

"He did fly after that."

"What and where?"

"Scott, how sure are you about this line?"

"Reasonably sure."

"I'll take your word for it. He was flying a black project out of Nellis Air Force Base near Las Vegas. He was out at the area."

"I know where it is. Twelve thousand square miles of nothing wrapped around a nuke test site. I spent enough time there."

"Remember the 'Have Blue' program out at Dreamland? That plane was classified so deep in the black that Defense didn't even have a numerical designator for it."

"Right, it was a fighter-bomber with Stealth characteristics. The Nighthawk project. I remember that. The pilot was killed."

"That's what I'm telling you, Scott. The Nighthawk pilot wasn't killed. The chase pilot was killed. The Stealth pilot ejected. It was Glassman."

"No shit."

"Test pilot's word of honor."

"What's he been doing lately?"

"Scott, you know I'd do anything for you, right?"

"Sure, buddy."

"Well, I just broke about a hundred regulations making this call. We never spoke, right?"

"Right," Cartwright said. "And be sure to look me up when you're out my way, Stu. We'll go fishin'."

"You got it, buddy."

Cartwright backed the Corvette out of Droopy's gravel lot and swung by the Mojave Airport. He drove past the hulks of Korean War–vintage aircraft in an elephant graveyard for airplanes. He cruised past hangars with airplanes parked in front that looked so sleek and new, they were already leaving the twentieth century behind. At the end of the hangars were the charter firms. They still flew DC-3s to haul freight and an occasional load of sky divers. The office for Royal Flush Air Freight was at the end of the hangar row. It was closed up tight with a "Back Soon" sign taped to the dirty window. Outside the office, there was a forlorn Huey helicopter with the faded letters AIR AMERICA stenciled on the tailboom.

Cartwright drove the thirty miles back to the Antelope Valley Inn, trying to collect his thoughts about Major Adam Glassman and his old pal Dick Moody. When he returned to his room, Glenda Moody was gone. Some pink lipstick on his bathroom mirror declared, "Maybe next time."

6

WEST LOS ANGELES

Cynthia Atkins looked back over her shoulder before she turned the first key in her apartment. There had been a man in the neighborhood who followed women into security buildings, scuttling in before the heavy steel gates could swing shut. She fumbled with the tear-gas key ring and opened the dead bolt. Then Hakim grabbed her from behind and pushed her inside.

"Don't make no noise, pretty lady," he hissed in her ear as he cupped his massive hand over her mouth. With his free hand he shook loose the keys so they clattered on the apartment floor.

Twisting Cynthia's right arm up to her shoulder blade, Hakim walked her to a reclining chair. He sat her down hard.

"You be quiet now, girl," he said. "I'm gonna take my hand off your mouf."

"You're the one who comes in through the gate,"

Cynthia whimpered. "I'll do what you want. Just don't hurt me."

"What the hell you talkin' about, girl?"

"Cynthia, it's me," Khalil said from the darkness of the kitchen.

"Khalil?" she asked, her voice quavering.

"I come with my friend," he said, rushing forward and putting his hand on her cheek. He kissed her lightly on the forehead.

"Khalil, what are you doing here? I heard about you on the radio. You're in trouble."

"That's right, honey lamb," Hakim hissed as he methodically tied her hands with a lamp cord he had cut with a kitchen knife. "He be in big-time trouble. And you're gonna help him out of it."

"Khalil, you should give yourself up," Cynthia gasped.

"Don't be ridiculous," Khalil snorted. "They would lock me away forever, like Sirhan."

Hakim stepped back from the chair and inspected his knotwork and the girl. He smiled. "Not bad," he said quietly. "Not bad at all, little brother. She got pretty yellow hair and soft skin."

"Please go away," the girl whimpered, hanging her head.

"Cynthia, this man is my friend," Khalil said as he pulled a bottle of milk from the refrigerator. "He does not hurt you. But you got to help us. We've got to get away."

"How can I help?"

Khalil drank the milk and carried the telephone on its long cord from the kitchen. "You got to talk to my other friend. We will call him. You are to ask for Mr. Hamza and ask about the rug, the red rug."

"Why don't you call him yourself?" she asked wearily. "You can do anything you want. You always did."

Khalil slapped her once, and Hakim grinned.

"Cynthia, I don't want to hurt you. But you must do what I tell you. You talk to Hamza and ask about the red rug. If he asks is it the one from Azerbaijan, then it's cool.

Everything is okay, see? If he asks is it the one from Turkestan, you shake your head to let me know and I hang up fast, okay?"

Khalil dialed and held the phone to the frightened girl's ear. Cynthia asked Khalil's question in a small, halting voice. She nodded reassuringly at her former boyfriend, and Khalil picked up the line.

"My brother, I am free," he exclaimed joyfully into the telephone. He listened for several minutes, and his face clouded with worry. He hung up.

"What's wrong, man?" Hakim demanded.

Khalil paced the room and wrung his hands. He shook his head and slapped his hips like a toy soldier. "They should not make me do more work," he cried. "I am already in trouble. They should have made it so I could go home."

"What we doin' instead?"

"I have to make contact with one of their men. They say I must work for him, or I can never go home."

"Well, I can tell you one thing, little brother. We got to get our ass out of here. They gonna come looking here if they know you close with the bitch here."

"Cynthia," Khalil said, grabbing her bound wrists. "You must help us."

"Elsewise, we got to kill you," Hakim said.

Cynthia breathed deeply and recalled all the rape survival training classes she had taken. Improvise and survive, she decided silently.

"I can take you to a safe place," she murmured. "My parents have a cabin. If you don't hurt me, I can drive you there."

"How far?" Hakim demanded.

"About seventy miles. It's near a little town called Wrightwood. It's a ski resort, but nobody's there during the off season."

"Sounds good. Let's do what she say."

"Okay, okay. Let's go," Khalil said.

"Hey, little brother. Who be the dude you got to do the job for?"

"He is from the homeland. He is a dangerous man."

"Why should you give a shit about all that? Why'n't you just bug out?"

"I must do what the brothers say, for the revolution. Or I am a dead man, and all of my family."

DOWNEY, CALIFORNIA

Four men waited in the gathering smog at the helipad outside Mercury's windowless "Beaver Works" building. Each was punctual, with habits instilled from a lifetime of working with slide rules and calculators. They had all arrived a few minutes early to wait for the helicopter shuttle that would carry them over the San Gabriel Mountains from the squat, ugly, buff-colored building to the firm's sleek new offices at Plant 36, a nine-square-mile network of runway, hangars, and assembly facilities for fighters, spy planes, sub chasers, and the nation's most advanced bombers.

Each Mercury man wore an identification badge and a pocket protector for the array of pens in his Sears-purchased Perma-Prest shirt. Each man wore his hair cropped short, reflecting a military background—except for Wendall Evans, the deputy projects manager, who was younger, more fashionable, and much envied for his jaunty BMW, which once sported a "BVRWKS" vanity plate before plant security unceremoniously removed it.

"Well, men, what do you think is in the wind with our blue-suit friends from the air force?" the manager asked.

"They're probably going to sharpshoot us about the delays, Wendall. We just have to be ready to get bitched out," said Bix Samuels, a contract performance officer.

"I doubt that," said Randy Jefferson. "I hear one of these guys is a big gun."

"We're going to get chewed on about document control," said Dan Lowell, a senior projects engineer and the eldest in the group. "And they've got a right to bitch. This would never have happened in the old days."

"Please, please, Dan," said Evans, the manager, raising his hands helplessly. "No more talk about the old days when people could keep a secret."

"Well, it's true," Lowell snapped. "We built four generations of spy planes, right here in Downey, and nobody ever found out about them."

"Until one was shot down over Russia," Evans said wearily. "We know that story. It was in the newspapers."

"When that story was in the newspapers, you were in grade school, Evans," Lowell said. "But the facts haven't changed. We can't seem to keep a secret anymore, and the air force ought to be damn mad."

Evans placed his hands on his temples and shook his head in frustration. He looked to the sky, hearing the hollow, chopping sound of the approaching helicopter. He looked forward to the day he could cease air commuting with the numbers-cruncher crew. For the weekly trips to the desert, he had requested use of the executive jet. For reasons of economy the request had been denied. It was an indignity he looked forward to putting behind him as soon as he made executive vice-president.

The men kept their heads down as they walked out to the Bell jet 'copter. They clambered aboard and hooked their seat belts as though they could have done it in their sleep. Evans stared out the Plexiglas window, attempting to impose some mental space between himself and his subordinates, although secretly he would have liked to be included in their conversations.

"How's your wife, Dan?" Jefferson asked over the whine of the engine as the jet 'copter built up RPMs for takeoff.

"Ginna's losing what sensation she had left below the knees," Lowell replied matter-of-factly. "She's gonna need another operation."

"That's tough," said Bix Samuels. "How many will this be?"

"Too damn many."

In a few minutes they were airborne, flying over the brown smog of the San Fernando Valley toward the clean vastness of the desert, where the secrets were kept.

PLANT 36

Cartwright guided his Corvette through the Plant 36 parking lot into the space next to the government-issue Dodge that Glassman drove. Glassman stepped out of the car, came to attention, and saluted.

"Good morning, sir."

With Glassman in tow, Cartwright returned the salute carelessly and kept moving toward the security gate, where a paunchy civilian-uniformed guard shared the duty with an air force guard in a blue beret.

The men were signing in when a civilian in a snappy navy blazer approached. By way of a smile, the man bared his teeth, which were bright enough for a dentist's lecture on the benefits of flossing. His hand was outstretched in greeting to the general.

"You must be the man, sir," he said, shaking Cartwright's hand heartily before the general had a chance to respond. "By gosh, it is a pleasure to meet a genuine hero like you, General."

"I ain't so sure we've met just yet. Who the hell are you?"

"General," Major Glassman said, "this is Holden Cunningham. He's Mercury's vice-president for corporate communications. He'll be taking us through the Mercury operation, and he's cleared to be anywhere in the plant."

"Pleased to meet you, Mr. Cunningham. Now tell me one thing. Where did all the damn documents get off to? I'm reading about your security leaks in the newspapers.

Are your people trying to give away the store, or did you just lose track of it?"

"General, sir," the man said, flushing a deep red and losing his toothpaste smile, "please understand. I am not involved in that part of Mercury's operation. I can only say that our own internal security investigation, in cooperation with the air force, is proceeding."

"How long you been with Mercury?"

"Five years, General."

"And where were you before that?"

"I was in New York with Kelly, Johnson and Masters. It's one of the biggest advertising firms in the East."

"Never heard of it. You a flier?"

"No. No, I'm not, General."

"Why are we talking with this guy?" Cartwright asked Glassman as the vice-president for corporate communications fiddled with his yellow tie, looking as though he would like to be on another planet.

"Classified briefing on new mission technology, sir."

"You know," Cartwright said, adjusting his aviator's glasses as he inspected the corporate figure, "I was flying test on Mercury planes when Bernie Jackson rolled his first spy plane out of the Beaver Works. And they never lost track of any secret paperwork then. Maybe I should be briefing you, Mr. Cunningham."

"I hardly think so, sir," the executive replied, pulling his tie even tighter, ruining the French knot. He dabbed his forehead with a monogrammed handkerchief. "We have a fine program on hand for you today."

Cartwright looked Cunningham up and down. He gave the vice-president a small, playful shove, the way a lion might push a cub. Then he clapped him on the shoulder. "Never mind me, Cunningham," he said, laughing. "I was just busting your chops. Now, you take us on your little tour and show us the new Mercury Corporation."

The trio walked across the tarmac toward Mercury's biggest hangar, a structure the size of an apartment complex that towered five stories above the desert floor.

"This is where the work gets done," Cunningham said cheerily.

"Final assembly, you mean," Cartwright said.

"That's correct, General. Final assembly. We've got twenty-five hundred jobs tied up right here."

"Old Bernie told me the work gets done up here," Cartwright said, tapping his forehead. "Well, let's go see what the worker bees are doing."

They stepped into an elevator and rode it to the top floor, then stepped out onto a steel catwalk. Another civilian guard joined by an air force security man armed with an M-16 waited on the platform.

Leaning on the guardrail, the general inspected the work going on several stories below. People the size of ants carried parts and tools in and out of the fuselage of a sleek-looking bomber-sized aircraft.

"This is Mercury's pride," Cunningham said. "We think it's going to give taxpayers more bang for the buck than the B-1 ever did."

"It looks like a B-1," Cartwright snapped.

"It's faster and quieter," said Cunningham. "It can fly lower and climb higher, if need be. And it's a damn sight better as a penetrator than the B-20X could have hoped to be."

Cartwright watched workers using powered buffing machines on the wing. They were applying black-striped material on the leading edge of the bomber's wing.

"That's radar-absorbent material," Glassman said, noting Cartwright's interest. "The strips are composite material made of graphite and various plastics. The trick is to use enough of the stuff so that it can soak up the enemy's radar beam."

Cartwright nodded and turned to Cunningham. "Tell me something. Is Reggie LeFever still chief test conductor for Mercury at Plant thirty-six?"

"Yes, General, I believe he is."

"Raise him for me on the radio, will ya? I've gotta talk to him."

Looking puzzled, the vice-president asked the civilian guard for his radio and made a call. He handed the walkie-talkie to Cartwright.

"King, is that you?" Cartwright asked into the microphone.

"This is King. Who are you?" the voice inquired through the scratchy static.

"This is Eagle. I'm on the fifth floor, and I want to come to your location."

"Roger that, Eagle. I'll give you directions."

Looking alarmed, Cunningham turned to Glassman, who shrugged. The vice-president reached for the radio.

"General. Pardon me, sir. But what are you doing?"

"Shut up, Cunningham. I'm taking directions," Cartwright said, keeping his ear to the radio.

"General, what is the problem? Is there something I can help with?"

"That isn't the plane," Cartwright said, pointing at the fuselage on the floor hundreds of feet below.

"General, what are you saying?"

"I'm saying thanks for the swell tour. Let's go, Major," Cartwright said, handing the guard his radio as he stepped back into the elevator.

"General, you can't do this. You've got to stay with me," Cunningham said, his voice rising in alarm.

"Let me say this real polite, Cunningham. I think I've got more friends at Mercury than you do. Try to follow me and I may have to punch your lights out."

Glassman jammed himself through the elevator door as it was closing. "With all due respect, sir...what the hell do you think you're doing?"

"We're cleared to walk anywhere in this plant, Major?"

"Yes, sir. But we should be with Cunningham."

"And get danced around all day? I don't think so."

"Cunningham is part of our cover, General. That was my plan, and you are ruining it."

"Major, if you give me a phony briefing on a phony plane, our Moscow friends will sense the ruse."

"What the hell are you talking about, General?"

"That isn't the plane, goddammit," Cartwright said, banging his fist on the elevator wall. The door opened, and he marched out across the assembly area toward a steel door with a security booth next to it.

"General, you're making a mistake," Glassman said.

"Maybe," Cartwright said. "And maybe you're a horse's ass. Keep the veil on Stealth for Russia, not me."

He strode across the plant floor past workers scurrying around the bomber fuselage. He banged on the window of the glass shack, and the guard inside rose. Seeing Cartwright's stars, he saluted.

"Get the chief test conductor and tell him to open the goddamn door, airman," Cartwright ordered.

"I'm sorry, sir. You're not badged for access to this part of the hangar."

"Son, do you know Reggie LeFever by sight?"

"Yes, sir."

"So do I. Black man. Mid-fifties. Wears two gold rings. One wedding, one air force. Favors sky-blue leisure suits. He'll vouch for me. Call on conference so I can hear."

Hurriedly the guard called inside. "Let him in, airman," LeFever answered. "If there's any flak, I'll take it."

The steel door opened, and they stepped into a brightly lit hangar the size of a high school gymnasium.

"Welcome, Eagle," boomed a voice from a loudspeaker. Immediately recognizing the source of the greeting, Cartwright looked up at the long, glassed-in booth built high above, like a press box in a sports arena, but the engineers at work behind the glass were not visible.

Cartwright quickly turned his attention to the massive matte-black boomerang-shaped aircraft that occupied the center of the hangar floor. Sitting sturdily on its delicate-looking tricycle landing gear, the craft resembled an enormous manta ray.

Cartwright stepped off sixty paces, using his soldier's stride to gauge the plane's wingspan. It had virtually no fuselage and no tail. Where the sharp angles and irregularities that define the shape of a jet usually were, there were only smooth, obsidian-colored surfaces and an occasional red-stenciled warning: "Hands Off—Radar-Absorbent Surface."

The general, completing his measurements, paced beneath the bomber, looking up into an open bomb bay. Deep inside the bomber's fish-white belly hung eight B-83 thermonuclear gravity bombs, each containing a one-megaton warhead suspended in a rotary launcher above Cartwright's head. No engine nacelles or exhaust ports protruded from the plane. Dark holes in the aft marked the location of the propulsion systems. Cartwright walked slowly back toward the nose and examined the sleek windowed cockpit, a slight rise in the leading edge of the craft.

"That, Major, is the goddamn plane," Cartwright said, crossing his arms in satisfaction.

The general ascended a metal staircase to the engineer's booth. Glassman followed Cartwright up the stairs and into the booth, where a row of engineers busily monitored data on glowing computer terminals. A huge black man stepped down from a seat mounted on a platform above the engineers and approached Cartwright, grinning.

"I wondered when you'd get your nosy big old beak poked inside all of this, Eagle," he said, shaking Cartwright's hand vigorously.

"Major Glassman, meet Reggie LeFever," Cartwright said. "He's chief test conductor for black projects at Mercury, no pun intended."

Glassman shook LeFever's hand awkwardly. "I wasn't aware you were fully briefed on black-project level information, General," he said.

"Old Eagle here's probably just been reading the trade publications," said LeFever. "If he's within a mile of a hot plane, he'll find it. If he can't see 'em, he can smell 'em."

"LeFever here is called King," Cartwright said. "You can see that from the throne he perches on. No one can run ground test on a plane better than this man. We flew Super Sabres together in Germany. You probably wouldn't be interested, though, Glassman. They were old airplanes."

"So what do you think of the new plane, General?" LeFever said, guiding the pair over to the windows overlooking the jet.

"Gimme the dope on her."

"The wingspan is about a hundred and eighty feet," LeFever said. "Tell me, General, does it look at all familiar to you?"

"Looks like the plane Glen Edwards was driving forty years ago at Muroc when he augered in."

"That's right. The Flying Wing."

"General, we really should be getting out of here," Glassman said. "We're overdue to meet the Mercury design team."

"At ease, Major," Cartwright said. "Don't be more of a pain in the ass than you usually are. Forgive him, Reggie. Now show me what your airplane is all about."

"No problem. Look over here, Scotty," LeFever said, punching a series of keys on one of the engineer's computer keyboards.

The computer imaged a schematic of a B-52 bomber flying across a radar scope.

"Look at that," LeFever said. "It was a hell of a strategic bomber, but it couldn't penetrate Soviet air defenses. It's almost as big as the Korean Air Lines 747 they shot down in eighty-three, and almost as easy to track, even with a full electronic countermeasure load."

He punched more keys, erasing the B-52 and conjuring up the image of a B-1 bomber. It was much smaller, and the wavy green lines of radar activity flowed around it in concentric circles.

"See that? The B-1's radar signature is a fraction of the B-52, even though the plane isn't really that much smaller."

"It's a good airplane all right," Cartwright said, looking intently at the screen.

"Try this," LeFever said, entering a series of commands that wiped the B-1 from the screen and summoned a manta-shaped schematic from the computer's memory. The glowing green shape faded quickly, becoming a barely discernible blip crossing the screen. The wavy lines that symbolized radar scanning beams appeared to pass directly through it.

"That's it, the STB-1," LeFever said proudly. "The Stealth Technology Bomber, capable of penetrating enemy airspace at any altitude."

"That's bullshit," Cartwright said. "You can't do it. The goddamn plane is almost invisible."

"It's not bullshit, Eagle. It's Stealth. And we're the only ones who have it, baby."

"Okay, Reggie. You gave me your magic lantern show. Now crunch some numbers for me. How do you do it?"

"You probably know the principles as well as I do, General."

"Yup. Stealth is achieved when radar waves flow over a flight surface rather than bouncing off it."

"Correct. But it's the aircraft's shape that makes up about eighty percent of the battle to achieve Stealth characteristics. You could have enough paint, epoxy composite material, and all the radar-absorbent material it would take to coat the Statue of Liberty, but with all that you couldn't hide the lady, could you?"

"Nope. She's got too many angles and points."

"Right. Paint her up with antiradar supergoop and you still have a highly distinct radar signature because the beams are gonna bounce off every curve and bump, the same way they would on an airplane that's got big intakes, big scoops, and highly irregular angles on its wings and stabilizers. You take a good look at the Stealth plane. We've eliminated all that stuff."

"If I remember right, the Flying Wing never made it as an operational airplane because it was a highly unstable flying platform. Remove the airplane's tail and it doesn't fly so good."

"That was 1949, Eagle. We've gone to the moon since then. Weren't you hotdogging around out over Rogers Dry Lake in that Grumman plane, the X-29, the other day?"

"Word gets out. Yeah, I drove it around some. It's a sweet plane."

"The wing on the Grumman plane is swept forward, right? Just like a bumblebee, it isn't supposed to fly well, but it does. How come? Same principle on the Stealth bomber. It's not going to fly with hydraulic controls that depend on muscle to push the plane around. Digital fly-by-wire, computer-controlled impulses directed on a hand control from a capable pilot will enable that unstable flying platform to handle as sweet as a two-year-old filly."

"You're saying your fly-by-wire can make this beast handle like an F-16?"

"She won't turn as tight, but she won't auger in."

Cartwright gazed down from the computer booth to the manta-ray shaped creation a few dozen feet below and whistled. It occurred to him that in his lifetime the world had moved from propellers and pistons into a brave new world of winged wonders capable of supersonic transport or of ending all progress.

"What's the deployment schedule for your superplane?"

"Imminent."

"How's the budget allocation?"

"Ample, unless all the money gets sucked into Star Wars at election time."

"They're always gonna need an air-breathing bomber."

"That, old friend, depends on the mood in Congress."

"Congress, my granny. There's been nothing yet that could beat Uncle Sam's being able to drop the big one down a smokestack and still be able to call it back if we need to."

"Hope the country agrees."

Glassman fidgeted behind the two men, looking constantly at his watch. "Begging your pardon, General," he said. "We've got to leave. Now."

"Hold your horses, Major. One more question, Reggie. What stage of development is the prototype here advanced to?"

"Shit. You saw it. It's carrying its war load."

"You mean the sumbitch is ready for rollout?"

"Affirmative."

"Who authorized an onload of H-bombs in a research-and-development facility?"

"You've already told the general too much, Mr. LeFever," Glassman said. "Really, General, we've got to go before they come looking for us."

"Reggie, disregard my junior officer. You know me. You can believe me when I say I am cleared that it's true. Spell it out. And no bullshit."

LeFever ran his fingers through his graying hair and breathed deeply.

"The onload was authorized at the highest level. If push came to shove, the president would rather use it than lose it. This one airplane might be our only shot at a decapitating strike. This is a test plane, but for practical purposes it is loaded for the bear."

"How long do you plan to keep it here?" Cartwright asked, ignoring Glassman.

"Not long. It should be at Area fifty-one in Nevada soon. We got a hardened hangar waiting for her there."

"I hope you know you got a hot potato here, King."

LeFever grinned and said, "Here's hoping it never gets baked."

IRAN, THE INNER CHAMBER

Avadek and the Green Flight pilots, whose heads were bound in the red cloth of sacrifice, bowed before the Imam and his son. The Persian letters on their headbands read, "On to Paradise." Avadek rose from his knees to a sitting position. The silence and austerity of the chamber reminded him of how remote he was from the scenes of dying he had witnessed at the front, where, again, the enemy had used gas. Flying their Soviet Sukhoi fighter bombers, they mowed down legions of women, children, and old men like blades of wheat. But this room was clean and quiet, like the martyrs' hospitals.

"You are ready then to leave for America?" the Imam inquired.

Avadek bowed to the floor in assent.

"And these you have found, they are worthy of the task?"

"These young ones live," Avadek said. "That is the measure of their worth. The enemy tried to chase them from the skies, but still they live. They fly the American planes, the Tomcats. They are the best holy fighters I can find."

"Maybe it is wrong that they live," the Imam's son grumbled. "The heroes of Islam are martyrs. They should have gone to paradise waging war in the marshes of the front."

"Some martyrs are more precious than others," Avadek said dryly. "These martyrs can fly." As he spoke, Mehdi, bowing, suppressed an urge to smile.

"Truly, then, it is hoped that they are worthy to be chosen," the Imam said, bringing his hands together and closing his eyes.

"We wish to depart, Imam Safavi. We ask only your blessing."

"Blessed are they who battle the unjust. Blessed are they who take up arms in the struggle of the poor and the weak against the evil and the powerful."

"Then, truly, we are blessed," Avadek said.

The eyes of the ayatollah fixed on the colonel. Avadek found himself captivated by the shrouded, sitting figure.

"Where is the young one, the one who gave you the treasure?" asked the Imam.

"He has gone ahead, to prepare the way," Avadek answered calmly. Inside himself he felt a wave of cold fear. Had Issam's body been found in the laundry hamper?

The old man's gaze persisted and penetrated, until finally the colonel believed that every secret thing about him must be known. Avadek, the unshakable, shivered. But the shrouded elder finally nodded his head and smiled gently.

"Hear me, now," he declared. "You know I am the giver of the laws. If your cause was not just, Avadek, your head would rest on a plate."

"It should not be otherwise, Imam," Avadek murmured.

"The plane of the evil ones will fly in the cause of Islam," the Imam said matter-of-factly. "You will bring it to the bosom of Islam. It will be our sword and shield. We will use it to end the struggle and to deal with the two Great Satans."

"We are honored," Avadek said.

"The journey before you is the pilgrimage of the just."

"My father," the Imam's son cried out, "I fear this undertaking is folly. If we seize this plane, we shall be bombed by the Americans. They will smite us."

"There can be no bargain with evil, my son," the old man said softly.

As the holy man spoke, the building shook. Cracks sundered the white walls, and paint dust showered like powder from the ceiling. All the men kneeling in the room looked about them, their hands on the floor, grasping at it nervously as though awaiting an earthquake or storm. There was a rumble, this time farther away.

"The Russian missiles," the Imam said quietly. Alone among them, he had not moved. "Every day the hated one fires more of them. The oil is in danger. The revenues are insufficient. The time for boldness is now."

"My father, would you risk devastation for our lands?" the son exclaimed, cocking his ear to listen for the thud of another SCUD missile.

"Boldness," the Imam said almost inaudibly. "Boldness carried the Imam Khomeini from his place of exile to the seat of triumph. Can we do less? Our Colonel Avadek and his warriors give us the opportunity to act with purity and decision."

"But Father," the Imam's son persisted, "if the Americans discover who has taken the plane, they surely will destroy us."

"You tremble, my son," the Imam said, smiling kindly. "They will not destroy us. I am told that the American plane flies very fast. On the day of Colonel Avadek's triumph, we will announce it to the world. They will look on us in awe and wonder."

"And what will keep them from launching their missiles, those even more frightful than the Russians'?" the son implored.

"Because we will have the plane," the Imam said, clapping his hands together like rolling thunder. "It will be rampant, flying free and full of its power to destroy. But first they must find it." The old man twirled his index finger in the air like a small whirlwind. "And we will tell the world that if any attempt is made to attack our holy lands, we will use the plane immediately. We will use it to lay waste the Saudi infidels' oil fields."

The Imam's voice was calm, but his eyes blazed with the certainty of decision. "Let every man fear the warriors whose cause is righteous. Tell me again, my Avadek. What was the code name given this airplane by the foolish Americans?"

"Aurora," the colonel said.

"Ah, yes. Aurora, the name for the light of dawn. For us, it shall be the dawn of Islam triumphant," the ayatollah said, placing his hands together and closing his eyes.

The men in the white room bowed deeply, including the Imam's son, who finally trembled at the wisdom and power of his father. A few miles away another missile fell, shaking the beams in the roof.

"I fear this day of decision," the Imam's son declared.

"There are other things to consider, things of this world," his father replied.

"What are you saying, revered one?" the son asked.

"The flow of arms to the enemy is uninterrupted. Our armaments have diminished to a trickle. We need a decisive weapon. The enemy is at our gate."

"You speak wisely, honored one," Avadek interjected.

"I am not finished," he said curtly. "No plan can be perfect. There must be an alternative. The opportunity of the plane must not be lost to us. We will be martyrs if called upon. But we will not be martyred for nothing. If an interception of the plane is likely, you will use its power against an American city."

The fliers raised their heads and looked at one another and at Avadek, who kept his gaze steady on the Imam.

"Certainly each of your families would endorse this action," the Imam said, smiling gently. Each flier knew the meaning of his words. They looked to Mehdi, their leader, whose face was expressionless.

Another missile fell, raining more dust on the men in the room. Each, deep within him, felt the power of the blast and then the heat. The city was on fire.

Avadek believed the fuse was lit, and the fire was burning its way across the gulf.

7

SAN FRANCISCO

Romanovich strode into the Edo Hotel on Market Street in San Francisco, barely concealing his rage. It took two tall bottles of warm sake from room service and a foot massage given by one of the expert Japanese women who frequented the hotel to calm him. Tatiana sat on the edge of his futon bed, her legs crossed demurely. She smiled patiently, appearing half-amused as the tiny kimono-clad Osaka girl walked on the major's back. When she finished, the masseuse smiled daintily, stepped off the major, and quietly left the room. Romanovich reached for his cigarettes on the black lacquer side table. Lighting one, he rolled off the bed, allowing the towel to drop. His Soviet brethren might be prudish, but he did not give a damn if a fellow operative gazed upon him in a state of nature. Perfunctorily he walked around the room, tapping wall surfaces in an inspection for listening devices.

"You are a new Soviet man," Tatiana said dryly as he walked about. Romanovich laughed and put out his cigarette in an elegant ashtray. He opened a Gucci bag, took out some bikini underwear, and put it on. Then he slipped into slacks and a LaCoste shirt.

"Interesting that the comrade has cultivated a taste for capitalist luxury," Tatiana said.

"The massage? That young lady's art predates capitalism and Marx, comrade," Romanovich said. "She practices a tradition that precedes the march of history. I experienced it during assignment in Japan."

"I have always wished to serve the state in that country."

"Forget it. The pace is grueling. I had more than pretty girls on my back. There are too many secrets in that country, and too little control on them. Get a dozen and Moscow Center wants one hundred. That is just how it is."

"Center will surely be demanding results on this mission," Tatiana said, taking one of Romanovich's cigarettes and lighting it herself.

"Of course. But we are fortunate to have a real mission, instead of just sucking up every bit of data within reach," he said, pacing like a panther. "That is all the stations do. Not one of them understands operations."

"You are critical of the stations?"

"Don't get political with me, little bird. On this operation, all that scheming and maneuvering matters little. Results count. None of the bastards at the stations in Rome, Beirut, and now San Francisco appear to realize that. They think their cousins or uncles are the reasons for keeping their jobs. When they are recalled to the motherland, they will change their tune," he said, stepping out the precise meter of a man who has spent time in a cell, awaiting further instruction. "Repeat for me, please, the Los Angeles file."

Romanovich settled back on the futon mattress and reached for the sake jar. He poured the clear fluid into the tiny glass and drained it. It was Tatiana's turn to pace.

"The Aurora source has been under control of a scientific exchange officer given permission to study at a

Los Angeles university, with his research limited to what the imperialists call noncritical technology," she said, reciting from memory like a schoolgirl. "This officer initiated the contact with Aurora and the Polish trade officer."

"I know that, Tatiana," Romanovich snapped. "Bring it up to date."

"The officer assessed Aurora's needs and serviced them accordingly."

"Prostitutes?"

"Precisely. And gambling," she said, blowing a last puff of smoke and stubbing out the cigarette.

"Traitors are rarely original," Romanovich said wearily. "That should help us, however. The scientific officer will process his request again, applying appropriate pressure in the form of fear and terror, and we will regain our materials."

"It will not be that simple. Our resource is simply too fearful. He knows what he has done. We are told he cannot summon the nerve to do it again."

"Then, I understand, it is your function to give him that courage," Romanovich said. "The director has told me you are capable."

"I am," Tatiana said, stepping behind a screen decorated with the serene beauty of Mount Fuji.

"How, then, will you accomplish your task?"

Stepping away from the screen, Tatiana placed her hands on her hips and swiveled slightly. Standing before Romanovich naked as an egg, she shook her blond hair from its elegant coif onto her bare shoulders. "Give me your cock and I'll show you how, Volodya," she said, smiling.

The KGB officer gazed on Tatiana and sighed. "Oh, hell," he muttered. "There's a time to lead and a time to follow."

She nipped playfully at his neck, then his ear. For the next hour she gave Romanovich a whirlwind course on practically all aspects of her expertise. At the end, Romanovich believed the girl could draw secrets from a rock.

PLANT 36

As Cartwright and Glassman entered the secure conference room deep inside Plant 36, the Mercury engineers rose, except for Evans, the deputy project manager who wanted to let the celebrity general know he was senior man on the team.

"At ease, men," Cartwright said easily. "No need to stand up. You're civilians."

The engineers laughed, while Glassman stood by, fidgeting, and Evans finally got up. The general shook hands with Randy Jefferson and Bix Samuels. Cartwright looked at Dan Lowell for a moment, then shook his hand warmly.

"Didn't you work on spy planes with Bernie Jackson a long time ago?" he asked.

"Sure did, General. I was there when you flew test on the Blue Bird out at Groom Dry Lake."

"Watertown Strip. Those were fine times at the ranch, and that was a fine plane. Good to see you again. It's Dave, isn't it?"

"Dan, sir. Dan Lowell, but you were pretty close."

Evans was the last to offer his hand to Cartwright. "We try to be error-free with our government work at Mercury, General," he said, adding a nervous chuckle.

"Fine, son. That's what Major Glassman and I are here to talk about."

"We have the men here who can account for cost overruns down to the penny," Evans said, exuding confidence he didn't feel.

"Don't worry, son. We're not auditors. Let Congress and the GAO pencil pushers do all that. We're here to talk about the airplane."

"So perhaps, General, we should get down to cases. I have the materials for the Mercury team to examine," Glassman said, reaching into his attaché case.

"Never mind that, Major. I'll be delivering the briefing orally. You just set yourself down," Cartwright said.

"But sir," Glassman said.

"At ease, Major."

"Sir..." Glassman persisted.

"That's enough, Major," the older man said, smiling at the seated group of engineers. "My aide wants his day in the sun. Forgive him."

The Mercury men laughed nervously, and Cartwright stepped over to a chalkboard. "Gentlemen, we are going to talk about Stealth today," he said, clapping chalk dust from an eraser.

"Sir, you realize that we are not authorized to discuss the project you describe or even to acknowledge its existence without proper authorization," Evans said, coughing.

"You're a little late, but I understand," Cartwright said, smiling. "Major, open up your damned case and show this young man our clearances."

Evans gave the documents a cursory inspection and nodded his approval.

"If we're all squared away, I will continue. Gentlemen, in case you were wondering why you were gathered here today, it was not to observe my official recall to active duty," Cartwright said. "You are here because Stealth is in trouble. The project is in danger of being compromised."

More than one member of the Mercury team gasped.

"General," Lowell said, "we find that hard to believe. We know there have been attempts to compromise security, but they have been thwarted. They even arrested a man a few years ago who thought he was selling secrets to KGB. Turned out it was an FBI sting operation."

"I understand, Dan. Air force and FBI are even satisfied that the crummy document security at Downey hasn't resulted in the compromise. We believe CIA would have detected something cooking on the other side of the pond if there was a leak. The threat of compromise is coming from another corner. In fact, it's another contractor."

"What are you talking about?" Evans demanded.

Cartwright picked up a piece of chalk and drew a series of circles similar to the radar beams the chief test conductor had summoned up on his computer screen. In the center of the circles, he chalked out a crude dot.

"I think I understand Stealth," Cartwright said. "Hell, a kid who reads *Popular Mechanics* would. There's not much secret that stays secret anymore."

"Just what are you saying, General?" Evans snapped.

Pointing at the chalk dot, Cartwright said, "There's your plane. Its surfaces are supersmooth and constructed of radar-absorbent material. It's carrying a sophisticated electronic countermeasures package."

"You're damn right, General. We think we've licked the radar signature problem."

"Fine, Dan. Fine. But there's a hole in Stealth."

"Would you mind telling us what it might be?" Randy Jefferson blurted out.

"Just this. Ivan is onto Stealth."

"What the hell do you mean? We're years ahead of their air defense," Lowell said. "I'd stake my life on it."

"That's affirmative, General Cartwright," Evans said. "I think you're off base."

"I'm glad you'd stake your life on it, Dan," Cartwright said. "Because that is exactly what our pilots will be doing if they have to fly a penetration mission."

"So what's the hole?" asked Jefferson.

"If the Russkies can't beat us in design, they'll steal what they need," Cartwright said.

"Well, damn it, we know they haven't stolen Stealth," Evans said. "So what is the problem?"

"The Soviet air defense forces are not going to find your airplane with radar, men. Instead, Ivan will use an infrared detection system he swiped from your competitors in Redondo Beach. It's about the size of a golf ball, or a Stinger antiaircraft missile warhead, just right to fit in the nose of a MiG interceptor. Or, if you cover a football field the size of the Krasnoyarsk radar with enough of those golf balls, you can just about protect the approaches to the Moscow air defense region. Then it's bye-bye Stealth."

"Jesus," Lowell said.

"I don't like it, either. But that's the way it is," the general said.

"Jesus," Lowell repeated again. "How do we know this is true?"

"You boys read the papers and keep track of the rumor mill. You heard about the Northram Aircraft bust?"

"We know about it, General," Evans said sourly. "The guy was trying to peddle papers about the Snakeye missile. It was chicken feed. Old stuff."

"That was the cover story from FBI," Cartwright said. "So far, it's holding."

"Shit," Lowell said.

"Look, boys. I'm not here to rag on you. Your firm has enough trouble with the FBI right now. You been hemorrhaging documents for two solid years, and even you don't know what's missing."

"That's a cheap shot, General," Evans said.

"It's true," Lowell said. "Okay, General. If you're not here to rag on us, what are you here for?"

"Danny boy, as far as CIA and Defense can tell, Stealth technology has not been blown. But if the Soviets can't find you with radar and Mainstay planes, they'll try to track you with passive radiation detection. Your job is to work up an effective countersystem."

"We're going to need the specifications of our competitor's infrared package," Evans said.

"You'll get them."

"When?" Evans asked eagerly.

"Soon as I can deliver 'em. At the moment, I am the Pentagon's highest-ranking messenger boy. This ends my briefing, gentlemen. I suggest you get your sweepers in here to remove any trace of my show-and-tell."

Cartwright shook hands all around, executed a smart about-face, and exited the room. The air-lock doors *shushed* open as he walked down the hallway with Glassman following close behind.

"Sir," Glassman said breathlessly, "your briefing was brilliant. Better than the one I prepared."

"Thank you, Major. That's comforting."

"It was also total bullshit. Nothing about passive radiation was stolen from Northram. It was all Snakeye stuff."

"The Mercury guys don't know that. They worry more about security against competitors than they do about the KGB."

"So how are you going to furnish competitive data on infrared tracking? The stuff I had in my case was a black-box modification we already studied and rejected."

"I've got a pal inside the beltway who can trick out something that will hold up long enough for the mole to leave his hole and swipe it."

"Does your guy know my guys?"

"Maybe," Cartwright said, grinning. "Maybe when I get back from Washington we can all do lunch."

"I'll go with you."

"Nope. I want you here at Plant thirty-six. That's an order," Cartwright said, and left the building.

Glassman watched Cartwright stride away. For a magazine-cover flier, he thought, the general certainly seemed to know a lot about spooking.

WASHINGTON, D.C.

The C-141 Starlifter banked ponderously on final approach to Andrews Air Force Base outside Washington. As the huge plane dropped through the cloud cover, Cartwright peered through the cockpit glass, enjoying the early morning view of the Capitol dome, the White House, and Washington Monument and the mighty snake of the Potomac as it wound past the Pentagon. Every time he descended toward Andrews, he cherished the panorama.

The mighty turbines of the Starlifter lowered pitch as the plane swooped toward the rapidly blinking landing lights.

"Just one question, General," asked the pilot, a young captain.

"Sure, what's on your mind?"

"What's a hot pilot like you doing hitching a ride with MAC?"

"Aw, hell. I needed the first freight out of Dodge, and that buddy of mine who runs the show over at Edwards wouldn't cut loose with one of his precious F-16s," Cartwright said, chuckling.

"Well, glad to have you, sir. Hope you had a pleasant flight," the transport pilot said as the giant plane screamed in and bumped onto the tarmac so fast that it had to deploy parachutes to brake its landing.

"There was a day when all us fighter jocks looked down on you cargo jockeys," Cartwright said. "The young ones probably still do. But your bunch, guys like Dick Secord, put me down on a hot and short field in Vietnam enough times for me to realize the kind of guts that takes. We're all in the same air force."

Before the Starlifter rolled to a halt, Cartwright was out of the cockpit. He made his way through the cargo bay and out onto the ramp, jogging, then breaking into a dead run. Spotting the stars on his blue forage cap and flight suit, a guard in crisp fatigues and blue beret at the foot of the control tower snapped to attention and saluted sharply as Cartwright breezed past.

He sprinted to the duty table and said, "Sergeant, I need a secure line, pronto." Before the sergeant could stand, he placed a phone in the general's hand. Cartwright dialed.

"Evergreen, that you? This is Eagle. I'm in your town. Let's meet in Alexandria for breakfast. They got good corned-beef hash at our bistro in Old Town."

He hung up and returned the phone to the bewildered sergeant. "Sarge, ring up the motor pool. Tell 'em ... hell, I don't care what you tell 'em. Just make sure they know you got a one-star here who needs a lift."

It was raining by the time Cartwright parked his government-issue Chevy in an underground lot off King Street in the Old Town section of Alexandria, just across the Potomac from the capital. He wore his uniform and blue topcoat to be less conspicuous. A stone's throw from Washington, Alexandria was a military town and nearly an annex of the Pentagon in nearby Arlington.

Brady Daniels, chief of the CIA, was waiting at a table in the back dining room of the colonial-style Holiday Inn. He looked like any of the silver-haired gentlemen who breakfasted regularly at the red-brick mansionlike hotel built on the site where the first shots of the Civil War were fired in Virginia. His predecessor, Bill Casey, would have been quickly spotted, being a political man whose massive frame was often before the cameras trained on congressional committees.

Daniels, on the other hand, shunned the cameras. He was an intelligence professional, therefore indistinguishable from the legions of lawyers, professors, and administrators who formed the mandarin class of official Washington. Often he had been mistaken for Archibald Cox. Both Daniels and Cox, the constitutional scholar, adopted the natty bowtie and severe brush haircut that was a mark of their prewar Ivy League class and of their breeding. Daniels rose and smiled as he saw Cartwright approaching. "Damn good to see you, Scotty," he said.

"Same here, Brady. Let's talk like old combat buddies."

The men sat down to a steaming silver pot of coffee. The waitress, decked out like Dolley Madison, took their orders and returned with plates of hash, eggs, and rashers of bacon. The orange juice was fresh-squeezed.

"Okay, Scotty. Put your cards down. Are you closing in? The president goes to the UN next week, and the Russians are going to be there. The president and State are going to dicker with the chairman on some pretty sensitive issues. Our man needs to know whether we've been compromised on the bomber."

"I'll tell you what I think we've got and what I'm gonna do, but first you've gotta talk straight with me."

"About what?" Daniels said through a forkful of hash and eggs.

"I need to know some more about Major Adam Glassman. The partner you've saddled me with is an unusual young man."

"Scotty, everyone in the world knows of you as an astronaut and a hot test pilot, right?"

"Damn right."

"But you know, and I know, that you've helped out the Company damn near since we got started."

"If you mean that OSS thing you got me into in France during the war, I guess you're right."

"But you've never acknowledged the help you've given us, right?"

"You know better than that. Even when I flew for you boys out of Iran, I was still a blue-suiter. I was just on loan."

"Then you've got to understand why I can't fill you in on Glassman."

"Nope. It won't wash, Brady. We're too close to the heart of this security breach right now. One of the boys FBI has spotted is a turncoat. I can feel it. I need to know what that boy Glassman is going to do when we smoke our quarry."

"And just how close are you on that?"

"I'm setting the trap, and Glassman is up to speed with me. He's a bright boy. I need some technical help from your boys at the Farm."

"Name it."

"I want 'em to dummy up some specs on passive infrared tracking devices. Use the Stinger warhead as a technical base, but load up the summary with some equations that need proofs to verify the research data."

"Maybe you'd like the real thing? Maybe you want a black-bag job done over at General Technologies? Maybe I'd even like to oblige, but those days are over, Scotty. Too much damn oversight."

"I know it. I just need something that looks too good to pass up. Your young major wanted to bait the trap with a black-box modification. I just wanted to come up with something the bad guys would feel like they've gotta have."

"So you like Glassman's work, but you have doubts about him personally. Is that it, Scott?"

"I'd like to say he has my confidence," Cartwright said, pouring a generous dollop of Tabasco sauce on his eggs, "but I don't know him. You and I buried the silk together and cut some throats during the real war. I gotta trust you. Tell me about this young fella. Is he up to the job?"

"If he wasn't, the president wouldn't have entrusted him."

"Bullshit, Brady. The president didn't pick him. You did."

Daniels sighed. He grinned like a parchment mummy and pushed the last of his eggs around on the fine china plate. "You play hardball, Scotty."

"My game's poker, Brady. I want to see your cards."

"I would trust Major Adam Glassman for superior performance with any job the government assigns him, with the exception of flying a high-performance military aircraft."

"That's an odd fitness report for a fighter pilot," Cartwright snorted.

"You know about the Syria business."

" 'Course I do. I've got my sources."

"I imagine you do," Daniels said as he packed his old briar pipe with his thumb. He used a silver pipe lighter and blew a dense cloud of musty-smelling Balkan Sobranie tobacco toward a ceiling fan.

"You know, Scotty, they were pretty rough on him."

"Yeah, I heard. They sweated him. What's that got to do with flying?"

"He's Jewish, you know. That's probably one of the reasons he got on so well with the Israelis. He's all American all right. But Glassman and the Israeli fliers, they were of one mind. He's fluent in Hebrew and a Middle East scholar, and I mean scholar in the classical sense. So when the Muslims got him, and quickly discerned his ethnicity, you can imagine what it might have been like."

"But by your account he didn't roll over."

"No, sir, he didn't," Daniels said, forming a puff of smoke into a neat ring, a prep school accomplishment he had never abandoned. "He came through like an ice man. And he gave us some great stuff on their interrogation technique. The air force reward was to put him on test flight at the Dreamland area at Nellis. He was handling the most secret plane in the Deep Black program inventory. Quite a feather in his cap."

"I know about that, too. His chase pilot augered in. He didn't. A pilot gets over that."

"The chase pilot was his brother. His younger brother, Ben. It had been their dream to fly together. When the major handled himself so well over in Fatahland, the air force wanted to do Adam Glassman a favor."

"Damn."

"Yes, sir, Scotty. That's about how I'd put it myself," Daniels said as he fiddled with a pipe tool and relit the briar. "The flight surgeon says Glassman suffers vertigo. The only reason he's wearing wings is that the cover for this job required it."

"Good God, Brady. I tried to get that boy to take the stick of a Starfighter I put into a flat spin the other day."

Daniels's jaw sank in surprise, causing his pipe to drop from his teeth and spill hot ashes on his wool slacks. "I would say you're both damn lucky to be alive," he said, sweeping the embers off his pants. "That man cannot fly."

"Now you tell me."

"He passed over on loan to Defense Intelligence Agency after his brother's death," Daniels said, regaining his composure and repacking his pipe. "They kept him because he's brilliant. And now we're using him. Do the country a favor and keep Major Glassman on solid ground, will you, Scotty?"

The dirty weather that had threatened the mid–Atlantic region all morning turned into a downpour. Inside the doctor's office in Arlington, Cartwright leafed through an old copy of *Newsweek*. The cover story was on the Soviet naval buildup in the Indian Ocean. The second story was about a new crop of high-ranking enlisted men who sold the Soviets the cryptographic analysis materials needed to most effectively deploy their fleet. Cartwright shook his head angrily as he read.

"The doctor will see you now," the pretty receptionist announced. Cartwright figured good doctors must hire such perky women to keep the patients in an upbeat mood, but for him the reaction was opposite. He distrusted professional cheer.

Without being told to do so, he stripped to the waist and climbed onto the examination table. During the past dozen years, in every area where Cartwright was stationed, he had retained a private physician. He knew he had outlived the flying days of most officers. It was always his plan to know about a medical problem before NASA or the air force could use it as an excuse to make him fly a desk instead of a fighter.

"I haven't seen you in a few years, General," the silver-haired physician said as he entered, reading Cartwright's records.

"There's been no need, Doc," Cartwright said, inhaling deeply and expanding his chest as the doctor tapped lightly on it. "I've been fit."

"You've been living in California, haven't you?"

"Yes. It's my wife. When she left England, she said she wanted to live in the sunshine. I like the hunting. The game is richer than the Smoky Mountains on the eastern side of the Sierras."

"And I thought all they did out there was take cocaine and cultivate a deep and dangerous tan."

"That's a different part of the state. Where I live, I can find a good-sized buck in less than half a day's drive. It's meat on the table. The fishing is good, too."

"Yes, sir. That sounds like a great life," the doctor said as he tightened a blood pressure strap around the general's heavily muscled arm. "So what are you doing here today?"

"Doc, you can keep this quiet, right?"

"You should know better than that, General. Our relationship is privileged."

"This is a national security matter."

"I understand, sir. I am a Virginian."

"I'm blind in one eye, Doc. My right eye. At least once in a while I am. It comes and goes. Sometimes I see just fine."

"Let's have a look at that," the doctor said, flashing a penlight in the general's eye. Cartwright blinked rapidly.

"Don't do that. Try to keep both eyes open, please."

The physician peered into the general's eye and grunted. He put down the light and scribbled a few notes on Cartwright's chart.

"Would you mind telling me what the hell it is, Doc?"

"Just guessing, I would say it's a sliver of aluminum or some other metal that is floating in your cornea."

"Oh, hell. Musta been some FOD that kicked up off the tarmac in the desert."

"FOD? I don't believe I know the term."

"Foreign object debris. Dust. Flying junk. You try to keep it the hell away from airplanes and spacecraft. But it's damn near always windy on the desert, and sometimes the stuff kicks up. It can bugger up the works of a good plane."

"Or a good pilot. It's correctable. We can remove it. But the eye will be out of commission for a couple of weeks."

"I can't do that, Doc. I gotta be at battle stations for

the next little while. I need this eye for the next few weeks, as much as I can use it, anyway."

"Well, you darn sure can't fly a plane, soldier. If I were a flight surgeon, I'd ground you."

"I guess I can stay on the ground for a little while. But I can't afford any hospital time," Cartwright said. "I'm fully engaged for the present."

"There's an additional danger that you could lose the eye if the condition persists," the doctor said coolly and professionally. "If that sliver, or FOD, or whatever you want to call it, continues to float, it could detach your retina and cause severe damage. You'd be grounded for good."

"How long have I got before that happens?"

"Honestly, I can't tell. It could be days or weeks. You should see a specialist, today."

The rain pounded outside. A fresh cloudburst dumped drops so heavy they sounded like hail or machine-gun fire, pressing the shrubbery against the office window and blowing the branches of a tree against the glass like a skeleton's hand. The room was overheated, but Cartwright shivered.

"Not a word about this, Doc."

"You have my word, General. But go see that specialist, if you want to keep the eye. That pair of good eyes has been an asset to the nation."

"You're telling me. If I can't see, I can't shoot."

"Don't put off the visit to the specialist."

"Doc, I've got to make a flight to the coast this P.M. It'll have to wait."

"Don't let it wait too long, General. And stay out of the cockpit."

Cartwright left the doctor's office cursing under his breath. At the same time he prayed he would keep his vision. He knew the time demand of his mission and that he could not perform it from a hospital bed. As he often did in similar difficult circumstances, he put his trust in a flier's luck. It had served him before.

8

LOS ANGELES

Major Adam Glassman sat in his car watching the small groups of men emerge from the temple in the Fairfax district of Los Angeles. Most of the men were old. A few of them were quite elderly, and Glassman knew they had begun their days in Russia or in Poland when that country was part of Russia. Some had survived the czar. Others had survived Hitler. A few young boys followed the men. Their side curls bounced gaily beneath their skullcaps as they followed their fathers and grandfathers, who walked with a dignified, somber gait. Major Glassman swallowed hard and blinked, remembering a time when he had been a boy with side curls who followed his father home from temple.

Glassman emerged from the car and adjusted his dark suit. He pulled down the brim on his fedora and followed his father once again. He caught up to the older man who was shuffling toward a bus stop on Fairfax.

"Shalom, Papa. It's me, Adam."

The old man turned and stared at his son through

thick spectacles, giving no sign of recognition. He stroked his long salt-and-pepper beard a moment. He adjusted his wide-brimmed black felt hat so the sun was not in his eyes. Then he turned away and continued walking.

"Papa. Father, wait. It's been so long. I need to speak to you," Glassman said, following after him.

"I have no sons," said the older man.

"Papa, listen to me. I'm leaving the service. I'm getting out."

The old man stopped again. He looked upon his son. Traffic whizzed by on Fairfax, and smoke from a rapid transit district bus filled the air as it pulled from the curb. The old man sat down on a bus bench, and Glassman seated himself next to him.

"How can I talk to you?" the old man said, gesturing rhetorically. "How can I even know this man who talks to me is my son? I don't even know his name."

"I am your son, Papa. I am Abraham Rabinowitz Glassowicz."

"No. Once you were that person. When you were a boy, studying Torah and the ways of God. Now you are some big-deal air force major with a name chosen by the goyim. Very impressive. You changed your name. You changed your God."

"Papa, I wanted to be an American. A real American. There was nothing wrong with that."

"American is fine. We all are American. But you were one of God's people. You changed your name. When you did that, you left your people," the old man said.

"Papa, I did what I did. That is history. I wanted to help my people. I wanted to help America. And if it was possible, to help Israel, too."

"Do not speak of that. That is an abomination. There is no Israel until the Messiah comes. Besides, that was only of secondary interest to you, the big shot who wanted to fly airplanes. What you did was not right," the old man said, shaking his head.

The brakes of a bus screeched as it pulled to a stop. A

few people, mostly elderly, got off. The old man remained on the bench as the bus departed, leaving a fresh cloud of diesel exhaust hanging in the air.

"I'm getting out, Papa."

"So," the old man said, sighing. "So, the big air force hotshot is admitting a mistake, maybe."

"There was no mistake, Father. I had to go and do what I did. I just cannot do it anymore."

"You mean it is not fun for you, now that you have killed your brother," the old man said.

Glassman jumped awkwardly to his feet and began to walk away. He turned and growled like a tortured animal, "I did not kill Ben."

"You didn't? Who did, then? Like maybe he would not have run after his big brother, the big-deal air force man? Look at yourself and face the truth, Mr. Adam Glassman of the United States Air Force."

"Papa, I want peace between us."

"You are alive. Life is not for peace. The grave is for peace. Life is for struggle and for truth."

Without looking back, the old man boarded a bus that swung from the curb like an angry beast.

"Shalom, Papa," Glassman whispered.

The air force major and former Talmudic scholar shuffled to his car, walking like a man much older than his thirty-six years. He settled into his government sedan and swung into the heavy traffic that impeded his progress all the way to the Federal Building on Wilshire Boulevard.

Glassman parked in the restricted lot, entered the undistinguished government building, and took the elevator to the offices of the Los Angeles bureau of the FBI. He stepped out of the elevator into a hallway lined on one side by windows. Through them he surveyed the thousands of rows of white crosses in the Veterans Administration cemetery across Wilshire Boulevard from the Federal Building. Among the sea of crosses were hundreds of Stars of David. One belonged to Glassman's brother. He turned from the window and walked toward the massive oaken doors of the bureau.

After displaying his pass to security, Glassman walked past a row of agents' desks to the office of Supervising Agent Tucker Adams.

As the door to the supervising agent's office opened, several tall Los Angeles police officers emerged. Their chests bristled with medal ribbons, and their collars shone with brass.

The policemen left together, marching in lockstep. The supervising agent and Glassman's contact, the agent from the FBI's Washington bureau, remained at the door. Seeing Glassman, the supervising agent waved him into the office.

"On your way to a funeral, Major?" the agent asked, noting Glassman's dark suit.

"I've been to temple this morning," Glassman said matter-of-factly. "My family is Orthodox."

"Yes, I understand," Adams said, although he didn't. "You know Mr. Benson, here from our Washington office."

"Yes, we've met," Glassman said, shaking hands with Benson, a bald man with the sandpaper voice of a former marine officer.

"Well, if you don't need me, I have a few things to do," the supervising agent said. He waved cheerfully as he stepped out, not wanting to admit he was being kicked out of his own office.

"He's got his hands full," Benson said, fiddling with an attaché case that had a complicated series of locks.

"We all do, Benson. What were the police doing here?"

"They were being briefed on something you should be aware of."

"I've got a pretty full plate right now."

"Washington realizes that, Major. The LAPD brass were here to get briefed on a terrorist threat. The suspected point of origin is Iran."

"You have my full attention."

"Good," Benson said, removing a file from the attaché case. Glassman perused it.

"CIA doesn't have many resources left in Iran. What they've got is precious," Benson said.

"I'm surprised they shared this," Glassman said, reading rapidly.

"Believe me, if your assignment wasn't priority, they would not share it."

"What was the source?"

"I don't know, and I couldn't tell you anyway. But as a professional, I would guess it to be someone high up in what's left of the Iranian general staff."

"What's this got to do with the Plant thirty-six operation?"

"Probably nothing. But it's going to distract the entire field office here. We think the Iranians may be planning some sort of suicide assault in Los Angeles. There's a U.S.-Soviet heat to prepare for the Olympics going on at UCLA next week. A truck bomb would be a good way to screw it up."

"If you reduce the manpower we need for surveillance, the Plant thirty-six subject could slip," Glassman said urgently.

"You've still got the Washington team for surveillance on your Plant thirty-six subjects, and your high-ranking partner is flying in tonight with a package. But Southern California is going to be lousy with Soviet agents traveling with diplomatic immunity."

The FBI agent sighed as he walked to the window. He looked at the palms of his hands as though he knew they were full, also. "There also is, as you know, the major military exercise being conducted in the Southern California desert and coastal region," he continued. "The Desert Thunder operation will deploy ten thousand men, two hundred ships, and six hundred aircraft. That's a lot for Ivan to get an eyeful of, Major. They will be getting everything they can, with satellites and human resources."

Benson wiped sweat from his forehead with a handkerchief. "FBI will have all it can do to keep track of them and monitor the threat from Iran. That's why we're activating LAPD's antiterrorist division."

"Can you tell me what group of geniuses scheduled military maneuvers at the same time as an expected penetration of California by Soviet agents?"

"It's glasnost, Major. We couldn't cancel the heat. We asked the Russians to come."

"What else do you know about the Iranian operation?" Glassman demanded.

"We don't know anything except what you've seen on the flimsy. It's Iran, and they are coming to, or are already in, California."

"Well, I can tell you something about their operation."

"What might that be, Major?"

"I know him," Glassman said, pulling two photographs clipped to a dossier from the file.

Glassman gazed at the photographs of Colonel Asrar Ajami Avadek and shivered involuntarily. One was a grainy shot of the colonel in civilian clothes emerging from Tehran's Independence Hotel. The other depicted a younger Avadek in a khaki police uniform.

"You know this guy?" Benson asked incredulously. "He used to work for CIA in the shah's day. The second shot was taken at Langley."

"He's got new friends. I met him in Lebanon. If you catch him, you'd better kill him."

Glassman looked Benson in the eye and pocketed the photographs. Benson looked back into Glassman's hard green eyes and decided not to raise an objection. After all, FBI held the negatives.

FAYETTEVILLE, NORTH CAROLINA

Master Sergeant (Ret.) Luke Brennan sipped the watery mess-hall style coffee they served at the Dixie Cafe truck stop and lit another nonfilter Camel. He knew he wouldn't walk a mile for a cigarette, but he'd probably kill a man for a smoke if he really needed it bad enough. As he sat in the truck stop on the interstate outside Fayetteville listening to the strains of Alabama wailing away on the jukebox, he reflected that cigarettes were about the only thing he needed that he could pay for.

Nearing the milestone age of fifty, Luke Brennan was not finding retirement sweet. When he chanced to check in at the Special Forces Club, it only reinforced his notion that he was not part of it anymore. The Kennedy Special Warfare Center at nearby Fort Bragg might as well have been a thousand miles and a hundred years away from him.

He looked at the other booths filled with a mix of rednecked long-haul drivers and fuzzy-cheeked kids from the Eighty-second Airborne Division wearing the Saturday uniform of blue jeans and denim jackets. They beat the work detail rap by sneaking off base early before their squad leaders could round them up for painting and cleaning chores. One of the troopers sported a black silk jacket with embroidery that boasted "Grenada: I Was There." With the concentration of a soldier trained to fire wire-guided TOW antitank missiles, he battled a legion of star monsters on a video game. Brennan tried to remember what it was like to be as young as the kid in the jacket. Had he ever been that young? He stroked the walrus mustache he had decided to let grow in Angola until it was a droopy masterpiece. It was nonregulation, and in the old days he would've busted any man out of the special warfare school who dared grow such an appendage. But for Brennan, times had changed. His life had changed with the onset of graying hair and the absence of victory. Phuoc Long was two decades behind him. Laos was done with. Nicaragua went sour after Gene Hasenfus blew the network with his perilous descent into celebrity. Listening to the deafening grind of the sixteen-wheelers pulling up to the Dixie Cafe, Brennan realized he was bored and broke and getting old. He stubbed his cigarette in the ashtray, and the waitress brought his ham steak and eggs with biscuits swimming in heart-threatening gravy. She also laid down his side order of a dozen strips of bacon. When he wasn't in training, Brennan was a big eater. But he could still run eight miles daily. Any fat he was carrying rippled over heavy, corded muscle.

As the retired master sergeant was deciding whether or not to mix his eggs into his home fries and grits, Angus McCain settled into the unoccupied half of his booth. Wiping sweat from his prominent forehead and sweeping back a shock of blond hair, he said, "You're Luke Brennan, A-308 Civilian Irregular Defense Group, right?"

Brennan looked at the big grinning man and felt a tingle. He recognized the tingle as suspicion or as the possible end of boredom. He hoped the big bruiser opposite him wanted more than just to check in on an old war buddy.

"I know you. You were with the Company," McCain said, his eyes hidden behind pilot's dark glasses.

"I don't know what company you're talking about," Brennan said, neither admitting nor denying his affiliation.

"You did short airstrip jobs for Air America in Laos, as I recall," McCain insisted, signaling the waitress to bring him coffee. "And your file says you did some good fast boat work in the Congo."

"The Congo," Brennan said bitterly. "That's back when we fought to win. Couldn't talk about the few we won, though."

"Killed a lot of communists, as I remember," McCain said. "Fact is, I'm with a team that still likes to win."

"Who might they be?"

"I can't name the customer. But the pay is good."

Brennan nodded, considering. He knew already that he would take the job if the big man was on the level. He was lonesome for action.

"Would Uncle mind my working for such a customer?" he asked, casually flicking a gnat from the orange hair on his arm that failed to conceal the garish green-and-pink

"Airborne" tattoo with the jump wings of an army parachutist emblazoned above it.

"No worries. Uncle is backing my customer."

"It's a Company-sanctioned project, then?"

"You figure it out."

"What's the nature of the job?"

"Nursemaid for a photo opportunity. The client cracks a building, takes some pictures, and gets out."

"Sounds like a piece of cake. I bet it isn't, though. Where'd you get my name?" Brennan asked, wolfing down his eggs and grits after first stirring them in the congealed grease from the bacon.

"The old-boy line. Band of brothers, you know."

"Well, nobody ever called me a good old boy, but if the pay is right, I might be your man. I've worked with a team or two. Might do it again," Brennan drawled.

McCain clapped Brennan on the back. "That's the spirit," he said.

"So, I need details," Brennan said.

"I'd like to say it's a piece of cake, Sarge, but I won't try to bullshit you. The job involves penetration, cover, and extraction. We gotta run interference for the customer. Can you assemble a team for that?"

"I hear things around. Prob'ly a couple of Cubans looking for work."

"Gee, Cubans. I don't know," McCain said, shaking his head.

"They're good people. Reliable. And I hear there's a few boys from Yellow Fruit on the market. They're still pissed off that the army told 'em to walk, but they're probably looking for work. We stacked up too many sneaky-Pete outfits these last few years. Then they shut 'em all down sudden after the Iran-contra thing. It's a buyer's market."

McCain nodded sympathetically as he cleaned his large white molars with a toothpick. "Well, reliable is what we need. Couple of ordnance guys. Heavy-weapons team. Some light-weapons specialists. I need a reinforced infantry squad. Maybe a dozen guys. Everybody you'd want for a hot LZ."

"You're right, buddy. It don't sound like a piece of cake."

"Can you do it?"

"You know the old airborne spirit. All the way. My guys can go Spanish and tolerable French. Do you need linguists?"

"Nope."

"No linguists, huh? Where's the job?"

"For the moment, that's a 'need to know' hitch. But it's in the lower forty-eight. I can tell you that much."

"Never heard about a job for Uncle that we did in-country."

"It's important, or I wouldn't have the brief."

"What'd you say was the pay again?"

"It's in the high fives."

"That's a good payday."

"It's a good job," McCain said, cracking his giant knuckles.

Brennan nodded reflectively and listened to the tractor-trailers grinding their way back onto the interstate. He smiled to himself. For the first time since his unwilling retirement, Master Sergeant Luke Brennan felt as though he were going places.

VAN NUYS AIRPORT, THE 146TH TACTICAL AIR WING

Glassman waited for a four-man team of weapons and ammunition handlers at the flight line of the 146th Tactical Air Wing in Van Nuys. The three airmen were led by a master sergeant. They stood as ready as the offensive line of the Los Angeles Raiders, only they were fewer in number. They scanned the evening sky, exhibiting none of the tension they felt.

"You'll want to put that field jacket on, Major," the sergeant said. "It can get mighty drafty in a Hercules."

Glassman already wore the comfortable blue pullover sweater with the elbow patches the Pentagon had acquired from the Brits a few years before. He shivered slightly as a Huey chopper lifted off from the flight line at the small base in the middle of the crowded San Fernando Valley.

"Thank you, Sergeant," he said. "I was forgetting myself. I've hitched a few rides in these birds before."

"Maybe so, but probably not one stripped down like this baby. It's rigged for short turnaround ammunition drop."

"What does that mean?"

"It means the doors are open, on landing approach and in flight," one airman said. "When it unasses its cargo, the Hawk comes howling in at about a hundred miles per hour. It gets drafty."

"Then I guess I'll bundle up," said Glassman, putting on the field jacket over the sweater.

"Good idea, sir," the chief said. "And be ready for a bumpy ride. Here's your parachute."

The chief spotted the plane first, turning from the west, a black speck with the sun setting behind it. "Here she comes. Get the pallets ready."

The men dispersed along the flight line, clenching their fists and jerking their arms up and down in signal to the men at the yellow skip loaders. The engines revved, and orange safety lights twirled.

The Hercules grew from a speck to a great dark shape. The team leaders ran forward, waving their flashbeams, and the skip loaders followed. The plane hit the tarmac. Its prop wash nearly blew off Glassman's blue forage cap, and he leaned forward in the chilly blast. The cargo ramp lowered, and there was Cartwright, waving like a schoolboy.

"Glad you could make it, Major," Cartwright shouted

over the engine roar as he adjusted his parachute straps. "This is gonna be fun."

"Haven't you ever heard of a direct flight, General? I could've picked you up at Edwards."

"This was the first taxi out of Andrews. Besides, the loadmaster here's lettin' me assist."

"Assist what?" Glassman yelled as the last of the ground crew's skip loaders backed down the ramp minus their cargo.

"The ammo drop. We're flyin' the opening sortie of Desert Thunder."

The ramp closed with a hydraulic whine, and the red lights went on inside the transport as it lifted off and swung heavily into the dusky sky. The entire operation had taken less than four minutes.

Glassman looked about him inside the aircraft and saw several men whose faces were dabbed with black paint. They wore speckled brown desert camouflage clothing and were armed like invading Martians.

"What's this got to do with us?" Glassman asked.

"Major, I want you to meet my son, Captain Scott Cartwright, Jr. He's just back from helping some holy warriors in Southwest Asia. Afghanistan, ain't it?"

"I will neither confirm nor deny that, sir. No such operation exists."

A hand dabbed with paint thrust itself forward in the darkness. Glassman couldn't tell what the face behind the paint looked like.

"Pleased to meet you, Major," said the young captain. "Hope this ride doesn't get too bumpy."

"Captain, I've got to tell you something. Every ride with your dad is bumpy."

The younger Cartwright laughed and said, "Well, it should smooth out after we unass this aircraft. My team's making a night drop over the Marine Corps Air Desert Combat Center at Twentynine Palms."

"Let me guess," the major said. "Your son is the loadmaster."

"Shit, no, Major Glassman. He's team leader of the Special Operations Group. The sarge over there is loadmaster," Cartwright said, pointing to a rangy man who was climbing up along the webbing.

The plane roared on in the darkness, and Glassman surveyed the crates packed on the pallets. All around them the heavily armed Martian men were huddled quietly. Each stared ahead, lost in his own thoughts.

"What's my father got you doing?" the young captain asked Glassman.

"He's got me doing paperwork so he can fly all around the country," Glassman said.

"That sounds like my old man. You've got to excuse me. We're on jump run." A red light began flashing. "Five minutes," Captain Cartwright shouted.

The loadmaster dropped down from his webbing and made final checks on the securing of the pallets. He hooked himself to a safety line, spoke inaudibly into his microphone, then listened, taking direction from the pilot. He motioned the captain over to the opposite side of the cargo door and gestured for the general and Glassman to hook their own safety belts. He punched a green button in the bulkhead, and the cargo door yawned open like the jaws of a great fish.

The freezing wind that crew chiefs call "the Hawk" rushed in, and Glassman shivered. He looked aft and saw the stars dancing brightly outside in the freezing night. Captain Cartwright, dressed in insulated flight coveralls, looked like a top sergeant who had been kicking cargo all his life. A buzzer sounded, and a rear light turned from red to green. The general and the loadmaster pushed the first pallet down the ramp, and it shuddered slightly as it separated from the rumbling plane. The canopies of the giant cargo parachutes popped open, and the pallet resembled a giant jellyfish drifting gracefully toward the moonscape thousands of feet below.

The SOG team pushed the second pallet forward, and the loadmaster gave it a final shove. The aircraft banked sharply. Glassman felt beads of sweat popping from his forehead as he clung to the webbing of the forward end. He looked behind him and saw the blackened faces of the SOG men. Having finished their cargo drop, they were all seated again in their webbed benches. They looked as calm as cigar-store Indians.

"Two minutes," Captain Cartwright shouted as the transport executed a sharp, steep turn. "Stand up! Hook up! Sound off for equipment check."

The men clicked static lines to the wire above their heads. They adjusted chin straps on their helmets and pulled the hooks and snaps on their buddies' chutes. "All okay!" the men barked in one voice.

"One minute," Captain Cartwright announced, standing by the portside door and the howling sky. A black top sergeant jogged back to join the captain at the starboard opening. "Shuffle to the door," he ordered.

Obediently the men shuffle-stepped to the black, empty, howling cavities. The buzzer sounded, and the red light turned green.

"Go! Go! Go! Go!" both men shouted as the SOG team disappeared through the doors, dropping silently into the night below. Then Captain Cartwright and the top sergeant vanished through the door, leaving the elder Cartwright with Major Glassman and the grinning loadmaster, who signaled a thumbs-up at them.

Cartwright, with his safety belt still hooked to the wire, rushed toward the portside door and clung to the inside. Half his body leaned out as the aircraft banked away from the falling men whose parachutes looked like tiny flowers fluttering toward the face of the moon.

"Did you ever see such a thing?" Cartwright shouted jubilantly as he swung himself back in the shaking airplane. "That's my son, goddammit. If those ain't the bravest young men, Major, I don't know what-all."

"I can tell you something, General," Glassman shouted over the engine noise. "Every country has those brave young men. And the world's no better for it."

"Is that you trying to get deep with me, Major?" the general shouted. "Or are you just pissed off because you used to be one of those young men and can't cut it anymore?"

Glassman sat in silence, ignoring Cartwright. The loadmaster buzzed the hydraulics, and the doors swung shut. The plane flew on in the night, turning toward its final destination.

Cartwright made his way over to Glassman and handed him a soft leather helmet, similar to one he was wearing. "Put it on. Regulations."

As soon as Glassman complied, the red light for jump run flashed again, and the ramp lowered. Methodically Cartwright hooked Glassman's static line to the wire above his head.

"What the hell is going on?" Glassman barked.

"One minute," shouted the loadmaster.

"All okay," Cartwright responded, holding Glassman's harness with one hand and hooking his own static line with the other.

"What the hell are you doing?" Glassman screamed.

"Go!" the jumpmaster shouted as the light turned green.

Cartwright pushed Glassman backward on the ramp and shouted, "If you can jump, maybe you can still fly." With that, he dropped the major into the darkness and followed him.

Both chutes popped open.

"You son of a bitch, Cartwright!" Glassman shouted into the night.

"Turn on your helmet strobe, so the Plant thirty-six security team doesn't shoot ya," Cartwright yelled, his voice clear as a bell across the dozen yards that separated them. Their strobe lights made them look like falling stars.

Glassman, sensing the dark earth rushing at him, bent his knees and collapsed in a ball as he hit the ground. Cartwright, a few yards away, bundled his chute and walked toward the major, chuckling.

"How'd ya like it?" he asked. "Ever done a night jump?"

"That's the last time I get in an airplane with you, you crazy bastard, sir," Glassman exclaimed, still panting.

As both men bundled their chutes and began to trudge across the runway, a small pickup truck with a security team rushed toward them. The men in the truck jumped out, their rifles ready.

"Halt and identify yourself," one guard shouted.

"Stand at ease," Cartwright ordered with easy authority. He lit a pocket flash so that it displayed his Plant 36 ID. The young guards advanced warily and inspected it. Then both saluted.

"This was a drill, men. You passed. Now give us a lift," Cartwright said, throwing his parachute in the pickup bed and climbing in.

"Yes, sir," replied the senior guard. Glassman followed Cartwright into the pickup.

"FBI says you've got the package," Glassman said as they approached the lights of the plant.

"Yup."

"Are you going to let me see it, General? With my engineering background, I should be able to discern if the Mercury team will figure it's bogus."

"Mebbe I will. I'm about ready to tell Brady Daniels to yank you."

"Are you, really? Because I don't inflate your general's ego. That's it, isn't it?"

"Nope," Cartwright said, hopping from the truck and marching toward his Corvette. "I'd have you pulled because I don't think you've got what it takes."

"I analyzed the leak, General."

"I know. Brady told me," Cartwright said, tossing his kit bag into the sports car.

"He told you?" Glassman said incredulously.

"That man would tell me anything. I half carried him to Spain when he was hurt bad during the real war. Hop in, Major."

Glassman glared at Cartwright. He looked around him in the desert night that cloaked the giant hangars. Then he shrugged and got in the general's car.

Cartwright flashed his gate pass at the guard shack and gunned the engine, pulling out onto Sierra Highway and depressing the accelerator. The wind whipped around the open car, sounding like a flight of quail on the wing.

"You're staying at Edwards, aren't you, Major?"

"Right. Bachelor Officers Quarters."

"Sounds lonely. But then, you're a lonely guy."

"I'm told that helps the work I do," Glassman said sourly.

"Maybe it does, and maybe it doesn't. You're not out in the cold for the Company right now. You're out in the cold with yourself."

"General, you're a sage."

As the car passed the winking lights of the desert town of Lancaster, Cartwright pushed the powerful Chevy over the 100 MPH mark. It slipped through the night like an obsidian arrowhead flying toward an unseen target. Within minutes they pulled up at the back gate of Edwards, where the sentry motioned them through.

"I love this desert," Cartwright said, stretching his free hand into the wind as he drove with the other. "I set down shuttle *Atlantis* over there on the dry lake, you know."

"I know, General. I read."

"But you don't know how I did it, Major. I did it by being the simply best fucking airplane driver there nearly ever was. I heard you were pretty good, too, once upon a time."

"You were misinformed. I was never a professional hero like you. I just happened to get shot down."

"Yeah, I heard about that. Some Nazi bastard shot an airplane out from under me once. But I got away," he said, making a turn onto a dusty road that led off into the moonlit emptiness of the prehistoric lakebed.

"You missed the turn for the BOQ."

"I know it," Cartwright said, wheeling up to a sandy

bluff and spinning the car around so it sat like a cannon guarding a hilltop.

Miles away, the lights from the desert air base glittered. A NASA crew was pulling late-night duty at the space shuttle gantry, which looked like a glittering wedding cake casting an eerie glow on the moonscape of the base. Cartwright gazed silently at the spot where he'd brought a spaceship home from its voyage to the heavens. He sighed.

"I know this place like the back of my hand. I landed my rocket ship right over there," he said, motioning to a point in the emptiness. "The Indians would call that a power spot, where the natural forces gather. The desert holds endless mysteries for me, Major. It is a combination of the seen and the unseen, like a shimmering mirage, promising water where there is none. You're like that a bit yourself, Major. You're a riddle. Things I can't understand, I tend to pick apart, until I understand 'em better."

"Maybe we can talk about our work, General. My personal life is of little importance, really."

"Buddy boy, your personal life is damn important to me when I may be under fire with you," Cartwright said, reaching into his kit bag. He produced a bottle of Jack Daniel's, took a swig, and tossed it to the major.

"I don't drink, General."

"Try it," Cartwright said. It was an order.

Glassman grimaced, took a short swallow, and coughed.

"Time was when all the fighter jocks handled their whiskey as well as they did their women and their planes."

"That's all very interesting, General. I saw all those movies, myself."

"You liked them old movies, right? John Wayne. Jimmy Stewart. Gable. Ever see *Jet Pilot*?"

"Sure, I'd sneak out after Torah, with my brother," Glassman said. "We weren't supposed to watch movies."

"Yeah, I heard about your brother. I know a lot about you, Major. But I don't know you."

"What's to know? I failed."

"You people carry a heavy load around, don't you,"

Cartwright said, pulling from the bottle and handing it back to Glassman, who looked at it reluctantly and then took a long pull.

"Yes," Glassman replied. "We tend our guilt like a garden."

"I want to tell you something about your brother, Glassman."

"What would that be?" the major asked, taking another long swig and looking up toward the billion winking lights of the Milky Way.

"Your brother wouldn't want you to turn pussy just 'cause he augered in."

"What the hell would you know about my brother?" Glassman said, slurring his words just a bit.

"Not a hell of a lot. But I know something about mine. I watched him go down in a blaze over Berlin. I was flying escort in a P-51, and he was in a Flying Fortress."

"So you couldn't save your brother," Glassman said, gazing intently at the bottle.

"Nope. He burned."

"My brother crashed. I ejected."

"Major, goddammit. That wasn't your fault. And losin' my brother, Bud, wasn't my fault. Time was I felt like it might have been. But that kind of thinking does no good. We all got to get on with it."

"So what did you do to get on with it?" Glassman asked, looking straight at Cartwright.

"I hammered the Nazis. Every one I could get in my sights. And after I hammered 'em, I drilled 'em. That's what you got to do, Major."

"I think that war was a long time ago, General," Glassman said.

"It never ended, Glassman. Same war. It's the eternal showdown between the good guys and the bad guys. And we got to get on with it."

Glassman sighed. For a moment he rested his head back on the seat and looked up at the indifferent, blazing firmament. "When I was a little boy, my people told me about the Holocaust," he said quietly. "My father told me everything. He was at Auschwitz. He heard the rattle in his brother's throat when he hung himself to escape his torment. I was a little boy in America, but I saw the death camp chimneys in my dreams. When I got older, I swore I would not let such a thing happen ever again. What was it like, flying out there against the Nazis?"

"We gave better than we got. We beat 'em."

"I would have liked that fight.... General, I think I'll have another drink, if you don't mind."

If in wine there is truth, sometimes in whiskey there is revelation. And the skull-splitting brotherhood of a hangover. They talked until dawn. They talked until they trusted one another. The general nearly told the major the secret of his eye. But finally he decided it was a whiskey secret he must keep.

9

TIJUANA, MEXICO

As dusk fell, turning the dusty ground from brown to purple, the soccer field in the Colonia section of Tijuana began filling with people who arrived in groups of six or eight apiece. A group of Salvadorans began an impromptu game, kicking a battered empty gasoline can up and down the field.

Soon the field was swarming with hundreds of people in their separate groups. Guatemalans. Many more Salvadorans. Nicaraguans. Mexicans from the south. Mexicans from the north. And a few Iranians.

Avadek and the men of Green Flight clustered on a rocky knoll, watching the multitudes warily. Like the other pilgrims preparing to cross the border illegally, they wore a patchwork assortment of garish polyester shirts and tattered trousers. The designer clothes they had worn on the flight to Mexico City when they were traveling as an OPEC petroleum engineering team lay abandoned hundreds of kilometers to the south in a bus station.

Avadek's men could not be distinguished by color or

dress from the hundreds of others who would cross at the soccer field that evening. Unless they spoke. So they remained silent and shook their heads and waved away the old man who approached them with a tinkling bell to announce the sale of the *helado* and *nieves*, the sticky ice creams for sale from his pushcart.

Already it had seemed a strange journey, through many different worlds. The lights of San Diego winked in the distance, shining with the seductive promise of *el Norte*.

By the time darkness was complete, the field began to empty. The groups of six and eight people known as *pollos*, or little chickens, were greeted by their guides, the coyotes. Some of the coyotes would collect their money and keep their bargain to deliver the *pollos* to the promised land. Others would just collect their money, leaving their little chickens to die in the heat of a locked freight-train car or a sealed van. Still others among the gap-toothed treacherous fraternity of coyotes would deliver their charges to the *bandidos* who infested the canyons and arroyos separating Tijuana from San Diego.

Avadek had other plans for his unusual band of *pollos*. Alone among them he carried a 9-mm pistol given to him at his country's embassy far to the south in Mexico City. The consular officer there had traveled north and made the arrangement for this night's rendezvous with the coyote.

The bus trip had been dusty and fearful for the fliers, but no one had taken notice of them. Mexico was a country of people ever moving restlessly to the North.

As Avadek and the men of Green Flight waited, he removed a compass from his trousers and took a bearing. He checked his military watch, the only valuable thing any of the men appeared to be carrying. He handed the compass to Captain Mehdi Mahan, who verified the bearing.

"All will be well," Avadek murmured in English. Mehdi nodded assent, and the men of Green Flight also nodded and grinned. They were feeling the tension of military men who feel themselves close to the time of action.

With the field nearly empty, the men waited. Finally

a man appeared in front of them. Until he was upon them, he was silent and nearly invisible. He grinned widely, so that his gold tooth could be seen even in the darkness.

"*¿El Norte, muchachos?*" he asked cheerfully.

"*¿Habla inglés?*" Avadek asked.

The man in the leather Elvis jacket and blue jeans nodded. "Sure, I speak English. You want to practice? Come with me."

The two men had exchanged their passwords and smiled, ever so cordially, at one another. Avadek nodded and gestured that it was time to go. The men of Green Flight rose as one and followed him into the darkness, trailing the coyote by a few feet.

"You don't have to be scared," said the guide. "I will take you safely across."

Avadek nodded. The others followed, wending their way into the moonlit arroyos, stumbling occasionally on the sharp rocks and stepping heavily through the brush and litter scattered about. They were fliers, not commandos.

"Don't worry, I'll take care of you," the coyote assured them repeatedly.

They trudged on for what seemed like hours. Suddenly they heard the *whop*ping, throbbing sound of a helicopter. But it passed far in the distance, shining its powerful search beam a kilometer or so to the north. The coyote waved them on, and they continued.

They walked into a dry wash, a moonlit wasteland of ruined tires, rusting barbed wire, and emptied water cans. Suddenly they heard the sound of an owl hooting.

"Stop," Avadek said. "That is it."

Out of a shadow stepped the massive frame of Angus McCain. The moon shined on his forehead and his lips were set in their perpetual grin. He wore a woven poncho, the kind called a serape. He offered his giant hand to the coyote.

"*Buenas noches*, partner," he said, gripping the coyote's hand firmly. "You brought me my *pollitos. Muy bueno.*"

"Don't bullshit me, man," the coyote said angrily,

withdrawing his painfully crushed hand. "Give me the rest of the money. The *dinero.*"

McCain smirked and reached into his pocket. He handed the coyote a crumpled wad of bills while Avadek and his men stood by silently. The coyote unfolded the wad of five one-hundred-dollar bills and rubbed them between his thumb and forefinger to determine their texture.

Looking up at McCain, who towered over him, the coyote said defiantly, "You got more. I think you better give it."

"Is that so, little partner? Who says so?"

"I got my amigos over there, gringo," the coyote said, inclining his head to the shadows. In the darkness there was movement. The shapes of three men emerged, at least one cradling a rifle and the others carrying long dark shapes that could only be machetes.

McCain shook his head uneasily. "Well, amigo," he said, "it looks like you got us. I'll give you the dough. Just let me and my boys go."

"Sure, gringo. Now give it."

Wordlessly McCain lifted the Ingram MAC-10 machine pistol that hung from a strap beneath his serape. He fired a silenced burst of twenty rounds into the three men in the shadows. The weapon made the noise of an air gun removing a tire in a repair shop. The men screamed as they bled and died. But there were always screams in the canyon. And blood was a familiar sight on the stones and sagebrush.

"The Lord helps those who help themselves," McCain said, looking at Avadek and the men of Green Flight lying flat on the ground. Lying next to them was the coyote, who was whimpering.

"Hey, you, gringo," he said helplessly, holding his arms over his face as he crawled in a semifetal position. "You don't kill me, okay? I give you the money back. We call it quits, okay?"

"Sure thing, amigo," McCain drawled easily. "My clip is about empty anyway, and what with nine-millimeter going for nearly twenty cents a round, you probably ain't worth killing. Gimme the money."

The coyote held the crumpled bills toward McCain, who took them lightly and rubbed them for texture. The coyote was crawling backward on his knees, holding his hands out in a pleading gesture.

"Just one thing, amigo," McCain said.

"Whatever you want, chief," said the coyote.

"Like I said, I wouldn't want to waste the ammo," McCain said, thrusting a powerful roundhouse kick into the side of the coyote's head, killing him instantly with his steel-toed boot.

Avadek rose slowly and dusted himself off. The others did the same. "If he had taken the agreed-upon payment, would he have lived?" Avadek asked dryly.

"Nope. You can't trust people who just work for money, Colonel," McCain said, grinning. "They always want more. They've got no sense of professionalism."

"But you are not like that, right?" Avadek asked lightly, patting McCain on his massive shoulder.

"Right," McCain said. "I enjoy my work."

With that he signaled the men of Green Flight to follow him. They marched on into the shadows, and when they came to the top of a moonlit mesa, they spotted a Chevy Suburban truck, a rugged vehicle big enough to carry a road crew or a gang of migrant workers. As they climbed into the truck, McCain handed them crumpled green cards that gave them legal status to work in the United States.

"You'll need these," he said. "You all speak English, right?"

The men nodded.

"Well, welcome to *los Estados Unidos*. The United States, land of opportunity."

The men settled themselves into the truck and soon were asleep as Angus McCain drove them from the border toward the San Gabriel Mountains on the edge of the Mojave Desert.

WRIGHTWOOD, CALIFORNIA

Angus McCain wheeled the Chevy Suburban truck expertly up the twisting mountain highway that led from the Los Angeles basin high into the San Gabriel Mountains. The well-paved highways of the United States bored him after years of driving jeeps in the Congo, Laos, and Nicaragua.

"This is pretty country, ain't it," McCain said, grinning his toothy death's-head grin.

"We have mountains in Iran," Avadek answered wearily. He, too, was tired from the journey, and he wanted to bathe. It had been years since he'd engaged in this sort of fieldwork.

"You got mountains all right, but not like these, old buddy. These mountains are for skiing, when the snow packs in. Yours are only good for a bunch of damn goatherds."

"How long have we known each other, McCain?"

"Shoot, more than thirty years, I'd say. Ever since the company put the shah back in."

"Do me a favor. I will not tell you how to spend the money my government pays you. You can spare me your observations on the quaintness of my people and culture. Besides, in Iran we ski."

"Sure thing, buddy. No skin off my neck," McCain said as he downshifted gears on a steep grade. "Just makin' conversation."

They drove higher into the mountains. The road was nearly deserted.

In the back of the Chevy Suburban, the Green Flight pilots slept. Avadek and his men still wore the clothing of the *pollos*. Their carefully guarded G-suits and flight coveralls hidden in their *pollo* bundles were stowed in the truck's cargo compartment. Their garish polyester disco shirts were soiled, and their pants were filthy from the journey past the nightscopes and helicopter surveillance of the border patrol. McCain, in his khaki shirt, faded jeans, and baseball cap, looked like any of the thousands of job contractors and ranchers who every day carried such men to low-paying jobs in the southwestern United States.

"Not that it matters to me," McCain said, "but why the hell do you people want to crack an aerospace plant?"

"You are paid well not to ask questions."

"I've got to give my team a cover story, old buddy. You bought a reinforced infantry squad, two fire teams of four men each, and a hard-striper to top-kick 'em inside. They are ex–Special Forces out of Fort Bragg. They are not dumb, and they're going to want to know what they're up against."

"We are working for the Jews," Avadek said, poker-faced.

"Say what? I don't think I heard that right."

"Our job is for the Mossad. The Zionists want photographs of new American airplanes."

McCain snorted in disbelief. "Doesn't your boss want to drive those folks into the sea?"

"It is simple. The Zionist entity wants photographs. We want armaments and replacement parts to vanquish the Iraqis. We need missile batteries, rockets, and electronic systems. We need air-to-air missiles. They will give us all these things for the right set of photographs."

"Shit, Avadek. They'd use their own people. They're the best."

"And you are a chauvinist asshole who believes the Zionist line. It is true that they are fine operational personnel. But politically they cannot use their own people. Zionist spies infuriate your Congress. So, while your government believes they are facing terrorists, I take photographs and files."

"God damn," McCain said. "A first class false flag job."

"You get us in and out. Do your job."

McCain whistled. He wheeled right off State Highway 2 and downshifted again as the Suburban climbed a steep, narrow road. The truck rolled past a cluster of rustic ski cabins, and the road narrowed again.

"Your advance man picked a good spot, Colonel," McCain said. "Not much traffic up here."

"Like yourself, McCain, I try to be thorough."

At nearly the top of the mountain, there was another dirt road and a cabin. An American flag fluttered on a pole mounted on a wooden deck.

"This must be the place," McCain said. "Looks right as rain."

A screen door swung open, and the forbidding figure of Hakim, the escaped convict, appeared, cradling a twelve-gauge pump shotgun. "Who are you all?" he demanded.

Almost motionlessly McCain reached for the slender Colt Python revolver in his boot. He figured by the time the man in the door swung the shotgun he could empty it at him and finish the play, if need be.

"Friends of the dove," Avadek answered through the open passenger-side window.

"That's right. You can come in," Hakim said, lowering the weapon.

"Is your man inside?" McCain asked.

"Unless it is a trap," Avadek said. "But I doubt it is. Let's go inside."

"You go ahead, I'll start unstowing the goods."

Avadek shook the young men in the backseat. The pilots blinked awake and looked about curiously. After years of war in the skies above their native land, flying and fighting at a velocity faster than the speed of sound, these past few days were surely the strangest they had witnessed. At Avadek's direction they got out of the Suburban and followed him up the steps to the cabin.

Avadek approached Hakim, who gazed at him warily, holding on to the shotgun all the while.

"You helped our brother," Avadek said, spreading his arms and raising his palms in a gesture of supplication.

"I be Khalil's friend. He's inside," Hakim said, raising the weapon level with Avadek's chest. "Now, if you don't want me to blow away whitey down there, get him the fuck away from the back of that truck."

"You are careful. That is good," Avadek said, lowering his hands.

He called out to McCain, asking him to step back from the truck. McCain grinned and obliged, stepping back and in one smooth motion shooting Hakim in the head with his revolver. Mehdi and his fliers swung around, aghast, and looked to Avadek, who shouted orders in Farsi. They looked at each other, then at the black man whose blood and brains were spattered across the redwood decking. Mystified, they looked to Mehdi for the next move. Mehdi looked at Avadek. Avadek kicked Hakim's body off the deck so it fell with a clump.

Khalil raced outside, shouting, "What is this? What is this?"

Avadek embraced him in a bear hug. "Little brother, we are here," he said, kissing the terrified Khalil on both cheeks.

Khalil broke the embrace and backed away. "What have you done with my friend?" he cried. "He was my friend. He helped me."

"There are no friends," Avadek said. "Only brothers in struggle. Who is here?"

"There is the girl. She gives us this place."

"McCain. Inside," Avadek said.

"Sure thing, pal," McCain said, replacing a cartridge in the revolver.

"No!" Khalil shouted. "Her parents, they are in Europe. They know she is at this place. They call. They call every day. If she does not answer, they will know something is wrong."

"I will go inside and see her. Then I will decide," Avadek said. "We may need her alive for a few days. In a little while, you will see to your friend's burial."

Avadek instructed the pilots to help McCain unload the truck. McCain opened a storage panel under the backseat and began handing them cases of C-4 plastic explosive, which the pilots carried onto the deck. After that, McCain sprayed Hakim's blood from the deck with a garden hose. The pilots, having finished their work, searched the sky for the direction of the sun. They bowed and prayed. McCain sat on a tree stump and quietly smoked a cigarette.

Avadek pushed Khalil inside the cabin, which was

dark, since the shades were drawn. Sitting tied to a chair in the gloom was Cynthia. She was blindfolded.

"Khalil, is that you? Who's there? I heard a shot," the girl murmured lifelessly.

"It is me," Khalil said, his voice trembling. "You must tell my friend about your parents. Tell him how you must take the telephone call."

"Who is this, Khalil? Where is Hakim?"

Sobbing, Khalil shrieked, "Tell my friend about the telephone!"

"They call about six in the evening, every day or so," the girl answered into the darkness. "They want to know how I am."

Avadek moved next to her in the darkness. He kneeled beside the chair. "And what do you tell them?" he asked gently.

"I tell them I'm fine," she said, her lip quivering. "I tell them I'm enjoying the peace and quiet." She sobbed.

Avadek patted her on the shoulder. "What is your name, little one?" he asked.

"Cynthia," she said haltingly.

"Cynthia," Avadek whispered, stroking her hair. "You are with friends. You are very safe. It is not good to worry. Soon you will be let go, and you can be with your family again."

The girl cried, filling the small room with the sound of her sobs and sniffles. Avadek and Khalil turned away from her when McCain rapped on the screen door.

"Hey, buddy. C'mere. I want to show you something."

Avadek lit a cigarette, blew smoke through his nostrils, and stepped outside the cabin, leaving Khalil to comfort his girlfriend. Avadek followed McCain down a slope to a small clearing. Looking down thousands of feet at the foot of the San Gabriel Mountains, he surveyed the vast, arid flatland of the Mojave Desert.

McCain handed the colonel a pair of binoculars. "Can't say I think much of the help you hired," he said. "But he couldn't have picked a better place. Look, off there on the flatland. See that big-ass building?"

"I see it. It looks like a factory."

"It's a hangar. Biggest one in the valley. Damn near the biggest in the world. That's your target, Colonel. Plant thirty-six."

As they spoke, an AWACS aircraft lifted ponderously from the plant airstrip. It carried radar and sensors that could spot an enemy hundreds of miles away—if the crew was on enemy alert.

MOSCOW

Deep beneath the Kremlin, the dozen members of the Politburo were engaged in debate over the career prospects for Rudenko, the KGB's director for North American operations. His options were continued employment, the Gulag, or the basement firing wall at Lubyanka.

As soon as he was called to the subterranean chambers of the Soviet government's ruling body, Vassily Rudenko realized his career and even his life were in peril. Unlike his protégé Romanovich, the North American director was not fortified by vodka. He believed alcohol to be the Russians' curse, but now he wished he had a drink. The director resisted an impulse to loosen his collar as he sat on the uncomfortable wooden chair in the overheated chamber that was ventilated poorly by ducts that circulated a stream of warm, stale air.

Seated like a line of stone idols, the dozen old men stared at Rudenko. Without flinching, the director returned the stare of the Communist party secretary of the Soviet Union, Comrade Mikhail Alexandrovich Kirilenko. The secretary was the youngest of the group and was reputed to be the hardest and wiliest among them.

Dimitrov, the KGB chief, spoke first, realizing the probability that his neck was as much at risk as that of

Rudenko. "So, comrade, discuss please the failure of your directorate in allowing this grave lapse in guarding the state," Dimitrov said, speaking like a stern father.

"Thus far there has been no failure of security resulting from the unresolved status of the Aurora project," Rudenko told the chief of state security, evading his question. "We remain in the process of retrieving important information from the main enemy."

"Your summary is not accurate," Kirilenko, the Party leader, said tersely, never taking his eyes from the North American director. "We are aware that you had the materials on the Aurora bomber, and you lost them."

"It is true, Comrade Secretary, that some technical information was taken by bandits in Beirut, but the materials they seized can be duplicated and returned to the motherland, I am told," Rudenko said, feeling small beads of sweat on his forehead. He hoped this was true.

"How did this happen?" asked Grigoriev, the Party's theoretician, an ancient from Stalin's day.

"One could only believe it would not have happened if the Committee for State Security were not straying from its political responsibilities," grunted Marshal Ivan Ligachev. The defense minister breathed heavily, causing his rows of decorations from the Great Patriotic War to ripple like wheat on his barrel chest. "As is well known, a project such as the new American bomber should have been designated a target of the GRU," he said, his voice rumbling. "The army and its military intelligence organ is as yet still ready to assume this commitment, if it is the Politburo's wish."

Dimitrov looked around him, then lit a cigarette and puffed in the direction of Ligachev, knowing that the marshal of the Soviet Union had been forced to give up tobacco because his lungs were corroding like a battle tank left too long in the weather. "It is a lawless world outside of the Soviet republics," he said, blowing a thick cloud of smoke. "Already I have dealt with the resident officers in Rome and Beirut who witlessly allowed the compromise of the Aurora material. They are in a place where they may reflect on their failure." As he spoke the KGB chief gazed through his spectacles at the army marshal, implying subtly that there were an abundance of places for those who failed to meet the standards of the Chekists. His cigarette dangled from his lips, and an ash that had accumulated fell on the table that Stalin had once used for his predawn staff briefings.

"A KGB action team has been dispatched to Beirut," he continued. "Its work is almost done. It may well be that the Aurora materials can be recovered there, in which case the director for North American operations can recall Comrade Romanovich, who is presently assigned to this matter and is working with our comrades at the San Francisco consulate."

"The GRU is aware of the actions of KGB's team," said Marshal Ligachev, covering his mouth to cough viciously. Clearing his throat, he added, "Of course, Dimitrov, the KGB must also be aware that the body of the courier kidnapped on the Rome flight was found in Beirut yesterday morning?"

"The Party was not apprised of this development," Kirilenko screamed, slamming his fist on the table.

"This development is being assessed even as we speak," Dimitrov said. He glared at his subordinate, Rudenko, who had failed to inform his chief.

"The body was found," the old marshal continued between deep coughs. "It was found in many pieces, enclosed in a sack delivered to our embassy. Some of the courier's remains were too small to identify clearly. There were, however, no materials found regarding the American bomber. The army would like to add that this strategic warplane, which represents the technology summit of the main enemy, is a grave threat to the motherland. Once it is deployed, our radars cannot detect it."

"Your radars cannot find a young boy in a small airplane," Dimitrov snapped.

"Those responsible for that grave breach are punished. We are speaking of the threat from a strategic nuclear bomber. I wonder how deeply the Committee for State Security is aware of this threat," Marshal Ligachev said, reaching for a cigarette pack on the table, then reluctantly pulling his hand away from it.

"The army also wonders where the plans for the American Stealth bomber are at this moment," Ligachev continued. "We already know where the courier is."

Rudenko wished he knew Romanovich's whereabouts.

PLANT 36

The air-lock doors *shush*ed shut behind Cartwright and Glassman, and they stood within the Stealth bomber's domain, looking up at the green, glowing panels of glass that masked the work area for the test engineers.

"King, I want to take her up," Cartwright said.

"Can't do it, man," said LeFever. "You'd need clearance from the secretary of the air force to even climb inside the cockpit."

"He's got that," Glassman said, producing a document for LeFever's inspection.

The chief test conductor whistled. "According to this, you can fly any damn thing you want," he said. "But I've got to get authorization for a check flight at the project director level."

"Do it, King."

"Company brass might not like it."

"Keep it simple for them," Glassman said with quiet authority. "The Pentagon wants the general to ride the new plane. Tell the brass at Downey their payment schedule might depend on that ride."

"I'll tell 'em," LeFever said, climbing the steel ladder and disappearing into his throne room.

As they waited, the two men walked beneath the smooth, flat fuselage of the bomber, which sparkled dully as the cool lights of the test chamber bounced off its black radar-absorbent skin. Its wings drooped gracefully toward the floor and its spade-shaped nose protruded menacingly from the manta ray configuration. It was a thing of forbidding, vaguely reptilian beauty. "How's it feel to look at a half-billion dollars, General?" Glassman asked.

"This thing looks evil, Major," Cartwright replied. "But, that's why we need it. It's a wicked world. I'm just looking for the rivets." Cartwright ran his fingers across the sharklike surface of the plane's underbelly. "I started flying when they were still counting airplane dollars in the thousands. All I knew was that I was responsible for all those dollars every time I flew."

"I guess you never really know how responsible you are until you lose one," Glassman said.

"Damn right, Major. But even then, if your luck runs right, you live to fly another day. I did. So did you."

Glassman nodded absently and walked forward to the aircraft's leading edge. He looked up at the gleaming bubble of the cockpit.

"It looks like something out of Jules Verne," Glassman murmured. "It looks like a living thing, a metallic bird of prey."

Cartwright edged up next to Glassman, looking at the plane in wonder, and said, "O brave new world."

"Huxley," Glassman murmured.

"Nope. Shakespeare. *The Tempest*, Major."

LeFever scurried down the ladder and ran toward them. "Downey wants to know the purpose of the flight. They assume you want to take the stick, Scotty."

"You tell Downey that we don't have to announce the purpose," Glassman said. "We already bought our E-ticket. We are informing them we need the airplane for a couple of hours as a courtesy."

"If that plane rolls out of here, it's going to be carrying a warload of nukes," LeFever said. "That's what the White House asked for, and that's what we gave 'em. This flight is not scheduled. Downey has to know who's gonna be responsible if we drill a hole in the desert and lose Nevada."

"The air force, damn it," Glassman snapped. "We're the customer, aren't we?"

"Whoa, fellas," Cartwright said. "Reggie, tell your bosses it's a check flight for telemetry workup and that you're going to fly. I'm aboard for observation 'cause I want a look at the radar cross-section data."

LeFever hurried up the ladder again, and when he returned he was all smiles. "Draw your G-suits, your bladders, and your bone domes," he said enthusiastically as he donned his own helmet and pressurized flight gear. "We're gonna drive us a Stealth bomber."

Cartwright and LeFever laughed. Glassman remained silent and was strangely pale.

"We'll suit up, Reggie," the general said, slapping LeFever on the back. "You call in frequencies to NORAD. I want the air defense net lit up from here to Cheyenne Mountain. We'll see if the fighter jocks can find your plane."

LeFever hurried away, and Cartwright turned to find Glassman laboring not to tremble. "I can't do this, General," Glassman said. "I want to, but I can't. As God is my witness, I am simply too afraid."

Cartwright grabbed the major by both shoulders. Instead of shaking him, he clutched him tightly. "Adam," he said like a father. "I know you are afraid. But as of today, you are a bomber puke. My bomber puke. I need you with me. You won't be required to do anything you can't handle, understand?"

Glassman swallowed hard and nodded assent.

"Let's suit up," Cartwright said quietly, and the major followed him.

The STB-1 Stealth bomber cruised at sixty thousand feet above the desert, sailing through the Mach 2 barrier at about fifteen hundred miles per hour. It seemed to Cartwright to glide through the high thin air like an arrow in flight.

"Let's take her down in the canyons and see what she does on the deck," Cartwright said to LeFever through his microphone. "I like altitude as much as the next guy, but I want to see what the avionics do flying nap of the Earth."

"Not necessary, Eagle," LeFever said, using the hands

on throttle and stick control to bank the aircraft to head toward the vast, empty reaches of the bombing ranges near Nellis AFB in Nevada. The sophisticated HOTAS stick resembled nothing so much as a handgrip trigger on an arcade video game.

"What do you mean, not necessary?" Cartwright demanded. "I want to see what she does down in the weeds."

LeFever edged the throttle forward, at the same time pointing the plane even higher into the upper atmosphere. Glassman, sitting in the defensive avionics officer's seat, monitored the bomber's progress on a bank of computer terminals.

"You remember the bomber penetration evaluation they did on the B-1 at Nellis in seventy-nine?" LeFever asked Cartwright.

"Hell, yes. The NORAD boys never found her till she popped up on target approach. That's what I'm saying. Let's take her down. I need real data to crunch, and I won't get it on a milk run."

"This ain't no milk run, General," LeFever said, grinning sagely. "Ask your major how many bandits he's got on his screen."

"Let me hear it, Major," Cartwright ordered.

"I identify eleven—no, twelve," Glassman said, monitoring the dancing lights of the displays. "Ranges vary from five zero to one hundred and fifty miles. There are target acquisition radars lit up all over the sky, but none has a lock on us."

"They're looking for us, Eagle," LeFever said. "But they can't find us. We're in the high-level penetration mode SAC hasn't been able to pull off since we had to scrap the XB-70 after Ivan shot down the U-2."

"What are you telling me?"

"Low-observable technology. It works, babe. In a stealthy mode we are practically invisible."

"Affirmative, General," said Glassman. "We have zero bandits on hostile approach. They're wandering."

"You mean the aggressor detail is loaded up with a

state-of-the-art electronic warfare suite, and they can't find us floatin' around up here?"

"They'd need a visual ID, and by then we've delivered the package."

"Damn."

"Do not swear in my microphone, General," LeFever said, his rich baritone swollen with mock seriousness. "We may be flying stealthy, but the government frowns on broadcast obscenity."

"How far are we from target simulation?" Cartwright asked, gazing ahead at the curve of the Earth, a rich brown horizon cut by a shimmering purple line.

LeFever nudged his control handle and banked gently, giving Cartwright a test pilot's smug grin. "Son, my eggs are dropped, and I'm heading for home. My data picture has us over target. Our package would have made every kilometer from Moscow to Kiev uninhabitable for the next hundred fifty years or so."

"Is that so, King?" Cartwright marveled. "Then thank God this is ours, not Ivan's."

"Amen," said LeFever.

The return flight to the hardened hangar at Plant 36 proceeded without anomalies. And Major Adam Glassman suppressed cold panic.

10

THE MOJAVE DESERT

Richard Moody dropped the wheels on the ancient C-123 Cargomaster and scanned the horizon for small planes. Seeing none, he signaled his co-pilot to bring the creaking transport down onto the remote desert airstrip. Moody observed a threatening line of black clouds from a front moving in over the Tehachapi Mountains. He was glad they would land ahead of the storm front. Wind shear and lightning could make the old transport a memory as quick as a SAM missile over unfriendly jungle. The transport's shadow passed bumpily over Sierra Highway and then onto home base.

"It's Miller time," the co-pilot, a Cuban named Saldana, said cheerfully.

"I'm ready," Moody agreed. "Enough tropics for one week, huh?"

Saldana shrugged. The Cargomaster bumped onto the strip, taxiing through the blowing tumbleweed toward the hangar that housed Royal Flush Air Transport, the airport's only major client. Once the roaring quartet of turboprop engines shut down, there was only the sound of the lonesome wind humming through the tie-downs that secured the Cessnas and Beeches.

Moody let Saldana make the log entries and dropped down onto the tarmac. He gave a thumbs-up sign to the crew chief, a Hmong tribesman from Laos who had been with Royal Flush when it was known as Air America in an earlier life and war.

"All okay, Dai Huy," the Hmong said happily. It had been a smooth drop with many Stinger missiles delivered to the rebels of Costaguana who were the agency's most recent beneficiaries.

"All okay," Moody responded. He walked toward the office, preparing to chew out the manager about the Cargomaster's faulty wiring, when he spotted a Willy's jeep speeding toward him. He stopped in his tracks as the jeep pulled up beside him.

"Been a long time, Dick," Angus McCain called out cheerfully, and motioned for Moody to get in the jeep.

As he recognized McCain, Moody's jaw dropped and he backed away as though he'd spotted a Mojave green rattler crossing the road. "I thought you were dead," he shouted over the wind.

"Come on, partner. We gotta talk."

"I'd sooner fuck a snake," Moody snapped. "Last time I saw you, you were flyin' over the hill in Laos. You left us."

"Had no choice, brother. Company orders. Now climb in," McCain ordered, offering a can of beer as he steered the jeep alongside Moody.

Moody batted the beer to the ground and spun around, walking in the other direction. McCain backed the jeep. "Don't play games with me, Dick," he shouted, steering with one hand and drawing his Colt Python with the other. "I'll shoot you, or I'll talk to you. Get in."

Moody stared coldly at McCain. Reluctantly he climbed in the jeep. They drove off as the first drops of rain smacked the airfield. As the horizon turned black, the jeep raced down a lonesome ribbon of sandy road. Raindrops stung Moody's face. In the distance he spotted a yellow neon sombrero blinking. Some optimist had plunked a Mexican restaurant down in the desert, waiting for the crowd that never came after the state highway bypassed a mile east. McCain wheeled into the dirt lot just as a cloudburst opened, soaking them both.

"Hell, we been wet before, ain't we?" McCain said.

"Yeah, and usually for no good reason," Moody yelled, running in under cover. "You know, if Dick Secord had made that run for the Hmong extraction, he would have got those men out."

"You've got a long memory, partner," McCain said, opening the door to the restaurant's dim lounge and shoving his revolver under his leather jacket.

"It was a long war, and I'm not your partner," Moody said, seating himself in a booth. He didn't think McCain had come to shoot him.

A sun-wrinkled waitress delivered a bowl of tired tostada chips and salsa along with the sauce-speckled menus.

"Bring us a couple of tequila shooters, some lime, and some beer," McCain ordered.

The waitress brought tequila and Carta Blanca. Then she drifted back behind the cash register, where she perused a *National Enquirer.* The neon sombrero winked bravely while desert lightning illuminated the dusky sky. Thunder boomed like artillery on the Plain of Jars. Neither man wanted to discuss that memory.

"Rough break you got with the bomber crash a while back," McCain said.

"You here to share my sorrow, Angus? Forget it. I'm not complaining."

"You wouldn't, pal. It's not your style."

"That's right," Moody said, biting a lime and tossing back the tequila so it filled his throat with its fiery balm.

"Still, it was a bum break," McCain said, downing his own shot. "*Salud,* partner. I've got a job for you."

"I'm busy."

"I can see that. Looks like you're making the Ilopango run. Uncle always needs a short runway jockey. And now they got one back after the aerospace contractor dumped on its best test pilot. What's Uncle paying you?"

"You know the etiquette. I don't discuss customers."

"Neither do I, pal," McCain said, smiling. "But the pay is better for my job."

"I wouldn't fly for you if my life depended on it. You left a lot of good men hanging. The Pathet Lao cheered when they saw you fly away."

Continuing as if he hadn't heard, McCain said, "We only need you for a couple of days. You'd be doing the old outfit a favor."

Moody drank from his long-necked bottle and gazed at McCain with distaste. "You ought to be dead, you know. I heard you were dead, once. Then I heard you were on the run from the feds. A wanted man."

"Everybody wants Angus," McCain said as he finished his beer. "They want results. I provide."

"You're a bad dream, McCain. Now why don't you just fade away like one?"

McCain shook his massive heard, smiling. "You ain't listening, brother. We got this job where the customer wants to put a team inside Plant thirty-six. Photo recon."

"I knew you were a back-stabbing shit. I didn't think you were nuts, too. Tell me why the outfit would want to spy on itself?"

"Favor for a foreign friend. You know, they're obliged. Scratch each other's backs."

Moody picked up a tortilla chip and chewed it carefully. "Suppose I had you checked out?"

"Don't even think about it," McCain said, losing his reptilian smile. "I need you, Dick. Don't make me get mean."

"I can get mean, too. We can't work together, McCain. We're different."

Moody got up to leave. As he reached the door, McCain whistled and said, "Seen your wife lately?"

Moody turned and glowered. "What the hell are you talking about?" he said, moving quickly across the room and grabbing McCain by the collar of his leather jacket.

"I just asked if you'd seen Glenda lately," McCain said, making no move to resist. "Take a ride with me, Dickey."

Moody clutched McCain's collar and hissed, "I got friends a mile from here who would cut you and flip for drinks while you bled to death."

"I know it, amigo," McCain said, putting his rocky hands gently around Moody's wrists to loosen the grip. "But you'd never see your old lady again, would you?"

Reluctantly Moody released the renegade. McCain threw down a quarter tip, and Moody followed him outside into the rain and gathering darkness.

VENICE, CALIFORNIA

The pain spread in a red wave from the man's lower back to his buttocks. He could see nothing. Blackness surrounded him like a velvet glove. His tormentor struck a new blow, and he watched a thousand stars burst like a galaxy being born. His heart pounded, and he feared he would die. The sound could be the gentle waves of the Pacific, rolling in somewhere nearby. Or it could be his own blood, echoing in his ears. He lived in a black room filled with white noise where there was no time.

He tensed for yet another strike. But his interrogator waited until he relaxed and then struck, so that the pain would be a surprise. He groaned, and his body sagged.

Inch by inch the chain bearing his leather wrist restraints lowered until his toes nearly touched the floor. His interrogator removed the gag from underneath the velveteen hood.

"Again," the man pleaded breathlessly.

"Worm," Tatiana hissed, tapping his buttocks lightly with the riding crop. "That is all you get until we reach agreement."

"I need more!"

"You don't deserve it," she said contemptuously. She turned a lever on the wall of the uniquely appointed apartment, and her subject fell to the hardwood floor.

"You're better than the others," the man gasped.

"I am more stern, if that is what you mean," Tatiana said, circling the man, tapping him lightly with her crop. "That means you must comply with my demands, worm."

"I can't," the man whimpered.

"If you don't, we must play for real, my little man."

"What you want is out of my reach. The window of opportunity is closed. It was a one-shot deal."

Tatiana knelt next to the man and straddled herself across his chest. She removed the hood slowly so that he could look upon her in the dim red light. Then she applied the crop across his throat until he nearly ceased breathing. She was stronger than most men. The man tried to resist. He kicked, but she was dominant. Suddenly he feared death. This terrible woman with her hot breath in his face was real. Too real.

"You will try again," she whispered, pressing the crop yet harder against the man's throat. "Repeat after me: 'I will get the Aurora papers.'" Then she pressed the crop harder and released it.

Coughing, the man uttered the demanded phrase. "I will get the Aurora papers."

She rose suddenly and removed a small cassette recorder from the drawer of a side table. Smiling at her quarry, she pressed the rewind button and replayed the tape.

"I will get the Aurora papers," the man's hoarse, recorded whisper repeated. The man on the floor moaned and wept softly. He had not compromised himself on tape before.

"Bitch," he grunted.

"Don't you love it, though," Tatiana said, unlocking his leather wrist restraints expertly. "I will expect to hear from you within the next few days."

"I'll do what I can. It may be impossible to do it again."

"Succeed, worm. The men who lost the material you took are dead. You are a spy. They don't play these nice games in prison. And we can think of worse fates than prison, I promise you. Now, get dressed. You disgust me."

The man's face formed a sickened smile. He did as he was told and left.

After he was gone, Tatiana removed her hose and leather accoutrements, hanging them on a hook in the closet. She stepped into the shower and bathed herself for nearly half an hour. Then she removed her neatly folded sundress from a chest of drawers and drew it over her curvaceous, completely nude body. After stepping into a pair of espadrilles, she walked out of the apartment into the blinding white light of a sunny Venice day. As she descended the steps of the elderly beachfront apartment, a pair of tanned, muscular roller skaters turned and whistled at her. She smiled coyly at the young men, who rolled on down the promenade.

LOS ANGELES

Romanovich, adjusting the lines of his nicely tailored Brooks Brothers suit, stepped into the dimness of the restaurant, leaving the traffic noise and smoggy heat of Olympic Boulevard behind him. The restaurant was called Uncle Jerome, a pungent, musty place with an adjoining motel set up for overlong lunch appointments between executives and their executive assistants. A discreet waiter, the only kind who worked at Uncle Jerome, consulted the reservation list and guided Romanovich to a curtained booth.

Tatiana waited in the booth, smiling daintily. She sipped from a Black Russian and giggled.

"What, may I ask, is so humorous?" Romanovich asked after the waiter departed.

"Really," she said. "How long have you worked abroad? You must be the fiftieth Smith on the maître d's list. And it is not yet afternoon."

"In this place, all reservations are for Smith. They keep track with initials. Now, how is your Mr. Smith?"

"Frightened, but ultimately cooperative. I have a thing I do with strings."

"I'll bet you do," Romanovich said. "When, please, will delivery take place?"

"He is being evasive."

"Fix that," Romanovich snapped. "That is your job. Our boss needs Smith's material, and quickly. Unless we provide it, the committee will authorize a retrieval attempt by another organization. Of course, you realize the consequences of such a decision."

Tatiana looked at her drink, then at Romanovich. With her pretty green eyes blinking wide, and somewhat frightened, she bore no resemblance to the snapping vixen who had dominated the hooded man earlier that day.

"This drink is too sweet," she said suddenly. "I need something stronger than an American lady's drink."

Romanovich snapped his fingers, and the waiter appeared. The KGB major whispered an order, and the waiter nodded approvingly. He returned a moment later with a bottle of Stolichnaya vodka, the kind obtainable only abroad or in the special Party stores of Moscow. Since the outrage over the invasion of Afghanistan had faded, it was again a popular brand in America.

LANCASTER, CALIFORNIA

Glassman rolled aside the metal door on the E-Zee Storage rental garage and motioned Cartwright to step inside. A few yards away traffic whizzed by in the simmering heat that radiated off Sierra Highway.

"You're full of surprises, Major. First you tell me to pull on my civvies, and next you run me out to a garage sale. Say, I don't think we've ever conspired together out of uniform."

"Yeah. Here I am, over thirty and still wearing jeans," Glassman observed as he pulled a tarp from the top of a drafting table and some government steel filing cabinets.

"You look like a graduate student," Cartwright remarked. "Out of your blue suit, you look like one of those brainy kids I met in the Student Union when I was gettin' my master's degree."

"Caltech, wasn't it, General? You probably looked like a *Field and Stream* cover when you were a big man on campus. Let me tell you something, General. I was a lot of things, but never an all-American college kid. I was a neurotic Jew. The only one at the academy that year." Glassman smiled, seeming to savor the memory. "But when I got in an airplane, General, I was one mean boy."

"You probably still are, Major."

"I doubt it. Anyay, welcome to my inner sanctum."

Glassman stepped deeper into the dimness of the rented space and turned on an overhead fluorescent lamp. He rolled shut the metal door to the outside world and turned on an electric fan. A scorpion skittered between his hiking boots.

"How did you settle on this place?" Cartwright asked.

"Simple assessment of security needs," Glassman replied. "When you want to keep something to yourself, never, ever, trust the government. Do what the dope dealers and money washers do. Rent from the private sector."

"Makes sense."

Glassman spun the dial on a small safe, opened it, and extracted a manila file folder filled with papers and photographs. He removed photographs of several men and arranged them before him on a portable table like tarot cards. "The Mercury Aviation for lunch bunch," he said. "Samuels, Evans, Jefferson, and Lowell. Arguably one of the best management-and-design teams in the country. And our friend Cunningham, the vice-president for corporate communications. One among them is a traitor. What are your thoughts, General?"

"It ain't the PR guy. He hasn't got that kind of access. Jefferson I would doubt. Same for Samuels. Solid families. No debts. Good service records."

"My compliments, General," Glassman said. "You've done your own checking. My guess, then, would be the same as yours. For a variety of reasons, it could either be Lowell or Evans."

"Evans is a big spender. He's one of those, whaddayou call 'ems."

"He's a materialistic bastard. In Torah study, perhaps we would have called him a man without values. One who serves Mammon. These days, I think we would call him a yuppie."

"That's it. Newest stereo. Newest clothes. Newest car. Maybe new loyalties?"

"It's possible. But he's making nearly enough money to pay his way. He expects a promotion. What about Lowell? You mentioned that you knew him."

"That was nearly thirty years ago. The younger man is sometimes different from the older one."

"So tell me, General. Who was the younger man?"

"Good designer. One of the best. He carried Bernie Jackson and Joe Lathrop over the top on a lot of Beaver Works special planes. I think he thought he was going to go straight to the top."

"But he didn't," Glassman said dryly, looking down at the typed security report on Lowell. "The dream fades. He is passed over by younger, less talented men. And his wife succumbs to debilitating illness. She needs constant care. He has too many debts and many needs."

"You make a run of rough luck sound like a prescription for treason," said Cartwright. "I'm not sure I buy that."

"I evaluate from experience."

"Well, that's the cynic's argument," Cartwright said heatedly. "Tell me something, Major. Did a rough streak make you turncoat? I seem to recall that when the going was tough, you got tougher."

Glassman nodded. "The mole isn't necessarily your old friend. We should keep watch on both men. They're both suspects. I will press FBI for enough surveillance, even with their attention divided by their damn terrorist threat."

As Glassman refiled the photographs and documents, a sixth photograph fluttered out from a file, like the Death card in the tarot deck.

"Who's this guy?" Cartwright said.

"He's a private project of mine," Glassman replied. "It's personal." He resumed assembling the file.

"Let's keep our dealings professional, Major. No bullshit. What's this guy to you?"

Glassman sighed resignedly. "FBI believes he's an infiltrator, setting up an attack on the upcoming Olympic heat in L.A. His suspected presence is drawing available personnel away from our surveillance of the Plant thirty-six leak." The photograph, a personnel file shot dated 1960 and taken at the International Police Academy in Washington, pictured a young Avadek in his police uniform. Cartwright examined it closely and saw that another picture was stuck to the back of the print. He peeled the photographs apart. The second picture showed Avadek emerging from a hotel Cartwright recognized as the Tehran Hilton. It was a grainy surveillance shot of a much older man who looked as solemn and determined as the young man pictured in the first photograph.

"You didn't answer my question, Adam. Who is he to you, personally?"

Glassman faced Cartwright. "After I was shot down, he was my interrogator," he said, his face forming an empty, emotionless mask as his eyes returned to the picture. "He wanted to cut off my arm, you know. They have a machine for that. They have a lot of machines. It was just luck the Syrian army raided his compound and ended up rescuing me. I never thought I'd be grateful to *them*," he added, chuckling bitterly.

"Maybe FBI will nab him in Los Angeles, and you'll get a chance to testify against him."

"General, you know the satisfaction you took in shooting down Nazis? That's the kind of satisfaction I'd get out of laying my hands on this bastard," Glassman said, slapping the photograph.

"Well, Major," Cartwright said, patting Glassman on the shoulder, "like the one buzzard said to the other buzzard, 'Patience. Patience.'"

Glassman looked at Cartwright, then burst out laughing. The general had never heard Glassman laugh. He smiled to himself, realizing that laughter might be the beginning of healing.

WRIGHTWOOD, CALIFORNIA

Glenda Moody tightened her tummy and raised her legs, attempting to perform an isometric exercise intended to toughen the abdomen. She lowered her legs gradually to the dusty plank floor, breathed deeply, then repeated the motion, struggling against the ropes that lashed her to the old metal camp bed. She smelled the pines outside and shivered from the draft that blew under the crude cabin door. A tight blindfold of rough canvas chafed her eyelids.

"What are you doing?" Cynthia whispered.

"I'm keeping my body fit, so I'll have it when I need it."

"What do you mean?"

"Honey, the only good thing I can say about whatever it is that's happened to me is that I've had a few days to dry out. When I get my chance to run for it, I want to be in shape."

"What are you talking about?" Cynthia said. "We'll never get away."

"You never know, honey. My old man was a POW. He never gave up thinking he was gonna get away."

"Did he escape?"

"Nope," Glenda said, lifting her legs again until she nearly strained her gut. "But he survived. Three years in the Hanoi Hilton. If he'd ever gotten the chance, he'd have gotten away. Dick said he exercised every day, and he thought about me. He told me that was what kept him from going crazy. So that's what I'm doing."

"I think you *are* crazy."

"Maybe so. But I ain't dead—not yet, anyway."

"We might as well be," Cynthia said, and began to cry.

"Hush, honey. Instead of going to pieces about that big son of a bitch, try to hate him. Give yourself something to hang on to."

"Every time he comes at me, I think I'm going to die," Cynthia sobbed. "And then I don't die. I just think about it and remember and dwell on it. I just wish I would die."

"What you ought to be thinking about is how to get that little weasel that brings us the food to get us out of here."

"Khalil can't help. He's as scared as I am."

"Shoot," Glenda said, "he's not tied up, is he? That boy brings us another plate of cottage cheese and I'm gonna kick him in the balls. Then he'll have something to be scared of."

The women heard footsteps coming up the hill. Once, every couple of days, Cynthia was led down the hill, about the time her parents normally called from their holiday spot in Gstaad. The man called McCain would hold a gun to her head, and she would lisp a few words of affection to her faraway kin. They would hang up, and he would take her to the woods and rape her. It was all done in a couple of minutes, carelessly. The big man would chuckle. Then he would hitch his pants and carry her back up the hill.

They heard the rapid footsteps of a man running. It was Khalil.

"Cynthia, are you all right?" he gasped as he burst into the shack.

"How do you think she is?" Glenda snapped.

"Shut up," Khalil said, grabbing Glenda Moody by her wrists, which were tied to the metal camp bed. He worked feverishly to untie the knot. "You've got to get up," he said, pulling her up on her bound feet.

On her feet, Glenda could feel the breeze as a window was pushed open, creaking on its ancient hinges, and she could feel Khalil's breath on her neck.

"Sweetheart, is that you?" a man's voice called out from down below.

"Good God, Dick, is that you?" Glenda shouted.

"Have they hurt you, Glenda?"

"Sweet Jesus, not yet. But I wouldn't bet on their good intentions. Are you all right, Dick?"

"I'm okay, sweetheart. I'm going to bring you home."

"When, baby?"

"I've got to do something for these people. Then we'll go home."

"That's enough. You've seen her," a man said. Glenda recognized the voice as that of the big man who had shoved her in the trunk of her car.

"I'll come get you," Dick Moody shouted. "Don't worry, honey."

"I want to go home, Dick," she cried, her strong voice faltering for an instant.

"Take her out of the window, boy," McCain shouted to Khalil, who pushed her to the floor, quickly retied her wrists, and shackled her to the bed frame.

"You little bastard," Glenda snarled. "God help you when my husband gets his hands on you."

"Cynthia," Khalil said, on the verge of tears, "tell this wretched woman to shut up."

"Why, Khalil?" the girl asked vacantly. "Why should I?"

"I don't know who you are, you little bastard," Glenda said, "but you better start thinking. These people are gonna kill you, too. They're going to kill all of us."

"Shut up. Shut up," Khalil said. He sank to his knees and began to weep.

"Oh, for God's sake," Glenda said. "What a pair you two must've been."

Avadek watched McCain and the American pilot Moody drive down the road in the jeep and heaved a sigh of relief. The colonel needed time alone with his men. He ordered Khalil to stand sentry outside.

"Now the American mercenary and his lackey are gone," Avadek announced simply to Mehdi and the men of the Green Flight. "When they return, they will bring more mercenary commandos. Like yourselves, they are professional warriors. But unlike you, they prize only money.

"There is little time to finish your training. Quickly now, you must learn. Learn from me, my brothers, or fail."

"We will learn," Mehdi said confidently. "Show us what you have."

Carefully Avadek removed a stick of gum from its pack and set it on the table. The fliers gathered around, fascinated, as he used a penknife to remove a tiny sliver from the dot in the "i" on the gum wrapper.

"Give me a torch, Captain Mahan," he told the senior pilot, who handed him a pocket flashlight.

Delicately Avadek placed the tiny sliver on a white sheet of typing paper. He removed a pair of thick, bifocal glasses in a case from the pocket of his work shirt. Expertly he popped one lens from the frames.

"Shine the light on the dot, Mehdi."

"It is a microdot," the pilot stated.

"Shine the light. Take the lens, Ali."

Ali Rezai took the thick lens and examined the tiny dot on the paper.

"This last bit of knowledge had been withheld from you for purposes of security," Avadek declared. "Do you know what you are looking at?"

Ali shook his head, looking puzzled.

"Pass the lens. All the children must see the prize."

Each of the fliers examined the dot. They murmured to each other.

"Tell them what it is, Avadek," Mehdi said as the men huddled like soccer players discussing a play.

"This is your final lesson," the colonel said. "Will someone venture a guess as to the nature of the device you have examined on the microdot?"

Sidi volunteered eagerly, "It is a detent mechanism for dropping ordnance. Iron bombs, I would say. Two-thousand-pounders."

"And tell me, how does it differ from equipment such as you have used in the past?" Avadek asked.

"The arming device in the cockpit makes use of keys turned in a black box. Two keys, one for the weapons officer and one for the flight engineer."

"And what do you deduce from that?" the colonel persisted.

"Your microdot contains the schematic, code, and arming sequence for the detonation of a thermonuclear weapon," Sidi said, like a clever student. "And since we are in America, I deduce it to be an American warhead."

Avadek smiled and lit a cigarette, a Lucky Strike. "When you are on pop-up approach to a selected target, the weapons officer and engineer turn the keys simultaneously. The weapon is armed," he said, smiling fiercely. "If all goes well, this weapon will be in our hands within a week. The plane you have been trained to steal contains eight nuclear free-fall weapons. The Americans have them now. But soon we will be the power to reckon with."

As the men of Green Flight pondered these words, Mehdi beckoned Avadek outside.

The pair walked in silence into the woods above the cabin. The air was fresh and cold and smelled of pine, like the mountain villages where Avadek lived as a boy. The stars gleamed coldly in the heavens.

"Your conspiracy is intricate, Colonel Avadek," Mehdi said.

"True," said the colonel, puffing his cigarette. "And yet, like all successful plans, at its heart it is simple. We must take the plane."

Avadek seated himself on a rock, his face a contented mask. Mehdi crossed his arms and looked down, trying to read the colonel's face in the light from the glowing cigarette.

"Military necessity I understand, Colonel Avadek. But I do not understand you."

"You needn't," Avadek replied. "It is more important that I understand you, and your men. I think I do. You are patriots."

A breeze lifted up suddenly, carrying a song through the trees. Mehdi heard a branch snap, and he looked back toward the cabin, realizing it was Khalil, the toady, rustling about down below. Mehdi turned to Avadek. "Before I commit my men to possible extinction, Colonel," he said, "there is a thing I must ask."

"Ask it. It is your right. I will choose whether to answer."

Mehdi reached into his pocket, and Avadek shifted uneasily, as though to reach for his own pistol. But Mehdi signaled quickly that he meant no harm. He pulled a battered passport from his tattered worker's jacket.

"You gave me these travel papers before we journeyed to Mexico City. The name on this passport is Issam, the same as the assassin you brought with you when we trained at the camp."

"Just so," Avadek said, inclining his head.

"Where is that man now?"

"He is dead," Avadek said simply.

"Colonel Avadek," Mehdi said, dropping to one knee, "behind you, you leave a trail of death. It is on your breath. Why did this man die? And why was I given his name?"

"He was more than an assassin. He was my guard.

He took direction from the religious cadres, the komitehs. So I had him eliminated and gave you his name for cover."

"And you are not guided by the komitehs?"

Avadek's nostrils flared, and his shaggy eyebrows arched. "Are you, my friend?" he asked, smiling.

"I am a soldier and an airman."

Avadek nodded contemplatively and lit a new cigarette with the glowing end of the one he had finished. Then he patted Mehdi on the knee affectionately. "That is why you were chosen. By me. I serve no god or devil. I serve no American, no Russian, and by heaven I serve no shah, no komiteh, and no holy men who live in another century from mine."

Mehdi was stirred by the colonel's words. He struggled to comprehend their meaning. "Then who or what do you serve?" he asked.

"History," Avadek said decisively. "And our right to claim it."

"What are you saying?"

"I found you in the desert, Mehdi," Avadek hissed. "I read hundreds of files, and I chose you and your men. I believe that I chose the best. I have survived many years and many regimes by making the right choices in men. You are the men whom I chose to offer power.

"We Persians were once a great people," the colonel continued, gesturing animatedly. "Our men marched with Alexander. We ruled from horizon to horizon. It can be so again. We will serve no one, neither American, nor Russian, nor holy father. Our nation has oil. We need only a weapon that will be an equalizer against the superpowers."

Mehdi shook his head and sat down on the pine needles. He looked up at the winking lights of the heavens and down at the glowing power grid of the lonesome cities in the desert below the mountains—the cities filled with people whose lives turned on the work at Plant 36.

"I have trained you well, Mehdi," Avadek whispered. "Take the plane. Take the plane and use it. But don't lose it. We will never get another chance like this one again."

"What are you saying, Colonel?"

"Once you have the plane, do not give it away. Do not barter it away. Prepare to dictate terms. Do you understand?"

"You are either mad or the sanest man I have ever met," Mehdi said in wonder.

"Trust me. And act wisely."

Mehdi felt a chill, whether from the rapid drop in temperature that came with night or from the colonel's words it was impossible to tell. He turned around and reached for the cigarette Avadek offered. The pilot lit the cigarette and smoked. He looked off toward the horizons, seeing everything and nothing, the riddle of the future.

Late into the night Mehdi's fliers drilled, answering dozens of technical and tactical questions to meet the standards of Avadek.

"Tell me again the plane you fly against the Iraqis," Avadek demanded.

"F-4 Phantom and F-14 Tomcat," they answered in unison.

"You will fly the Tomcat again, Sidi," Mehdi declared. "You and Reza are to fly escort for the bomber. There will be Tomcats on the flight line. Should they be disabled when the raiding party attacks, you will seize F-16s, which are also scheduled for propulsion trials at the American plant. Upon failure to seize an F-14, your radar operators will be left behind to fight their way out with the American team."

The radar officers nodded agreement, evincing the same stoic attitude displayed by the pilots. Mehdi turned to Sidi and Reza. "You will engage the American fliers, and at all costs protect the escape of the bomber," he said. "You will probably die."

The fliers nodded.

"Why do we attack in daylight, when the factory is crowded with workers?" asked Ali Rezai.

"The confusion will be greater. Was not Pearl Harbor a daylight attack?" Avadek replied. "The bomber will be ready for operations at that hour. It is tested daily in its hangar."

"My colonel," Ali persisted, "what is Pearl Harbor?"

Hearing the sound of approaching vehicles, Avadek ignored the question. He rapidly replaced the microdots on their spots on the gum wrappers, pocketed the pack, and strode to the window.

The Chevy Suburban followed McCain's jeep. It was filled with a dozen large white and darker-skinned men with grim expressions on their combat-hardened faces. Avadek emerged from the cabin as the vehicles pulled up in front. Climbing out of the truck, the big men carried high-powered rifles and heavy satchels laden with a variety of weapons stolen or devised by the team.

"Boys, meet Avadek," McCain said. "He writes the checks."

THE PRIZE

11

PLANT 36

The members of the Mercury design team—Evans, Lowell, Jefferson, and Samuels—all looked up from their seats like expectant schoolboys. Glassman turned on an overhead projector, and Cartwright pointed to various characteristics of a schematic illuminated on the screen.

"The principles are clear as mud," Cartwright said. "You propose to invade an enemy's airspace by employing an aircraft with a radar cross section so negligible as to escape detection. That's fine as far as it goes. But what are you going to do about infrared signature? This baby tracks IR, and we have reason to believe the Soviets are fairly far along in the same area."

"General, you're going to have to show us that the Northram Corporation's workup can do what you say it can," said Wendall Evans. "You're talking about a significant design modification to fix something that we don't really know to be broken."

"I understand, Mr. Evans," Cartwright said, snapping

shut his collapsible pointer. "You need to do some numbers crunching."

"You're damn right," Evans said. "The slightest change at this stage of development means tens, maybe hundreds, of millions of dollars."

"And a breach in the integrity of the aircraft's defensive system means it's a sitting duck for Soviet surface-to-air missiles," Glassman said.

"We don't know that," Evans insisted.

"Have you ever been shot down, Mr. Evans?"

"He's right, Wendall," Dan Lowell said as he chewed on a pencil. "The airplane has got to be in the zero-defect parameter or it's just a flying Edsel."

"Thanks, Dan," Cartwright said. "Major, why don't you open up that personal computer you lugged over here and show these men some numbers."

Glassman unzipped an Apple Macintosh computer from its gray canvas bag. He set it up on the table, inserted a small disk, and booted the computer to clicking, whirring life. Lowell and Jefferson leaned forward as the gray-and-white screen snapped into focus. Methodically the men began scribbling notes as the equations danced in front of them.

"General Cartwright, my team is going to want to have a longer look at the Northram schematic," Evans said.

"I think that can be arranged, as long as it's understood the data doesn't leave this building."

"You can appoint one of us as custody officer. We all have the appropriate clearances."

"How about you, then, Evans?"

"I'm willing if you are, sir."

"Good. Have you got a copier nearby? We'll make four copies, for which you will be designated custody officer."

"The copy room is around the corner, next to the little-boys' room."

"Fine. Major, finish off here and I'll take Evans to copy the drawings," Cartwright said, handing Evans the schematics.

Glassman worked the Macintosh mouse control with the ease of an experienced hacker. He retrieved new information on the screen. Lowell scribbled furiously on a notepad, then turned to the general.

"May we ask the major to see some of the digital data?" he asked. "It would give us a model for the IR monitor's scanning patterns."

"Go ahead, have a ball. Evans and I'll be right back."

The men walked through the air-lock door that secured the briefing room and through a hallway that led to the copy room. The steel door to the copy room boasted an electronic lock, and a sign painted in red letters declared, "Authorized Personnel Only."

"Evans, I gotta take a leak," the general said. "You can't copy these outside of my presence."

"That's fine, General. The door to the copy room is secured electronically. I can key it, and there will be a delay while it identifies me. You can do your business."

"Fine," Cartwright said, opening the door to the men's room. As he stepped into the lavatory, he noted the time. He entered a stall and waited. He left the stall and washed his hands. When he emerged a few minutes later, Evans was still waiting for him.

"Still got a minute on the time delay, General," he said brightly.

"That door is a good idea."

"We installed it after the document flap."

"Too bad somebody didn't do it before."

"Security is a constant work in progress, General," Evans said airily as the door buzzed open.

"I'll keep that in mind."

In the copy room, Evans programmed the duplicating machine, a sophisticated Japanese copier. Four copies of the schematic popped into the tray, each with a different-colored number at the top of the page.

"That's neat," Cartwright said.

"Hard to beat the Japanese."

"I guess we'll just have to keep on trying."

Evans keyed the door, and it buzzed open. As the men stepped out of the copy room, Glassman paced rapidly toward them.

"Call from the Pentagon, General. You can take it in room L-1011 at the end of the hallway."

"Fine. Will you escort Mr. Evans back to the briefing room, Major?"

"I know my way around the building, General. Perhaps the major needs to go with you."

"You know better than that, Evans. We've got a custody chain on your drawings. Just go back with the major and I'll be along shortly."

"Have it your way, sir."

"I generally do," Cartwright said, his black low-quarter shoes tapping smartly as he walked on the freshly waxed floor.

The general entered the office of the superintendent of quality inspection. A receptionist, recognizing him, stood immediately and smiled.

"Yes, ma'am, I will autograph your notepad, for your little boy and your husband, too, but right now I need you to get me a cup of coffee while I take a call on your secure line. Now scoot."

"Certainly, General. Take my chair," the receptionist said, exiting into the corridor. Cartwright picked up the phone and pushed the button for the extension on the line that was blinking.

"I'm on time. Are you?" demanded a gravelly voice on the other end of the line.

"The air force is always on time, Benson. We're like you FBI guys. We pride ourselves on results."

"What have you got?"

"You want to alert the fox team at One Wilshire. We've got us a pair of bunnies to track. Both had motive, and we've just supplied opportunity. One of them is dirty."

"We've got a federal magistrate waiting to sign warrants. What are we searching for?"

"If it's bunny one, he'll have a copied document, a

schematic. Bunny two has a computer disk, or he'll be carrying raw notes. Either one should put them in the bag."

"Good deal. Nice work, General. The president will be pleased."

"Just don't let him slip. The bunny is only a bunny. We gotta find us the bear."

"Leave that to us. There's so many Russkies in town for the friendship games down at UCLA, we may just declare open season."

"My partner is worried you're gonna let that Middle East threat materialize. Any leads on the terrorism angle?"

"All we can do is try to prevent," the agent growled. "There's no guarantees. We haven't seen the hostiles since we got the report they were in country."

"Do what you can. My partner thinks he's got a personal stake in it."

"Yeah, he told me about the Iranian guy. We'll do our best. Depend on it."

"One more thing, Benson. I want to see the sorry son of a bitch that runs Mercury these days."

"I imagine that could be arranged upon debriefing."

"I want to see him now. I am quite firm on this, and I imagine the president will be, too."

The voice at the other end of the phone sighed, a gravel-throated sigh. "I'll arrange it."

Cartwright hung up. The receptionist returned with coffee in a Styrofoam cup. She handed it to Cartwright, who reached for it and grabbed empty air.

"General, are you all right?" the young woman asked, placing the cup in his hand.

"I'm fine, honey. My mind must've wandered," he said, putting the coffee cup on her desk.

He turned away from her and walked into the hallway. Slowly he passed his right hand in front of his line of vision. He was completely blind in his right eye.

Four of McCain's men played a desultory game of poker. The others seated on the floor by their bunks cleaned

MAC-10 machine pistols, giving them the attention a surgeon would his instruments. Dick Moody's frame filled the doorway. He crossed his arms and watched McCain with undisguised loathing.

Avadek's pilots huddled in another corner of the cabin, sitting by the window and muttering to one another. Neither circle of men had taken the other in yet.

"Let's take a walk in the woods," McCain told Brennan, the team leader. Brennan nodded, and Avadek rose to accompany them. McCain shook his head, and the colonel nodded his understanding.

McCain edged by Moody, and Brennan followed. Stepping outside, McCain lit a tipped cigar and offered one to Brennan.

"Who are these camel jockeys?" Brennan asked.

"Does it matter?"

"Not to me personally, but, like I told you before, I've got a couple of Cubans with me who won't work for commies. If it's Libya, they're out."

"When I recruited you, you said your men would go anywhere, anytime. I paid for people with operational backgrounds. Your men have been paid for this job."

"That may be, but my guys won't work for Libya."

"Then there should be no problem, partner," McCain said, smiling and putting one of his big arms around Brennan's shoulders. "Remember, this is a Company-sanctioned event. We're working for the Jews. Mossad wants a look-see at a new plane. It's a photo recon. Piece of cake. We're in and we're out."

"Shit," Brennan replied. "I think it could get bloody."

"Do your men trust you?"

Brennan nodded. "But they know we're not paid to go to tea parties. They're acting on the assumption this is a Company-sanctioned enterprise. We will use deadly force if needed to effect the extraction."

"Good. You just tell 'em this is for a friendly power. No commies. No specifics. Just a patriotic job that pays good. Shit, tell 'em it's for the contras. I don't give a damn. As long as they crack the plant."

Brennan nodded again.

"Can do," he said.

Retired Master Sergeant Brennan had fought with the men on his team on three continents, first for a cause and later for money. He had a seasoned team leader's confidence that the men would bring this one in for the big money. And for Uncle, too, of course.

Khalil trudged up the hill to the shack, carrying milk and bread for the women. He had taken to muttering to himself about his fate, his family's future, and the unfairness of everything. The Americans and Avadek had left him to feeding the women, a task that humiliated him. As the men in the cabin pored over charts, maps, and diagrams, he knew something terrifying was to take place, but he had no one's confidence or friendship. As the wretched American woman had told him, he feared his usefulness was ending. Every morning, before dawn, he was shaken awake by Avadek, the man who gave him bad dreams.

He turned the key in the rusting lock and shined a flashlight in the darkness. Cynthia and Glenda Moody sat, wide awake, tied to either end of the metal camp bed.

"How's our little rat today?" Glenda Moody asked.

"Shut up, wretched woman, or I do not feed you," Khalil grumbled.

"Aw, what would your bosses do then, little fella? They might snuff you and go get another houseboy."

"Be quiet, Glenda," Cynthia said. "I want to eat."

"That is better," Khalil said, stooping down to pour some milk from a carton into Cynthia's mouth.

She suddenly leaned forward to kiss him. Instantly he drew away. "Cynthia, do not do that," he exclaimed, standing up.

She looked up at him innocently and said, "You liked it before."

"You cannot do this," he said, but he did not move

away as she rubbed her head against his thigh and then nudged toward his crotch.

"This is disgusting," Glenda Moody said, turning away as far as she could with her hands tied behind her. "I'll close my eyes. You can't make me watch."

"Oh, shut up, Glenda," Cynthia snarled, rubbing her head more insistently against Khalil's pants as he began to grow erect. "I'm getting to like this. Why shouldn't Khalil get a little?"

"You try to trick me," Khalil hissed, but he sighed heavily and found he could not pull himself away from the girl's lips.

"It's not a trick, Khalil," Cynthia gasped. "What if your friends kill us? What if I never make love again? Khalil, I want you inside of me."

He dropped to his knees and kissed her. She responded, pressing her tongue into his mouth.

"Take off your pants," she whispered, biting at his shirt and licking the lobe of his ear.

Khalil unsnapped his pants and began to pull them down as Cynthia bowed her head to meet him. He pulled her toward him and began to groan with pleasure, closing his eyes. As he opened them he saw the big iron bed rolling over on top of him as Cynthia and Glenda jumped up together with all their might.

The weight crushed him against the floor as the bed and the women fell on top of him. Cynthia rolled her body across his slight legs, and Glenda rolled all her weight on top of the mattress she held down on top of his head. Khalil gasped and choked. He tried to push Cynthia from his legs, and she bit his extended fingers with all her might. His screams were muffled by the mattress, until at last he didn't scream anymore. Glenda kept her weight on him. When she relented, Khalil was unconscious.

"Good girl," she whispered to Cynthia. "Now hitch yourself around and get into his pockets."

The girl whimpered slightly, then twisted herself around and thrust her fingers into the pockets. She shuddered as she fished her hands around on the limp man's body. She pulled a crumpled green card and dropped it. She dug deeper into one pocket and shrieked joyfully when her fingers touched the cold steel of a pocketknife. "I've got it," she grunted.

"Good girl. Roll yourself back here and cut away."

LOS ANGELES

Tatiana padded lightly to the window of Romanovich's hotel room on Olympic Boulevard and opened the blind partway, letting in the brown light of morning in Los Angeles. She crossed back to the bed, where she picked up a black nylon stocking and rolled it slowly over her ankle and finally up to her milk-white thigh. Daintily she placed her toes in the absurdly angled shoe with the spiky heel. Romanovich watched approvingly. She repeated the procedure with another stocking and another shoe, and then she did a slow turn in front of the bed where Romanovich lay, so he could examine the white of her back and buttocks, which had a pleasing mole on the left cheek.

"You are happy, Volodya?"

"What man would not be?"

"Well," she said teasingly, "you are a man of the people, but first you are a man."

"Was the issue ever in doubt?"

"Not really. I am glad to have been able to work with such a man. Good in so many areas of his work. Am I not a good agent?" she asked, completing the turn so that she stood naked in front of him, except for stockings and heels.

"In fact, you are excellent," he said, smiling.

"I didn't mean that way," she said, pouting. "I mean, am I not good at my work?"

"It is true either way," he said. "But where were you this morning? I needed to contact you."

Touching herself gently and then more firmly, to

Romanovich's great approval, she said, exhaling, "I was shopping."

"Where?" he asked, beginning to breathe heavily.

"It is a place called Rodeo Drive in the Beverly Hills. It is the name of a street like the cowboys of the John Wayne movies, but it was so much nicer than Paris, where everyone shoves," she said, continuing her handiwork. She sighed finally and leaned over to grasp Romanovich, then mount him lightly first, then heavily.

"This is all very capitalist," he said, groaning with pleasure.

"We are doing our work, are we not?"

"Yes," he cried as she rode him. "Yes, we are doing our work."

"Then," she whispered, nipping his ear, "a few moments' pleasure does not matter."

"Yes," he said, relaxing as she withdrew from him and rolled onto her back. She pinched his nipples, then bit them.

"Where did you learn this?" he asked weakly.

"Well," she said, licking his ear, "it was not at Moscow State University. I can tell you that much."

Romanovich kicked his feet in the air and stretched his arms in back of him as far as they would go. "You are on my account," he said. "Where is money to spend on this Rodeo Drive?"

"The little American man pays me well."

"You have been charging him money while you bully him to steal secrets?"

"He cannot seem to keep the money we give him. We have paid him, and now, for me, he gives the money back."

Romanovich shook his head. "I do not understand Americans. Never will. They are a guilty bunch."

"I understand them," Tatiana said, pulling lightly at the wisps of hair on Romanovich's chest. "Men are the same."

"Are we?"

She lit a cigarette and placed it in his lips. Then she lit one for herself. "Yes. All of you. You are the same."

She got up and strode to the bathroom, where she washed herself from the sink. She frowned in the mirror and dabbed a powder puff on her underarms. She had shaved there, to be like the American women in the magazines, but she found the custom slightly repellent.

The telephone rang.

"Who would have this number?" Romanovich asked.

Tatiana rushed to the telephone. She listened for a moment, then hung up. "It is our friend," she said breathlessly. "There is a demand for a crash meeting. He says it must be the both of us."

"How the hell would he even know about me?"

"He is not stupid. He knows I am not alone. He expects a man."

"Untie me, damn it. And put your clothes on."

Professionally, Tatiana Ivanovna unbound Romanovich's wrists, and they began to dress.

WRIGHTWOOD, CALIFORNIA

D-Day 0300 Hours Local

In the cabin, in the woods above Plant 36, a single, dim light burned behind makeshift blackout sheets. Avadek pored over the diagram McCain had penciled for him and compared it with the plant layout that was set up like a toy village on a sand table. A few feet away Mehdi's pilots and McCain's men snored, deep in the slumber of men readying themselves for action. Brennan lit Moody's cigarettes, and the two watched McCain and Avadek quibble over details, keeping silent until they would be asked about their component of the operation.

"Tell me again, McCain," Avadek ordered. "Details of insertion."

"Before first light, my teams accompanied by your

people will enter the subassembly site at Vortex Components," McCain said, using a pointer to indicate a wooden model of a hangar located just outside the plant's perimeter.

"What is there?" Avadek demanded, pointing to the model.

"We've only been over it a dozen times," McCain said, sighing. "Well, hell. You paid your money. Let's do her again. The Vortex hangar will serve as the staging area. As you know, Vortex was responsible for assembly of a tail section for the C-6 transport. Their contract is finished, with the tail sections assembled across the street on the plant proper. They have one tail assembly plug left and a caretaker crew."

"How many caretakers?"

"Enough to provide badges for Sergeant Brennan's fire teams," McCain said, grinning. "As the Vortex crew arrives to hand off from the night watchman, we will disable them, in the same manner employed to disable the night watchman."

"You skipped a step," Avadek snapped.

McCain sighed. "We seize the gut wagon and use that to gain entry to the Vortex hangar."

"I'm not familiar with this term, McCain."

"Gut wagon. You know, dammit. The doughnut truck. The lunch wagon."

"I understand. You have disabled the Vortex personnel. What then?"

"Then my men will affix their photographs to the security badges of the Vortex caretakers," Brennan drawled. "My lead man, Refugio, does good work. He can dummy up a passport in twenty minutes. Shouldn't take him more than ten mikes to do the badge work.

"The rest is easy, Colonel. We load your people in the tail section plug like a bunch of wetbacks in a railroad car. We ferry the tail section across the street and through the gates."

"The Trojan horse," Avadek said.

"Easy as makin' goat cheese, old buddy," McCain said, grinning.

"We better go over the extraction," Avadek said sourly.

"My boys raise hell on the flight line at the plant," Brennan said as he inserted a wad of Mail Pouch chewing tobacco and bit down on it. "We fire up a lot of flash bangs and set off plenty of willy peter, white smoke. We should have the security team there outgunned, in case they don't scatter. McCain's survey indicates their training is spotty. We resort to deadly force only if necessary. If we raise enough hell, it might not be needed. Brother Moody here brings the chopper in when we fire the red flare."

"What do you mean, raise enough hell?" Avadek demanded.

"Nothin' fancy," Brennan drawled. "Disable every aircraft on the flight line, spray down the landing gear with some thirty-caliber, and blow a couple of Claymores to discourage the curious."

Avadek shook his head. "These aircraft," he said, pointing to a series of "X" marks on the diagram, "will be left unharmed."

"The hell they will," Moody snapped, gazing darkly at the huddle of heavily armed men surrounding him. "Unless McCain's team takes out every aircraft on the flight line, we'll be on a chopper ride to hell." He stared at Avadek. "We maybe can avoid pursuit from Edwards, Norton, and March air force bases if we fly nap of the Earth under the radar. But if there's anyone on our tail with a Sidewinder missile, we're dead meat."

"My men will fly these two planes," Avadek said, smiling as he pointed at the "X" marks. "They will protect us on our way out."

"Shit, I can see those boys of yours protectin' us," Moody snorted.

"Listen to me, American," Avadek said quietly. "Those boys, as you call them, they fly, and they can fight. You don't have to be American to fly a plane, you know."

"Is that right," Moody said.

"Look," said Avadek, "would you rather leave this American defense facility flying a lone unarmed helicopter, or would you like a fighter escort so we give your wife back and everybody goes home okay?"

"Shit," Moody said. "Take the fighters. This is a mad tea party any way you look at it."

"Right," McCain said. "Then we all shag ass to Mexico. If things go right today, you get a happy family reunion, and I get to spend my money."

"You can start countin' the days you gotta watch your back, buddy. We get done with this, I'll be out there. You can make book on it."

"Don't be sore, Dick," McCain said, lighting a cigar. "You'll hold up your end. I know that."

"Well, know this. If we get through this day, I'm gonna track you down," Moody said. "The sorriest thing you ever did was grab my wife. You'll live to regret it."

"I'm shakin' in my boots," McCain said, blowing a smoke ring. "You better take off, amigo. You got work to do."

The test pilot looked long and hard at McCain, as though trying to memorize the renegade's features. Then he stepped quietly from the cabin.

As Moody's truck drove down the road, Brennan motioned that he was going outside. "I'll check the perimeter," he said.

McCain offered a cigar to Avadek, who shook his head, then reached to his pocket and shook out a pack of Lucky Strikes. Both men smoked in silence, finally having nothing to say to one another.

Suddenly the door of the cabin opened, and Brennan strode in, tugging anxiously at his handlebar mustache.

"You got problems, McCain," he said.

"What're you talking about?"

"The bitches you had the raghead watching are gone."

"What the fuck do you mean?" McCain said, stubbing out the cigar and rising from the table.

"I waited outside, till your flyboy buddy took off,"

Brennan said. "Figured he'd lose his enthusiasm if he knew his old lady was loose."

"What is this?" Avadek demanded.

"It's like I said, the bitches are gone. I couldn't track em in the dark," Brennan said. He stepped outside the door and pulled the limp body of the unconscious Khalil into the cabin.

"Here's the raghead, Angus. He's down, but he ain't out. Not yet, anyway. Guess we gotta decide whether we're gonna hit or split."

"Shit, Brennan, we gotta search the woods."

"We could do that, but it's gonna eat up some time we ain't got," Brennan said. He crouched down, inspecting Khalil as though he were game meat.

"It's your party," McCain said to Avadek. "Security's gonna blow anytime. We can abort and beat it for the border."

"In that case, you do not get the remainder of your fee," Avadek said. "And I do not accomplish what I have planned."

"Then let's do what we come here to do."

"What about the little guy, here?" Brennan asked. McCain jerked his head and turned his thumb down. In one motion Brennan cut Khalil's throat with a Gerber combat knife, as quickly as though he were cleaning a fish.

Brennan rolled the body off the deck in front of the cabin. McCain and Avadek watched as the mercenary walked down the steps and rolled the body next to the woodpile under the cabin.

"I better wake the men," Brennan said, climbing back up the steps. "I guess you'll tend to your own people," he said to Avadek.

The colonel nodded. "They are ready to ride in your Trojan horse, Sergeant. Let there be no more mistakes."

PLANT 36, OUTER PERIMETER

D-Day 0445 Hours Local

The guard for Keystone Security Services, Inc., stirred awake as his Casio watch beeped insistently. He always set it for quarter to five, in case he drowsed, and usually he did drowse. As he gathered his senses the radio alarm on his desk buzzed, then switched to country music. The guard stretched and rose from his folding chair. It was nearly the end of another night watch.

The telephone rang, as it always did, just before 5:00 A.M.

"This is station six," the guard answered perfunctorily. "Everything A-okay."

The guard hung up the phone and took a few steps just to get the kinks out. He started trudging a slow circuit around the C-6 tail section, to get the wrinkles out of his khaki slacks. He walked around the fifty-foot superstructure of the cargo plane's tail and looked up into the shadows his desk lamp cast in the beams and spars of the hangar. The tail section rested, secured with steel bands, on the flatbed of the eighteen-wheel truck that would carry it ponderously across the street to be attached to the half-finished fuselage of a giant military transport. It was the last in line on a billion-dollar contract. The guard was a bit melancholy that the Vortex contract was finished and he would soon be transferred to another station. The hangar duty had been pleasant. Security checks at the subassembly plant had been infrequent. No one had bothered him.

Outside in the darkness, a bell clanged. It was the gut wagon, the catering truck that brought breakfast sandwiches, doughnuts, and coffee for the morning shift. The guard checked his watch. It was about an hour early. But his stomach rumbled with hunger. He stepped out into the gray light that blanketed the desert before dawn and blinked. The lights were still blazing across the street at Plant 36. The bell on the gut wagon clanged again, and he stepped into the darkness, eager for a doughnut.

LANCASTER, CALIFORNIA

D-Day 0615 Hours Local

Cartwright picked up the pace as he jogged toward the railroad tracks separating the town of Lancaster from the edge of the Mojave Desert. A thin trace of star-speckled aquamarine blue separated the sky of morning from deep space above. Cartwright felt the sun on his back as his legs pumped up and down like pistons. He jogged on the right-hand side of the road to compensate for his loss of peripheral vision. Working up a good sweat, he picked up the pace again and heard the clang of the bells on the candy cane at the railroad crossing ahead and the rumble of the approaching locomotive's diesel engine.

Leaping like a hurdler, he sailed over the lowered crossing guard as the lights flashed and the bell continued to clang its warning. He raced across the gleaming tracks, his Nikes barely touching the roadbed gravel. The diesel horn was deafening, but no more so than a Pratt and Whitney turbofan screaming to life. Cartwright crowed a joyous victory shout as he slackened his pace and the freight train rumbled past the crossing, with the engineer leaning far out of the diesel and yelling, "Ya crazy?!" Cartwright, his hands high in the air, twirled in a small victory turn and continued jogging toward his room and a shower at the Essex House, one of the principal hotels in town serving the air force and the aerospace community. It was not quite 6:00 A.M.

He ran easily along Avenue J past the neat, tree-lined streets of midtown Lancaster, hooked left on Tenth Street West and slowed to a walk about a hundred yards away from the Essex House, where the morning commuter traffic was already clogging the street.

In his room Cartwright showered briskly and, wrapped in a towel, was about to treat himself to a room-service breakfast when his telephone rang. He picked up the phone after a single ring.

"Benson here," announced the gravelly voice on the other end.

"What's up?" Cartwright said.

"Where are you?" Benson shot back.

"Anywhere you need me, fella. What's up?"

"Our boy started moving in an unfamiliar direction about forty-five minutes ago," Benson said. "Fox team is on his tail."

"What'd he do?"

"He drove from Burbank to Torrance, slipping in and out of three or four major freeways. He stopped at South Coast Plaza and made a phone call. Then he kept moving. We are following."

"I'd say it's time to bring in the top table at Mercury on this," Cartwright said.

"I agree. The company CEO will be ferried out to your location within the hour. I assume you and your partner are handling."

"You've got that right. Soon's I get out of my skivvies, I'll be on a beeper. Keep me informed."

"Affirmative."

Cartwright stepped quietly into Major Glassman's room, which adjoined his own. He flipped on the light, by now knowing better than to surprise his partner. He turned on the television set to a morning news show, and Glassman shook himself awake.

"You're sopping wet, son," the general remarked.

"Bad dream. They are frequent, but I handle them."

"Man shouldn't sleep like that. You don't get any rest."

"It's something I'm working on," Glassman said, swinging his legs off the bed.

"Well, we got work to do. Pull on your class As, Major."

"What's happening?" Glassman asked eagerly.

"Benson tells me the bear's going to go for the honey. He thought we might like to ream out the president of Mercury Aviation Corporation before the Justice Department does."

"And how," said Glassman. "Who's the leak?"

"Benson wouldn't tell me over the house line. My bet is we'll know by lunchtime. Let's go, Major."

The two men, decked out in their dress blues and mirror-shined, low-quarter shoes, tapped smartly out to Cartwright's glistening Corvette. As they walked toward the car, Cartwright tossed the keys to Glassman.

"You drive."

"General," Glassman said, shaking his head.

"Go on. Do it. You been puttering around in that piece of government junk. This ain't a hot plane, but it's the best damn production roadster in the U.S. of A. It's the four hundred twenty-seven cubic-inch V-8 with cross-fire injection. Put this baby out on the highway and punch it."

Glassman looked at the general and smiled crookedly. "Okay. It's your funeral."

The men climbed into the angry-looking car, and Glassman gunned it all the way to the plant. Cartwright watched the major handle the wheel with confidence. He would have liked to evaluate him when he was on flight status. As the speedometer edged past eighty MPH on the Sierra Highway, the general decided Glassman must have had natural talent. What he'd lacked at different times in his life was luck.

SANTA MONICA, CALIFORNIA

D-Day 0800 Hours Local

The breeze blew gently through the palms on the

cliffs above the Pacific Coast Highway. Traffic whizzed by below but passed by sedately on the street that fronted the cliffside park in the pleasant coastal city of Santa Monica. A wino approached the park bench where Romanovich sat reading the *Wall Street Journal*.

"Spare a quarter, mister?" he said.

"Get lost if you want to keep your legs, pal," Romanovich said in unaccented English.

"No hassles, brother. It's cool," the drifter said, wandering away into another orbit of the park.

Romanovich turned to finish the article.

"What are you reading, dear?" Tatiana asked in the bell-sweet, middle-American tones she had developed by mimicking the anchorwoman on the *Today Show*. She gave his arm a little squeeze and giggled, imagining herself to be a young American woman out in the park with her lover.

"It's a good article," Romanovich said. "Leave it to the *Wall Street Journal* to do a bang-up piece on the Red Flag squadron."

"Who are they, darling?"

"It's a U.S. Air Force unit. They adopt Soviet flying tactics to train their own fighter pilots."

"What an original idea," Tatiana said, pushing a wisp of her straw-blond hair beneath her beret.

"Sure was. I'll hang on to the article. It could come in handy," he said, proud of his command of American slang.

Couples, bums, bag ladies, and roller skaters made their way past on the promenade. Finally a nervous-looking man in khaki slacks and a navy-blue blazer sauntered past the bench. Like Romanovich, he carried a copy of the *Journal*, opened to the page with the Red Flag article. Tatiana kissed Romanovich on the cheek and followed the man across the street to an outdoor bistro called the Cafe Casino.

Romanovich watched Tatiana seat herself at a table. The man in the blazer seated himself next to her, carrying coffee and croissants on a tray he brought from the cafeteria. He nearly spilled the tray, and Tatiana put her hand on his wrist, gently, as though to calm him. Romanovich finished reading his article, chuckled, and folded the paper. He scouted the traffic coming in either direction on Ocean Avenue and watched the signals change a few times. Then he rose and walked across the street.

He made his way through the white tables and Italian wire chairs. Much of the clientele was also imported, the morning crowd drinking espresso and sampling newspapers from Japan, Iran, the Philippines, and France. Romanovich seated himself at the table next to Tatiana and offered his hand to her breakfast companion.

"Mr. Lowell, so glad to meet you, sir," he said, grinning like a Midwest college boy and shaking the engineer's hand with a hearty grip. "That jacket looks good on you. You should get it taken up at the cuff, though."

"We've got to talk money," Lowell rasped.

"Certainly. That's what we're here for."

Romanovich offered Lowell a cigarette, and the engineer accepted eagerly, allowing the Russian agent to light it for him. He had given up smoking years before but he had resumed in recent months. The term "job stress" held many meanings for him.

12

WASHINGTON

D-Day 1145 Hours Local EST

The president's massive desk in the Oval Office was
bare of ornamentation, except for the picture of his wife,
her radiant smile a source of strength for him, and the
model of an LST landing craft presented to him years
before by war buddies from the Inchon landing. He did
not make a career out of reliving his Korean exploits, but
he found it useful to remind everyone from Pentagon
advisers to Capitol Hill adversaries that he, like Jack
Kennedy, had been a bona fide war hero before he became
a politician.

By midmorning he had concluded his routine. During
his breakfast of orange juice, poached egg, and dry toast, he
had digested the *New York Times*, the *Washington Post*, and
the early final edition of the *Los Angeles Times* flown from
the coast. The papers were full of congressional fallout
about the recent air strikes in Lebanon. A *New York Times*
editorial complained that the United States was becoming

a warrior state like Sparta, and the president chuckled in disgust.

Arriving in the West Wing, he received the national security briefing from Madeline Murdoch, who told him that except for the usual wretched state of affairs in the Middle East, the world was no more or less dangerous than when he had gone to bed the night before. He received the new ambassador from Nigeria and suffered through five minutes with the pool photographers. Unlike his predecessor, he detested photo opportunities.

The president had no sooner returned to the Oval Office when David Runyon, his adviser on domestic policy, arrived with the Secretary of the Treasury. Both launched into an oration on the need to adopt a sound monetary policy that would at least make a small nick in his predecessor's staggering budget deficit. The president, nearing his seventieth year, was a vigorous man, but he had to suppress a yawn.

A sharp rap on the door startled the chief executive from his drift. "Who is it?" he asked calmly.

The Secret Service agent at the door announced, "It's Dr. Murdoch with FBI, sir. It's urgent."

Hastily the president excused his cabinet secretary and the adviser as Madeline Murdoch and the FBI director entered. Outside in the hallway, the somber man holding the Football sat on a French antique chair. Madeline Murdoch and the Judge walked past him as though they did not see him. He was like the furniture.

"I apologize for interrupting, but you wanted to remain informed on the Plant thirty-six case, sir," Madeline Murdoch said, smoothing a wrinkle in her Harris tweed jacket.

"Of course."

"We think we've got the bastard," the Judge said, grinning fiercely.

"Yes, sir," said Madeline Murdoch, retaining her usual poise. "There are developments on the coast."

MOSCOW

Mikhail Alexandrovich Kirilenko, chairman of the Politburo and general secretary of the Communist party of the Soviet Union, put first one foot, then the other, on the floor of his apartment deep within the forbidding walls of the Kremlin. The room, of course, was warm. Unlike the overheated, common apartments of Moscow, this apartment was heated with an electronic room control imported from the West, so it gave the chamber a pleasant, toasty warmth without steaming the windows.

The chairman stretched, blinked slowly, and regarded his retainer, Yusupov, an able personal secretary who had served him since his days as a factory director haranguing workers on to higher efforts in the service of socialism. His assistant held a silver tray with steaming coffee on it. The tray was czarist, the coffee a fine Colombian roast.

Kirilenko sipped his coffee as he walked to the window to observe the pair of elite Red Army guards goose-stepping in ceremonious march across the floodlit courtyard below. Like his most feared predecessor, the chairman was nocturnal, beginning his workday when most souls were asleep.

The sight of the soldiers in the courtyard comforted him the same way that the regularity of a clock's ticking in his grandfather's house once did. That was before the terror of Stalin. Before his youth in the Komsomol.

The guards, finishing half their circuit, snapped to a left-face, presented their assault rifles with fixed bayonets to the cold, empty night air, then continued their march with clocklike precision. Since his grandfather had disappeared, the chairman knew his only safety lay in protection from men who could march with the regularity of clocks.

Yusupov finished laying out the chairman's clothing and drew the water for his master's bath. After bathing, the Party leader rubbed himself to a pink blush with towels of deep pile bought in Paris so that the leader of the people would not suffer the raw skin of a worker or peasant. As he emerged from the bath chamber, the black telephone beside his massive bed was blinking its red light.

"Leave it," the chairman snapped to Yusupov, who walked quietly to the door and moved his hand toward the silenced pistol that he carried in his subtly tailored coat. He knew his master feared assassination above all things.

Kirilenko picked up the telephone and uttered a few guttural growls in the affirmative. Then, with Yusupov's aid, the chairman dressed hastily. Moments later Ligachev, the minister of defense, entered, and Yusupov slipped back to the window curtains like the shadow he was. The minister's face was ashen.

"Give me bad news directly," the chairman ordered, sipping his coffee and gazing on the minister with his well-hated fish-eyed stare.

"The action team has done its work in Beirut," the minister croaked.

"And so?"

"The Aurora materials have departed the Lebanon."

"How do you know this?"

"A GRU interrogation team have questioned all known living fanatics of the militia that kidnapped the Soviet citizen courier."

"What do the Muslim thieves say?"

"Whatever materials the courier carried are believed to be in the hands of the Iranians."

"Fuck your mother," the chairman snorted. "How in hell did that happen?"

"It would appear that an Iranian agent operating in the Lebanon would have discerned the documents have an intrinsic value," Ligachev said, his hand shaking as he rubbed his chin. "It is improbable that they would know what is contained in the Aurora materials. These are primitive people."

"Just so. Have we had an offer of ransom?"

"No communication whatever."

"What resources do we have in Tehran? Are the Tudeh networks active?"

"They were neutralized by order of the KGB, Comrade Chairman. It was a favor to improve relations with the Islamic regime," Ligachev said lamely.

The chairman's face darkened. "Yusupov, come here," he ordered. "Take no notes. Just listen and remember."

The retainer nodded as the Party chairman growled orders.

"We will convene the Politburo in emergency session," he said. "I will need the army's support on this. The Beirut station will be temporarily under active jurisdiction of GRU, the army service. In Beirut, this will be enforced by the Spetznaz troops."

The defense minister nodded and attempted to conceal the smile that fought its way to the surface of his rough features.

"Yusupov, you will compose a directive over my signature for the organs of state security," the chairman said as he paced restlessly. "KGB station in Damascus will attempt to open a channel to the Iranians for discussion of the materials they hold. We will use the Syrians to help us influence those damnable rug merchants."

"And if that should fail, Comrade Secretary?" Ligachev asked quietly.

"Then we tell the Iranians we will give the Iraqis enough ground-launched cruise missiles to make the rubble bounce in their outlaw nation."

For the past several years the newest chairman had acted cautiously to discharge the Soviet Union's subsidy and support of terrorist groups, while still trying to keep the Soviet state sympathetic to movements of national liberation. He wished now that he had moved more quickly and boldly.

SANTA MONICA, CALIFORNIA

Tatiana returned to the table carrying a tray with fresh croissants, which both men ignored. Lowell reached nervously for a cup of coffee on the tray.

"The question of money is simple, Mr. Lowell," Romanovich said. "But we must have your documents now, not later."

"You don't understand," Lowell said, the coffee cup shaking in his trembling hand. "The material you asked for is irretrievable."

Romanovich's face darkened. "What are you saying?"

"The Stealth stuff was a one-shot deal. I couldn't access that cache of material again if my life depended on it."

"I can assure you, Mr. Lowell, your life may very well depend on your ability to retrieve such materials. Certainly your freedom does," Romanovich said.

"Your people blew it, not me," Lowell snapped.

"That is irrelevant. If this is the case, what is the purpose of your demand for such an unwise meeting?"

"I have with me stuff that is as valuable as what I took previously. You can have it, but you've got to meet my terms. I am a desperate man."

"It is normally unwise to deal with a man in a state of desperation," Romanovich said, sipping his espresso. "It is difficult to believe you possess material of equal value to what you previously obtained."

"It's something you want all right."

"Describe it."

"It's an active infrared scanning system that could counter a Stealth aircraft."

Romanovich's eyebrows rose in interest. If the Aurora material were truly irretrievable, he thought, this could be the ticket for safe return to the motherland. Otherwise, he knew it would be wise to seek out a good plastic surgeon in the capitalist enclave of Beverly Hills. The incompetence of others had rendered Romanovich a desperate man.

"Why would I believe that you have such a prize?" he demanded.

"Because some of the material has already traveled East. But I have a personal guarantee from an air force general that the drawings I hold are perfected, and still secure."

"Name this general."

"The astronaut General Scott Cartwright."

Tatiana watched Romanovich carefully for his assessment of a deteriorated situation. Hearing Cartwright's name, the Russian whistled softly. "What do you propose?" he asked.

"I have with me one-half of the materials I described. The second half is deliverable to you upon my receipt of a Costa Rican passport, with correct visa and receipt of three hundred thousand dollars to an account in the Grand Caymans that will be controlled by my wife's conservator, a person I shall designate."

"All of this takes time."

"Take it or leave it," Lowell said. "But don't take long."

"Darling," Tatiana said, squeezing Romanovich's arm, "Mr. Lowell has helped us often in the past. Can't we trust him, just this one time?"

"That's right, bitch," Lowell snarled. "Tell him how it's gotta be. No visa, no documents."

"Hush," Tatiana said. "Mother will spank."

Lowell stared at her for an instant, his eyes full of hate. Then he looked down at the smooth surface of the white enamel-coated table, seeming to study its every detail.

"It's a deal," Romanovich said tersely, offering his hand to Lowell, who passed him an envelope under the table.

As the three rose to leave, a helicopter zoomed low overhead, its rotor blades roaring and leaving a prop wash that blew flowers, cutlery, and linen from the tables. A bullhorn blared, "Everybody down. Everybody down on the ground. This is the FBI!"

Dozens of diners scrambled to the ground, and Romanovich dived for a hedge that divided the sidewalk cafe from Ocean Avenue. As he rolled onto the sidewalk, the strong hands of a pair of men in trim gray suits laid hold of him. Romanovich was handcuffed, and when he was brought to his feet, he saw another team of agents handcuffing Tatiana, whom they had caught running toward the rear exit. He couldn't help thinking that she was no stranger to handcuffs.

It was Supervising Agent Benson who put the cuffs on Dan Lowell and moved him along briskly toward one of the government sedans that blocked Ocean Avenue.

"Oh, my God," Lowell said, lumbering along like a man walking underwater. "What have I done?"

"You know what you did," Benson said, shoving him roughly into the backseat of the car.

After Tatiana and Romanovich had been placed in separate sedans, a young agent in a jogging suit ran toward Benson and shouted, "Where's the party? One Wilshire?"

"Nope. We need a couple of hours before the lawyers and the Soviet consulate ride in. We convoy to the LAX Plaza Hotel. Make sure we read these turkeys their rights."

"And then?"

"Then," Benson said, "we gently persuade them that they got no rights."

He turned and peered through the bulletproof glass at Lowell. The engineer had vomited. Lowell turned his head to see Benson staring at him and quickly averted his eyes as the car pulled away from the curb.

PLANT 36

D-Day 0845 Hours Local PST

The day-shift traffic backed up for nearly a mile from the Plant 36 main gate. A security guard at the gate shack waved the workers through after giving their ID badges the once-over. Cartwright's Corvette rumbled impatiently, with Glassman tapping nervously on the steering wheel.

"It ain't as much fun sittin' in traffic as it is opening that baby up on the highway, huh," Cartwright said.

"When you're right, you're right, General," Glassman said. "So I've been missing out. I'll have to buy a hot car one of these days."

"And fly a hot plane. And chase some hot women."

Glassman sighed and said gently, "You never give up, do you, sir? I've got to tell you, I think my flying days are over. Flight surgeon called it vertigo. He said I've got no sense of time and altitude."

"Bullshit. You just got shook up. Hell, if I had a nickel for every time I had to dead-stick it onto that lakebed over there, I'd be a rich man," Cartwright said, pointing to the wasteland where he'd landed the space shuttle.

A pair of F-16 Fighting Falcons passed low over the plant, leaving a trail of transonic noise in their wake as they roared back toward Edwards Air Force base. The lead plane turned a slow aileron roll, and the wing man followed. The fighters climbed toward the empty blue, then hit the afterburners, and some of the workers driving convertibles cheered and whistled watching the planes vanish.

"Shit, son, don't you want some of that again?" Cartwright asked, shading his eyes as he watched the jets form contrails. "There's only one thing better."

"I never flew for that kind of glory, General. My pleasure was oriented to the mission."

"Don't give me that line of bull, Adam. It's in your blood."

"After we put the Mercury ring in the bag, I'm resigning my commission, General."

"Shit," Cartwright snorted. "What kind of thing is that for a man to do?"

"My reasons are sound to me, even if you don't understand them. I regret that you don't know me as well as I thought you did, General."

The cars edged forward slowly toward the gate. The Corvette was two cars behind an eighteen-wheeler truck carrying the completed tail section of a C-6 Transport on its flatbed. The truck rumbled forward, belching diesel from the pipe above its cab. The cars ahead of Cartwright's Corvette waited for it to get a few yards ahead before pulling up behind it again.

"You ain't a coward, Glassman. I know that. But you ought to solve this thing, and I don't think you can do it running away."

The cellular phone in the Corvette burbled its electronic tone, and the general picked it up. "Cartwright here."

"This is Benson," announced the gravel voice. "We got the bear. A pair of 'em, actually."

"That's good. Damn good."

"The bad news is the mole was an old-timer. He's cooperating so far without aid of counsel, but he gave them a lot. His name is Dan Lowell."

"Oh, hell. I was hoping it would be the younger guy."

"It's Lowell. And something else has come up," Benson said, his voice blanked for a moment by static. "Do you know a woman named Glenda Moody?"

"Sure do. What's up?"

"Seems she was kidnapped. We don't really have the whole story yet. I got a sketchy report from a duty officer about terrorists, the CIA, and God knows what. She was pretty badly banged up, but she asked for you."

"Soon as we clear the site here at thirty-six, I want details," Cartwright said, speaking to Benson as though he were an aide.

"Affirmative. We'll talk at One Wilshire this afternoon."

"Cartwright out."

Passing through the gate, the Corvette wheeled left toward the Mercury office complex and the executive helipad that fronted it. The truck carrying the twenty-foot-high tail section rumbled slowly to the right, driving toward the hangars. As the truck pulled the tail section, a giant hangar on the opposite side of the field rolled open, revealing a glimpse of the space shuttle *Victory*, the latest in the fleet. Plant 36 was a place of multiple wonders.

Cartwright and Glassman parked at the edge of the

helipad and, like airmen everywhere, kept their eyes on the horizon. Glassman turned the radio on and moved the dial to a station carrying big-band hits, and Cartwright nodded approvingly. As they looked skyward a great dark shadow descended from their nine o'clock. It was a thing of majesty.

"Habu plane," murmured Glassman.

"The quick and deadly snake of Okinawa overflight. Since you'll be a civilian, you might as well start calling it a Blackbird. That's what the taxpayers call 'em. Ever fly one?"

"No, sir."

"It was glory. Still is. Flies at Mach 3 plus and takes a couple of hundred miles just to swing it around. It's got the only pair of engines that burn red hot. See it in the skies over Colorado and you think you're tracking a UFO."

"If you like the Habu, then take a look at that," Glassman said, pointing to a dark spot in the distance.

"It doesn't look familiar," Cartwright said as the spot grew to an accelerating profile of wingtip and fuselage rocketing over the desert floor.

"No reason it should. That's the demonstration model of the Advanced Tactical Fighter. The Blackbird was probably trying to keep up with it over Colorado a few minutes ago."

"Balls."

"That ATF is the next century's fighter, General."

"Looks wicked. Ever fly it?"

"Yes, sir. Once," Glassman said, and a ghost of a smile crossed his lips. "It's called the Rampant."

The fighter jet scissored over the landing field and swung around in a 6-G turn tight enough to make a pilot's nose bleed. Then the pilot appeared to stop the plane so it hovered in midair about five hundred feet above the tarmac. Four thrust vector nozzles locked into position under the plane's delta wings and blasted angrily, setting the jet down on the field vertically, like a spinning top.

"That thing hauls butt at Mach 3 and hovers like a chopper?"

"Yes, sir."

"My granny."

"O brave new world."

"You're right, Major. It looks like the future. To think I started in props."

As the prototype fighter rolled to its hangar, the Mercury executive helicopter zoomed overhead and descended to the helipad.

LAX AIRPORT PLAZA

"You're the skunk at the garden party," Supervising Agent Benson told Tatiana Ivanovna.

He offered her a cigarette, which she refused. Then he opened the curtain so it would show the panorama of Boeing 747s departing from Los Angeles International Airport. His best chance of getting a confession, he knew, lay with the beautiful woman, whom he sensed to be an opportunist. And his best opportunity for turning her would be in the first ten minutes of the interview.

"Look at those planes, sweetheart," he said carelessly, lighting a cigarette. "We call them freedom birds. But for you they're a one-way ticket to the Gulag."

She crossed her arms. Then she uncrossed them and toyed with her hair. Benson smoked and paced. "You're well dressed now," he said, waving his cigarette. "That won't last. Get used to trousers made out of wood fiber or whatever it is they use over there. Wood pulp grinding on your fine white ass. I hate to even think about it."

"I am exactly what I appear to be," she said, speaking for the first time. She sounded cool, her tones creamy. "I am trade representative for the Ukrainian Socialist Republic, with diplomatic status. Please contact the Soviet consulate and arrange for my immediate release."

"Didn't they tell you, honey? You're on commercial status. You've got no immunity at all. But that's the least of your problems. See, I'm not what you have to worry about. It's your boss in the next room you've gotta sweat," Benson said. "Party membership is no good to you now. You failed. He's gonna get out of this jam." Benson pointed to the room presumed to hold Romanovich. "That man is already arranging his story so that when he goes home, you get the blame. He's done it before. Your comrade is gonna need a goat. And it's going to be you."

Tatiana Ivanovna stared straight ahead. A jumbo jet screamed skyward, its engines sounding not unlike the wind howling across the tundra.

"Give me a statement now, and we'll protect you," Benson growled. "You can forget about the wood pulp panties."

"Do you think I am a common whore?"

"Partly," he said, rubbing his bald bullet head. "But I think you're smart, too. My offer is good for five minutes. Then we have to talk with your boss. If he rolls over, you and I have got no deal."

He left cigarettes and a lighter on the coffee table and walked out. Tatiana looked at them for a long minute. Then she shook the pack and lit a Marlboro, inhaling deeply. Like most good communists with the opportunity for travel, she loved American cigarettes.

PLANT 36

D-Day 0930 Hours Local

The man stepping from the Bell jet 'copter looked like what he was, a cover subject for *Forbes* magazine. Duncan Avery, the latest president of Mercury Aviation Corporation, was followed onto the tarmac by Wendall Evans and the company's vice-president for corporate communications, who nervously fingered his yellow power tie. With the rotors still whirring, Avery stepped away from the helicopter, the wind blowing his silver-blond locks like an advertisement for men's hair products. He grinned boyishly, walking toward Cartwright.

"Good to see you, General," Avery said, extending his hand. "We met at the Air Force Association dinner last year."

"Get rid of them," Cartwright said, jerking his head toward Evans and the public relations chief. "We've got to talk alone."

Avery stopped in midstride and cocked his head to one side, not unlike a prize Doberman he owned. "I beg your pardon?"

"Your flunkies are a security risk, Mr. Avery," Glassman interjected. "What needs to be said is for your ears only."

"I don't know you, young man," Avery said equably. "But I think whatever the general tells me should be on the record and appropriately discussed in my office."

"Evans, take a hike," Glassman ordered.

"Now, wait a minute," Evans protested.

"You heard the major," Cartwright said. "Beat it. And take your pal with the custard tie."

"This is really outrageous, gentlemen," Duncan Avery said as Cartwright took the executive by one arm and Glassman took him by the other. Gently but firmly they began to walk him down the flight line away from the Mercury offices.

"What is this all about?" Avery snapped.

"Your project security," Cartwright said.

"We're not talking in your office because it hasn't been swept for bugs, Mr. Avery," Glassman said. "Maybe not since Joe Lathrop himself died."

"This is ridiculous," Avery snorted. Cartwright and Glassman, having walked the executive a reasonable distance from his puzzled aides, swung him around in a manner like that of deputies who calm drunks before cuffing them.

"How long have you been president at Mercury?" Cartwright demanded.

"Two years. What's that got to do with anything?"

"More like eighteen months, I'd say. I know you, Avery. You're a takeover artist. You came here from a car rental company," the general said contemptuously.

"Really, General."

A pair of Grumman F-14 Tomcats roared in low over the flight line. They zoomed out of sight, then reappeared on final approach. As they wheeled toward a space on the runway allocated for servicing several other navy planes, a ground crew ran forward. Heat waves shimmered on the tarmac. Avery sweated uncomfortably.

"The FBI's got one of your Stealth project men in a hotel room right now, Mr. Avery."

"What's that supposed to mean to me?"

"It means he's a goddamned spy," Cartwright said. "It means he tried to hand over Mercury's best stuff, stuff that cost a million bucks an hour to develop."

"There are a lot of spies," Avery hissed. "Not least of all in the military. You've got a goddamned nerve to talk to me like this, General."

"If the chief exec isn't responsible for house security, who is? I know your sort, Avery. You ran a biscuit company, then you bought into rent-a-cars. Now it's aerospace. You think it's all the same stuff. Well, let me tell you, mister, Uncle Sam's airplanes ain't biscuits."

"I've had about enough of this conversation, Cartwright. You can be sure the secretary of the air force will hear of it."

"Put it on a gift certificate, Avery," said Cartwright. "When we get done cleaning your house, you'll wish you were selling crackers again."

Rolling to a stop, the navy jets whined as their Pratt and Whitney turbofan engines wound down. The distracted executive fixed his gaze on the pilots emerging from the cockpits. A pair of air force security guards armed with M-16s ambled by on their round, giving the general a wide berth and wary salutes.

"What do you want me to do?" Avery asked finally, sounding somewhat dazed.

"The security breach is severe," Glassman said. "Admit first to yourself that you are in over your head. Move quickly to pick a successor who is an industry veteran with no history of security breaches."

"Then plan on a housecleaning. The air force will assist," Cartwright said, motioning the shaken executive back toward the offices. "You'll probably even get to keep your golden parachute. It's the only kind of chute you boardroom guys need."

As Glassman and Cartwright walked with Avery, the driver of the eighteen-wheel tractor-trailer towing the Vortex tail section climbed from his cab, stepped onto a catwalk on the flatbed of the truck, and began unhooking a large tarpaulin from the maw of the C-6 tail section, which looked like a giant metallic shark's carcass. It was Glassman who first noticed the man had an Uzi submachine gun strapped to his shoulder.

"Something's wrong," Glassman said.

As casually as a pitcher on a pickup softball team, the driver tossed a concussion grenade a few feet from the two air force security guards stationed at the hangar door to the building that housed the STB-1 Stealth Technology Bomber prototype. As he did so, men with guns began running out of the hollow aircraft tail. The startled guards were watching the grenade as it detonated, knocking them senseless to the ground.

Shock waves from the stun grenade battered Glassman, Cartwright, and Avery to the ground, making their ears ring and their noses bleed.

The attack on Plant 36 had begun.

13

PLANT 36

D-Day 0934 Hours Local

Brennan's fire team Alpha had taken down the half-dozen blue-suiters who guarded the flight line. The Alpha team fighters tossed stun grenades and flash-bang bombs that blinded their victims. One air policeman managed to fire a short burst from his M-16. An Alpha team gunner shot him with return fire from an Uzi, making him the first casualty of the fight at Plant 36.

"It's a hot LZ," Brennan cried. "You are clear for deadly force. Fire! Fire! Fire!"

At Brennan's command, his fire team shot another air policeman.

Fire team Bravo, led by Brennan's man Refugio, was moving the Green Flight bomber crew, laden with their flight bags, toward the giant hangar. Taking the large key ring from one of the guards, Refugio methodically opened the small hangar door, leading Green Flight's bomber team, with Mehdi first, inside the building. As they ran all of them donned gas masks.

Refugio and his two riflemen burst through the air-lock door, the Green Flight crew crowding in behind, pressing their backs to the wall where it intersected with a small corridor that turned sharply right. Refugio, at point, lifted his silenced Walther PPK automatic and killed an air policeman before he could chamber a round in his M-16. The civilian security guard with the air force guard stood in mute horror as his partner slumped to the floor. For an instant the civilian guard gazed at the men in gas masks as he would at a snake poised to strike. Then Refugio was at the man's neck, pressing the Walther to his carotid artery.

"Dial up the door sequence and get us inside if you want to live, motherfucker," Refugio grunted through his mask. "I'm backing away out of camera range. But I'm right behind you, asshole. So do it right."

At the bend in the corridor, Refugio's rifle team dropped to their knees, each man cocking an M-206 grenade launcher, one with a green-painted aluminum round, the other with a red round. Behind them, hugging the concrete floor and clutching their flight bags, Captain Mehdi Mahan, Ali Rezai, and the two radar officers, Hossein and Hashemi, awaited their moment.

His fingers trembling, the guard punched the numbered sequence on the wall panel and the door swung open. As the guard stumbled forward into the Mercury black projects hangar, he was dropped to his knees and cut in half by a hail of fire from two Delta operators wielding Heckler and Koch machine pistols. If the Delta men had worn gas masks, they might have lived.

Refugio's fire team volleyed their grenades into the hangar, one creating a blinding flash and the other filling the chamber with incapacitating gas. One of the Delta operators was knocked to the ground by the flash bang. Refugio shot the other.

The engineers and checkout personnel who had huddled behind their workstations when the Delta operators called the alert coughed and choked. Some of them, blinded by the flash bang, screamed. But the screams were cut short as they inhaled deeply, then slumped flat behind their desks.

In the airtight test sequencing booth suspended from the catwalk above the STB-1 Stealth Technology Bomber, Reggie LeFever huddled, grunting the words "damn ...damn...damn" like a catechism. As the first shots were fired, he sealed the booth from inside and hit the floor. Hearing no more shooting, he ventured a peek from the bottom of the booth window with its panoramic view of the black project hangar. As he took in the view, he shuddered.

The smoky gas from the grenade assault was dissipating, and McCain's mercenaries were fanning out in the hangar, occasionally kicking a disabled plant employee to make sure he was down. LeFever gasped, sighting four men in flight suits accompanying the masked gunmen.

"You sons of bitches," he whispered. "Come to Reggie, and he'll give you a nice surprise."

LeFever edged backward on the floor toward his desk and slid the drawer open, taking out a 1911 Army Colt .45 automatic. He fumbled in the drawer for the clip and inserted it in the magazine, all the time watching the scene below from the bottom edge of the window.

Suddenly one of the intruders pointed in the direction of the test sequencing booth and sprinted toward the catwalk. The gunman fired a burst through the window of the booth's steel door, spraying a shower of shattered glass. He then tossed a grenade in the booth, and Reggie LeFever, bleeding from numerous glass cuts, watched it clatter across the floor. Making his decision quickly, he rose to his feet, ignoring the grenade, and fired the Colt, emptying his magazine into the gunman on the catwalk until the grenade exploded, tearing apart the booth and killing LeFever instantly.

Refugio's second operator ran up the catwalk and grabbed the gunman who had tossed the grenade. He waved down to Refugio and shook his head.

"He's dead," Refugio said to Captain Mehdi Mahan as he removed his gun mask. "So already I lose one good man cracking your plant, and maybe more. Get out your cameras and take your pictures. It's your party now."

"Yes," Mehdi said, taking a 9-mm automatic from his flight bag and shooting Refugio. "It is our party."

In unison, Ali Rezai, Hossein, and Hashemi dropped their flight bags and pulled out pistols, shooting the third man in Refugio's fire team. Then they removed pressure suits from their flight bags and suited up. Grabbing their helmets, Ali Rezai and Hashemi followed Mehdi to the ladder that hung suspended beneath the cockpit of the STB-1 Stealth Technology Bomber. Hossein ran toward the door panel and hit the switches to open the huge hangar. As the hangar door groaned open, desert sunlight streamed in on the winged form of the hulking bomber, making its dark, radar-absorbent surface shimmer.

Hossein ran to the ladder and joined his comrades. Once inside the cockpit, the fliers donned the helmets in their flight bags and connected the oxygen hoses and radio leads. Each man quickly settled in to his space, glancing hurriedly at his particular array of display screens and computer "black" boxes that made up the bomber's Electronic Warfare suite and flight controls. Like blind men reading Braille, the crew ran their fingers quickly across the dozens of buttons and toggle switches each was responsible for. There was no time to marvel at the futuristic simplicity of the cockpit's layout in which a few multicolored screens replaced hundreds of dials.

"Radio check, over," Mehdi said, keying the intercom in his helmet. Each crew member responded.

"Let's go," he said.

Eyes on the control panel, Mehdi hurriedly sought the button whose location he had memorized during the training in Avadek's camp. Finding it, he pressed down and the four modified General Electric F101 engines roared angrily to life.

Outside the hangar, Brennan was satisfied with the

raiding party's progress. He checked wind direction by eyeing a sock on the airfield and fired a pair of white phosphorous grenades from an M-79 launcher. The grenades hit the flight pad with dull metallic thuds. He aimed expertly, making sure the mushroom billow of deadly white smoke blew away from the fighter jets parked next to their weapons carts.

An alarm siren wailed. Several dozen plant employees ran from an open hangar into the cloud of white smoke. Some screamed in pain as the phosphorus burned their skin. Others ran toward the open desert. Machine-gun fire punctuated by glowing red tracer rounds raked over their heads, and some of the quick ones dropped to the tarmac. Others less quick were felled, moaning or screaming, by stray rounds.

Cartwright and Glassman held the panicked Avery to the pavement, tearing his expensive suit. The force of the blast appeared to have put the executive in shock. He lay squirming on his side, holding himself in a fetal position.

"It sure as hell ain't a drill," Cartwright said as he low-crawled toward the slain air policeman and grabbed his M-16. Using the youth's body as a rifle rest, he surveyed the airfield through the peep sight and found what he was looking for, the source of tracer fire that was raking the tarmac. The 7.62 mm fire arced from behind an air force pickup truck parked at the end of the airstrip. Cartwright clicked his fire selector to semiautomatic and popped off five rounds, silencing the gunner. Cartwright laughed and yelled, "Got ya." He crawled to the second slain guard and took his rifle.

"Come on, son," he yelled to Glassman.

"Where are we going?"

"We're gonna take as many of these bastards as we can."

"What about Avery?"

"Leave him," Cartwright said, running serpentine and tossing an M-16 to Glassman, who caught it neatly. "Lay down cover fire," Cartwright shouted, and he ran a few dozen feet in a short burst before dropping down on the airstrip.

A second automatic weapon, an M-60, had opened up farther down the field where the air horn from the main hangar blew. Cartwright didn't see any more blue suits.

"Don't leave me," Avery pleaded to Glassman. "Please."

Glassman, already crawling away and firing shot bursts from the assault rifle, said, "Don't move. If you move, you'll die."

Cartwright, using fallen bodies of plant workers for cover, moved back toward the office complex in short sprints. Some of the men he lay beside begged for help, but he couldn't stop. The general spotted three pilots in flight suits, huddled by a large air-conditioning unit next to one of the secondary buildings. Their service-issued .38 Smith and Wesson revolvers were drawn, but they could see no targets through the smoke.

Keeping his head well down behind the stout body of a plant assembler, the general shouted in his best command voice, "You men. I am General Scott Cartwright. Follow me." And, as he ran toward the building, they did.

"What have we got, sir?" a captain demanded as they huddled behind cover.

"Gotta be terrorists. Where the hell is plant security?"

A man in blue coveralls ran up to the group. He carried a nine-millimeter Browning pistol and wore oak leaves on his collar. "General Scott Cartwright," he grunted, "I am Major Roy Trueblood, Delta security element."

"Delta, huh. Where are the rest of your cowboys?"

"Some dead. Some are incapacitated by gas. The rest are trapped inside the Mercury black hangar. They will resist."

"Well, Major, our tits are in a wringer now," Cartwright said. "Who's commanding your unit?"

"I am, sir. Colonel David Donegal is dead." Farther down the flight line, a series of Claymore mines exploded with a deafening roar.

"What are we facing, Major?"

"Hostile penetration by one bad-ass team, sir. They are of unknown origin."

Glassman, his face streaked with sweat and cordite, ran up to the group. A WP grenade thudded on the airstrip, laying down a fresh cloud of poisonous smoke. Cartwright heard a long rebel yell.

"Glassman, I want you to lay down another burst while I scoot over to my race car," he said.

"What's the plan?"

"Gotta get to my car phone. FBI's Benson can alert the military. We gotta presume we're cut off."

"Better hurry, General," Trueblood urged.

"I know what I gotta do," the general snapped. "You men, spread out and kill terrorists. Get their guns and then kill some more."

LAX AIRPORT PLAZA

Supervising Agent Benson returned to the room where Tatiana was being held. She had finished her first cigarette and was daintily pulling a second from the pack when he entered.

"No more Amerikanski cigaretti in the land of the great frostbite," Benson said dryly. "You're going to have to make up your mind pretty fast, comrade. Your partner is considering asking for political asylum and submitting to lengthy debriefing."

"And so?"

"And so he is clearly the more valuable of the two of you. If we keep him, we ship you back. Just like that."

For the first time she smiled. "And you think he is more valuable? That is about what I'd expect from a fascist policeman like yourself."

"We haven't got time for this. I'm going to take the first one of you who gives me a reason to help them. The other one gets hung out."

Tatiana inhaled deeply. An agent the size of a linebacker burst through the door, and Benson whirled, furious at being disturbed.

"Sir, we have flash traffic from the general."

"The hell you say. I said no interruptions!"

"You've got to come, sir. There is a terrorist attack of some sort in progress. General Cartwright is taking fire at his location."

PLANT 36

D-Day 0958 Hours Local

Cartwright, pinned down on the pavement next to his Corvette, shot a running man whose rifle clattered on the concrete as he fell. He found that the blindness in his right eye had no effect on his marksmanship. He just mourned the loss of lateral vision. Reflexively he closed the eye. He had two clips of ammo left that he'd lifted from the slain guard. The M-60 gun continued to chatter away as Glassman, who had laid down covering fire for Cartwright, sprinted up to the car.

"How's your ammo, Adam?" Cartwright said to the winded major.

"I've got another clip. What did Benson say?"

"Thirty minutes flying time for the FBI antiterror team. And he's alerting Edwards, March, and Norton."

"We haven't got that long."

"I know."

"We need the cavalry."

With his good eye Cartwright spotted seven or eight men running down the airfield as though they were on a scramble. Several wore G.I.–issue desert camouflage, and four wore flight suits. He aimed and squeezed the trigger, knocking down the closest of the runners. Using Kentucky windage, he estimated he had a range of about four hundred meters.

The camouflaged men kept moving, and the four in flight suits climbed ladders to mount the F-14 Tomcats, which, Cartwright and Glassman knew, carried full weapons loads of Sidewinders and Sparrows. Cartwright fired three rounds and cursed. The planes lay just outside his effective rifle range.

"Listen," Glassman hissed.

In the distance, faint but growing louder, came the hollow chopping of Huey helicopters. Cartwright made them out as specks on the pale blue horizon. They became darker, larger, and louder.

"Well, we got cavalry," he said.

"Or more Indians," Glassman said, firing at the terrorist gun that kept him pinned down. "What the hell is the target? Are we at war?"

The helicopters touched down in the parking lot behind the assembly buildings. Four squads of air police piled out, hitting the ground running. They fanned out and moved to cover positions.

Cartwright heard the engines of the Tomcats turning over and watched the fighter jets taxi to the end of the runway. As the engines whined, building RPMs, Cartwright saw a red flare sail lazily into the sky from the other end of the runway. He heard the *whop-whop-whop*ping sound of yet another Huey helicopter. It zoomed over his head and dropped down in front of the main Mercury hangar.

The Huey whirred a few feet above the ground. It was a "slick" model with its doors removed and a faded AIR AMERICA logo painted on its tail boom. Cartwright looked up and saw Dick Moody at the controls. Several men ran forward and began climbing into the whirring chopper as two men gave covering fire. One of them was McCain. The other was Avadek.

Adam Glassman, seeing Avadek, screamed a primitive cry of recognition and hatred. "It's him!"

He fired wildly, missing Avadek and McCain, who climbed aboard the hovering helicopter. The Huey was rising off the apron as Cartwright slammed a fresh clip home and snapped his bolt.

He flipped his fire selector to rock 'n' roll and fired a long burst into the helicopter's rear rotor, bringing the chopper crashing a dozen feet to the ground like a wounded animal. Miraculously, Avadek climbed the torn metal of the wreckage and continued to fire his assault rifle. Glassman ran forward, firing at him, but the Iranian slipped away behind the mass of twisted metal. Two other men inside the wreck, one of them McCain, crawled out and began to run across the field. Cartwright slammed his last clip home and dropped the other man like a running deer. McCain vanished behind a building.

A shuddering mass of metal creaked and groaned as the huge door of the Mercury complex cranked open. Rolling forward slowly, but gathering speed, was the grim black manta-ray shape of the Stealth bomber. The hijacked Stealth was wheeling forward onto the airstrip. The great black wing rolled down the runway on its tricycle-carriage landing gear, gleaming dully like some prehistoric reptilian bird seeking prey.

The renegade Tomcat escort fighters gathered speed rolling down the secondary airstrip that flared off into the desert. The Stealth edged forward, its engines generating tremendous heat waves that shimmered from the tarmac.

"Son of a bitch," Cartwright whispered, and rushed forward to the downed chopper. He ran round the Plexiglas windshield of the cockpit and climbed atop the wreckage. Richard Moody lay trapped inside, still strapped to the pilot seat, dazed and bleeding amid twisted controls and sparking wires. He looked up at Cartwright and moved his lips soundlessly.

"Dick, what have you done?"

"Glenda. The bastards were CIA. They took Glenda," Moody groaned. "Said it was a Company job."

"You asshole, *I'm* CIA," Cartwright snapped. "These sons of bitches are rogues. Glenda got away from 'em."

Moody, bleeding through the nose, brightened for an

instant and smiled. Then he doubled in pain, clutching involuntarily in the mess of straps. Cartwright smelled fuel. He pulled up to lower himself into the cockpit. He heard a snapping spark and smelled rubber burning.

"Get out, Scotty," Moody gasped. "It's gonna go."

"Fuck you, Dick. Try to hit your release buckle."

"Forget it. I'm done," the pilot grunted. "Help Glenda and tell her I'm sorry."

The gasoline caught silently first, then made a *whump*ing sound that blew Cartwright backward off the chopper. He stumbled away and caught a blast of heat as the Huey blew, sending a cloud of black smoke and flame over the runway. Cartwright assumed that Moody had passed out because he heard no screams. Cradling his rifle, he ran back toward the plant complex.

The gunfire had slowed, and Cartwright spotted numerous air police in blue berets fanning out across the plant grounds, their rifles at port arms. He ran toward a knot of blue-suiters who were standing over two men in handcuffs lying spread-eagle on the ground. A burly chief master sergeant was supervising, and he snapped a businesslike salute as Cartwright approached. The sergeant wore the silver parachutist wings of an air force commando.

"What have we got, Sergeant?"

"These birds," said the massive sergeant, holding Avadek and McCain by the collar as Glassman ran up to the group. "We knew they weren't friendlies."

"Do you know 'em?" Cartwright asked Glassman as the major caught his breath. In one motion Glassman was on his knees, punching Avadek in the face.

"I've got Geneva Convention," Avadek shouted as Glassman pummeled him. Laughing, he spat and said, "You are dead American assholes, all of you. Dead!"

As the major gave Avadek a wicked kick, Cartwright grabbed Glassman from behind and pulled him away. "You can't do that, Major," he grunted, hoisting Glassman by his collar.

"We aren't arresting this son of a bitch, General. It's

war!" Glassman shouted. "You want me to read him *Miranda?*"

"Goddammit, it may be Armageddon if we don't work something out fast. We got no time for old scores," Cartwright shouted. "I want you to walk away. I mean it. Walk away!"

Glassman looked at the general, his face contorted with a dozen remembered torments. He looked at the man on the ground in disposable handcuffs, his torturer. And then he followed Cartwright's order and walked away.

"Sergeant," Cartwright shouted.

"Yes, sir."

"Drag that piece of white trash you got over here to me."

The sergeant complied, picking up McCain like a bag of cement. McCain, lying on his back with his arms thrust behind him, grinned at Cartwright.

"You know me, Scotty," he said. "I'm a Company man."

"You used to be, you son of a bitch. Do you know what you've done?"

"Photo recon for a friend," McCain said, spitting blood as he spoke. "Langley will clear it up."

"The hell you say. You just mighta lit the fuse on World War Three."

McCain leaned forward, close enough so his foul breath was in Cartwright's face, and said, "Do yourself a favor and let me go, General."

"Fat chance," said Cartwright.

McCain grinned, stomped the air force sergeant's foot with his heavy boot, and sweep-kicking him to the ground, ran serpentine down the flight line. Cartwright raised his rifle, drew a bead, and shot three rounds, dropping McCain so the big blond man fell to his knees and then onto his back. The commando sergeant ran forward to McCain's slumped body. McCain lay still, then raised his head, grinned, and spat in the sergeant's face. The sergeant knocked him out with a single powerful blow. Looking at the wounded renegade, the sergeant pulled off his beret and applied pressure to McCain's bleeding leg.

"General," he called out, "his leg wound's a gusher. You must've hit an artery. He won't last."

"Triage him, Sergeant," Cartwright yelled back. "We need him. We need some answers."

The sergeant nodded and kept the pressure on the leg wound. McCain came to groggily. He grimaced at the sergeant and, dying, said, "I'm killed, you stupid son of a bitch."

"Sergeant," Cartwright shouted, "is he dead?"

"Yes, sir!"

"Then run your fastest man on over to that Corvette yonder. I got a cellular phone there, and I need it."

As the runner returned with the phone, the general punched the flash traffic speed dialer and picked up Benson on the Los Angeles secure line for the FBI.

"Don't talk, Benson. Listen. I need a patch to NORAD at Cheyenne Mountain," the general ordered. "They will have to handle the White House relay. When you ring off, move your communications base to the Federal Emergency Command Center in Los Angeles."

"Sounds like your party," Benson said. "Your line is clear for NORAD."

The earpiece crackled with static for an agonizing two minutes, then a bell tone rang once and a voice came on the line. "This is Armacost."

"General Armacost, this is Scotty Cartwright at Plant thirty-six. Do you authenticate my voice?"

"I authenticate. What is your situation?"

"You will open a line with the White House immediately, and authorize a continental scramble for all TAC forces," Cartwright said. "Additionally, you will move SAC up to highest defensive condition. Do you read me, over?"

"On whose authority? I say again, what is your situation?" demanded the taut voice on the other line.

"My authority. Authenticate with the president. One of our bombers is loose. And God help every one of us."

Lieutenant General Kenneth Armacost knew Cartwright well enough to realize the retired astronaut did not waste words. He began issuing orders to execute a DefCon-4 alert.

LAX AIRPORT PLAZA

Supervising Agent Benson dragged Tatiana into the room with Romanovich. He pulled her in by her hair and threw her, handcuffed, to the floor. Then he punched Romanovich to the ground. The other agents in the room watched Benson in horror, but they made no move to stop him.

"You bastards!" he shouted at the Russians. "You want a war? I'll give you a war, goddammit. I'll put the boots to you, and you'll be the first casualties."

"What madness is this?" Romanovich demanded, attempting to roll clear of Benson's kicks and punches. The woman cringed and assumed the fetal position.

"You stole the goddamned plane, did you? What could you have been thinking of?" Benson yelled. "There is a nuclear bomber airborne with a hijack crew flying it!"

"We stole no plane," Romanovich gasped. "We stole plans."

Benson slapped the Soviet agent with his hard open hand. "Then, asshole, tell me this. Who has the goddamned plane?"

"It was the Arabs," Tatiana Ivanovna hissed. "This is KGB's failure."

"Say nothing, woman," Romanovich ordered.

"It was the KGB," she said, speaking to Benson. "I am not KGB. I am Soviet military intelligence."

One of the agents whistled and said, "The bitch is GRU."

"This operation was a KGB failure," she groaned. "Arabs, I don't know, Persian terrorists. If the plane is gone, they took it. They stole Stealth plans from a KGB courier in Beirut."

Benson grabbed Tatiana, lifted her, and threw her back on the bed. He held her by the fabric of her blouse and breathed hard in her face, baring his teeth. "What are you telling me, bitch?" he snarled.

"This must be terrorists flying your plane. They took diagrams, operational plans, weapons delivery procedure, everything," she gasped.

"Do you know what this means?" the agent said, his voice almost pleading. "You may have started a war with the United States."

"Call Soviet embassy immediately. Demand conference call with your president and Ambassador Grelnikov. No one else. I must talk with them."

"You whore," Romanovich shouted. "You were GRU?"

"You are a fool, Volodya," Tatiana said, shaking her hair and attempting to ease her hurried breathing. "All Chekists are fools."

14

FLIGHT

D-Day 1004 Hours Local

Captain Mehdi Mahan lifted the pickle-shaped HOTAS control stick and nudged the throttle forward, pushing the bomber so it shuddered slightly as it passed Mach 1. He marveled at the responsiveness of the Stealth bomber's fly-by-wire controls. A plane that looked as though it might not fly at all cut through the high, thin air like a sharp knife. He had never dreamed of flying such an aircraft. Now, looking ahead through the Plexiglas bubble of the cockpit that formed the leading edge of the wing, he felt as though he were flying straight into the future as the bomber pushed effortlessly through the clouds.

Ali Rezai looked at him wonderingly as the machine they took climbed toward the heavens, where the sky turned a deep azure hue. "Why do you climb, Mehdi?" he asked. "We should get to low level to avoid the radar."

"This plane will avoid radar at any altitude," Mehdi said, smiling. "As the holy men would say, it is satanic."

"We have no fear of radar?"

"No radar will find us," Mehdi said, scanning the layout of computer-generated graphics on the panel of display screens. He was searching for his escort of hijacked Tomcats. He then monitored the head-up display screen and found the pair of dancing holograms he was searching for. The Tomcats were close by.

"We need only worry about American interceptor aircraft, which we will avoid by flying to maximum altitude and setting an evasive course," he said.

"We did it," Ali Rezai murmured with quiet awe. "We took the American plane."

"The American leaders put all their faith in technology," Mehdi declared. "We believe in what people can do. You, Ali, and I have flown more years in combat than any pilots flying in the world today, do you know that?"

Mehdi pushed the throttle forward and marveled at the airspeed indicators that showed the aircraft accelerating beyond Mach 2. He whistled. "You remember what the American trainers told us," he said. "They were wiser than their Pentagon masters. They said the bravest, best pilots will win. We are those pilots."

"I need directions for a heading," said Hossein, methodically exploring his display panels and instrumentation as Hashemi familiarized himself with the aircraft's defensive and offensive avionics systems.

"The immediate course heading is for the Gulf of Mexico," Mehdi said. "We will adjust course after in-flight refueling."

"Why set course for Mexico?" asked Ali.

Mehdi smiled and said, "By crossing into Mexico, we avoid sweeps of American continental defense aircraft. We fly by means of stealth."

The men inside the supersonic craft barely heard the quiet whine of the bomber's engines.

"The adjusted course will take us across the North Atlantic and North Africa. I will submit coordinates on arrival at our first destination. We've got to find our flying fueling station and hope Avadek was right about its location."

PURSUIT

"What is your situation, General?" the president asked calmly, his unmistakable voice clear through the satellite transmission.

Standing in the chaotic midst of medics, stretchers, sirens, running men, and ambulances arriving at Plant 36, Cartwright spoke loudly and evenly, "Simply, sir, an armed Stealth bomber has been stolen. Real time elapsed by my watch is four minutes."

"Who did this?" asked the president.

"It might be the Russians. The attacking force hijacked a pair of Tomcats. Besides us, only Iran flies Tomcats, but it still could be a Soviet endgame."

"Your advice?"

"Move to DefCon-4. Then attempt continental AWACS surveillance and be ready to move, sir. By that I mean you must move the White House to preserve the chain of command. You must assume, sir, that you are the target."

"You said *attempt* AWACS surveillance, General," the president said.

"Mr. President, the Stealth bomber will be a needle in a haystack. It is designed as a radar-evasive aircraft. There is no countersystem once it is airborne."

There was a pause on the other end of the line. Cartwright believed that he heard a deep sigh from the commander in chief who sat in the Oval Office on the other side of the continent.

"Scotty, shall I activate the Looking Glass?" the president asked, referring to his airborne command and control platform operated from a Boeing 747.

"You must decide on that, sir. But once you're aboard

Looking Glass, you will lose hot-line communications with the Russians. It's a tough call."

"What are you doing, Scotty?"

Cartwright looked at the smoke, wreckage, and bodies that surrounded him. He looked at Glassman, who was directing ambulance traffic on the flight line, and he looked down the runway at the Advanced Tactical Fighter prototype.

"Nothing I can do here, sir," he replied. "You'll need the joint chiefs and NORAD to manage the scramble. I am in pursuit."

"Scotty, I didn't hear you," the president said through a sudden patch of static. "Please repeat."

"Gotta go, Mr. President. Cartwright out."

Cartwright handed the cellular phone and his M-16 to the sergeant who was guarding Avadek and ran toward Glassman.

"Can you still fly that thing?" Cartwright yelled, pointing to the bullet-shaped fighter prototype.

Glassman looked at Cartwright incredulously. "Are you crazy?" he said.

Cartwright pointed at the manacled Iranian lying on the tarmac. Avadek, unshaken by the chaos around him, smirked at Cartwright and Glassman as though he were Iago, exposed but unbowed.

"We did it, you know," he said. "You Americans did not think we could. But we did."

"That son of a bitch took one of our planes, Major," Cartwright shouted. "You gonna let him?"

Glassman looked at the ground, then at the empty skies where the Stealth bomber flew undeterred.

Cartwright grabbed the major by his collar. "Let me put it this way, hotshot. Can you save your country and maybe what's left of your whole fuckin' family?"

"General, as God is my witness, I don't know if I've got the hands or the eyes. I don't want to fly and fail. Why not you?"

"Because I'm half-blind, goddammit!" Cartwright shouted. "If it's not you, it's over. That's all."

"Blind?"

"I got no peripheral vision. I got no right eyeball. Now, what about it? Are you combat-fatigued, or are you able?"

"Can you read a radar scope?" Glassman asked urgently.

"Yup."

"I need a weapons officer."

"You got it. Let's go."

Cartwright beckoned two pilots who had been helping the beefy sergeant guard Avadek. At his order they hastily clambered out of their flight suits so that he and Cartwright could don them.

"Gimme yer bone domes," he ordered, and they tossed him their helmets.

Glassman raced toward the ATF fighter the way he had run during an Israeli air force scramble, with Cartwright close behind. They ran as though the fate of the world depended on how fast they reached the cockpit. They knew they were nearly six minutes late.

THE WHITE HOUSE

D-Day 1310 Hours Local EST

The president spread his hands on the rich hardwood of his desk and examined them. They trembled. He turned his chair so that he could survey the view he had come to love of the Washington Monument and the ring of flags that blew briskly in the wind on the Mall. The thousands of tourists that milled by every day, he knew, were his responsibility. He tried to imagine the monument and all the people gone in an instant but could not. He breathed deeply and turned to Madeline Murdoch.

"Let's review options, Madeline," he said.

"The Stealth bomber is carrying eighty gravity-release single-megaton bombs, sir," she said crisply. "Any one of them is the equivalent of nearly one thousand of the bombs used to destroy Nagasaki. The bomber's war load could end all life in an area the size of Great Britain."

"And they could be dropped anywhere," the president whispered.

"At Hiroshima and Nagasaki, people within two miles of ground zero survived," Murdoch said, dispassionately. "Any weapon measured in megatonnage will end all life within eight miles of the blast. At the eight-mile range, all those not vaporized will be burned severely. Their eyes would melt. Supposing the target were Washington, sir, the firestorms would consume the Virginia and Maryland suburbs."

"There's nearly a million people, Madeline."

"Yes, sir, that is anyone not moved to the hardened shelter of a command post. Those survivors would be people in the defense loop, sir."

"Define our defensive capabilities against such aerial attack."

"There are none, sir. President Nixon scrapped plans for defensive systems in Washington allowed under the ABM treaty. We must plan for the worst."

"Dr. Murdoch, establish the hot-line link with Moscow. Notify Defense and State and put them on a conference line on the gold phone. We'll need Dr. Farkash to interpret."

Since the early years of the Reagan administration, various upgrades in the communications link to Moscow had been installed. The Teletype printers at the Pentagon across the Potomac still functioned, with each side sending greetings several times a day. But in addition to the printers, the president did actually have a red phone with a direct voice link to his Kremlin counterpart. The phone was carefully maintained, unlike the days of the Kennedy administration when a decorator for the First Lady had the red phone removed because its color clashed with the desk.

Dr. Farkash, a deputy to the national security adviser, entered the Oval Office looking puzzled. Farkash had never received such a hurried summons. He was a Hungarian expatriate who had fled Budapest in 1956. He prided himself on his mastery of Slavic languages, precisely because they were so different from his native Magyar.

"How can I be of help, Mr. President?" the interpreter asked, bowing formally like a man of old Europe.

"Dr. Farkash, quite simply, this is the most important conversation that has taken place in this office, ever," said the president. "You will be in direct communication with Secretary Kirilenko. Any mistake of nuance, any misapprehension of my stated meaning, could very well mean the end of civilization."

Dr. Farkash nodded, unruffled.

"It goes without saying that any account of this conversation stays in this room if we should succeed. If we fail, it doesn't matter."

Madeline Murdoch held high the gold phone, signaling that the secretaries of the Departments of Defense and State were on the line. The president pressed the conference button on his interoffice phone so that he would not have to hold two receivers.

"Boys," he addressed them, "we are in a hell of a mess."

"Mr. President, the air force has been alerted, and there is a continentwide TAC scramble in progress," said Robert MacLaine, the secretary of defense. "General Armacost has given me a few details, but not the big picture."

"Mr. President," the secretary of state said testily, "I must beg your pardon, but I am in the dark on this thing. This is, again, a matter of not keeping State informed."

"We have Moscow on the line," Professor Murdoch said, lifting the red phone and handing the receiver to Dr. Farkash.

The president pushed the button on his own console and listened as the linguist made the preliminary authentication. A moment later the leader of the Soviet Union came on the line.

"Kto eta," he said, asking to whom he spoke, then identifying his own designated interpreter.

"Ya Lazlo Farkash," the interpreter said, then explained he would speak on behalf of the president of the United States.

"Dr. Farkash, put this in the plainest terms possible," the president ordered. "One of our nuclear bombers has been stolen by a hostile power. You must tell Secretary Kirilenko that any nuclear detonation on the territory of the United States will be considered an act of war fomented by the Soviet Union."

Farkash translated, and he believed that he heard a gasp at the other end of the line to Moscow. He looked at the president and listened.

"He says this is not possible, Mr. President."

"Tell him we have people in custody whom we suspect of having initiated this operation, and that they are Soviet citizens, espionage agents of the KGB."

More hurried conversation followed, with Farkash scribbling notes on a small pad, then turning again to look at the president. "These agents you speak of, Secretary Kirilenko admits they exist. But he says they were sent to steal technical data on the Stealth, not an actual plane. He gives you his word."

"Tell the secretary as bluntly as you can, Doctor, that I do not believe him."

Farkash spoke, delivering the president's message accurately but without emotion. Then, turning to the president, the interpreter said, "The secretary tells you that he speaks the truth. But it is possible a third power, a Middle East country, is involved. The KGB team was sent to repeat its recovery of data already liberated from a California munitions plant, which was lost in the Middle East."

"Already liberated. Good God."

Farkash translated. There was no response from the Kremlin to the president's exclamation.

"Tell the secretary, tell him that the theft of such materials could be considered an act of war in itself. Ask the secretary what he would do if he were in my place," the president said, barely containing his anger.

Farkash gave the message and listened. He scribbled hastily, breathed deeply, and read from his notation. "The secretary beseeches you in the name of peace not to misinterpret his suggestion. Allow the armed forces of the Soviet Union to assist in any way possible in bringing down this plane."

"Inform the secretary," the president snapped, "that any appearance of Soviet aircraft within the airspace of the continental United States will be considered a hostile act."

Farkash translated and listened. He turned to the president. "The secretary suggests you use the AWACS aircraft to direct the air forces of the Soviet Union in the Caribbean. They will follow your every instruction, and if the bomber is identified, it will be destroyed."

"Tell him thanks for nothing. Oh, hell. No, don't tell him that, Farkash. Tell him we will consider the offer, but that our forces worldwide are being placed on maximum alert."

"Mr. President," Madeline Murdoch said urgently, "we don't have time to consider the secretary's offer. Either we go along, or we reject it and go on a war footing. We don't have any other alternative."

"So that's it," the president said, sighing and rubbing his forehead. "It's peace or war, and maybe the devastation of American cities. And it was those bastards' fault in the first place. Their offer could still be a trick."

"That is certainly possible, sir," Murdoch said. "But I think if they were going to attack, it would be with a massive strike, not a rogue bomber."

"There is no precedent for this," the president said, his voice quavering for the first time.

"Sir, actually such a precedent does exist," Madeline Murdoch said. "During the Cuban crisis, Dr. Guevara urged Castro to seize the Soviet missiles. The Soviet ambassador informed Castro of the likelihood of his assassination if any attempt were made to interfere with removal of the missiles. Our situation could be similar. An unknown third power could be seeking nuclear parity by taking the bomber."

"Secretary Kirilenko is awaiting your answer," Farkash said.

"Tell the secretary we accept his offer. In the name of peace," the president said bitterly.

"The secretary says he thanks you for your understanding and goodwill."

"Thank the secretary also, Dr. Farkash. And tell him that if the bombing begins here, it will likely not end here."

The president looked out his window toward the windswept mall. A bus full of schoolchildren was unloading at the Washington Monument. It was time to move the command to the Situation Room.

ABOARD THE ATF

D-Day 1015 Hours Local

General Scott Cartwright eased himself into the backseat of the Advanced Tactical Fighter prototype, connecting radio leads and oxygen hoses as the Plexiglas cockpit bubble clunked down. When the ground crew disengaged the air crew boarding ladders, Major Adam Glassman punched a single button that gave the experimental jet a hot start like a B-1 bomber. Its advanced-design engines ignited with a huge hollow roar, and Glassman taxied onto the main runway.

"Gimme the short course, Major," Cartwright ordered as he surveyed the array of consoles, indicators, and cathode-ray tube screens in front of him. As he hastily checked for popped circuit breakers, the general listened to Glassman's heavy breathing over the internal mike that connected them.

"Sir, have you flown the Tomcat?" Glassman asked calmly, his breathing slowing as the jet rolled down the tarmac, gaining speed by the second.

"Boy, I've flown everything from a Focke Wulf to a Foxbat. You just give me the systems briefing, and I'll make 'er work."

"Roger that, General. Pretend you're in an F-14 and consider the systems to be analogous," Glassman said as the plane left the desert flightline and soared into its element, its engines blazing.

"Okay, so I got a Phoenix radar system to contend with here," Cartwright declared, pushing the weapons control system knob to standby and also the lighted button that cooled the electronics on the radar.

"It's not exactly the Phoenix system, General, but it's similar," Glassman replied as he edged the aircraft into a steep climb, leaving the San Gabriel Mountains and Plant 36 behind in the distance.

"It's actually an entirely new generation of avionics, General," Glassman said, adopting his briefing manner. "This system backs up the newest missile in the inventory, the advanced medium-range air-to-air missile."

"AMRAAM, huh? Well, hell. That's good news, anyway. We'll maybe get a rifle shot at the bastards. I hear the AMRAAM's got its own little radar as good as the one on the F-18 Hornet."

"It can effect a kill within ten miles of target with its own radar system, independent of the fighter's target acquisition equipment. But we're seeking a radar-elusive aircraft. To kill them, we've got to find them first, sir. I'm afraid we'll need visual contact. It's a needle in a haystack."

"One problem at a time. Just one more thing, Major. Have we got a gun?"

"By your left knee, sir. We've got a Vulcan rotary cannon that fires uranium-tipped bullets. This aircraft has a lot of lift and carries a big weapons load, so you've got nine hundred rounds. You've also got a Phoenix missile complement. There's Sparrows, even a couple of Sidewinders. And General, I've got no idea in bloody hell where we're going."

"Hell, son, I thought you had more sense than that. Point this bird to the border. We're goin' to Mexico."

Obediently Glassman edged the nose of the aircraft to level flight at fifty thousand feet, banked slightly to starboard, and pointed the plane on a southerly heading.

"I'll bite, sir. Why Mexico?"

"I just figure if I were a Chicom bandit in a MiG-17 with a sky full of Sabrejets on my tail, I'd haul ass for the Yalu River and denied territory above the Thirty-eighth Parallel. These boys won't do any different. Now let's goose it."

As the sleek fighter blazed across the skies over the cactus wastelands, Cartwright methodically manipulated the stick in the cockpit center to move the ATF's nose-mounted antenna across the spectrum of sectors he was scanning in search of the black plane and its deadly escorts. The green screen glowed in front of him, telling him nothing. Fearing the battle might be lost before a shot could be fired, he pointed the radar antenna to look-up position, look-down, and then straight ahead.

Suddenly his identify friend-foe panel alerted him. Cartwright's heart raced, then sank. It was the first time in his flying career he bemoaned the sighting of friends. He monitored a formation of F-4 Phantoms, piloted by the Air National Guard, plugging along just above Mach, trying to catch up to the ATF.

"This is Zulu Flight leader to Eagle-Rampant," the F-4 leader announced. "We understand you are in pursuit of a bandit, over."

"Have you seen the black plane?" Cartwright shouted into his mike.

"Negative, Eagle. But my backseater did eyeball a pair of Tomcats that declined to identify and authenticate. From what NORAD tells us, they ain't from Miramar Naval Air Station."

"Cut the bull and give me a fix on your last sighting, Zulu," Cartwright demanded.

"Roger. According to your present heading, Eagle,

you are already in pursuit," the Zulu Flight leader replied. "Can we assist?"

"That's negative, but thanks, Zulu One. Maintain your patrol sector and patch into NORAD. I got a message for 'em."

"Roger, Eagle."

"Message follows. Alert NORAD that Eagle-Rampant is in hot pursuit into international airspace. Also, notify Cheyenne Mountain to light up the board with TAC scrambles across our southern border, to include all air bases and naval air stations assigned patrol duty over the Gulf of Mexico. Do you roger, over?"

"This is Zulu One, roger, that's a good copy. Anything else, over?"

"Yeah. Pursuant to the alert order, they better ground all Tomcats in the inventory. Anything we can see with that configuration is likely to be a bandit, over."

"Roger, Eagle. Good hunting. Zulu One out."

With his good remaining eye, Cartwright peered forward toward Glassman in the front seat. The general was gaining confidence in the major's aircraft handling.

"General, you must be aware that if we are sighted, the Mexicans will likely scramble some of their Freedom Fighters."

"The F-5's a dandy little plane. But shoot, son, when's the last time we got worried about the Mexican air force? We gotta kill us a Stealth bomber."

"Any suggestions?"

"We gotta find the Tomcats. They're the key."

"What if the Tomcats are a diversion?"

"No way they'd go to the trouble to steal that package without giving it escort. What we've got to figure is whether the bomber is tasked for fight or flight. It's either gonna drop its eggs, or it's on a flyaway mission for later use. If it's gonna fight, we may already be too late."

"And if it's flight?"

"Then there's a tanker out there somewhere. If we find the tanker, we'll get a crack at our rifle shot. From a tactical standpoint, we've got outstanding visibility today, Major."

"General," Glassman said, his voice crackling in the mike, "I've got nothing but empty sky ahead of me on my display screens. I don't mind telling you I'm goddamned scared."

"There's no time for that attitude, Major. Most fighter jocks would give their left nut to be flying this plane."

"I'm not afraid to die, General. But failure terrifies me."

"Tell me something, Major," Cartwright said quietly as he scanned the glowing screen in front of him. "In your best military opinion, can this aircraft catch a brace of Tomcats with a two-hundred-fifty mile lead?"

"Sir, compared to this plane, the Tomcat's a hog," Glassman said.

"That's better, son. Keep your eye on the HUD and watch your six. I'll find the bastards, and you kill 'em."

"Yes, sir."

The ATF prototype zoomed along on its southerly course, racing through cloudless skies that carried the riders of the Apocalypse just beyond the horizon. Like a grand master deciding on a chess move, Cartwright considered the options, moving the radar antenna housed in the stubby nose of the ATF across the search quadrants so that its powerful beam would search the sky for the black plane. As he maneuvered the stick feverishly, the antenna would look up, look down, look sideways, and look straight ahead.

ABOARD THE STEALTH

Hossein, the assigned Stealth flight engineer, entered a new series of digital commands into the STB-1's navigational boxes. Then he cross-checked them against the coordinates given him by Captain Mahan. Something in him made his breathing quicken and his chest swell with pride as he handled the sophisticated equipment. It was wondrous machinery, and he was master of it. For a fleeting second he relaxed in the deep seat, which was more comfortable than the Phantom and the Tomcat ejection seats. As the Stealth bomber cruised sixty thousand feet above the Mexican desert state of Chihuahua, Hossein realized all the cockpit fittings of the STB-1 were built for the long haul of transcontinental flight.

"Our data is verified, Old Man," he told Mehdi. "If the serpent Avadek did not lie to us, tanker rendezvous should be established about three hundred nautical miles east of Mexico City, over the Mexican Gulf."

"I think Avadek was the father of lies, but he would not bend the truth in this case," Mehdi said. "We will make our rendezvous with the tanker. The question is, will he know what we are when we appear?"

Ali Rezai, Hashemi, and Hossein laughed nervously.

"We have come a long way," Ali Rezai said as he monitored the bright-colored display of CRT screens that held his attention in the co-pilot's seat. "I did not think we could do it."

"All things have been made possible for the men of Green Flight through bravery and brains," said Mehdi, who was not given to making speeches. "I am so proud of you brothers and fighters. You are true fliers. We go home covered in glory."

Grinning proudly, Ali Rezai never took his eyes from the screens he monitored. He wondered how a nation as powerful as the United States of America could develop such machinery and then, through carelessness or greed, allow it to be stolen away. All of the on-screen information corresponded accurately to the plans and flight manuals that had been provided by Avadek. The thief at Mercury had done his work well.

"Activate the laser radar," Mehdi instructed Ali Rezai. "We need a readout from all points on the clock."

The laser radar, designed to make a maximum information survey while keeping its radar signal reduced to the narrowest-possible spectrum of observability, beamed its signal, altering for the briefest moment the shield of invisibility that cloaked the Stealth plane. Computer imagery on the CRT conjured up a layout of the signal's data.

On the pulse doppler look-down radar console, Ali Rezai quickly identified the Tomcat escort interceptors piloted by Sidi and Reza. They were flying in a welded-wing formation twenty-five thousand feet below the Stealth bomber's high-level cruising altitude. One hundred miles ahead on the horizon, the radar's signal fired back the reassuring shape of the tanker from the homeland, which was cruising at thirty-five thousand feet over the Mexican coast, near the port city of Vera Cruz. The computer-generated image fed back by the laser signal was so distinct that it showed everything except the blue-and-green Trans-Continent Airways paint job and markings that disguised the support aircraft beckoned from the homeland the previous night using McCain's UHF transmitter.

"Give me one more laser sighting for a completed verification," Mehdi ordered.

"Should we risk that?" Hossein asked as he charted the formation's progress on the inertial navigation system's lighted computer display. "The more we operate on passive systems, the safer we will be from detection."

"Little brother, I want a smooth refueling operation," Mehdi said decisively. "I feel we are safe. Let's take another look."

Ali Rezai complied and activated another laser radar signal. He tracked the screen and verified position on the loitering tanker, and then his eyes darted to the bottom of his display. "There is an intruder aircraft on my screen, Mehdi," he said urgently.

"What range and type?"

"Range is one hundred fifty miles and closing. There is no classification for it in the computer's data bank. But it is, without doubt, an American interceptor."

"What speed?"

"It is flying in excess of Mach 2," Ali said, his voice

rising. "It is tracking Sidi and Reza. It is firing a powerful radar signal."

For a second Mehdi stared at his co-pilot. Then he tapped his external microphone pedal and broke the radio silence maintained since the raid, only an hour past but now a seeming eternity behind.

"Green Flight elements Hot Dog and Tough Guy," Mehdi said in the smooth English that was the international language of pilots. "Be aware you are the target of hostile pursuit. Break right and engage. Green Flight leader is continuing to rendezvous point."

Silently acknowledging the Green Flight leader's emergency transmission, the Tomcat fighters piloted by Sidi and Reza rolled and dropped away, turning to face their pursuer.

ABOARD THE ATF

Cartwright blinked. In the space of that blink, he found what he was looking for on the green screen, which was sweeping its powerful beam in the long-distance range-while-search mode.

"Found the bogeys, twelve on the clock and high at one hundred ten miles."

"General, are you certain the bogeys are not third-country neutrals?" Glassman asked urgently. "We don't want to down a Mexican plane."

"Fairly certain, son. My system verifies a Phoenix missile separation from both bandits. They're after our ass. We are under attack."

"Roger," Glassman said, initiating a steep climbing maneuver similar to the one Cartwright panicked him with in the Starfighter. Through the climb, he kept his right hand steady on the fly-by-wire hand control. "I am evading."

As he maneuvered, the hostile acquisition tone buzzed insistently, raising the blood pressure and adrenaline level in both men. Glassman engaged the afterburner in a nearly vertical climb.

"We lost one and found one," Cartwright said coldly, noting that one of the missiles was still locked on approach.

One missile sailed by, thousands of feet below, its guidance system failing the final factory test of air combat. The other, still sounding the hostile tone, headed toward the ATF fighter's nose and intakes.

"Engaging gun detector mode," Cartwright said, flipping the knob that would allow the aircraft's Vulcan cannon to track independently.

"Taking my snapshot," Glassman said, firing a two-hundred-round spray of uranium-tipped bullets and watching the dancing holograph of his heads-up display to check for result. A yellow airborne explosion twelve hundred meters to starboard ended the missile threat.

"You work close, Major."

"Wouldn't want it any closer, General. Status of bandits?"

"They're maneuvering for another shot."

"We've got to fight, sir."

"Negative, son. We've gotta sink the *Bismarck*. Give chase."

"The Tomcats are the immediate threat."

"Don't argue, Major. Goose her and go. We can't waste time and fuel dogfighting. The Stealth bomber is out there somewhere in the same sky. The Tomcats will return to their mother ship."

Cartwright popped the radar system into the shorter-distance track-while-scan mode, watching the hostile aircraft maneuver as Glassman hit the afterburner again and blazed across the Mexican sky. For a brief moment the bandit Tomcats were within range to fight, but they lost the opportunity when Glassman lit the twin candles of the afterburners and zoomed past Mach 2 on wet thrust, leaving them behind. Altering his search mode momentarily, Cartwright spotted a large blip on the screen.

"Bingo. We got us a tanker loitering off the gulf."

"It could be an airliner, sir."

"I'll bet you a doughnut it's the bandits' flying Texaco," Cartwright said. "Let's nail it."

"Not without a visual ID! We're not the goddamn Russians, sir."

Glassman accelerated the ATF to the edge of its flight envelope, pushing the fighter off the edge of the Mexican coastline. He crossed above the cresting waves of the gulf, where schools of flying fish leapt, ignorant of the combat above. The silhouette of a commercial plane appeared, first in the heads-up display, then in Glassman's line of vision.

"My God, it is an airliner," Glassman cried, spotting the green-blue commercial paint job of an American carrier.

"Wag your wings and give 'er a flyby, Adam," Cartwright ordered. "Give 'er a closer look."

"Trans-Continent Airways plane, this is Air Force Eagle-Rampant. Identify your flight number and destination, over," Glassman demanded on the external radio frequency as the ATF pulled even with the airliner.

A few seconds passed without a response. Then the pilot answered, "This is Trans-Continent Airways Flight one-five-five-zero. We are on course for Mexico City. What is the problem, over?"

Glassman strained for a sight of the commercial pilot in the airliner cockpit. The pilot's tone of voice was neutral. His English was proper, but not American.

"Drop down, Adam. I want to see something," Cartwright ordered. The jet dropped back and descended two hundred feet.

"That airliner is trailing a fuel boom, Major," the general shouted on the internal mike. "It's the Stealth bomber's ticket to home base. Nail the sumbitch!"

Glassman unhesitatingly triggered the Vulcan, exploding the tanker's port engines, tearing off its wing and sending it in a fiery metallic shower into the Gulf of Mexico thirty-five thousand feet below.

"God forgive me if we were wrong," Glassman said.

"Stay frosty, partner. We're on the track," Cartwright

said, scanning the horizon with his single sharp eye. "Watch the sky and keep your powder dry. We'll snare the bastard yet."

ABOARD THE STEALTH

Fifteen miles northwest and twenty thousand feet above Cartwright and Glassman, the batlike ebony form of the Stealth bomber hovered, with Mehdi and Ali Rezai watching the passive detection display screens intently.

"The tanker was our passage home," Ali Rezai murmured. "What are we to do now?"

"The men in that plane will kill us if they can," Mehdi said. "They are men. Since we cannot go home, we must fight."

"But Mehdi," Hossein piped in, "this plane is a bomber, not a fighter."

"Then we must bomb."

"What are you saying?" Ali demanded.

"We need a target," Green Flight's commander said firmly.

"What do you mean?" Ali said, his voice rising.

"If we are shot down, our training, this mission, will have meant nothing," Mehdi said, gritting his teeth. "I will not allow it." He breathed deeply and sighed. "Take the plane to America."

"This is madness, Mehdi," Ali shouted.

"Do you realize what we have?" Mehdi growled, grabbing the younger man by the collar. "We ride the Apocalypse! We must use this opportunity or lose it."

Mehdi looked at his men and in an instant felt the certainty of a Bonaparte, a Genghis Khan, or an Alexander gazing to infinity and ruling everything within sight.

"Where to in America?" Hossein asked, casting his lot with the leader.

"The heart of America. Washington."

"Madness," whispered Ali.

"Strategy," Mehdi hissed back. "If we survive, we will land and refuel while America reels. Then we will fly home as masters, not slaves. We will be patriots. We will rule."

The co-pilot stared in awe at his commander. The radio amplified the breathing in each man's oxygen mask. Hossein punched navigational coordinates into the STB-1's computer, and it fed him back a lighted path to Washington.

Rejoining the Tomcats near the refueling rendezvous point, the black plane waved its wings and changed course.

THE CARIBBEAN

Flight Captain Yuri Petrov turned the controls of the lumbering TU-95 Bear aircraft over to his co-pilot Misha and walked toward the rear of the plane where the radar operators were stationed. He reached into his bulky flight jacket for a small, tightly wrapped Cuban cigar, but then thought better of it. He loved the rich taste of the cigars but believed that smoking affected his visual acuity.

The massive Russian Bear bomber-reconnaissance plane roared over the Caribbean, its huge eight-bladed propellers giving off a radar signature that could be picked up all the way to Eglin Air Force base in Florida. But Petrov knew that his own exposure was not the problem. On highest orders, the Bear and every Soviet and Cuban aircraft available were scanning the skies in their sector.

"Our sector is clear from horizon to horizon," the senior radar operator told Petrov, never taking his eyes from the light sweeping a glowing array of scopes. "We have the MiG-29 squadron in its assigned zone. Otherwise nothing, Comrade Captain."

"You know what you are searching for, Sasha," Petrov said. "You are looking for a brace of imperalist fighters, Tomcat class. Make that identification, and I will make sure there is base leave for every man on the flight."

"It is curious, Comrade Captain," Sasha said, still monitoring the scopes. "The skies are empty of the imperialist's air forces. Never have I seen a sky without some of the aggressor aircraft on our tail."

"That makes your task easier. Most of the planes aloft should be ours. Just find the imperialists," Petrov said. "I don't know what the command wants, but they have made it clear this is not an exercise."

Petrov, inured to the deafening rumble of the Bear's engines, made his way forward to the cockpit. He found Misha grinning like a schoolboy, ever happy for his chance at the controls. Petrov seated himself behind the massive cockpit console and was again contemplating lighting his cigar when the radio crackled in his helmet.

"Comrade Captain Petrov," Sasha exclaimed excitedly. "I have identified the aggressor aircraft!"

"How many, Sasha?"

"It is as you said, two of the interceptors."

"Sasha, listen. This is orders. Search for a third aggressor."

"I am looking, Captain Petrov. There is no third aircraft."

"Give me their position," said Petrov, who had taught aircraft recognition courses at the Air Defense Command.

"Aggressor position, Captain, is three o'clock, high, and passing over at range of eighty kilometers. Speed indicated is well over Mach, Captain."

Scanning the horizon through the cockpit window to his rear, Petrov ordered Misha to climb. The aircraft lumbered aloft as Petrov mentally ticked away the seconds needed to make a visual identification. On the very edge of his vision he caught the silver, metallic glint of the Tomcats streaking across the sky. Then he saw the dark thing.

"Misha, do you see it?" he shouted excitedly. "There are three! It is not a flight of two. It is a line abreast formation of three, as they said."

"I see nothing, Captain Petrov," the co-pilot said

nervously, holding the controls as though he were a small child behind the wheel of a car. "I am flying."

"Fuck your mother, Misha. You have never flown. Radar, this is Petrov. Identify number of aggressor aircraft."

"It is two aircraft," Sasha replied through the crackling microphone. "Their separation is one thousand meters. Their general direction north and east at twelve on your clock, Captain Petrov."

"Three, damn it! It is three," Petrov growled. "Radar, alert fighter command to draw the MiG forces to Sector four-zero-three."

Petrov, his hawk's eyes zeroed on the gleaming horizon, watched the metallic glint disappear into a range of puffy cumulus cloud cover. He spotted the silver wings emerging, and then he saw the dark thing again.

"I was right, Misha," he gasped. "It was three, and I saw it."

Lieutenant Alexei Antonovich and his wingman banked left silently, then plunged their NATO-designated MiG-29 Fulcrum fighters into a slow, graceful roll, corkscrewing from an altitude of thirty thousand feet. On spotting the glints of metal moving away toward the horizon, they opened throttle to close. The wingman, Medvedev, followed his flight leader into a climb to assume maximum advantage in firing position. He confirmed his position on his look-down radar, the design of which had been liberated from a California aircraft firm.

"The target is identified," Antonovich reported by radio to the Air Defense Command complex outside Havana.

"Give visual identification of aircraft types and description, Red Flight leader," the metallic order returned over Antonovich's microphone.

"Two interceptors, American navy, and one unknown aircraft," Antonovich replied as he opened throttle in the climb.

"*Pazhalsta*, describe third aircraft," the voice ordered calmly.

"It is large and black, Comrade Commander. It looks like a bat."

"Red Flight leader, you are authorized to attack. Destroy the targets."

Antonovich and his wingman ignited their afterburners, pushing their powerful titanium swept-wing fighters past Mach 2 on their speed indicators to close with their quarry to a range of less than five kilometers. Antonovich gazed in wonder at the giant bat-winged aircraft. At nearly the same instant, the Soviet flight leader and his wingman pressed their weapons firing system buttons and let fly with a pair of Atoll air-to-air missiles.

Mehdi, confidently handling the controls of the hijacked Stealth bomber, looked in alarm at his display screens. A tone alerted him to the Atoll missiles streaking toward his flight. He opened throttle and dived at maximum acceleration, skimming the waves of the Caribbean. He hoped desperately that what he had read about his strange craft was true, that the baffles on the engines would help protect it from the homing mechanism of the heat-seeking missiles.

"Brothers, we must fight," he announced calmly over the microphone. "There are MiGs. They have engaged us."

Sidi, the Tomcat flight leader, spotted the Atoll missile attack at the same instant that Mehdi broadcast his warning. He rolled his interceptor and dived, then initiated a steep climb. The flesh on his face compressed deep into his skull as the G-pressure increased in the cockpit cabin to six times the force of gravity.

Sidi, who had downed a dozen MiG-21 fighters in aerial combat over Abadan, swung his swept-wing interceptor into a hard turn and faced his enemy, the pilot Antonovich, in head-on engagement. At a range of less than a mile, with the aircraft charging each other like locomotives, Sidi fired a burst from his M-61A Vulcan rotary cannon. The spray of rounds shredded the MiG, which burst into a shower of metal and flame.

"Allah Akbar," Sidi and his radar intercept officer shouted in unison as they soared aloft. "God is great."

"Sidi," the radar officer cried out as he scanned his screen, identifying the lumbering Bear aircraft flown by Captain Petrov and Misha, "there is a bandit aircraft at fifty kilometers, at four on the clock and low. It is a Russian reconnaissance plane. It is directing the attack."

"I will kill it," Sidi replied simply, firing a long-range Phoenix missile.

The Phoenix missile, with an advertised eighty-four percent kill ratio, sailed faultlessly toward the Bear reconnaissance plane.

Aboard the TU-95, Sasha looked at his scopes in horror. For a fleeting second he regretted the loss of the base leave to Havana; then as the missile ignited and ravaged the plane, he tumbled seaward in the exploded, burning aircraft.

Sidi broke off his attack and observed the wreckage of a second MiG floating in the waves. He realized that Reza had done his job and killed the other Russian plane. He glanced to the rear and saw his radar man busy at the screen in the cockpit seat. In another minute they would need to deactivate their radar beacon, which made them a visible target for all patrolling aircraft. But he wanted enough data to rejoin his wingman so that they could resume their mission to escort the holy plane to its ultimate destination, about thirty minutes' flight to their north and east.

The data of the air combat south of Florida was monitored by an AWACS sentry plane patrolling off the coast of North Carolina. The air force radar man shivered as he observed the Bear vanish from his screen.

"This is Blue Light operator," the staff sergeant announced. "We have bogeys, apparently one five zero miles northeast of the Cuban coast. It looks like they're mixing it up."

The data was relayed to the National Military Command Center in the Pentagon complex on the Potomac. An interservice task force of intelligence analysts quickly assessed the data, and their analysis was relayed to the joint chiefs. Air Force General Harold Kuhner read the flimsy and picked up his gold phone. When the president came on the line, Kuhner said, "My advice, sir, is that we activate the Looking Glass aircraft code-named 'Nightwatch' while we still retain that option."

"General, you realize if we do that, we lose the link with the Russians."

"I realize that, Mr. President. The moment has come, however, when we must preserve integrity of the command structure in the event of the worst case."

The president, suddenly angry, smashed his powerful hand on his desk. He looked at the illuminated maps surrounding him in the Situation Room and felt overwhelmed by the enormity of events. He looked at the array of sophisticated communications gear at his command and raged that it could do so little to save hundreds of millions of people.

"The fools!" the president told his advisers. "If they are lying, they are beginning the war. And if they are telling the truth and this was all a bloody botch, they are still probably beginning the war."

The red phone in the Situation Room rang, and Dr. Farkash and the national security adviser waited for the president to pick it up. The president's hand trembled as he reached for the phone. Simultaneously the interpreter picked up his own extension.

"Dr. Farkash," the president said almost gently, "inform the secretary that we have no choice other than to move to preserve the chain of command. Inform him also that we will act with maximum restraint, but that we will maintain all of our options as a sovereign nation in the event of attack."

"Yes, Mr. President," the translator said, observing the frantic look in the president's eyes.

15

WASHINGTON

D-Day 1515 Hours Local EST

In the musty upper-floor chambers of the National Press Club, Leon Chapman ambled over to the wire service printers that were spewing their budget of communiqués at fourteen hundred words per minute. He sampled the offerings of the Associated Press, the United Press International, and Reuters. And he sampled his bourbon.

David Willers, the *Flight World* reporter, walked over from the bar to join Chapman at the printer stands. In all his years of frequenting the rooftop club a block from the White House, Willers had never gotten a scoop. But he always found a few aging reporters ready to bend an elbow and spend an afternoon talking about how they spent their lives riding the Washington merry-go-round.

"What have you got?" Willers said.

"Some bullshit monitored from the radio listening post at Nicosia," Chapman replied. "Iran says they're gonna really lay it on the Iraqis this time."

"They're probably gonna start dropping kids with bombs strapped to 'em," Willers said sourly.

Chapman turned away from Willers at the sound of sirens outside the building. A couple of reporters ran from the bar to pop open the French windows and leaned out to look over the balcony below. Chapman and Willers ran to join them. They watched a convoy of black Cadillac limousines followed by Secret Service vans passing below on Fourteenth Street and turning onto Pennsylvania Avenue. As the convoy passed, Chapman heard the familiar whir of a Sikorsky helicopter engine. The green-and-white helicopter flew past the needle of the Washington Monument.

"What do you figure, Leon?" Willers asked.

"That's Marine Corps One. Something hellish big is up," Chapman grumbled as he pushed back through the small crowd and ran toward the elevator.

As he pressed the button to descend to street level, the wire service printer bells were ringing with terse paragraphs of bulletin traffic announcing the unannounced and unexplained departure of the president from the White House.

ABOARD THE ATF

The Advanced Tactical Fighter prototype Rampant flew east in a designated air corridor of twenty thousand feet, cruising at a speed slightly in excess of Mach 2. Cartwright observed that Major Glassman was handling the stick competently but conservatively.

"We're burning a lot of fuel, son."

"That's correct, sir. If we proceed at present speed and course, we will have virtually no loiter time over the target, or at least what you think is the target."

"I'm right about the target."

Glassman banked the stubby-winged fighter slightly to starboard and zoomed, monitoring his heads-up display unit all the while. With the advanced target identification systems designed for the ATF, the pilot could identify twenty-four enemy targets and attack six different threats at varied altitudes and distances. But so far the skies were ominously empty.

"What makes you so certain about the bomber's destination, General?"

"Washington is the only target that matters. If they don't decapitate, the exercise is only senseless slaughter. These boys want more than that. They've worked too hard to acquire the weapons delivery system that we let 'em snatch away from us. They want the grand slam. I know it. I can feel it."

"We can't fight without fuel, sir."

"Punch the NORAD frequency, boy. I'm gonna fill us up with ethyl."

Glassman brought the NORAD command frequency on line and announced his position. Cartwright keyed his mike and spoke.

"Cheyenne, this is Eagle-Rampant, maintaining course for presumed zero target one, do you copy, over?"

"Roger, we copy, Eagle," the voice at Cheyenne Mountain replied dispassionately.

"You got a SAC base in Texas, and I assume a sky full of B-1 bombers on airborne alert status, over."

"Roger that, Eagle. How can we assist, over?"

"Just park a silver sow nice and steady at about thirty thousand feet whilst we cross over Lubbock, and you can put me on the ledger for a case of Lone Star the next time I'm in the Rockies."

"That's a good copy, Eagle. One KC-135 refueling bird coming up, and we'll call you at the club on the beer."

Glassman banked the ATF slightly and adjusted his course setting for Lubbock. He sucked deeply on his oxygen and moved his lips in silent prayer that his hand would remain steady.

WASHINGTON

D-Day 1532 Hours Local EST

The streets of the capital city were quiet. Tourists on the Mall crowded into the Smithsonian Institute to hear radio and television coverage that was being piped in on public-address systems. The ubiquitous snack trucks and tacky souvenir stands stood empty, their vendors abandoning their workplaces along with the tourists. A scattered stack of "Oliver North for President" T-shirts tumbled onto Constitution Avenue and blew about in an empty wind.

In millions of homes across America and in office buildings and factories, people were crowding around television sets and radios to hear the live coverage from the capital and wonder at what sort of new national calamity was in progress. The television reporters, doing their stand-ups in front of the familiar back lawn of the White House, told their viewers portentously that there were more questions than answers.

"What we know, Charles, is this," the White House reporter in the trench coat told his New York anchorman and the rest of the nation. "There has been an explosion and fire at an aerospace plant in California, where it was believed a nuclear Stealth bomber was under construction ...and there has been the departure of the president from the White House. What we don't know is if the events are somehow related."

Charles Corwin, the silver-haired anchor, tore another sheet of wire copy and slammed his fist on his massive desk. "Bob, what are we getting from the Pentagon? What are we getting from State? Can you make any sense of the larger picture?"

"From what we can tell at this point, Charles ..." the reporter stammered. "Well, hell, there is no larger picture. They're all gone, dammit. They're gone. The spokesmen at

Pentagon and State don't know where their bosses are, and we don't, either."

Another wire service bulletin was handed to the anchorman. Corwin looked at it and gasped.

"Can we confirm this?" he demanded of his off-camera staff. "I can't read this until we get our own call through." Corwin crumpled the copy and tossed it aside, then grabbed at his collar and looked haggardly into the eyes of millions of viewers. "The situation is—" he said, his voice cracking. "The situation is simply that there are more questions than answers at this point in time. We shift now to our reporter in Los Angeles."

The crumpled wire service bulletin had announced that the president had departed Andrews Air Force Base, reportedly aboard the Boeing 747 Looking Glass aircraft code-named "Nightwatch."

ABOARD THE ATF

The funnel from the KC-135 refueling boom snaked itself seductively a few feet in front of Major Glassman's face. Watching, hypnotized as he gazed into the bright sunlight reflected through the cockpit glass, something deep within him recalled the memory of an interrogator holding a rubber knout in a basement dungeon. And he reflected on the horror he felt at loosing a missile on a plane displaying the paint and markings of an American commercial carrier. His vision blurred, and a small moan escaped his throat, echoing through the hot mike that connected him to his backseater, Cartwright.

"Major, snap out of it," Cartwright shouted through his microphone. "Marry that male plug to the female end, and let's gas up."

Cartwright peered forward and saw Glassman's hand trembling on the stick. "What the hell's the matter with you, Glassman?"

"I can't, General. I just can't," Glassman said through clenched teeth.

The two planes, cruising on dry thrust, hovered near one another in a graceful airborne mating dance. But the pilot of the fighter was unable to complete the dance.

"This is Casey at the Bat," the tanker pilot announced on the SAC frequency. "We are ready to discharge fuel for Eagle-Rampant. How you, over?"

"This is Eagle," Cartwright radioed back. "Give us a minute to check our trim and we'll be right with you, over."

"That's a good copy, Eagle," the tanker pilot drawled. "Awaiting your signal, out."

"Well, boy," Cartwright boomed over the fighter's internal mike, "are we gonna fuel up, or we gonna fall outta the sky and die?"

"You do it," Glassman snarled. "I'm grounded."

"Not at thirty thousand feet you ain't. We been down this road before. It's your airplane, Major."

"I can't!" Glassman exclaimed.

"You've got to."

"I'll fail."

"Fuck you, Glassman. Try."

The funnel dropped ahead of the cockpit, and the separation increased. Glassman looked at the whirl of dials and indicators on his console and then at the wide expanse of blue sky above. He looked at the tanker cruising so near, and something within him told him the refueling hose was friend, not foe. He eased the stick forward and mated the fighter to the fuel boom.

"I knew you wasn't a pussy, Glassman," Cartwright snorted. "Now take this plane the fuck off of autopilot and let's do some flying. We're late."

"Roger that, General," Glassman said, his voice registering through the microphone in the pure, calm tones of a fighter pilot. "I'm going to be okay."

He uncoupled the ATF fighter from the tanker and waved his wings at the KC-135. Then he fired the afterburner and zoomed east toward zero target one, the city of Washington.

THE NORTH ATLANTIC

Alerted by the patrolling AWACS aircraft, a pair of F-15 Eagles from the Fifty-ninth Tactical Fighter Wing out of Eglin spotted the rogue Tomcats flying at an altitude of twenty thousand feet, north of the Grand Bahamas and east of Cape Canaveral.

"We got a pair of bandits, nine o'clock and low, distance fifteen miles and closing," Captain Clayton Wilson, the fighter leader, declared, leading the pounce.

Wilson and his wingman dived and closed the distance on the Tomcats. As the Eagles ignited their afterburners, they zoomed to an indicated airspeed approaching nine hundred MPH.

"You're right on top of them, Race Horse leader," announced the AWACS operator who had earlier witnessed the destruction of the Bear reconnaissance plane. His voice betrayed no loss of composure. "You should have visual identification."

"Roger that," Wilson radioed back. "I got eyes." He triggered a Sidewinder air-to-air missile as soon as he heard the acquisition tone humming in his helmet earphone.

As Wilson let the missile fly, he watched the Tomcat leader roll over, then climb. The rogue plane's radar intercept officer released a shower of flares in an attempt to dodge the missile by flooding the sky with deceptive heat emissions.

"They're dogfighters," Wilson declared, watching the Tomcat leader break through cloud cover at thirty thousand feet. "They're gonna try and dodge it."

Reza, the Tomcat leader, lit his afterburner and pushed his plane into a vertical climb with the Pratt and Whitney engines pouring out nearly twenty-one thousand pounds of thrust. Whipping his twin-tailed aircraft into a hard left turn, Reza then dived to meet the brace of Eagles, firing his twenty-millimeter Vulcan rotary cannon as he plunged, approaching nose to nose with Wilson's wingman.

"Hello, Americans," Reza announced. "Meet your maker." A splash of cannon rounds shattered the Eagle driver's cockpit, sending the F-15 pitching toward the sea in a fiery splash of metal and fuel.

"Damn," Wilson raged, pushing his Eagle into a series of tight turns. "Sons of bitches can fight." He fired a second Sidewinder heat-seeking missile.

Reza twisted and dived, swooping a few hundred feet above the waves. "Allah Akbar," his wingman in the other Tomcat exulted. But Sidi's joy was premature. He uttered his war cry just as Wilson's second Sidewinder found his tailpipe and sheared through the high-speed turbofans. The Tomcat piloted by Sidi twisted crazily and smashed into the unforgiving chop of the North Atlantic.

"Race Horse two is down," Wilson radioed to the AWACS Sentry. "I have killed one bandit. Location of second bandit unknown, unknown."

"Roger, Race Horse leader. A navy S and R team has been dispatched. Any sighting of the rogue bomber element during contact?"

"Negative. Tend to my downed wingman. I will press the pursuit. Race Horse leader out."

The Eagle driver headed north, searching for a renegade Tomcat and an invisible plane. The Stealth bomber, flying out of sight of the AWACS sentry at an altitude of sixty thousand feet, accelerated to its maximum speed of Mach 2 plus and crossed the North Carolina coastline near Wilmington.

Reza, pilot of the remaining escort Tomcat, slipped through the AWACS net flying nap of the Earth just behind the STB-1. Slightly less than two hours had elapsed since the attack on Plant 36. Monitoring his CRT screens which inched the bomber closer to target like an illuminated bouncing ball, Mehdi turned to his co-pilot and smiled. "We are almost there," he said.

"We are ready," Ali Rezai said solemnly, staring his commander in the eye.

Captain Mehdi Mahan looked resolutely ahead, toward the horizon, then down at the displays with the lighted symbols dancing before him like an equation for conquest. "Let's go," he said, edging the throttle toward maximum speed.

ABOARD THE ATF

D-Day 1547 Hours Local EST

Cartwright radioed the AWACS sentry plane sent out from Langley Air Force Base to clear a search sector as the ATF flew over the rolling green of the Piedmont region of Virginia. The bullet-shaped ATF swept by the state Capitol in the heart of Richmond and quickly crossed over the earth-colored brick homes of the suburbs, punctuated by graceful old white frame houses.

The aircraft sped to the Potomac and traced a path along its twisting banks, wagging its wings in greeting to a formation of F-16 Fighting Falcons patrolling the skies above the Pentagon.

The Capitol dome was majestic and unmolested, and the great obelisk of the Washington Monument glinted proudly in the afternoon sunlight. The streets below were empty of traffic, although some thousands of cars appeared to have been abandoned by motorists who'd heard radio bulletins and run for hasty shelter. All flights from Dulles and National airports were canceled, leaving thousands sitting on their luggage listening to radios or crowded into lounges to watch the television news.

"We've failed, General," said Glassman. "We'll never find it. We designed the devil's own machinery, and it will be our undoing."

"Don't go biblical on me now, partner. We ain't dead yet."

"The Stealth bomber hasn't been identified since it got loose. That was twenty-four hundred miles and two hours ago."

"Take this scooter on upstairs, will ya? We got to get near the ceiling, or all we're gonna see is a gravity bomb sailing toward the White House."

Pulling back on the fly-by-wire hand control, Glassman throttled up past fifty thousand feet, leaving the city and suburbs of more than a million people in miniature below.

"They could have already dropped payload anywhere along the line, General,"

"Shit. Eglin downed the decoy off Florida. What do you think they want, the final destruction of Sarasota?"

"They're people just the same. These men could destroy any number of people."

"No one has been hurt yet. We're loitering on the target. Our job is to not fuck up."

Glassman banked the ATF into a sweep to a vector of the airspace over CIA headquarters and the northern Virginia suburbs.

"Fucking up is a strong possibility, General. Finding the bomber may be impossible."

"Fly the airplane, Glassman. That's your job now. Enough folks already fumbled the ball before we got our chance. We can still make it right."

Cartwright marveled at the ATF's display screens. Instead of the murky graphics of earlier models, they offered an accurate, near photographic display of the horizon and a split-screen view of the ground terrain far below. Suddenly the panel lit up with the approach of an intruder aircraft. It was a Tomcat, coming in low on the deck from the direction of the eastern shore of Maryland.

"You got the bogey at six o'clock and low," Glassman shouted.

"Roger that."

"I'm diving to engage."

"The hell you say. The Tomcat's decoying now. Climb, dammit."

Glassman banked the ATF, preparing to zoom down toward the Tomcat.

"Goddammit, I said climb!" Cartwright screamed in the mike.

"It's my airplane, General."

"Damn right, and that's your capital down there. The real bandit is gonna be sailing in on approach at max ceiling. Trust me."

Glassman pulled back on the stick and throttled the ATF so it burst above the clouds, mounting Gs as it climbed.

"Activating all radar systems," Cartwright said, throwing on the aircraft's short-range beacons.

"You're making us a sitting duck, General," Glassman said, his voice under control.

"Damn right. And a half-blind one at that. Maybe if we can't find the plane, the plane will find us."

Glassman throttled the fighter through the clouds into the upper air corridor that formed the southernmost sweep of the military district of Washington. As Glassman and Cartwright patrolled about forty miles south of Washington, the radio crackled on a clear frequency.

"Eagle-Rampant, this is Nightwatch, do you copy, over?" the calm voice of the president inquired.

"Roger, this is the Eagle-Rampant."

"The Sixty-first Tactical Fighter Wing is engaging a low-flying Tomcat that has been identified as a hostile. Any status on the intruder Stealth aircraft?"

"Negative, goddammit, sir!" Cartwright shouted. "And I suggest you all clear the net and leave the fighting to us."

For an instant Cartwright looked up from the radar scope, and immediately his one good eye was riveted to a spot in the western sky, an approaching black mass that was growing by the second. It looked like a wing, a black wing with no tail and a shark-line nose gliding through the sky as a great dark manta ray would swim above the sandy ocean bottoms. It crested the clouds, soaring undetected by the ATF's aura of radar beams, leaving no signature on the radar scopes of countless interceptors searching for it.

"Good God," Glassman whispered into the microphone. Transfixed, he watched the dark shape approach. "There she is."

Like a furious winged predator, the Stealth bomber hurtled toward its target zone.

ABOARD THE STEALTH

D-Day 1604 Hours Local EST

Inside the STB-1 bomber, Captain Mehdi Mahan instructed Hossein and Hashemi to begin the arming sequence that would activate a B-83 gravity-release weapon, a twelve-foot-long bomb that would descend to earth by drogue parachute and unleash a nuclear hell worse than the fire that rained on Japan nearly fifty years before.

Eyeing one another levelly, each flier punched a key code and removed a platinum key from a pair of sliding drawers located adjacent to the crew seats. Simultaneously Hossein and Hashemi inserted their keys into a black box sitting between the flight engineer's and weapons officer's seat. A red light lit up, and the box emitted a warm buzzing sound not unlike the purring of a cat.

"Shall we continue?" Hossein asked, his voice trembling slightly. As he spoke all four crewmen could hear the hydraulics of the rotary launcher in the weapons bay grind as the first bomb locked into dropping position.

"Proceed with the alphanumeric coding procedure as indicated in the training sequence," Mehdi said. "We are nearly home, brothers."

The black plane continued on its heading toward the triangle of earth that encompassed the Lincoln Memorial, the dome of the Capitol, and the White House. They formed the geographical core of a city from which a plume of blast, heat, and radiation would emanate, destroying or burning every living thing inside the beltway that ringed the capital city.

ABOARD THE ATF

As Glassman maneuvered the ATF, Cartwright furiously manipulated the radar stick, trying to get acquisition for a missile shot at the advancing bomber.

"What have you got, sir?" Glassman demanded.

"I've got shit. We're too close for a Phoenix shot, and I can't lock on for an AMRAAM."

The bomber swept past them, as unheeding as a great whale sounding for the depths. Glassman opened throttle and climbed, putting the ATF into a six-G high-barrel roll that brought the plane into attack position behind the bomber.

"I've got a weak trace indication on my forward-looking infrared detector. I'm firing a Sidewinder."

The short-range missile arched crazily down toward the bomber and sailed harmlessly past the advancing plane.

"The goddamn baffles on the engines of the thing sure as hell work. They even gum up the IR signature," Cartwright snarled. "Let's get a gunshot at it. The radar is in gun director mode."

The Stealth bomber banked slightly after the missile shot and swooped, then rose to higher altitude.

"The sons of bitches can fly. Take your shot, Adam ...now!" Cartwright shouted.

Glassman squeezed the cannon trigger, and it made a snapping sound like a dry twig. "Nothing," he said. "Jammed."

"Pitch another Sidewinder."

"It won't work."

"It's all we got. Try, dammit!"

Glassman loosed another Sidewinder missile, but it

was like throwing a rock at a kid on a bike. It fell short, and the black plane flew on.

As the bomber pushed on toward the low-slung horizon of the Washington suburbs, Cartwright's scope alerted him to a new threat. The Tomcat flown by Reza that had come in low from the Maryland shore had gained altitude.

"We got a bandit high and on our tail," Cartwright announced. "The bandit's playing cat's paw for the bomber. We've got a Sidewinder on acquisition tone coming after us. Evade. Evade. Evade."

Glassman pitched the ATF nose down and dived, trying to zoom away from the missile, which continued sounding its menacing acquisition tone. After diving deeply, accumulating G-forces pushing the skin tight down against the fliers' faces, Glassman opened throttle and climbed high in an Immelmann turn perfected seventy years earlier by a German World War I ace. Still the missile tone sounded.

Glassman moved the throttle to a near stall mode. The ATF slowed in midsky, nearly hovering, and the Sidewinder sailed by, overflying the fighter. Ahead, the Stealth bomber was receding to become a tiny black spot on the horizon.

"Open her up or we're gonna lose it, Adam," Cartwright said.

Glassman accelerated, building speed that left the clouds and finally the sound barrier behind. And then the plane pushed on again through a second sound barrier. Still the Tomcat was following.

"I'm going to reposition on the bomber," Glassman said. "If I can pull it off, I'm going to put us in a vertical reverse and dive. I'm going to ram the bomber, General."

"Roger, Adam. It looks like our last shot," Cartwright said coolly through the hot mike. "Do what you think best."

Glassman pushed the ATF into a high-climbing attitude to bring his fighter over the bomber. As he did Cartwright spotted the Tomcat advancing on the rear of the ATF plane in a wide-angle lag pursuit. Then, as Glassman banked briefly before edging the plane into nose-up attitude for the vertical reverse maneuver, Cartwright could see the long, low white buildings of official Washington below. And looking up above, he could see the dark shadow of the black plane. Suddenly another missile tone sounded from the pursuing Tomcat.

"Climb this son of a bitch, Adam, or we're gonna have a Sidewinder up our tailpipe and nothing to show for our efforts."

Glassman lit the ATF's afterburners, and the flying bullet soared vertically.

Cartwright's nose bled, and the vision in his good eye went gray as the G-forces mounted. Suddenly Glassman brought the ATF over the top and dived. The fighter dropped like an elevator out of control. The Sidewinder missile tone faded, but Cartwright, straining at the neck, turned his head to look back behind him in the cockpit bubble and saw the angry intakes and nose of the Tomcat in close pursuit. He could see the pilot, his goggled face a death mask.

"Dive and turn, dammit!" Cartwright shouted, looking down to see the black flat upper wing surfaces of the bomber directly beneath the nose of the ATF.

"I can't evade," Glassman yelled.

"Turn," Cartwright groaned as the Gs pushed his lips across his teeth in a feral grimace. "Turn and dive!"

For a fleeting spot of time, Cartwright looked straight down through the cockpit dome of the Stealth and saw the air crew of the rogue bomber reaching for the black box that carried the arming keys for the weapons payload.

At the last possible instant, Glassman twisted the control handle, veering from the collision course with the bomber. The ATF rocked sharply as its wingtip grazed the forward edge of the black plane.

The Tomcat piloted by Reza crashed squarely on the black plane's upper surfaces, striking the intruder plane like a thirty-ton meteorite. A fireball of flame, hot plastic, metal, and explosive ordnance showered across the sky, but there was no mushroom burst. The payload lacked its final instruction to detonate.

Burning graphite, shattered titanium, and various other metals flared across the sky, dropping a comet's tail of destruction in a three-mile swath from northwest Washington to the rolling green hills of Fairfax County on the northern Virginia shores of the Potomac. The rotary carrier with its deadweight payload of nuclear weapons plunged menacingly to earth and buried itself deep in the red clay of an open field south of McLean, Virginia.

Buffeted by shock waves from the collision and explosion of the intruder aircraft, Glassman worked the stick furiously, but the ATF's fly-by-wire impulse controls were dead and the plane continued to pitch out of control, losing thousands of feet of blue sky as the altitude indicator plunged ceaselessly to earth.

"It's time to get out, son," Cartwright said, patting his gloved hand over his bleeding face.

"It's my plane, goddammit," the major cried as the fighter sank toward the wildly spinning ground below.

"It's the government's plane, sonny. It's your life," the general yelled. "Hit the eject!"

"Oh, hell," Glassman shouted, pulling his ejection lever.

Simultaneously the fliers blasted high into the air, and their parachutes blossomed like great blooming flowers over their heads. They hung suspended, a few dozen feet from each other, two small men dangling like marionettes.

"You did good, Adam," Cartwright yelled, his voice sounding hollow in the empty, silent air.

Glassman, descending in parallel motion with Cartwright, nodded and signaled a faltering V for victory at the older flier, his face streaked with cordite and blood from the ejection.

Suspended peacefully under the canopy, Cartwright marveled at the quiet of the lower air currents and the wind whispering through his helmet. To him it sounded like prayer. Suddenly he wished he were home, drinking coffee with his wife, Gloria.

With the earth rushing toward him and the horizon

welling up suddenly in the last few dozen feet of the parachute's descent, Cartwright bent his knees gently and put his feet together as he watched a treeline rise up. He bounced to earth, rolled over, and then rose to his full height, as he had in occupied France and Korea and a dozen other places where he'd flown and fought for his country. It was harder to get up now. He was older.

He walked toward Adam Glassman, who was untangling himself from the shroud lines of his own canopy. Clumsily Glassman extricated himself from the harness.

"You want to take care of that face of yours, Major," Cartwright said, reaching into the pocket of his flight suit for a first-aid pad. "That's a nasty gash."

Glassman sat down in the deep grass and breathed deeply. "We've alive, and they're dead," he said, exhaling.

"For us, that's what counts," Cartwright said, applying the pad to Glassman's bleeding forehead.

"What's to be done about the people who sent the plane?"

"We're gonna have to fight it to the death with 'em or find some common ground and talk sweet reason. I can't say which would be best. It's a dangerous world."

The general hoisted Glassman's arm over his shoulder, and together they began to march toward the road. "I'd like a beer," said Glassman.

"Me too, brother."

EPILOGUE

WASHINGTON

D-Day Plus 180

The National Security Council analyst's memo was delivered by hand and Madeline Murdoch considered it along with her cup of Morning Thunder herbal tea. She dismissed the NSC analyst, wishing to be alone with his summary and her thoughts.

The analyst's evaluation would form the core of her own response to the president's Foreign Intelligence Advisory Board, which was completing its own postmortem on the Stealth hijack, as were innumerable congressional committees, each seeking its own pound of flesh. She respected the opinion of E-23 (name excised), but would ultimately have to make her own decisions on how to present the analyst's conclusions to the committees and the president. She opened the overleaf to the analyst's report.

CLASSIFICATION: MOST SECRET—BLACK
DISTRIBUTION: MURDOCH, EYES ONLY
SOURCE: MAGIC 13, DESK E-23
SUBJECT: STB-1 DISPOSITION

With the destruction of the STB-1 Stealth bomber and its war
load, America, Iran, and the Soviet Union have stepped back
from the brink. The outcome represents an uneasy draw between
powers and leaders who see the world through vastly different
eyes. Mutual understanding eludes us and the danger this
represents escalates daily.

Still, a cold peace is the only thinkable alternative to a hot war
for all disputed parties.

Destruction of the Iranian refinery at Kharg Island a week after
the STB-1 hijack should be considered the appropriate measured
response unless future hostile acts occur. The destruction,
accomplished by commandos wearing no national insignia, was
complete. The result—elimination of twelve percent of Iran's
refining capacity—was laudable.

In the weeks following the destruction of the Stealth Technology
Bomber, the president's address to the nation on the status of
U.S. counterintelligence capabilities was generally well received
as indicated by surveys and polls.

Congress convened its select committees for lengthy hearings
on Middle East relations, Soviet espionage, and lax security in
various of the defense industries. The meetings continue without
discernible effect on policy.

Sufficient "face" has been restored among the disputing parties.
The mullahs of the Islamic Republic trumpeted another
humiliation for "The Great Satan." The president has announced
a triumph of American arms and told the American people that
"the system worked."

General Scott Cartwright's vision has been repaired with laser surgery. His return to active duty must be counted a plus. Major Adam Glassman has returned to flight status. It is lamentable that for security reasons, their identities cannot be disclosed. The National Intelligence Medal is recommended for both combatants.

One politically explosive issue remains. It was deemed best to secure defector status for Colonel Asrar Ajami Avadek to ensure an orderly and thorough debriefing. We are now faced with a dilemma. Testifying under his grant of immunity, he has become the star witness in closed sessions of all committees exploring the ramifications of the Stealth hijack. Frankly, he has captivated his interrogators, on the Hill and in the intelligence community.

He is becoming a popular lecturer at seminars and training sessions of the CIA and other agencies. He has expressed interest in American citizenship.

Your thoughts for action on this, Dr. Murdoch?

Sincerely,
E-23 (name excised)

It was still early in the day, too early for whiskey. Madeline Murdoch shook her head and laughed in wonder at Avadek's gall. She placed E-23's memo in the burn box, incinerating it instantly. She wished that her decision on the Iranian colonel's status could be accomplished so easily.